THE BUTLER DEFECTIVE

A BUMBLING BRIT ABROAD MYSTERY, BOOK TWO

D. R. LOWREY

Late Bloomer Books

Editing by The Pro Book Editor

Beta read by Peter Anthony

ISBN: 9781734108262

1. Main category—Fiction

2. Other category—Humorous/General

Second Edition

Dedicated to my dad, George Lowrey, a World War II veteran who was not the inspiration for Grumps.

1

NEW BUTLER, NEW BODY

"Reporting for duty," said Nigel while standing at attention in his stiff new butler suit and snapping a crisp salute. "Nigel Blandwater-Cummings at your service."

A new career has but one first day, and Nigel wanted his to go down smoothly.

"Bring me a tequila," replied his new boss, hunched over her desk, projecting the topside of her cap to the attentive Nigel.

Mrs. Sandoval's mornings, Nigel would learn, never went down smoothly. Nevertheless, he pushed up his right eyebrow to its fullest extent and pursed his lips. He'd long rehearsed this expression—the Haughty Butler, he called it—in front of the bathroom mirror. It was during one such session that the notion of butlering first loitered in that warehouse between his ears.

"Forgive me, madam, for being presumptuous, but was it not my understanding that you had sworn off alcohol before noon?"

"Not today. I'm feeling unnerved." Her morning constitutional appeared to have taken a toll. The sunlight perhaps had been too dazzling, the birds' songs too energetic, or the flowers too smelly.

"Oh, dear, sorry to hear that." Indeed he was. An unhappy employer is a demanding employer.

"Cut the sympathy," said Mrs. Sandoval, cradling her fore-head. "Sorries don't soothe the bulldog. Pour me a strong one." Then, after groaning like a ship hung on the rocks, she added, "And tend to that body in the garden."

The previous statement required clarification. The tequila bit was well understood, but that part about the body... Surely, foreign objects on the grounds fell under the remit of the gardener. He asked, "Pardon me. Did you say 'that body in the garden'?"

Mrs. Sandoval uncoiled herself into an extreme recline, affording Nigel unobstructed sightlines into her nostrils. Looking down her nose at him, she continued, "Before I said 'that body in the garden,' I said 'bring me a tequila.' If you're going to work here, you need to keep things straight."

"Yes, madam. I'll fetch the tequila."

Nigel returned brandishing a silver tray topped with the crucial tequila shot, which he'd diluted slightly with water. Mrs. Sandoval had proudly declared her temperance between the hours of midnight and noon, so if she found it hard to live up to that promise, he felt obliged to aid her just a little.

"Your tequila, madam."

In a well-practiced sweeping motion, Mrs. Sandoval grabbed the slender shot glass from the serving tray, lifted it to her lips, and flipped it bottoms up. The golden elixir leaped toward its destiny, hopping off the tongue, skipping down the esophagus, and jumping into the stomach where it cleaved into a thousand tiny court jesters ready to distract the agitated queen. She placed the glass back on the tray and expelled a toxic cloud of fumes over a rolled tongue.

"Is that the Padron Golden?" she asked.

"Yes, madam."

"Something's wrong with it. Contaminated. Water's gotten into the bottle. Fifteen percent, I'd say. Throw it out. Not worth drinking."

"Yes, madam." Lesson learned.

"Now, go take care of that body in the garden."

"If I may ask, madam, what kind of a body are you referring to?"

"A dead one, I think. At least it didn't move when I stumbled over its ankle this morning."

Maintaining one's composure, Nigel had recently learned, was a vital attribute in the butler's toolbox. *But damn! A body?* Projecting his best butlerly detachment, he asked, "Do we know who it is?"

"Speaking for myself, no. If you do, let me know."

"Yes, madam," replied Nigel, as per his training. "I will take care of the situation."

"One other thing, Nigel."

"Another thing?" said Nigel, hoping it might be another tequila rather than another body.

"The dead man has a toad in his mouth."

"A toad in his mouth?" repeated Nigel.

Nigel placed a hand to his chin and mouthed the words, "A toad in his mouth." His eyes brightened. "Ah! You're speaking metaphorically. You mean he has a frog in his throat. I see. I've never heard the phrase 'a toad in his mouth,' but it stands to reason. Perhaps he died of some respiratory ailment. But," continued Nigel, "how did you know he had a frog in his throat?"

"I did not say a frog in his throat. I said a toad in his mouth. Look in his mouth. You'll see a toad. That's what I call a toad in his mouth."

"I see. I'll get on it straight away."

"Oh, Nigel."

"Yes, madam."

"I'm glad you're here today. It's times like these when a butler comes in handy. Welcome aboard."

"Thank you, madam," said Nigel, exiting with a purposeful gait and stiff posture. Once out of Mrs. Sandoval's eyeshot, the self-assured stride crumpled into a stumbling lurch.

Nigel had hoped to slowly ease into his new job. A break-in period would have been nice. This was not to say he lacked confidence. Confidence he had up to the gills after his intensive two-month course from Old Winpole's Online College for Butlers. The old school provided a comprehensive, dual-tracked buttling *programme* covering all the technical aspects—beverage preparation, laying out of clothing, Excel—and the behavioral aspects—obsequious servitude, haughtiness, and sly browbeating—in equal measures. Still, if any single point had been chased up a tree at the old alma mater, it was to expect the unexpected.

To demonstrate, Old Winpole related the story of his first job where, on his third day of employment, he'd learned of his client's habit of allowing a leopard to range freely about the premises. Old Winpole had to buck up and show that cat who was boss. The unspoken lesson in the tale was that people who hire butlers are sometimes lunatics. But at least Old Winpole, referred to as Scar by his associates, had been allowed a couple days to establish his bearings.

Nigel had been allowed scarcely a pair of minutes. On the bright side, the presence of an intact body indicated a scarcity of large cats roaming the estate.

Nigel, standing, and the policeman, squatting, stared down upon the body. None of the three appeared comfortable in the presence of the others. Nigel broke the ice.

"How long you suppose he's been dead?" asked Nigel of the policeman.

"Long enough," the officer said, poking around the body with a pencil.

"I would agree," said Nigel, running short of clever repartee. "I guess you see a lot of dead bodies in your profession, eh?"

"You talkin' to me?" said the policeman.

Nigel looked at the policeman and then at the dead man. "Yes."

"Nope," said the policeman.

Several seconds of silence followed.

"My wife was a police officer," said Nigel.

"Please step off the body, sir."

"What?"

"Step off the body, sir. Please try to keep off the body."

Nigel hadn't noticed that he'd been standing on the dead man's hand, now mashed into the soft garden soil. "Oh, sorry about that."

The police officer did not acknowledge his apology, nor did the dead man. The officer continued to poke around the body—a pocket here, a nostril there. An ambulance stood nearby, staffed by a couple of EMTs enjoying a tranquil moment by analyzing each other's high kicks.

"What are we waiting for?" asked Nigel.

"Detective," said the policeman, comparing his own shoe to that of the dead man's.

Before Nigel could think of what else to say, his attention was drawn to a man in a crumply trench coat loping toward the garden, trailed by a younger minion. Nigel wasn't familiar with the trench coat, but he recognized the head poking from it. It was that rubber-faced cop the townsfolk referred to as Barney. Winjack was his actual name, and he had somehow—nepotism, possibly—been promoted from patrol officer to detective. Past dealings with this officer had left Nigel highly unimpressed. This hayseed seemed better suited as a jail-sweep than as a detective. He suspected the trench coat had been bought the day of his promotion and slept in every night since.

The trench-coated Rubberface placed himself at the body's edge and assumed a Superman posture with feet planted wide apart and fists set firmly against his waist. He looked toward the horizon as if he might spot a killer lurking in the woods. The policeman looked up at the detective as if he'd spotted a nitwit lurking in a trench coat.

"What ya got here?" shouted Rubberface.

"Dead man," answered the officer.

"I see that," said the detective, rolling his eyes within their rubbery sockets. "Can you detect a cause? Any signs of a struggle? Foul play?"

"There's a toad in his mouth."

"A toad in his mouth? That could be your cause of death right there—poison toad. What's that over there?" said Rubberface, pointing at a shovel.

"Shovel," said the cop.

"I can see that. Why is it here? What was he doing with it?"

"Digging that hole, maybe," said the cop, nodding toward a freshly dug hole.

"Maybe," said the detective, "but that ain't much of a hole. If he was digging, he must have been interrupted. Or maybe someone else was digging, and he interrupted them. Maybe he happened upon someone digging a hole for an unseemly purpose, a confrontation ensued, and this man ended up dead."

"With a toad in his mouth?" said Nigel.

Rubberface slowly turned toward Nigel, appraising him with squinty eyes.

"Don't I know you?" he said.

"Nigel. Nigel Blandwater-Cummings. I'm the butler here."

"The butler, eh?" His intonation implied he had heard about butlers. He rolled his eyes over Nigel from head to toe. "Your shoes match these tracks," said the detective. "I would say a near-perfect match. You going to tell me that's a coincidence?"

"No."

"How do you explain your tracks being all around the body?" asked the detective, pointing at the footprints.

"Must have happened when I was walking around the body."

Rubberface looked down at the body as if searching for

another explanation. "Hold on a minute. Look at that there. His hand has been mashed into the dirt. That's important. That's desecration. We've got desecration of the body. A real sicko did this. Had you seen this before?" he asked the officer.

"Maybe," said the officer.

"What do you mean 'maybe'? Either the hand was desecrated or it wasn't desecrated."

"Maybe. I don't recall," said the cop in a tone reserved for pesky little brothers. "It became hard to tell once that guy stepped on it."

"I see. The butler has already contaminated the evidence. We'll treat this as a homicide scene until further notice." Rubber-face instructed his minion to take pictures of the body from various angles and collect the shovel as evidence.

The detective probed various aspects of the body, including the toad, with a small metal wand. As the body was loaded, toad and all, into the ambulance, the detective wrote vigorously in his notepad as the officer waited patiently to secure the scene, and Nigel looked on in wonder.

"Any theories, detective?" asked Nigel.

"Given that he had a toad in his mouth, the best theory is death by toad. But I've lived in Tonkawa County all my life and never seen anyone put a toad in their mouth, so we've still got a mystery."

"May I posit a theory?"

"So, the butler has a theory, does he? Everyone wants to be a detective. Go ahead. Amuse me. What is your theory?"

"I apologize that my hypothesis is not so intriguing as yours, but, what if the man died of a natural cause? A heart attack, embolism, stroke, whatever, and he fell down dead with his mouth agape—"

"A what?"

"Agape."

"What does that mean?"

Nigel dropped his jaw open which the detective seemed to

take as a kind of insult. "Open. His mouth was open. Then, sometime later, a toad seeking accommodation for the night found comfortable lodging in the unfortunate man's mouth."

The detective's face roiled as if thoughts were squirming just below his gummy hide. "Not impossible," he said. "But it still leaves many hanging questions. Why was the man here in the first place, and what was he doing? Also, what killed the toad?"

"Heart attack, old age, bad breath, whatever. All good toads go to heaven someday."

"My advice to you: stick to butlering. Meanwhile, I'll be identifying the victim. That may tell us why he was here. The coroner and the toxicologist should have a great deal to say about this case. By the way, you shouldn't leave town without notifying the police."

"Notifying the police? Why would I need to—"

"I'm just saying. Please, notify the police."

2

ONE MORE THING, OR TWO

As they carted the body off to wherever they cart bodies off to, Nigel observed Mrs. Sandoval watching from behind the porch railing. At various times during the proceedings, he had seen each of the home's four female inhabitants in that same location. The rotation of observers reminded him of one of those Swiss mechanical clocks on which a figure of a mouse pops out of a tiny door, circles the stage, and exits in time for the next mouse's entrance.

Before the cop's arrival, Nigel had been the observer on the porch as he watched the ladies view the body via a sort of corpse-viewing parade. First on the scene had been the estate's primary decision-maker, Mrs. Sandoval. Mrs. Sandoval, a well-maintained, middle-aged woman with a penchant for costumery, normally maintained a professional business-like demeanor between the hours of 9:00 a.m. and noon. Beyond those hours, when conscious, she drifted in a tequila-soaked fog. Wearing an approximation of a nineteenth-century Italian sailor's uniform, Mrs. Sandoval had stopped briefly in front of the body and said, "Don't he look natural?" Perhaps this proclamation was standard protocol from a lifetime of funerals or, perhaps, toad-stuffed corpses were "natural" among the Sandovals. Either way, being a gracious woman, she would not have drawn attention to the warty amphibian bulging from the man's mouth.

Mrs. Sandoval had been followed in the procession by her daughter. Stefanie was adored by members of the household, though also pitied for having inherited a mutation for normalcy. Her surroundings rendered poor Stefanie almost unnoticeable in a Marilyn Munster sort of way. She had a husband who also went unnoticed because he was away a lot, though not enough for most people. Stefanie's head had not swiveled as she approached the body, nor had her body twisted. The shifting pupils of her widening eyes had been the only body parts allowed to acknowledge the cadaver she'd come to see. That is, until her shoe had made contact with the body's outstretched foot. Then she had expelled a mouse-sized shriek and scurried past like a chill running up the spine.

Next in the procession had been the octogenarian, Abuelita, in her mechanized wheelchair. Not much to say about Abuelita unless you had a few weeks to kill. Life had been hard on her, and in return, she had been hard on life. Everyone else's life. She had one eye that drifted aimlessly, as if searching for an exit. The other eye was steady, purposeful, and evil, with a tendency to sear any flesh, bone, or willpower unfortunate enough to fall within its gaze. Abuelita had stopped her chair in front of the body and sneered. Anything else would have been a surprise. Sneering was her go-to move. She might have been sneering at Death, that weak-kneed rival whom she bested on a regular basis. She might have been sneering at a corpse who had the audacity to die on her property without her participation. Or she might have been sneering because it was a Monday.

She had been followed by Esmerelda, Abuelita's long-lost daughter who had recently returned. Essie had come back to Mama, but not quite the same as when she'd left. Forty years will do that. In a fit of teenage rage, Essie had run away to California with a boyfriend in hopes of joining a hippie commune. Arriving on the scene well after the highwater mark for hippie communes, the only receptive association turned out to be not just a commune, but also a coven. While Essie had never fully adapted to the occult lifestyle, certain aspects continued to cast their spell to this day. Looking down upon the body in her tie-dyed muumuu, she had danced a little jig, uttered an incantation, and then collapsed in a heap. After a dramatic pause, she'd popped back up, rotated her extended arms in broad circles, and hissed like a punctured inner-tube. She'd ended the exercise by pointing at the cadaver's head—or maybe at the toad—while reciting a limerick not featuring a man from Nantucket. After completing the verse, she had held this pointing position for a good three minutes, perhaps waiting to be handed a broom.

None of the ladies had ever seen the man before, not even in a dream or a hallucination.

That had all been earlier this morning. Now, the ladies were inside, waiting for Nigel. He'd have liked to keep them waiting, but he felt an obligation to minimize the dawdling since it was his first day on the job. He had already come to understand the ladies largely kept to themselves in separate parts of the house, yet he found all four members assembled in the salon.

"Hello, ladies," said Nigel to the silent horde. "Busy morning."

If silent glaring was a form of busyness, then it was still an action-packed day for the ladies. Nigel had the feeling of a fly caught in a web shared by four black widow spiders.

"Can I get you something?" he said.

Mrs. Sandoval replied, "Mr. Nigel, something has come up."

"I should say so," said Nigel. "Or gone down, might be the better term. It's not every day a dead body turns up on the premises, is it?"

The ladies looked at the floor and grumbled.

The lack of response unsettled Nigel.

"I was speaking rhetorically, of course, but just for grins, let me repeat the question. It isn't everyday a dead body turns up on the premises"—he awaited their reassurances—"is it?"

"Of course not, Mr. Nigel. That's not the issue we wish to address," said Mrs. Sandoval.

"No, of course not. I can tell that weightier matters are afoot," said Nigel.

"Weightier, perhaps not, but they are of great importance to us," said the oddly levelheaded Stefanie.

The ladies wore tight lips; they averted their glances. It was coming on to Thanksgiving, and Nigel imagined himself covered in feathers and peering out of a pen at Farmer Bill sharpening his implements.

"I think I'm catching the gist of this," said Nigel. "It was a quick hire. I understand that. If you've changed your minds, you've changed your minds. We can all be big about this and agree that it just didn't work out. Nothing ventured, nothing gained, as they say. Of course, there was that rather intense and costly butlering course, but I did learn how to tie an ascot and that, at least, is something to build on—"

"No, Mr. Nigel, we're not firing you," said Mrs. Sandoval. "Not yet, anyway."

Taking a moment to consider her reply, Nigel wasn't sure how he felt about this. He hadn't planned on being fired his first day, but if this dead body business happened even, say, semi-annually, he wasn't sure he'd found his dream job. "Are you sure?" he said. "Sometimes it's good to go with your gut."

"No, Mr. Nigel. We need your help now more than ever."

"Really? You've never had my help before. You might not realize what you're getting into."

Mrs. Sandoval started to speak before clamping her mouth shut. She looked to the other three ladies. She received three blank looks in return. "You see, there's going to be a wedding."

"A wedding? How wonderful. Congratulations. It's a very lucky man to win your hand, Mrs. Sandoval. May I be the first—"

"It's not me, Mr. Nigel."

"Not you? Well, your lovely daughter Stefanie is already off the market, am I right?"

"Yes, you are," said Stefanie.

"In that case, it must be the, um…unique…the one and only, Esmerelda. Congratulations. I'm sure you and your spouse will be so…unique together. Let me be the—" Nigel saw Esmerelda shaking her head. "Not Esmerelda?" He peered furtively in the direction of the vulturess, Abuelita. She had been engaged just three months before. That marriage had been put on hold after the groom's honeymoon plans were revealed to include bride-icide. "You don't mean—surely not…not *Abuelita*," said Nigel.

"What do you mean, *not Abuelita*?" said Abuelita, reaching into her pocket for a projectile.

"It's Abuelita?" said Nigel, preparing to leap behind the sofa.

"Yes," said Mrs. Sandoval. "Abuelita is to be married."

Nigel extended a very tentative paw. "May I be the—"

"Stay away!" shouted Abuelita. "I'm remaining chaste for my honeymoon. No lookee, no touchee."

With hands safely tucked behind his back, Nigel bowed. "I'm sorry, Abuelita. I merely wanted to congratulate you on this wonderful development. Someone will be very happy." *Though it's hard to imagine who.*

"It sure as hell won't be you, if you keep ogling me. Any monkey business and you'll be laid out in the garden with one toad down your gullet and one up your—"

"Abuelita, please," said Mrs. Sandoval. "Mr. Nigel is our new butler. He's here to help."

"Any way I can, madam," said Nigel, brushing wrinkles from his pants after standing up from behind the sofa.

"That's the spirit, Mr. Nigel," said Mrs. Sandoval. "You're in charge of the wedding arrangements."

"Me? In charge of the wedding arrangements? While I'd love to see Abuelita have an absolutely smashing wedding, do you think I'm the best person for such a task? I've never planned a wedding."

"Come now, Mr. Nigel," said Mrs. Sandoval. "How hard can it be? You are a butler, after all. You've been to some kind of school. Why, just this morning you disposed of a dead body, and I'm sure your funeral arrangements will be to die for—"

"My funeral arrangements?"

After a moment of apparent confusion, Mrs. Sandoval smiled. "I'm sorry. I must have startled you. I don't mean *your* funeral, silly. I mean for that dead person."

"But we don't know who he is. Why would we arrange for the funeral?"

"Well, Mr. Nigel, if someone else speaks up and wishes to do the honors, I suppose we acquiesce, but he did choose our property to die on. I feel we owe him a proper burial. We can put him in the garden."

Stefanie and Esmerelda puckered their faces as if the idea of a man underneath the ornamentals didn't sit well. Then they looked at each other and shrugged their shoulders.

"Bury him in the garden?" repeated Nigel.

"Play it as it lays," said Mrs. Sandoval. "It's fitting, seeing as how we occupy a former golf course. Maybe that can be the theme for the funeral, The Final Hole."

"No!" shouted Abuelita. "We're not burying him in the garden. You do that and the Laura Bush petunias will get trampled. Ain't worth it."

"I agree," said Nigel. "Think of the petunias."

Mrs. Sandoval apparently had not thought of the petunias. "Maybe you're right. The most convenient place, for the mourners' sake, would be close to the parking lot."

"Enough with the funeral, already," spouted Abuelita. "That stiff's on ice. He'll keep for months, if need be. What about my wedding?"

"What is the date for this blessed event?" asked Nigel, thinking that Halloween had just passed. "After the holidays, I take it."

"The fourteenth. November the fourteenth, a Saturday," replied Mrs. Sandoval.

"The fourteenth of November? But today's the ninth," squealed Nigel.

"No shit, Sherlock. You better get that ass in gear," said Abuelita.

"I don't know where to start," said Nigel, placing a hand to his forehead to control a series of mad twitches infecting his left and right eyebrows.

"Let's start with the wedding gown. I can help you with that," said Stefanie. "We'll find a nice lace gown in cream."

"Cream? No, ma'am," said Abuelita. "Not cream. Not for *my* wedding."

"Cream or off-white is traditional for older brides marrying for a second time," said Stefanie. "Maybe you were thinking white, but that's a symbol of innocence and purity that—"

"Crimson," yelled Abuelita.

"What?" said Stefanie.

"Crimson. Crimson and gold. Those are my wedding dress colors, and I don't want an argument. Ain't nobody can say I didn't earn those colors. And I want to show off my boobs. Lots of boobs. They been wrapped up like lunchbox burritos for decades now. They need one last coming-out party."

"It's your day, I guess," said Stefanie.

"I'll make some lotions and potions," chimed Esmerelda, framing her face with dancing hands.

"I feel ill," mumbled Nigel. The quiver infecting his eyebrows had meandered south, settling in for a lengthy stay among his digestive organs.

"It's too late to send out invitations," said Mrs. Sandoval. "But we'll need a registry. What is your fiancé's name?"

Abuelita stroked her chin.

"You do know his name, don't you Abuelita?" said Stefanie.

"Of course I know his name. It just escapes me at the moment. I don't call him by his name, anyway."

"What do you call him?"

"By his Twitter handle, at JakWad44. Of course, I have my own pet name for him."

"And that would be?" prompted Stefanie.

"That's for me to know and you to shut up about."

The grandfather clock in the atrium donged.

Nigel had heard of death knells, and now he'd felt one.

Mrs. Sandoval threw up a finger for each dong. When the number of thrown up fingers reached twelve, she shouted, "Tequila!"

Nigel's rush hour had arrived.

3

A FERAL BUTLER'S DAY OFF

Nigel awoke to his teeth clattering and his stomach fluttering. His trembling hands grabbed for the bedsheets, and he clenched his jaws, tightening his muscles to choke off the shudder. Once he'd stopped shaking, the bed stopped moving. All was quiet except for the sound of his shallow breathing and a rumble in his stomach, which he suspected was his soul curling up to die.

His beauty sleep had left him exhausted in his bed. Throughout the night, revolving thoughts of weddings, funerals, snide detectives, and stepping on a dead man's hand feasted on his mind like ravenous bedbugs. Thank God for nightmares so vivid that they wake you up.

Nigel would have been squeezing Annie for support had she been there, but she was an early riser. Especially, it seemed, on mornings when Nigel was being sucked into a bottomless maelstrom.

Sitting up in bed and waiting for the sweat to dry, Nigel thought of the previous day's events. This was the last thing he wanted to think about, but sometimes the last thing you want to think about is the only thing you can think about until you've thought about it. So, he thought about it.

Being new to the butler's profession, he'd had his share of

first-day jitters. Worrying, for instance, that he might be tasked with folding a fitted sheet, ironing triple-pleated trousers, or excoriating a scullery maid. Outside of those butler's banes, however, he'd approached the day with a reasonable degree of confidence. Unfortunately, disposing of dead bodies had failed to show up on Old Winpole's syllabus. The planning of weddings and funerals had also been neglected. Nigel had the sneaking suspicion that even if he'd signed up for the Butler's Deluxe course at twice the price, such topics would have scarcely been mentioned. He had hoped that for his first trip to the plate, he would have been lobbed a few ripe melons, underhand. Not, as it turned out, slung an assortment of scorching meteorites.

To make matters worse, he had competition of the kind that one cannot defeat. Gastrick, the previous butler, had set an impossibly high standard of service. Something Nigel had been reminded of on an hourly basis. Absent from these comments had been any mention of Gastrick, superlative butler though he was, as the central participant in a plot to murder Abuelita. Had old Gastrick's murdering skills matched his buttling expertise, Abuelita would by now be food for mushrooms, while Gastrick would be overseeing the estate's conversion to a country club with eighteen holes of golf.

Recent history notwithstanding, phrases beginning with "Gastrick used to," "Gastrick would," and "Gastrick would never," had became so annoyingly thick that Nigel, at the end of his first workday, had assembled the estate's occupants to reintroduce himself.

"I am Nigel," he had said. "Your new butler. I endeavor to provide you with the most outstanding service possible. Rest assured, I am fully cognizant that, as your new butler, my services may be somewhat at variance with recent conventions. Be that as it may, I wish to emphasize that two services I will never provide are: one, murdering you in your sleep; and two, altering your wills behind your backs. Thank you for your attention." Raising the tip of his nose, the right brow, and the left upper lip, he had turned and left for the day.

Being a butler had some positives. But that was yesterday. As bad as the night had been, and as bad as the day leading up to the night had been, today would be better. Sure it would. It was Tuesday, his day off. The unusual schedule of Tuesdays off and half-days Saturday and Sunday had been instituted by his predecessor, Gastrick, of course. The wife's dreaded to-do list of home improvements awaited, as always, but before he'd looked, the phone rang. Nigel fished his phone out of yesterday's pants and saw that Annie was calling, probably to add three new items.

"Listen, I know it's your day off, and you want to get to that to-do list," said Annie. She was smart but no mind reader. "But there's been an emergency. Mother needs your help with her hot water heater. It's sprung a leak. The water's draining okay, but she'll need a new one."

"Today?"

"Of course, today. She can't take a shower without hot water, and you wouldn't want to be around Mother if she can't take a shower."

"I wouldn't want to be around Mother—"

"Stop. Don't say it. Not now. Stanley would have taken care of this kind of thing, but now that he's gone, things like this just put Mother in a tailspin. You know she still blames you."

"For her hot water heater?"

"For Stanley walking out. So, consider this a chance to redeem yourself."

"Stanley left by his own good judgment," said Nigel. "I had nothing to do it."

"Maybe, but that's not what she thinks."

"Can't she call a plumber? That's what I'd do."

"She can't be alone in her house with a plumber. Just go over there and do what you need to do to fix it. In case you've forgotten, replacing the hot water heater is also on your list. You fix hers, score a few brownie points, and get some practice all at once."

"Okay. But it's not your mother I'll be collecting my brownie rewards from."

Frankly, Nigel found the image of Annie's mother in a tail-spin not that unappealing. Certainly not something needing immediate attention. The idea that he was "to blame" for Stanley's escape was ludicrous. Nigel took no credit. On the other hand, if Stanley felt he'd been instrumental, a kind mention in his last will and testament would not be rebuked. As for being "redeemed" in Mother's eyes, she'd treated Nigel like something to be scraped off a shoe for as long as he could remember. He hadn't seen a change of heart over the ten years of his marriage no matter what he did.

Having established who wore the jeans in the family, Nigel slipped on his bloomers and consulted the YouTube experts on hot water heater installations. Nothing presented seemed insurmountable for this recent graduate from butler college. After all, he'd installed a shower head, and it barely leaked at all. The biggest challenge would be getting the bulky tank into the attic, but thankfully, his mother-in-law was the strapping, athletic type.

Before stopping at the hardware store for parts, he made a side trip to Stanley's Pies and Desserts. The proprietor of this shop was none other than his mother-in-law's estranged husband, Stanley.

Stanley had left the old battle dragon a few months earlier, being declared middle-aged crazy by baffled friends. Nigel was baffled by their bafflement. Middle-aged *reasonable*, it seemed to him. The astounding bit wasn't his leaving, but what happened directly after. Stanley had become the current boy-toy for a local celebrity, Cam Logan. For those who knew Stanley and Cam Logan, nothing about that last sentence could ever sound right. As a pair, they were like Dom Perignon champagne with a tray of biscuits 'n gravy served with a plastic spork. I mean, when a faded, roly-poly, dough-faced, retired pipefitter shacks up with a rich, glamorous, multi-husbanded country music star, people say, "Whaaa?" and rightly so.

As if that were not enough, the relationship had stirred in Stanley a latent artistic soul no one would have ever suspected. His newfound creativity spewed forth in the form of baked goods. With Ms. Logan's backing, he'd opened an artisanal bakeshop, becoming the hottest entrepreneur in the county.

This was Nigel's first visit to the brightly lit emporium, which resembled what he imagined a modern art gallery to be like. The only objects that weren't white or shiny were the scrumptious goods themselves. Say what you will about Stanley, the man knew his away around a crust. His current offerings were built around a Van Gogh theme. The blueberry pie version of *Starry Night* looked good enough to frame. Assorted cherry tarts presented as discarded ears challenged consumers to reexamine societal taboos.

"Nigel, old man," shouted a familiar voice, interrupting Nigel's contemplation of a Van Gogh self-portrait rendered in cheesecake form.

He turned to see the approaching Stanley in his baker's whites, looking surprisingly mobile. Not only was Stanley uncharacteristically animated, but his hairline was on the move, having un-receded several inches down the forehead in a magical reversal of a longtime trend. The sprouts occupying these former wastelands must have had deep roots extending to a previously unexploited reservoir of auburn. Stanley's face appeared to have been ironed, or buffed, or steamed, or worked over in some heavy-handed way. Below this rigid, plasticine hide lurked a smile struggling to present itself. It was clear that Stanley had found his place in the world. And that place, when not producing pies, was next to Cam Logan at the cosmetic surgeon's office.

"What brings you in?" asked Stanley.

"A bit of business, actually. I've been put in charge of a wedding, and I thought you might provide the desserts."

"A wedding? So Annie's got you planning weddings, has she? I might have thought it."

Eager to disavow the notion of a dominant wife, Nigel replied, "No, no, no. I've taken the position of butler at the Sandoval place, and as part of my official duties, I'm making arrangements for a wedding to be held there."

"The Sandoval place?" asked a surprised Stanley.

"That's right. The old golf course."

"I gotcha. When's the soiree?"

"Friday."

Stanley cocked his head, rolling his eyes back to the sector of his brain that had the calendars. "Friday? Today's Tuesday. That's not much time."

"I understand that. It's a small affair, maybe a dozen. I don't expect much. Just some choice pieces from your usual batch would be sufficient. I'll let you decide."

"I'm supplying a cake for a boy's birthday on Friday. I can double it up."

"Fine. Whatever you have will be wonderful, I'm sure."

"You said you're working at the Sandoval place?" Stanley's eyes exhibited a strange concern, as if working at the Sandoval place came with a curse.

But what did Nigel know? With so little bendable skin, Stanley's face was hard to read. "Yes. Started yesterday. Probably not the best day to start."

"No?"

"Happened to be a dead body lying about. As a butler, I have to take care of dead bodies. Not many people know that about butlers."

Stanley's jaw dropped. A goose egg, should one have been available, could have been inserted into his mouth without touching lip. After a moment, the jaw regained its form. "Dead? Are you sure?"

"Well, I hope so. Else the autopsy will be a fright."

"Anyone we know?"

"No. A drifter, perhaps."

"Do they know who killed him?" asked Stanley in a low voice, as if the cherry tarts had ears.

"Who killed him? Let's not jump to any conclusions. My money is on natural causes. Not that I know about these things, but I saw no signs of a struggle, unless you count the toad."

Stanley wore a faraway look, like a baker in a hot air balloon. "Makes one think, doesn't it?"

"Does it? About what? Toads?"

"Here today, gone tomorrow. That sort of thing."

"Right," said Nigel, not realizing they'd veered philosophic. "You always surprise me, Stanley. I mean, when I talk to you, I never expect anything, and yet, there's always *something*. Hidden depths."

"Hidden what?"

"Depths."

"Oh," said Stanley, as if his balloon had just scraped a mountain top. Reestablishing a foothold on the *terra firma*, he added, "Listen, how would you and Annie like to come out to our place some evening? We're practically neighbors. We have a place out there."

"So I've heard. I'm sure Annie would love to meet Cam. Text me. We'll set something up."

The hardware store was across town from Stanley's bakery, a five-minute drive. The choice of model for the water heater was critical, a decision which, if badly made, would sabotage the entire operation. Most units on display were quickly deemed unsuitable, but one was the perfect fit. It fit in the back seat of Nigel's car. Perfect.

Having loaded up the heater, associated parts, and most of the tools he'd need, Nigel steeled himself for the installation by thinking of old St. George. That dragon-slaying saint had been a boyhood favorite of his and, after meeting his mother-in-law, an inspiration. Something about gas heaters and mother-in-laws had rekindled memories of the ancient hero and his fire-breathing foe.

"Hello, Mother," said St. Nigel to the dragon. "I heard you were in need of a water heater. I'm here to install you a new one." He unleashed a forty-watt smile, hoping she might detect the good cheer and hold back on the flames.

"You? You're going to install the hot water heater? You're joking, aren't you?"

"Not in the slightest, Mother dearest. I'm packin' a heater, and I'm here to install it. Just lead the way—"

She did not lead the way. She guarded the door as if he'd waved a foreclosure notice in her face. "What makes you think you can install a water heater? You may be a lot of things, Michael—"

"Nigel."

"Nigel, but handy isn't one of them. That's good, honest work—stuff you wouldn't know about. Before you polluted his mind, my husband did work like that. He had know-how. He was a pipe fitter."

Such a vituperative comment, especially one ending with the words pipe fitter, deserved a snappy comeback. Nigel would have one in a couple of days, but for now, he needed to install a water heater with minimal discord. "Okay, suit yourself. I'm sure you can call around to find a crew of burly installers ready to help out a lone female for a hefty price. You know how pipe fitters are."

"The hot water tank is this way, up in the attic."

Much to Nigel's surprise, placing the new water heater went quickly with a minimal amount of interference and abuse. The mother-in-law's combative spirit had been somewhat blunted by the physical toll of pushing the water heater up to the attic. Conversely, Nigel's enthusiasm soared as he watched the water heater reach its destination coincident with his mother-in-law's near-collapse from exhaustion.

Despite a few variances from the YouTube video, the installation went like clockwork. In no time, a fine new gas hot water heater had been signed, sealed, and installed. Nigel felt so good about the job he'd done that he bought a second set of identical parts and went to work at his own place. Two water heater replacements in one day would certainly impress Annie.

Talk about your brownie points, absolutely.

By four o'clock, Nigel had finished his second installation and tucked himself into the Lazy Boy to luxuriate in his own accomplishments. He was exhausted, but it came from a good place—a place he hadn't accessed much lately, where good, honest work could be flaunted for a personal advantage.

As his mind drifted into the clouds, his eyelids crept downward into the shuttered position that had eluded him the night before. He settled into an initial stage of sleep when, to his annoyance, an explosion occurred. He had the sensation of levitating for a split second before dropping with a thud into the chair. He didn't know the source of the calamity, but he knew where to look.

He rushed to the pull-down ladder leading up to the attic. The ladder did not need to be pulled down because just to one side, in the ceiling, was a large hole to be known henceforth as Hole A. Looking through Hole A, Nigel saw a lovely blue sky dusted with altocumulus clouds. Such a sight would not be possible without the roof having a significant perforation, hereinafter known as Hole B. He felt certain that neither Hole A nor Hole B had been present when he was installing the gas water heater.

Ah, the gas water heater, thought Nigel.

It should have been somewhere in his line of sight between holes A and B. It was not. He looked down at the floor. Could his home have fallen victim to an untimely meteorite strike or falling aircraft debris?

The lack of scattered metal parts or flaming stones suggested not.

Those scoundrels! thought Nigel. *They sold me a defective water heater!*

He had read somewhere that in such instances, one should remove one's self from the premises, so he grabbed his cell phone and headed out the front door.

As he walked down the street, Nigel noticed an unusual number of neighbors standing outside, looking back from where he had come. After putting a hundred or so paces between himself and the house, he turned to see what they were gawking at. In his front yard's live oak tree, some fifteen feet up, sat the steaming wreckage of a new gas water heater, unnervingly similar to the one he had just installed.

Nigel felt as though he should call someone. Out of an abundance of caution, he dialed his mother-in-law to alert her to the minor possibility that she too might have been sold a defective water heater.

"Hello, M-M-Mother."

"Hello. This must be Nigel."

Nigel was thrown for a loop. The mother-in-law never called him by his actual name. Usually it was Nile, or Niland, or Bonehead. A slip of the tongue, perhaps.

"How are things going over there?" said Nigel.

"Things are fine here. I just got out of a warm shower, thanks to you."

"Nothing unusual? No odd sounds or anything?"

"No, nothing unusual here. Why do you ask?"

"Oh, well, there was just something I wanted to mention about your new water heater—"

"Just a second while a light my cig—"

"Mother?"

Nigel heard a hollow sounding explosion followed by a noise like a cell phone impacting a solid object at high speed. There was also a scream, another scream, and then a yowl. While hard on the ears, he considered the screams and the yowls to be positive signs.

He hung up, dialed 911, and directed the operator to dispatch emergency vehicles to Mother's address for an apparently defective gas water heater incident. Then, after noticing more than the usual amount of smoke enveloping his own home, Nigel redialed 911 and told the same operator, in a different voice, to dispatch a fire truck to his own address for a defective gas water heater incident.

When the operator mentioned that just moments before he had received a similar call for a different address, Nigel professed his incredulity. When the operator mentioned the two calls had come from the same phone, he made a series of static-like noises and hung up.

4

UNWELCOME GUESTS

Considering that it was just his second day on the job, Nigel entered the estate with a frightful amount of trepidation. It was quite a favor to ask of an employer, but every proposed alternative had been summarily squashed. So it was that he plodded toward Mrs. Sandoval's office with Annie and her mother in tow. A little cheeriness from the pair would have bolstered his morale, if not his case. Bolstering, however, was not what they wanted to do for Nigel.

"Mrs. Sandoval, you are looking especially radiant today," said Nigel, buttering the crumpet.

Dressed as a gaucho, she pushed up the brim of her wide-brimmed hat with a riding crop to get a look at the crowd invading her office. "You've brought visitors?"

"Yes. Let me introduce these two wonderful ladies. You've already met Annie, the top investigator at Sniffer's Detective Agency." Nigel had previously concealed that Annie and he were man and wife. He felt no compunction at present to set the record straight. The fewer the complications, the better. "She, of course, was instrumental in saving Abuelita's life from that evil lawyer and your sinister butler, Gastrick."

"Sinister, perhaps," said Mrs. Sandoval. "But he knew his way around a cocktail."

"Yes, but now you can enjoy your cocktails without speculating on their cyanide content?"

"He also knew how to steam a hat. What's your point, Mr. Nigel?"

Nigel felt it best to plow forward. "Let me introduce this other fine lady. This is Annie's mother, Kayda."

Annie's mother presented a particularly formidable visage, even for her, with a turban wrapped around most of her head to conceal a head of hair that had been incinerated in broad swaths by the inconvenient heat of a gas explosion. She also wore enormous dark sunglasses that hid a missing left eyebrow. Other than that, she was her usual dread-inducing self.

"Kayda. That's an unusual name," said Mrs. Sandoval.

"It means dragon in Korean," spouted Nigel.

"You don't look Korean," said Mrs. Sandoval.

"I'm not. Nigel came up with that. My parents didn't know Korean."

"They obviously knew something," said Nigel. "Now, if I may get back to business, I have a proposal. Annie here is not only a private investigator, but also a former policewoman with the Houston PD. She is well-versed in matters of security and defense. In other words, she's handy to have around should a criminal element present itself."

"Are you implying that we have a criminal element in this house?"

"No, not in the house, but possibly outside. Why, just the other day a stranger infiltrated the grounds."

"Who?" said Mrs. Sandoval. She could be absentminded in the morning but was much better in the afternoons, between drinks two and four.

"The dead guy," said Nigel. "That corpse in the garden. He infiltrated the grounds."

"Do we need to worry about him? I mean, being dead and all?"

"Possibly not him, exactly, but someone else. If there's one, there could be more. We don't know what his intentions were. He may have been up to no good."

"Absolutely he was up to no good. He died in our garden. That's no good."

"Precisely. You don't want unknown persons wandering willy-nilly about the property and then dying. That's why I propose Annie stay on the property for security. Just for a while, mind you."

"You're proposing we pay her for on-site, twenty-four-hour security. Is that it?"

"Somewhat, but not quite."

Nigel hopped to the side, a response to the painful twisting of his backside flesh between Annie's thumb and forefinger. Something in Mrs. Sandoval's proposal had appealed to her, but he could not bring himself to charge his employer for a favor. Old Winpole wouldn't have stood for it.

Safely out of pinching distance, Nigel continued. "You see, Annie has rather suddenly been placed in the market for housing. When I heard about her dilemma, I suggested she might find housing here in exchange for her service as a security officer. Kills two birds with one stone, you might say."

"May I ask why she is in need of housing?"

"Gas water heater—a defective one. Damned thing exploded."

"I see. And what about her mother?"

"Yes, of course. Annie's mother, you see, also finds herself in need of housing on a short-term basis. She would be staying with Annie if not for that damned, defective, exploding gas water heater. My thought was that she could room here with Annie for the time being. She would be no trouble. She's quite unassuming," said Nigel, unconcerned, apparently, over the combustibility of his pants. "We could even put her to work cleaning, disinfecting...toilets and whatnot." He shuffled sideways again, this time to avoid the steam escaping from Mother's ears.

"I hate to be a thrower of wet towels, but two more people in the house, what with the upcoming wedding and the funeral, would be quite a burden."

"You haven't heard my full proposal," said Nigel.

"I haven't?"

"No, because I haven't proposed it yet. I propose that I too reside on the premises for as long as Annie and her mother are here. I could room in Gastrick's old quarters. You would, for the time being, have a live-in butler just as you had with Gastrick. I would deal with any extra messes caused by your temporary tenants. See how it all balances out?"

"*Does* it balance out?"

"With the wedding and the funeral coming up, I daresay, it will be useful to have me on site twenty-four seven." Though somewhat un-butler-like, Nigel batted his eyelashes for added effect.

"You may have something there," said Mrs. Sandoval, stroking her cheek with the riding crop. "Very well. Choose a room in the left wing and help the ladies get situated. Then, Mr. Nigel, I want a word with you."

Nigel did his best obsequious bellhop routine while showing the ladies to their room. When they bemoaned the lack of a butler-skin rug on which to wipe their tired feet, he excused himself to return to Mrs. Sandoval's office. While he didn't relish a fresh one-on-one with his gaucho overseer, he was quite relieved to escape the cat-o'-nine-tails tongue-lashing by his better half and her noxious hell-demon mom.

"At your service, madam," said Nigel, standing at attention in front of Mrs. Sandoval's burled oak executive desk. "Perhaps I should apologize for springing my plan on you so suddenly, but—"

"Don't bother about that now. We need to get busy. We're expecting Abuelita's fiancé this morning."

"This morning?" repeated Nigel. "This whole marriage thing is charging forward like a runaway freight train. Is the groom to be staying here until the wedding?"

"Yes, he'll go into the other spare bedroom. I'll be away this morning, so you must take care of things."

"Very well. What is the gentleman's name?"

"The gentleman?"

"Abuelita's fiancé?"

"Oh, him. For now, this 'gentleman,' as you call him, goes by At-Jakwad44. Abuelita can't seem to dig up a real name. I do have a picture of him, though. Here, take it."

Nigel looked at the picture up close, then far away, and turned it over to look for an annotation, like maybe a date. "You've noticed, I suppose, that the gentleman in this picture appears younger than our Abuelita by three or four decades?"

"I've noticed. I've also noticed the picture looks like a badly faded Polaroid. Out of date, I imagine."

Still looking at the photo, Nigel replied, "We can only hope. May I presume that the gentleman, when he arrives, will be wearing a shirt?"

"I would think. That topless photo, as I understand it, was sent as part of a reciprocal agreement, but it's all we've got. Or, I should say, it's the only picture Abuelita will let us see."

"Very well. When Mr. At-Jakwad44 arrives, whom shall I notify?"

"Get Abuelita down here. She's prepped and ready."

"Indeed. Leave it to me."

"And," said Mrs. Sandoval, punctuating her words with hand chops, "make sure you warn this guy about Abuelita's wheelchair."

"He doesn't know she's in a wheelchair?"

"I don't know. But even if he does, he won't know about her braking issues. Give the man a tutorial on how to sidestep a runaway wheelchair. Otherwise, he'll be taking his vows on crutches."

"Will do," he said, taking his leave.

Nigel was not supposed to bound during butler's hours, but bound he did, right up the grand staircase three steps at a time. The day was becoming busy, and he felt a need to keep up. Entering Gastrick's old room, where he'd deposited his suitcase, he began to unpack. While he was in amongst the socks, the doorbell rang. The backbone stiffened, the waistcoat tightened, and the socks, those not on his feet, would have to fend for themselves. Work called.

Nigel shuffled down the stairs at butler's battle speed and swung open the double doors to reveal a man wearing a shirt. Not a very fine shirt—not fine in any way—but a shirt nevertheless. That was but one difference between the man at the door and the man in the photo.

Indeed, photo-man seemed of an entirely different type and vintage than door-man. Photo-man was of the strapping variety —one of those athletic types who lived on a boat and only reluctantly put on a shirt when visited by a detective. If photo-man did wear a shirt, it'd be of the thin and tight variety to show off his muscles. If door-man wore a tight shirt, it'd be to keep his ribs in place. Photo-man had smooth, bronzed skin. Door-man appeared to be wrapped in beef jerky. Photo-man had a full head of hair. Door-man did not have a full head for hair to grow on.

Compassion precluded further comparisons as Nigel looked at the man and then the photo. The two visages suggested a separation of many years, and from the looks of it, very hard years they were, too. He wondered if a portion of those years might have been spent sealed in a sarcophagus or buried in a peat bog. The man had something of the mummy about him. And not those movie mummies, so full of zest, but more like the museum ones, admired for their staunch refusal to become dust.

"Guy Yeena?" said the man.

"No. The name is Nigel. I'm the butler. You are At-Jakwad44, I presume?"

"This is the Sandoval house?" said the man.

"Yes, you are at the Sandoval estate. Welcome, and come on in. You look as if you've been on a long journey."

A long journey indeed. He looked as though he'd spent the last two decades dragged about by a mangy lion with gum disease. The man carried a heavily soiled laundry bag, and his clothes looked like something a kind-hearted hobo might donate to a bum.

The man shuffled forward, turned himself in a circle once inside, and ogled the surroundings as if he'd been transported into a Martian palace.

"I've been instructed to fetch Abuelita upon your arrival," said Nigel. "I'm sure you're eager to see her. Follow me, please. Can I get you anything to drink?"

"Water. Clear, clean water."

"Very well. I'll see what I can do," said Nigel, thinking if that was his drink of choice, grounds for divorce had already been established. "Please have a seat here," said Nigel, presenting a spot on the Louis XIV loveseat.

Returning with silver tray topped with a bottle of water and a glass, Nigel set the works on an end table and began to pour. The man leered into the glass as if a mermaid were splashing in it.

The man roiled his lips in preparation, then hoisted the container to the proper orifice and downed the contents with a series of gulps. The residual overflow was remedied with a swipe from the back of his hand, and then he nodded while gazing into the empty glass. "So good. Don't have this where I came from," he said.

"No? Where might that be? Michigan?"

The man cackled while Nigel chuckled. After a minute, they stopped, realizing simultaneously that they'd been laughing at different things.

"Had to get back," said the man. "They whomped me, you know. Gave me this dent," he said, waving a finger around the left side of his skull, which indeed housed a noticeable cavity. "Bit too. Ate bugs. Lost my clothes, but I came back. Need to find wife. Do you know Guy Yeena?"

"No. I'm sorry I don't know a Guy Yeena, but maybe we can do something about that wife. If you'll pardon me, I will notify Abuelita that you're here."

Nigel hurried to Abuelita's room but was waylaid by Abuelita herself hiding at the top of the stairs behind some draperies. She was in her wheelchair, but her customary black granny dress had been ditched in favor of a blue satin number that must have contained some form of display-shelving infrastructure upon which had been hoisted Abuelita's bosoms. Either that or they'd been pumped full of helium. Either way, raising the war-ravaged relics to such unlikely altitudes should have required a 'For Display Only' sign. Not to be outdone, Abuelita's face had undergone major reconstruction, which involved serious quantities of spackle and multiple coats of paint.

"Abuelita, your fiancé has arrived."

"That ain't him. I've been watching," she said, holding up a pair of opera glasses. "He's old."

Nigel had never been in Abuelita's room, but her comment raised a suspicion that it must be devoid of mirrors. Several reasons why that might be came to mind. Aloud, he replied, "I'm sorry if you were expecting a college sophomore, but you're not exactly a spring chicken yourself. He's obviously come a long way to marry you."

"Send him away. He's not my type."

"You should have typed him before you got engaged. I can't send him away. He's got a dent in his head, and he's eaten bugs. You owe him the courtesy of an introduction at the very least."

"No. Tell him I've disappeared without a trace, and I'm not expected back. Tell him I've eloped with the pool boy. Tell him I have one of those diseases where I live in a bubble. Tell him anything, just get him out of here."

"Abuelita, I will not break off your engagement for you."

"Why not? You're the butler. Start acting like one."

In Nigel's butler training, Old Winpole had vividly described the consequences of butlers allowing themselves to be interjected in domestic disputes. He'd related a very personal tale of a family that had communicated their love, affection, and displeasure via slaps, which they would often compel the butler to administer. It wasn't until Old Winpole was instructed to perform such services on a string of unsavory leather-clad house guests that he'd realized his services as a butler were being rudely abused. Nigel was not about to fall into that chasm.

"I will tell him you are currently indisposed," said Nigel. "But breaking the engagement I will leave to you."

Nigel returned to the stashed fiancé. "I am so sorry, but it will be a little while before Abuelita is available. Is there anything I can get you? A beverage? Air freshener? Fudgesicle?"

"Clean, clear water, please. We don't have that where I came from."

"Of course. You'll be glad to know water flows here as if from a spigot."

As Nigel produced the water, he noticed, for the first time, the man's foot coverings. His "footwear," to stretch the term, was noteworthy for its improvisational character. In amongst conventional shoe components were sizable portions consisting of cardboard, leather scraps, and straw. One foot was covered in large part by the repurposed shell of an armadillo, which, thankfully, was sufficiently weathered to be free of tire marks. He decided the man would at least receive a shoe upgrade for his troubles.

"Excuse me while I run an errand. Please make yourself at home," said Nigel before heading upstairs.

5

A GUEST'S WELCOME

Nigel ran upstairs to the butler's quarters and flung open the closet. Apparently, an arrest for conspiring to commit murder doesn't allow time for clearing out closets. Gastrick's were positively stuffed with his effects. Far too many, in Nigel's opinion. Having requisitioned the room for his own temporary stay, he saw a golden opportunity to set a course for Gastrick's spiritual redemption with an act of charity. Perhaps in some future parole hearing, Gastrick could leverage the heartfelt gesture. That is, if he ever learned of it.

If anyone had clothes to spare, it was that incarcerated clotheshorse. His closet contained a week's worth of official butler attire in one section, atrociously colorful leisure wear in another, and what appeared to be a shoe and boot museum in another. A special section of vintage footwear, each identified with a copper nameplate, beckoned from a mahogany display rack. To one side sat what appeared to be a pair of mini refrigerators with glass doors. Flicking a switch illuminated their interiors. One was empty, but the other contained a pair of desiccated old knee boots of the kind worn by desiccated old horsemen. A shiny silver placard described the contents as "Wellington Boots c. 1823. Once owned by Beau Brummell."

Nigel wasn't interested in boots requiring refrigeration. Instead, he found what he was looking for on a lower shelf in a cubby tagged, "US Army Issue Corcoran Paratrooper's Boot, 1944." These boots held a special significance in the darker regions of Nigel's heart, as well as other areas not to be discussed in polite society. One might say that delicate parts of Nigel's anatomy had recently shared an uncomfortable moment with the toe of one of those boots. And now that the misused boots were destined for a new owner, those insulted body parts could finally rest easy.

Next, Nigel selected from the closet two pairs of socks, some underwear, a pair of slacks, two shirts, and some aviator-style sunglasses. He loaded the loot into an overnight bag also from the closet and then raided the bathroom for a bottle of cologne, some mouthwash, and toothpaste. When he noticed a mannequin head sporting a rakish driving cap, he threw that in as well.

On his way out, Nigel noticed a heavy gold watch on the bureau. The sinister butler Gastrick, in his new captive life, might need a calendar but certainly not a watch. Into the bag it went.

Carrying the boots and the overnight bag, Nigel descended the sweeping main staircase until he saw that his visitor had a visitor. Thinking Abuelita had enlisted a mercenary to deliver her rebuke, he stepped behind a pillar and stretched an ear to its limit.

The guest's visitor was that flaked-out woman-child, Esmerelda. Essie was a nice woman but also a disturbingly vivid example of the type of characters allowed to run loose in asylum Sandoval. She had a reputation around town as the crazy woman who read people's auras. These auras, in her view, contained all manner of personal data that she disclosed loudly and without hesitation. Many people around New Antigua, however, considered their auras to be their own damn business and reacted to Essie's pronouncements about as well as they'd react to someone reading out their credit card numbers.

This mysterious new guest was not, it appeared, one of those people. Not so surprising, considering the amount of loose wiring likely housed in his aura-factory. Essie and the visitor sat gazing into each other's eyes. One might have thought they were lovers preparing for a first kiss, but with his deeper insight, Nigel reckoned they were engaged in a telepathic experiment.

He heard the man mumble, "If that mockingbird don't sing...."

Esmerelda joined in on the next verse. "Mama's going to buy you a diamond ring." Then she put a hand to his cheek.

The doorbell interrupted their touching duet, prompting Nigel to drop the boots and bag and go answer it.

The sight of a distinguished, elderly gentleman standing at the door induced a flutter to Nigel's innards. Not that the man appeared formidable in any way, but the large suitcase by his side portended trouble of the worst kind, the kind that makes itself at home. The man leaped forward with an extended hand and toothy grin. Though they'd not met before, a few synapses in the back of Nigel's brain scratched their chins.

"Howdy. Jack Watt. Nice to meet you."

"Jack Watt?" said Nigel as a few synapses raised their hands. "I'm Nigel, the butler."

"The butler? And English too. Sweet! You probably know already. I'm here to meet my little sugar hen. If all goes well, we'll be married within a week." The man reached into his jacket and pulled out a photograph.

Nigel, not to be outdone, reached in his jacket to retrieve his photograph. "You're forty-four?" he asked.

"I thank you for the compliment, but I'm seventy-four. You might want to have them peepers checked."

"I mean, you're JackWad44," said Nigel, looking at photo, then at man, then at photo. The two images depicted disparate vintages of the same man, for sure. He just hoped Abuelita wasn't intent on receiving an exact replica or, for that matter, a reasonable facsimile to the photo Nigel slipped back into his pocket.

"Oh? The Twitter thing," said Jack Watt. "Yeah, that's me." He continued to ogle his photo the way the earlier guest had ogled the clean, clear water. After sweeping his tongue across the upper dentures, he exhaled with a "cha-cha-cha."

Nigel invited the man in and craned his neck to get a look at his entrancing photo. The image alarmed him. In terms of sensuality, none of the current females of the Sandoval estate held a match to the "lady" in the picture. The only aspect of the image carrying any sense of familiarity was the middle third. There Nigel saw a resemblance to what he'd seen earlier in the day, extruding itself from a blue satin dress. But the goods in the vintage photo looked fine as they were. More than fine, actually. In contrast, the updated version of the genuine article desperately needed some Photoshop. A disturbing pattern was emerging with regards to photographs.

"Follow me, please," said Nigel motioning him forward. "I trust your trip was okay? Nothing untoward? No subsisting on insects or receiving dents to the head?"

"Not hardly. The trip was grand. Couldn't complain," he said, hoisting his suitcase as if it were filled with feathers.

His attitude was refreshing. Nigel saw no way it would survive into the evening. Jack Watt was shown discreetly into Mrs. Sandoval's office, located across the atrium from the other visitor. Best to keep Jack Watt separated from as many people as possible. He would soon have his own issues to deal with.

"I will let Abuelita know you are here," said Nigel. He then turned and legged it toward Abuelita's room.

With the real fiancé in captivity, Nigel had to wonder, who was that first guy? Maybe he just wanted a tall glass of clean, clear water, but he'd have come a long way just for that. With the groom-to-be waiting in the wings, Nigel had no time to consider the matter.

At her door, Nigel whispered, "Abuelita!" following three soft knocks. "Abuelita, are you there?"

"You got rid of him?" came the response from behind the door.

"No, he's with Esmerelda. They're having a sing-along. Your fiancé is here now."

"I told you to get rid of him."

"There seems to have been a mix-up. The man you saw was not your fiancé."

The door cracked open. "You said it was."

"I was mistaken."

"What kind of a butler are you? This wouldn't happen with Gastrick."

"No, it certainly wouldn't. If Gastrick were here, you'd be supplying the worms their minimum daily requirement," said Nigel. "Who is that man? Do you know?"

"How would I know? And why would I care? I want to see my Little Wadkins. I need to freshen up, then I'm coming down."

"What about the other man? You can't come down until we get rid of him."

"Not *we*," she corrected. "*You. You* get rid of him. You let him in. You're the butler. If Gastrick were here, he wouldn't have let him in."

"No, of course not. Not unless he were peddling poisons."

"Do what you want with that other guy. I'll be down for my beau as soon as I touch up my face."

"Very well. Your beau awaits in the office."

Nigel returned downstairs. Guest #1 and Esmerelda were getting along like two old cellmates who had shared a padded room. When he arrived at Mrs. Sandoval's office, Jack Watt was leaning back in the office chair and leering at the photo of his betrothed. *Leer while you can*, thought Nigel. *Winter is coming.*

Leering as he was with his back to the door, Jack failed to notice Nigel's approach. "Man, oh, man," growled the ogling Jack.

"Ahem," interrupted Nigel. "Excuse me, sir. Abuelita shall be down shortly." He refrained from mentioning that she would have aged some fifty years in the interim.

Looking up from the photo, Jack replied, "I hope by Abuelita, you mean my Sweet Little Hen."

"I hope by Sweet Little Hen, you mean Abuelita."

It occurred to Nigel that he didn't know Abuelita's actual name. Abuelita, meaning Lil' Grandma in Spanish, probably wasn't the name she used for suitors. Sweet Little Hen sounded more plausible, given her flexible truth-in-advertising policies.

Following Nigel out of the office, Jack Watt rubbed his hands together as if about to place them in front of a fire. The two reached the center atrium just as Abuelita appeared in her wheelchair, perched at the top of the grand staircase. Since she had a ground floor room, Nigel had not expected such an entrance, but neither should he have been surprised. As a former burlesque star, she had a finely inflamed flair for the dramatic. At one time, so Nigel understood, a fraternal organization had formed exclusively of men who had been injured or arrested during one of her theatrical performances.

"Abuelita, I will meet you at the elevator," shouted Nigel, hoping to discourage any further foolishness.

"Nonsense," she cackled back, starting to extricate herself from the chair.

Standing for Abuelita was not a quick process, as it involved unbuckling her seat belt, scooching each alternate butt cheek forward one inch at a time, and then flipping herself over before straightening to a stand. She carried out this torturous process to scattered "oohs" and "ahhs" from the apprehensive crowd below, now consisting of Nigel, Jack Watt, the mystery guest, and Esmerelda. Eventually, she stood tall at the top of the stairs. It took her but a moment to realize her public was behind her. She shuffled herself around to face the gathering below. Standing in her blue satin dress as straight as her bones allowed, she looked as regal as she could hope to at this stage.

Taking in the whole picture, Nigel thought she had pulled off a minor miracle. To what end, he could not say, but in every respect she appeared a different person, which had to be a good thing.

Esmerelda put two fingers in her mouth and whistled.

"Galena?" said Jack Watt, reaching into his jacket to retrieve his photograph.

"Guy Yeena!" yelled the mystery man as if he'd just won the Guy Yeena jackpot.

Having completed her grand gesture, Nigel expected Abuelita to strap herself back in her wheelchair and zip over to the elevator. She, however, was just getting started. She shuffled on wobbly legs to the wide, swerving handrail on the left side of the staircase. She posed there for a moment, one arm resting on the surface of the smooth railing, face uplifted to display her profile. Very Bette Davis. She then faced the handrail, extended both arms skyward, and fell across it. Teetering on her belly, she began the great slide downward like a sideways Superwoman.

"Catch me," she yelled to a crowd frantically pointing at each other.

If Abuelita had performed this stunt before, it was likely not while wearing satin. The stairway's curvature scrubbed off a bit of velocity, but her rate of acceleration was frightening. She glided down the handrail like a brakeless tobogganist, yelling "Wheeeee!" all the way.

The railing on this staircase did not flatten gracefully at the end. No, this handrail ended with an ornamentation known as a finial. This particular finial was a round wooden sphere the size of a basketball. If the job of a finial was to discourage sliding down the handrail by sane people, then the Sandovals' finials served no purpose.

While not stated as one of his duties, Nigel felt a responsibility to prevent, if possible, deaths from occurring on the premises. He lined himself up for the catch, not knowing if, after striking the finial, she might fling to the left, to the right, or in both directions simultaneously.

Abuelita hit the wooden ball with a thud, sending it to the floor like a bowling ball while she spun through the air in a series of horizontal cartwheels.

No prescribed way exists to field an old crone that's been flung in such a manner. At least, not that Nigel had seen on YouTube. He braced himself, and first contact was with his head. Fortunately, the impact was cushioned by the only soft bits still in Abuelita's possession. Nigel's arms closed around the torqueing torso. Here, too, he was fortunate because his right arm slipped neatly around her shoulder while the left found the most secure position possible for clamping onto a transversely whirling female with extended legs. The pair twirled multiple revolutions across the floor until Nigel's twisted legs buckled, sending the entire mass into a swirling heap at the geographic center of the atrium.

Sometime during all the sliding, catching, and spinning, Mrs. Sandoval and Stefanie had entered through the front door. The group was further enriched by Annie and her mother, who had evacuated their rooms upon hearing Abuelita's first wail. The entire ensemble gathered around the tangled mass of humanity on the atrium floor.

"Galena?" said Jack Watt, his deflating tone embodied in a physical sense by Abuelita's chest after her dress's scaffolding had given out.

"Wattkins, is that you?"

Jack gazed at Abuelita, and Abuelita gazed at Jack, with him definitely getting the worst of it. Though Abuelita's face had come through the ordeal unscathed, not so the cosmetics intended to obscure it. At some point in the gymnastics, one side of her painstaking construction work had been sheared off, sloughed off, or shattered to pieces, revealing the corrugated hide below. One of her batwing false eyelashes hung from her eyebrow, and her glistening black hair lay at the base of the stairs.

Nigel had never seen anyone belch up his own liver, but Jack Watt appeared to be on the verge.

"Yes, it is me," he bravely admitted.

"Doesn't look like you," said Abuelita.

"And you…don't look like…anyone," said Jack Watt.

"What's going on here?" shouted Annie, glaring at Nigel.

Startled by Annie's voice, Nigel attempted to rise before noticing that his left arm was clenched tightly between Abuelita's thighs. He jerked his arm away as if from a cobra while she kicked him for good measure.

The mystery man in the armadillo shoe knelt down beside Abuelita. "Guy Yeena!" he said.

She stared at him for a moment before replying, "Valdemar?"

"Valdy?" shouted Mrs. Sandoval, making her presence known for the first time.

"Laura? Laura!" said the old man, turning toward Mrs. Sandoval.

"Papa! Oh, Papa!" shouted Stefanie, collapsing on the old man.

Esmerelda joined in the group hug.

The doorbell rang.

6

REINTRODUCTIONS

Nigel brushed himself off, shoved his nose into the air like a good butler, and limped to the door. "It's you," he said, standing opposite the rubber-faced detective who, in Nigel's opinion, appeared more rubbery with every encounter.

"Police Detective Winjack," he said, flashing a badge. "May I come in?"

"What for?"

"Police business."

"I'll let you in this time, but next time I want to see donuts," said Nigel, waving him forth before turning to all present. "Police Detective Winjack is here, he says, on police business."

The motley crowd—lying, kneeling, and standing—turned and stared.

The detective marched two steps in before catching sight of the loopy tableaux. He planted his feet and stood slack-jawed, like a fish seeing its first submarine. "Am I interrupting a party?"

Half said "yes," half said "no," and Abuelita spoke for everyone when she said, "None of your beeswax."

"Well," said the detective, turning to Nigel, who'd established a position to his rear thinking he would not turn that way. "What say you?"

"I am the butler, sir. I do not express opinions."

The detective stepped to Nigel's side. "Who are all these people? I don't recall so many when I was here before."

"The current residents of this household, temporary and permanent," said Nigel, sliding away from the detective.

"I see. So you can introduce them," said the detective, easing toward Nigel.

Introductions were part of a butler's job, but scanning the collection of players, Nigel realized he was missing a program. Even the principals seemed surprised at who was who and what was what. Unfortunately, a butler has his duties to perform. "Here goes," he said. "This is Mrs. Sandoval."

"We have met," said the detective. "And this one I believe I also know," he said, turning to Esmerelda. "Remind me, are these two sisters?"

"No. Esmerelda is the daughter of Abuelita," said Nigel, nodding toward Abuelita, who was seated on the ground. Kneeling beside her, rubbing her leg, was the mysterious guest.

"And who is that man fondling Abuelita's leg?" asked the detective.

"Why, that is...that would be..." stammered Nigel. He knew who he wasn't. He wasn't Abuelita's fiancé, and yet, this man had taken charge of her leg as if he owned it. If that wasn't fiancé-consistent behavior, Nigel didn't know what was. And Abuelita, reacting in a perfectly fiancée-consistent way, was not kicking his face in. Her actual fiancé, Jack Watt, was nowhere to be seen.

"This man..." stammered Nigel, taking up where he left off, "is none other than..." He waited for a miracle.

"Papa!" shouted Esmerelda.

"Papa?" muttered Nigel.

"Dada!" said Stefanie.

"Ex-husband," said Abuelita, patting the diligent hand kneading her thigh.

"My husband?" said Mrs. Sandoval.

"Got that?" said Nigel, turning to the detective.

"Just a minute. I am not quite getting this," said the detective. "I need to understand what's going on here." He paced across the room, pulling back his crumpled trench coat with a hand on his waist while the other massaged his forehead. A third hand, if he'd had one, would have been stroking his chin. "Let me get this straight," he said. "The old lady getting the leg massage is this man's ex-wife, while you"—he pointed to Mrs. Sandoval— "are his current wife. Is that correct?"

"I'm not sure," said Mrs. Sandoval.

"You're not sure the old lady is his ex-wife?" said the detective.

A blue low-heeled pump emitting a contrail of mothballs and corn squeezings sailed past the detective's head. Abuelita shouted, "I'll show you who's an old lady!"

"I'm sorry, ma'am," said the detective, waggling a finger at Abuelita. "No more shoes. Now, let me rephrase the question. The shoe-thrower is the man's ex-wife?"

"That positively *is* his ex-wife. But I'm not sure if I'm his *current* wife," said Mrs. Sandoval.

"What? Do you have amnesia? How do you not know if you're his wife?"

"He just showed up today after being gone for twenty years. We thought he was dead," said Mrs. Sandoval. Then she turned and addressed the crowd around her. "Didn't we think he was dead? Does a marriage have an expiration date? Isn't there some kind of 'use it or lose it' clause? I mean, I haven't seen the man in twenty years. Who knows where he's been!"

"Did you file for a divorce?" asked the detective.

"Of course not. You can't divorce a dead person."

"Was there a death certificate?"

"No. How can there be a death certificate without a body?"

"In that case," said the detective, "I now pronounce you still man and still wife." He turned to the mystery guest. "You there, Mister...?"

"Valdy," said the leg-caresser, sitting on the floor with his back against the large wooden finial ball.

"Valdy, you may stop massaging the ex-wife's leg and get started on this one." The detective nodded toward Mrs. Sandoval.

"Okay," said Valdy. "Does she have a cramp too?"

"So very interesting," said the detective, head down and hands aflutter. He circled the crowd with jerky steps, coming to a halt in front of the finial ball that had been bludgeoned off the staircase by Abuelita's torso. "It's interesting that a long-lost relative's return coincides with a mysterious death on the premises." He put a loafer-clad foot against the ball. "Interesting, indeed," he said, resting an elbow on his up-thrust knee with the fist forming a pedestal for his chin. Having assumed the Thinker's pose, he muttered, "Interesting," twice more.

"You there," the detective said to Valdy. "Tell me your story."

Valdy, alarmed at being addressed, stood up.

Losing its backstop, the finial ball skidded out of the atrium and into something audibly breakable. The detective's body attempted to follow the ball, crumpling into a lumpy sphere before unraveling after less than a full revolution. He came to rest in a supine position with his trench coat splayed across the floor like useless wings and his head uncomfortably close to Abuelita's unclad foot. The disoriented detective, seeing the gnarled talon, convulsively clawed at the air with all available limbs. For anyone struggling for the image, imagine a stricken June bug with a rubbery face reacting to an approaching boot.

"You dropped this," said Valdy, looking down at the detective while holding the man's peanut-butter-and-jelly sandwich.

"Place it in one of my coat pockets, please," said the supine detective. "I will conduct my interview from this position for a few minutes, if you don't mind. The extra time will allow my back joints to realign themselves." He retrieved a pen and notepad from the pocket of his trench coat. "Now, tell me your complete name."

The mysterious newcomer received the question and, before answering, looked in sequence at Mrs. Sandoval, Abuelita, Esmerelda, and Stefanie. "My name is Valdemar Guillermo Sandoval de la Huerta," he said, creaking out the name syllable by syllable, as if it had been in storage.

This was old news, of course, having been spilt minutes earlier, but was, nevertheless, received with a round of excited squeals.

"Let me see," said the detective, pen in hand. "That's V, A, L, T?"

"Here," said Mrs. Sandoval to the laid-out detective. "I'll write the name for you." She had no patience for an extended recitation of letters. She wanted to hear Valdemar's story, as did the other ladies closing ranks around him.

"Thank you," said the detective, handing over the notepad. "Now, how did you get here today?" he asked Valdemar.

"I walked."

"You say you walked here today. You've been gone twenty years, and that's your story? Surely, you didn't spend twenty years walking here."

"It's a long way," he said. "And it's Valdy, not Shirley."

"Okay," said the detective, obviously perturbed by the answer but also by the women standing between him and his subject. "I'll play this game. Where did you walk from?"

"Amazon."

"Amazon? They have a distribution center in San Antonio, don't they? You walked from San Antonio?"

"Brazil."

"You walked from the Amazon in Brazil straight here and arrived today?"

"No, sir."

"You didn't arrive today?"

"Yes, I arrived today, but I didn't walk straight here. The first couple of years, I walked in the wrong direction." By now, the ladies had established a regular habit of oohing and aahing at his replies. Esmerelda and Stefanie, positioned on either side of the man, kept busy with the handiwork, clutching a piece of upper extremity with one mitt while intermittently patting or rubbing with the other.

"For two years, you walked in the wrong direction?" asked the detective.

"I say two. Could have been three or four. Hard to tell. They don't have seasons down there."

"When did you find out you were walking in the wrong direction?"

"Chile. I came to a sign in the road that said 'Bienvenidos – Chile.' I had no map, but I knew that weren't right. I'd have discovered my error sooner if Bolivia was better with their signage."

The detective, scribbling in his notepad, appeared visibly annoyed. Perhaps because marble floors are poorly cushioned, or because his pen didn't write upside-down, or because his upright subject was receiving massages. Whatever the reason, his questions came with increasing amounts of spittle. "Okay, let's back this up. Why were you in the Amazon twenty years ago?"

"Forgive me, my memory is not so clear in that time. I remember a boat and some men, and this girl in Urucurituba dancing the wamba-tamba. Nothing more comes to mind from that period until I was awakened in the jungle by the moist tongue of a jaguar against the sole of my bare foot. Once I fought off the jaguar, I noticed I had this dent in my head. See"—he pointed to the dent. "From then on, it was mostly just me walking."

"You fought off a jaguar?" asked the detective. "With a dent in your head?"

"No, with an arapaima. I don't know how you'd fight off a jaguar with a dent."

"And what is an arapaima?"

"A big fish. It happened to be lying beside me at the time.

When this jaguar was licking my foot, I grabbed the fish and swung it around to whomp him on the head." The ladies, based on the volume of oohs, tightness of claspings, and frequency of pattings, took this to be an heroic act.

"And the jaguar fled?"

"No, he didn't fled. He's a jaguar. Lucky for me, he chose surf over turf. He grabbed the fish and ran off to eat his dinner."

"So this fish just happened to be lying beside you in the jungle?"

"Yep. I believe this dent in my head came from that fish. If you take a look at the dent, it's shaped like the head of an arapaima. Just how I got an arapaima-shaped dent in my head, I couldn't say, but maybe the arapaima lying beside me had something to do with it."

"Did you file a report with the police?"

"What police? It took years just to get out of that jungle. By then, the case would have been pretty cold, don't you think? In my experience, police aren't much interested in two-year-old, dent-in-the-head cases, especially when the main suspect is a fish. Tell me I'm wrong."

The old man went on speaking haltingly, sometimes pausing with a perplexed look before continuing. He appeared to be remembering and forgetting things as he spoke. Despite the difficulties, he methodically pieced together his story.

"So, you were alone for two years in the jungle," said the detective. "How did you survive?"

"Let me set you straight. I don't really know how long I was in the jungle. I didn't have a calendar. And I wasn't always alone. There were tribes around. I tried to steer clear of them, but sometimes I couldn't. One tribe captured me and kept me as a pet, and let me tell you, those people treated pets like dirt. I escaped pretty quick, but there was this other tribe that tried to turn me into wood."

"Turn you into wood?"

"Yeah, like into a human tree. They fed me some concoction

until my muscles stiffened up and my skin became like bark."
The ladies gasped as if a man turning into wood was an alien
concept. "Then they tied me to a log and left me as food for the
termites."

"I guess we can surmise that the termites weren't
interested."

"They ate my heel."

"Your heel? On your foot?"

The man scratched his dented head while considering the
question. "That's where I kept it. I used to have two, now I have
but one."

"But you escaped."

"Eventually, I became thin enough to slip out of the ropes. I
don't think the natives thought I'd last that long, but I was given
a stay of execution by an anteater."

"An anteater, you say?"

"I did say. An anteater wandered by from time to time and
slurped up a bunch of the termites. Kept them from going at me
wholesale. After a few days, I made my escape."

Since moving to New Antigua, Nigel had concluded that his
past lives in London and Houston had been abnormally
subdued. Hearing this man's tale was yet another reminder. In
fact, had Nigel received news of such exploits while living in a
giant metropolis, he might well have dismissed them as bloated
exaggeration. However, here in New Antigua, in the comfy
confines of the Sandoval mansion where people came in two
varieties, fruit or nut, the man's anecdotes made all the sense in
the world.

What might Annie make of all this? She could tell stories
from her marine and cop days that would burn your neck hairs
off. She'd seen some things. Nigel spotted her on the sidelines
wearing the kind of "uh-uh" face exhibited by policemen
hearing about broken speedometers. By contrast, her head-
swathed mother was winding the cuckoo clock with her tongue
sticking out.

"So, you walked all the way here with no heel?" asked the detective.

"Not exactly. In Colombia, I met a woodcarver who was kind enough to carve me a replacement heel in exchange for a gold piece," said the man.

"A gold piece? Where did you get a gold piece?"

"Found it along the way. Found a bunch of them, matter of fact. So I carried a few. Most got stolen—bribes and such, corrupt police."

"There were many gold pieces, but you took only a few?"

"I had no pockets or bags to carry them in. I was pretty much naked at that point and walking on one heel. There was no way to carry a bunch of gold coins. Gold is heavy, you know. Wasn't my priority."

"That gold coin probably could have paid your way home."

"Yeah, well, even if it could have, I still had to walk someplace, and without a heel, that'd be difficult. First things first, I've learned."

The detective sat up and, in one of his finer moments, appeared speechless. He peered down his nose at the man for an awkward thirty seconds before resuming the conversation. "That is an incredible story. Are you going to write a book?"

"A book? I ain't thought about a book. I mean, maybe it sounds exciting in the *Reader's Digest* condensed version, but it was pretty much a grind, let me tell you. I don't know that it would make much of a book. Edgar Rice Burroughs has written better ones."

"As entertaining as your story is, let me turn to the business at hand," said the detective. "As I arrived, I saw an elderly gentleman sprinting away from the house. Who was that?"

"I don't think you need to worry about him," said Nigel.

"He was on the premises. Of course I need to worry about him. Who was he?"

The detective must have seen Jack Watt sprinting the half-mile to the highway. Too bad it hadn't been timed, as it might have set a record for the age group. By now, Jack was probably in the back of some pickup truck, heading out in whatever direction that pickup truck happened to be heading. After seeing what had become of his voluptuous fiancée, his flight was hardly a surprise.

"Was he carrying a suitcase?" asked Nigel.

"He was not."

Wise decision, thought Nigel. *It will have to be shipped.*

"You must be talking about Jack Watt, Abuelita's fiancé," said Mrs. Sandoval to the detective.

"Really?" said the detective. "The current fiancé stepped out while the ex-husband fondled his bride-to-be's leg? What am I to make of that?"

"I don't know that you need to make something of it," said Nigel. "Jack's only just arrived. The ex knows his way around that leg far better than he does. Jack's probably one of these chaps who prefers to ease into things."

"Interesting," said the detective, "The ex-husband and this fiancé and a mysterious murder all converging on this property at the same time. I will need to speak to this Jack Watt. Does this Jack Watt know about Abuelita's previous fiancé?"

"What about Abuelita's previous fiancé?" asked Mrs. Sandoval.

"I mean, his little legal trouble," said the detective. "That slight case of conspiracy to commit murder, among other things."

"Nobody says nothing about that," said Abuelita. "You hear me, flatfoot?"

"I do not intend to intrude on your affairs," said the detective, "no matter how sordid. At any rate, I believe you are safe until the wedding."

"I agree," said Nigel. "Murder is far more likely after they get to know each other, especially if Jack's the patient type."

The detective spun himself around on his butt to look for

more inhabitants. "And who are these two ladies? It seems I've seen you before," he said, pointing at Annie.

Nigel shuffled over to the two to make the introduction. "This is Detective Annie Novak. You may recall she was instrumental in revealing Abuelita's previous murder-prone fiancé."

"Right. And why are you here today? Not for that case, surely."

"In light of the recently discovered corpse, I'm providing extra security for the house," said Annie. "And my name's not Shirley."

"Well, if there should be another body, you will be the first person I come to see, Miss Not-Shirley," said the detective with a smug smile.

"And this young lady," said Nigel, "is her mother, Kayda. Kayda means dragon in Korean."

Nigel noticed her nostrils flare and took a step back.

"And why the sunglasses and turban?" asked the detective. "Are you concealing your identity?"

"I was in an accident leaving me somewhat less than my normal beautiful self."

"Can you remove your sunglasses so that I might be able to identify you, if needed?"

"I could," she said between exposed, clenched teeth. "But then I'd have to kill you."

The sitting detective chuckled. "Very humorous," he said.

"She's not joking," whispered Nigel, waving a finger at the detective. "That dragon don't joke."

7

A FROG IN THE WORKS

The detective, in an uncomfortably vulnerable position, pulled himself up and straightened his jacket. At no one's request, he addressed the assembly. "It is most fortunate that I have you all together. I have an announcement concerning the body found on these premises last Monday." He stood with legs apart and hands behind his back, rocking up and down on the balls of his feet as if the upcoming announcement pulsated inside him like a gas bubble searching for an exit. "As most of you know, toad poisoning was suggested as a likely cause of death."

"How did you come to that conclusion?" asked Annie. As a former detective herself, she approached these county mounties with more than a hint of skepticism, especially this dough-face. Based upon previous encounters, she'd rated him as strictly crossing-guard material.

"The dead man had a toad in his mouth. This fact, along with the knowledge that some toads are poisonous, led the investigator on the scene to surmise toad poisoning as a probable cause, a straightforward and logical hypothesis."

"Who was the investigator on the scene?" asked Annie.

"A police Detective Winjack," he said, consulting his notebook.

"That's you," said Annie.

"Why is that relevant, missy?" asked Detective Winjack.

"Because, before I issue an assessment, I want to know how deeply I should cut. If it's your hypothesis, I'll go easy to spare you the embarrassment. If it's from some boob down at HQ, I'll feel free to let myself rip."

"My notes indicate it was me."

"Okay, here's what's wrong—"

The detective held up a hand. "I'm sorry to interrupt your berating, but it won't be necessary. The coroner has beat you to it. The man in question did not die of toad poisoning. The toad was not a poisonous variety. However, when the coroner removed the toad, he found this in the man's throat."

The detective reached inside his trench coat and pulled out a baggie, holding it high for the crowd to see. "Who can guess what is in this bag?"

The spectators were in no mood for guessing. A wrong guess would only incite ridicule, figured the bystanders. All but one.

"A greasy yellow spot?" said Nigel, describing with reasonable accuracy what everyone saw. "Is it mango?"

"No."

"Is it peach?"

"No."

"Is it ripe banana?"

"No, it is not ripe banana. Does anyone besides this imp of a butler wish to hazard a guess?"

An awkward silent pause suggested they were quite content to let the imp of a butler do the talking.

"What I have in this baggie," said the detective, waving the thing around at arm's length, "is a poison dart frog."

"He *did* have a frog in his throat," said Nigel. "I said he had a frog in his throat, didn't I, Mrs. Sandoval? I must be prescient. May I take a look?"

The detective handed the baggie to Nigel, who examined it from various angles before running his fingers across the yellow splotch. "It's a frog, all right," proclaimed a satisfied Nigel. He then pulled open the bag, stuck his face in for a closer look, and staggered backward. Coughing, he bent forward and held the bag at arm's length for the detective to take. "That is the worst smelling frog ever," he said between retches.

"You fool. It's preserved in formaldehyde."

"Well, that's the worst smelling formaldehyde ever."

The detective held the bag aloft. "We are awaiting toxicology reports, but we believe this poison dart frog was the cause of death, a likely murder."

The crowd gasped.

"Well, that's a relief," said Nigel.

"What do you mean, 'that's a relief'?" asked the detective.

"As shocking as it is to have a murder committed in our midst, it's reassuring that the culprit's been identified and the threat neutralized," said Nigel, gesturing to the baggie. "Bad frog!"

"You nincompoop! The frog is not the murderer," declared the detective, who appeared to approach life, or at least his murder investigations, devoid of a sense of humor. "The frog is the murder weapon. The murderer has yet to be identified. We are awaiting the toxicology report to confirm the manner of death, but the frog, according to Google, is a poisonous variety native to South America."

"So, both a toad *and* a frog were found in the mouth of the deceased," said Annie. "What does that tell you about the supposed killer?"

"It tells me this man, or woman, is comfortable working with amphibians. I hate to sound the alarm, but we should all be alarmed. I mean, this time a frog and a toad. What next? Newts and salamanders? Who knows what this fiend is capable of? If he were to expand into reptiles, whoa, Nellie! What then?"

"I meant," asked Annie, "what is the psychological profile of a person who would kill a man by placing a poisonous frog in his mouth?"

"The psychological profile? You're asking about the psychological profile? Is that what you're asking about? The psychological profile?"

"Now that you mentioned it, what about the psychological profile?"

The detective paced rapidly in one direction, then another. He was a pacer, this detective. And, while pacing, he pondered. And, while pondering, he patted his temple with a finger—one of his own. For several minutes he paced, pondered, and patted before a perspiring but persevering crowd. Suddenly, he stopped pacing, patting, and, presumably, pondering, long enough to pop a thumb into his piehole. There it stayed until a person publicly pooh-poohed the practice, prompting the pea-brained primitive to pull it out and park it under an armpit. For a moment, he had forgotten where he was.

"An interesting question, you ask," said the detective. "What was your question?"

"The psychological profile," said Annie.

"Ah, the profile. What is the psychology of a man who would do such a thing? This is no average man on the street who kills using guns or knives or hatchets. If that were only the case, we could rest easy. No, we have here an evil ogre, or perhaps an evil genius, who would sacrifice a cute little frog just to kill a man—"

"Or," added Nigel, "sacrifice a man just to kill a cute little frog! Have you considered that possibility?"

The detective's eyebrows did the wave in one direction, then the other, while he considered it. "This killer," he continued, "exhibits the traits of a thorough, cold-blooded professional. He takes no chances, thus the use of a toad as a backstop for the frog. I am no psychologist, thank God, but if I were, I'd say this man has a complex."

"Really?" said Nigel. "What kind of complex?"

"A...um...complicated complex," said the detective, inspecting the thumb he'd just found in his armpit. "Does that answer your question?" he asked Annie.

"Hardly."

"Very well, then, for this investigation, I will be interrogating each of you. Fear not, this is completely normal. Unless you've recently committed a fiendish act, you have nothing to worry about."

"Do you really need to interrogate everyone? Isn't there a way to shorten the process?" asked Mrs. Sandoval.

"Shorten the process? You mean cut to the chase, eh? Get to the heart of the matter? Is that it?" asked the detective.

"If you could."

"I'm glad you suggested that," said the detective. "That is a superb idea that had not occurred to me. So much better to wrap this up in ten or fifteen minutes rather than drag it out for days or weeks. Of course we can try a shortened process."

"I would be so grateful," said Mrs. Sandoval.

"Sure, no problem," said the detective. "Listen up, everyone. I'm looking for the fiend who killed a man by putting a poisonous frog down his throat. Did anyone here do it?"

Silence.

"No? Does anyone know who did?"

Silence.

"Well, I'm sorry," said the detective. "I tried, but no results. Back to the old-fashioned way."

"Excuse me, sir," said Annie. "Since no one here is fessing up, do you know what you're looking for?"

"What I'm looking for?" asked the detective. "What would *you* suppose I'm looking for? Clues, interactions, locations, preceding events, relevant data, information that may aid in solving the crime. You of all people should understand this."

"What I mean is, do you have specific physical data from the crime scene along with various case conjectures that you hope to validate or invalidate with the information provided in these interviews?"

"Yes, absolutely. Physical data: dead man with frog in throat and toad in mouth. Conjecture: he was murdered. Valid or invalid. Let's move on. I request from the owner of this house the temporary use of a private room for the interrogations. Can this be accommodated?"

"Yes," said Nigel. "We can provide you with a room."

The old grandfather clock to one side of the atrium began to gong. With each strike, Mrs, Sandoval held up a corresponding number of fingers, encouraging those in the room to count along. Coinciding with the twelfth dong, she shouted, "Tequila!"

Knowing Mrs. Sandoval's fondness for this noontime ritual, Nigel had set up a device to start playing the song "Tequila" coincident with the last gong strike. Even without the titular beverage, the reverb-drenched opening chords had the effect of a powerful tension reliever. By the time the saxophone kicked in, a conga line was snaking its way through the atrium and sitting area.

"My God, it's been a long day," shouted Mrs. Sandoval. "Nigel, do your duty."

"Yes, ma'am," yelled Nigel, breaking away from the line and leaving the detective as the caboose.

8

INQUIRING MINDS

"Here it is," said Nigel, flipping on the lights to Mrs. Sandoval's office. "I trust it befits your inquisitions." He hoped a couple of tequila squirts had oiled up the detective and de-starched that index finger he so enjoyed waggling at everyone.

"Not as spartan as I would have hoped," said the detective, pushing his thumb into the back cushion of an office chair while shaking his head. "I'd have liked something less hospitable, harder, more stuffy, less oxygen."

"Should I exchange the furniture for a footstool, replace the light fixtures with a dangling bulb, and pump in some carbon monoxide?"

"Could you?" asked the detective.

"No," said Nigel.

"This will have to do then. I'll start with you. Have a seat."

"With me?" asked Nigel. "I'm just the butler, and only since Monday morning, the same day the body showed up."

"Quite a coincidence, isn't it?" asked the detective, holding a penlight to his temple while aiming its powerful beam into Nigel's pupils.

"I don't know that it's a coincidence," said a squinting Nigel.

"My start date was scheduled weeks in advance. Bodies, as I understand it, don't have a schedule. They show up when they show up. Am I right?"

"And how do you know about bodies?"

"I've had this one all my life. Fortunately, I've kept it functioning, not like our uninvited guest."

"Why did you take the butler's job, Mr. Blandwater-Cummings? May I call you Mr. Blandwater-Cummings?"

"Do you really want to?"

"It suits you."

"As you please. I took this job because it was available. Between you and me, I had to get out of the house. The wife had this to-do list, you see. An absolute beast. Frightful. And the pay was practically nonexistent. This job was better than that job."

The detective pulled down on his face. He had the kind of face that didn't need pulling down. "I understand that before taking this butler's job, you broke into this very house."

"Well, that was a misunderstanding, really. I didn't so much break in as was pulled in by a couple of your police buddies. I was actually on my way out."

"On your way out?"

"Yes. I mean my intent at that point was to leave the premises, but the only way to do that was through the house—"

"So, you were in the house, trying to leave when they pulled you in? Makes no sense."

"No? Let me clarify. I was on the premises, but not in the house. I wanted to leave the premises, but the only way for me to leave the premises, at that juncture, was through the house. I was in the process of entering the house in order to leave the premises when your mates arrived and pulled me through. You see, I'm embarrassed to say, I had gotten myself stuck. There. I hope that's clear."

The detective leaned forward, placing his palms flat on the desk. He looked like one of those lizards about to spear a bug with his tongue. "Are you being evasive?"

"Evasive? I'm sitting right in front of you," whiplashed Nigel.

"So you became the butler on Monday. When was this breaking and exiting escapade?"

"About three months ago."

"I see. So, why were you on the premises then?"

"To catch a dog thief."

"Why would you be here to catch a dog thief?"

"Why?" said Nigel, finding it hard to believe the man was a detective. "Because the dog to be thieved was here."

"What dog?"

"The one the thief was after. You are a police detective, right? Could I see your badge?"

"You may *not* see my badge."

Nigel heard a grinding noise coming from the detective's tightly closed mouth. Might this be a contributing factor to the overall rubberiness of the man's face? That is, perhaps he'd ground down his teeth, resulting in an oversupply of facial skin around the jawline. Of course, that didn't explain the flaccid folds higher up or the sad, drooping hide around the eyes and off the nose. Perhaps some combination of excess skin along with gravity's unrelenting pull had resulted in a sort of landslide effect. A glacial dermal movement, to put it more precisely. Nigel wondered what kind of skin products this man had subjected himself to.

"What are you doing?" said the detective.

"Eh?" said Nigel, releasing a fold of his own cheek skin. "Just thinking."

"Well, stop. Answer my question."

"Which was?"

"Why were you looking for a dog thief on this property?"

"I was contracted."

The detective once again assumed the lizard pose. "They contracted a butler to find a dog thief?"

"Utter nonsense. Of course they didn't hire a butler to find a dog thief. They hired me."

"But you *are* a butler," said the detective, pointing an accusing finger.

"I am *now*. *Now*, I'm a butler. Not then."

"What were you then?"

"A private investigator."

The detective fell back in his reclining chair until he was looking at the ceiling. "You had a license?"

"An unlicensed private investigator."

The detective, recognizing an opportunity, leaned forward again. "That is unlawful."

"For a pet private investigator? I think not."

He huffed. "So, how long had you been a pet private investigator?"

"Starting from when?"

"From the time you were contracted by the Sandovals."

"A day, give or take."

"So, this was your first case?"

"My first *paying* case. I'd done amateur work before."

The detective began another round of face pulling. "For who?"

"For me. I had dogs. Sometimes they escaped. I found them, sometimes."

"Mr. Blandwater-Cummings, may I be blunt?"

"If you're asking for my opinion, I would say you are not just blunt but dull as well. Not that you should be too upset about it. My dad once said to me, 'We can't all be the sharpest knife in the drawer.' I didn't understand what he meant back then, but now I do. There was once this serial killer back home, went by the name of Henry the Head Smasher, and when they asked him why he preferred to use blunt instruments, he said, 'With the blunt instrument, it may get messy, but there's no mistaking whether you've completed the job.' I've often taken comfort from that quote. I hope you don't take me as some kind of bootlicker, but I believe the two of us—me and you—are a lot alike. We're just a pair of hardworking blunt instruments, and when we finish a job, people know we've been there. That's my observations so far."

A distinct creaking resounded from within the detective's mouth—tooth enamel undergoing pressurized deformation. "Mr. Blandwater-Cummings, in the few months since you've been in New Antigua, you've cultivated quite a relationship with this household. First, claiming some unknown privilege as a pet detective, you were found prowling on this property in the middle of the night—breaking and entering was how the police report put it. And then, not more than three days later, you were found in the company of two persons who were plotting a murder on this property—"

"Did you say, 'found in the company of?' They were trying to kill me! I foiled their plot and incapacitated the scoundrels, no thanks to you," said Nigel, straightening his tie in the most intimidating way.

"Be that as it may, it's a little hard to comprehend how a hapless pet detective found himself among such a band of cutthroats. And, once those cutthroats were safely behind bars, you returned to these premises as a butler, taking the place of the previous cutthroat butler."

"What of it? The head cutthroat was a lawyer, but you haven't seen me practicing law. I have standards."

"Do you? I'm not reassured that on your first day as a butler, a dead body turns up. And what do we find in the throat of that dead body?" asked the detective, unsheathing his index finger and waving it around like a magic wand. "A poison dart frog, Mr. Blandwater-Cummings. A poison dart frog. Do you know where poison dart frogs come from, Mr. Blandwater-Cummings?"

"Poison dart *tadpoles*?"

"South America, Mr. Blandwater-Cummings. South America. Do you know what else comes from South America?"

"Let me think... Parrots, Mr. Winjack. Parrots and capybara, Mr. Winjack. Capybara and caipirinha, Mr. Winjack. Caipirinha and—"

"Are you making light of this murder investigation, Mr. Blandwater-Cummings? I'm making a note," said the detective, and he meant it. He dictated to himself while scribbling in his notebook, "Suspect exhibits signs...callous disregard...serious nature...the crime...displays contempt for law enforcement."

"That's overreaching, isn't it?"

"It is my observation."

"A wrong observation. Contempt for law enforcement based on what? My interactions with you? Hardly a representative sample. Would I, for instance, proclaim that law enforcement officers have rubbery faces based on a single unfortunate incidence? No, that wouldn't be fair. On the other hand, if I limited my statement to—"

"Enough! Where was I? South America—"

"You were in South America? I'd have sworn you were here the whole—"

The groan of straining enamel was punctuated at odd times by the crunch of rupturing dentine. "South America," the detective growled. "Anacondas come from South America. Anacondas, like the one that you were found with, come from South America—the same region as poison dart frogs."

"I see where you're going with this."

"Do you?"

"Evidently to South America. We may as well conclude this interview right now. I have never been to South America, have no connection to South America, and don't know any South Americans. I am not your man!" To punctuate the statement, Nigel assumed the lizard pose and flicked his tongue, symbolizing how he'd just eaten this detective for lunch.

A grinding sound followed by a pop emanated from the detective. His eyes widened, and his hand slapped against his jaw. He spoke through a clenched mouth as if practicing to be a ventriloquist. "The common thread is not South America," he grunted. "But you, Mr. Blandwater-Cummings. You have been present when each of these unexpected creatures appeared. Not only that, you have been the thread linking the unusual crimes tied to this address. Before you came to town, New Antigua was a sleepy community with scarcely a South American creature or a murder plot to its credit. Now we have both. How do you explain that?"

"You, my dear detective Winjack, must be mad. My dear mother always warned me about men in trench coats, and now I know why."

After a knock at the door, Stefanie popped her head in. "I'm sorry to interrupt, but Nigel needs to take Abuelita and Jack to pick up their marriage licenses."

"Okay," said the detective through clenched jaw. "We're finished here."

Nigel exited the office into the home's entire menagerie loitering just outside.

"Don't worry, Mr. Nigel," said Mrs. Sandoval. "We believe you're innocent."

"It's good to know you have my back."

"We took a vote," said Mrs. Sandoval. "It was four votes for innocent, three for guilty, and one undecided."

The detective, clenching his jaw, stormed into the crowd. "Don't tell me you heard some of our conversation," he said.

"Not some," said Mrs. Sandoval. "All, I should think. How could we not?" She looked up at the home's twelve-foot ceiling, which towered above the nine-foot walls of the office. "You two are loud talkers."

"But why are you all here?" asked the detective.

"You wanted to talk to us. Where else would we be?" answered Mrs. Sandoval.

The police detective slapped his forehead, causing an uncontrolled shimmy to the lower part of his head.

"Mrs. Sandoval, I'll take you next," said the detective. "The rest of you cannot stay here. You must wait over there." He indicated a place on the opposite side of the atrium out of earshot. "If I find anyone over here, I'll book them for obstructing a police investigation. Now, away with you."

9

GETTING IMPLICATED

Nigel was stunned to learn not only that Jack Watt was on the premises, but that he was up for a marriage license. What kind of a desperate man was this? Was he a fugitive looking for a place to lie low? An escapee from a mental institution? A sufferer of temporary bouts of blindness? As a butler, Nigel wasn't allowed to ask such questions, but that wouldn't stop his pondering in the privacy of his own brain. For the moment, however, he put the thinking on hold to do his job.

Having alerted the future licensees of their appointment, Nigel waited for them in the atrium. Jack Watt arrived first, twinkling down the staircase like Fred Astaire late for a tryst with Lady Frankenstein. Abuelita's tardiness gave Nigel the opportunity to spend a few cordial minutes with the condemned. Jack Watt was a surprisingly jolly old fellow given the circs. Face it, any bloke marching off for a marriage license with Abuelita could be forgiven a fluttery lip, or, for that matter, a fluttery bowel. Had Nigel been in Jack's shoes, he would have downed a beaker of bleach, glass and all. But Jack Watt was not a glass-muncher, nor a bleach-guzzler. Not only did Jack Watt cheerfully absorb Nigel's lectures on wheelchair avoidance, he contributed to the science with a few of his own tips garnered from a familiarity with bullfighting.

"Bullfighting is a cruel sport, is it not?" asked Nigel.

"I wouldn't say that," said Jack. "Those toreadors have good working hours and a bountiful clothes allowance."

"For the bull, I mean."

"Not if it's done properly," said Jack, extending himself in a demonstration, "with the estocada technique—a sword plunged between the shoulder blades as the beast charges."

"Sword between the shoulder blades," murmured Nigel as a whir portended the arrival of the shin-shredding wheelchair.

Jack Watt handled his initial encounter with admirable grace —no bruises, and no sword. Nigel helped the pair into the backseat of the Town Car and confined himself to driving and listening for the remainder of the trip. Preferable, he thought, to having his cranium pummeled by a lady's shoe. The backseat combatants sat notably stiff in the early rounds, but once Abuelita broke out a bottle of the social lubricant, a jab-and-parry game ensued.

"My goodness," said Jack Watt after taking a swig. "What do we have here, *aguardiente* from Colombia?"

"Ouzo," said Abuelita. "From Greece."

"We do get around, don't we?"

"You only think you been around. You ain't seen nothing yet."

The action became heavier as the bottle became lighter. Abuelita, the pursuer, landed a number of sly suggestions, coy propositions, and double entendres straight from her vault. Clearly, she would have preferred the action take place in a phone booth, liking nothing better than to corner her opponent for a close encounter. And the sooner the better.

Jack, in contrast, used all the available space to dodge, deflect, and maintain a distance. He may have racked up points with charming banter, but the head and body appeared to be a no-contact zone. Parry, backpedal, and keep moving. Tire, frustrate, and then control seemed to be his strategy. He played the waiting game, though what he might have been waiting for wasn't altogether clear.

The trip to the courthouse came off as planned without the appearance of corpses, killer frogs, or flying satin tarts. After walking the two sloshed licensees to their respective quarters at the estate, Nigel headed to the kitchen. While preparing meals was not his responsibility, lording over the meal-preparer was. He found the chef torridly exercising her thumbs on one of those portable gaming devices.

"Well, Lynette, what's for dinner?" asked Nigel, leaning against the island, which he might have expected to be populated with dishes in various states of preparation.

"It's pizza night," she said, grimacing while her machine emitted a sad deflating sound.

"Pizza night? Is that a specialty of yours?"

She looked up at Nigel as if he were her no-good husband, "No, it's a specialty of Domino's, and they deliver."

"I see. I was under the impression that you, as the cook, actually cooked the meals. Was I wrong?"

"No, but if you hadn't noticed, there's a damned army around here today. If I'm supposed to cook for ten people instead of four, someone needs to tell me and, while they're at it, pay me."

"Understood," said Nigel, remembering it was the butler's responsibility to relay dining requirements to the chef. "I will try to come up with a head count for tomorrow's meals."

"And a dollar allowance. Don't forget the allowance. That's important."

"Absolutely," said Nigel, knowing he'd blown today's assignment. "By the way, where have all the inmates gone? Have they escaped? The place looks deserted."

"I believe they're gathered in the game room."

"The game room? Is there a ping-pong tournament? Why the game room?"

"Nobody tells me nothing, you understand, but I believe they may be listening in on that detective in the office."

"From the game room? It's nowhere near the office."

"The phone system, dummy. Someone left the line open in the office. But don't ask me about it, I'm just the cook. Nobody tells me nothing."

Nigel walked to the game room at the far end of the seldom-used Sanderson wing, so called for a chap named Sanderson, presumably. He must have liked playing games. The Sandovals, Nigel was led to believe, didn't, really.

In the game room, Nigel found assorted inhabitants huddled in the northeast corner around a desk phone. In his absence, someone had demonstrated the resourcefulness to liberate a bottle of bourbon along with the requisite accessories.

Nigel issued the butler's greeting, "Ahem."

"Shhhhh," came the collective response.

Abuelita's voice crackled from the speaker phone. "None of your beeswax!"

"It *is* my beeswax. I'm the law. I'm investigating a murder. Refusing to answer my questions does you no good," said the detective. "How did you meet your fiancé?"

"None of your beeswax. Hic. Next question. Hic."

"You've got the hiccups."

"So, you're a detective after all."

"Have you been drinking?"

"Damn right I been drinking, and so have you. I saw you throwin' down the tequila. Hic. And you're on duty. Hic. Ain't that right? A drinking policeman. Hic. There ought to be a law."

"My behavior is not your concern. Now, what can you tell me about the deceased?"

"Nothing. Never seen him before. Hic. I already said that."

"Do you know any reason for someone to be on your property at such a time, say, a repairman or a gardener?"

"Nope."

That cop might as well have been talking to a clam. He and

Abuelita had gotten on each other's bad side in a hurry. No surprise, considering they were two people with four bad sides. If not for his badge, the detective likely would have been fending off projectiles.

"Did you know the schedule for any maintenance or gardening work at the house?" asked the detective.

"Nope. Hic. That's the butler's job."

"Your butler, as I understand, has just been hired. What can you tell me about this butler, Nigel Blandwater-Cummings?" said the detective, spewing the name syllable by depraved syllable as if announcing Batman's newest arch-villain. Nigel's name had problems enough without being dragged over smoking coals.

"That butler's the one you (hic) ought to have your eye on," said Abuelita. "He's a sneaky one. Hic. He was all over me from the first."

"Really?" said the detective. "What do you mean, 'all over me'?"

"Physical contact," she said. "Inappropriate touching. Hic."

"Really?"

Nigel shuffled toward a far corner of the room where he pretended to be cleaning. He felt the tingle of accusing eyes about his person, a sensation akin to being crawled upon by hairy spiders wearing tiny spurs. Had there been a manhole nearby, he would have dropped himself into it.

"Don't look so surprised," said Abuelita. "The first time I met that English (hic) jackass, it wasn't five minutes before he was slobbering all over my hand. If I hadn't whomped him, he'd a been up my arm and onto…other (hic) things."

"My goodness," said the detective.

"The next time I saw him, even worse. He dropped down (hic) and stuck his head right in my…my regions."

"Your *regions*?"

"Hic. You know, my *private* regions. The pelvic area…my hoo-haw, for God's (hic) sake. You need a picture?"

Nigel needed no picture, nor a reminder. He remembered the unfortunate accident in nightmarish detail and would have given an appendage for the ability to forget it.

"I get the idea," said the detective. "Were there corroborating witnesses?"

"Hell (hic) yeah," she croaked. "He did it in broad daylight for the whole damn world to (hic) see. He don't care. That's the kind of pervert he is. Hic. Mrs. Sandoval was there. She can tell you, if she was still (hic) conscious. I don't know why he didn't go for her. She'd probably (hic) enjoy it."

Nigel felt a slight relief as one or two of the eye spiders hopped onto Mrs. Sandoval.

"Stefanie was there when he did his dirtiest work," droned Abuelita. "Hic. She can tell you what happened. And the old butler, Gastrick. He saw it all."

"Anything more about this butler?"

"Hell, yes, there's (hic) more! He broke into the house in the middle of the night. If he hadn't got (hic) himself stuck in the doggie door, he'd a got me. He told some ridiculous story about catching a dog thief. Hic. He weren't after no dog thief. I saw the look in his eye. Urges is what I saw—raging (hic) urges. Nothing was going to stop him. Except, of course, that doggie door. Hic."

"If I may ask, with all of his bad behavior, why was he hired to be your butler?"

"Talk to Mrs. Sandoval about that. Maybe (hic) she has the hots for him. But if that's what she's thinking, she can forget it. Hic. Once a sexhound like that gets a taste for the plum, he ain't settlin' for no prune. Hic."

Nigel refused to look toward the crowd, but he heard a gulp that would have been two ounces of bourbon finding its way into Mrs. Sandoval. He could have used such a fortifier. He felt himself drop into a familiar dream, where sat a younger version of himself, in class, stark naked, wondering how to leave without drawing attention. His teacher, the formidable Mrs.

Ratcher, had been replaced by his wife, the formidable Annie. Trapped like a naked rat.

"You've been most informative. Is there anything else you would like to tell me?" Nigel heard the detective ask.

"One more thing (hic) about that butler," said Abuelita.

Nigel felt his bones going soft.

"Yes?" said the detective.

"Maybe he meant no disrespect, but (hic) I heard that butler call you a rubber-faced Barney buffoon of a detective."

"Oh, did he?"

"I think it was him. Hic. There were a lot of people saying a lot of things, but I'll bet it was him."

"Thank you for that," said the detective. "I think that concludes this inquiry. You've been most helpful."

"Hic. They took away my pistols," she said.

"What?"

"I used to have pistols. They (hic) took 'em away after I plugged the television a few times. Now I have nothing to defend myself (hic) with except for some knives, clubs, and chairs. I might need a gun to protect my honor. Hic. Could you lend me yours?"

"I'm afraid that would violate department policy. Besides, I understand you're getting married soon. I'm sure your husband can protect you."

"I'm not sure about him yet. I would (hic) prefer a gun of my own, at least for the first couple weeks. I've never married without a (hic) gun before. Are you sure you won't let me borrow yours? Maybe you (hic) have a spare. Hic."

"I'm sorry, but no. Let me get the door for you."

There was no more conversation. Just the whirring of an electric wheelchair with the sounds of collisions and some masculine yelps.

10

A SHOCKING DINNER PARTY

Nigel slipped out unnoticed thanks to the distraction provided by a billiard ball ricocheting about the game room at high speed. Esmerelda declared the runaway ball, a six, evidence of a resident poltergeist. Had he stuck around, Nigel would have agreed wholeheartedly, the ball having leapt from his hand to pursue its free and independent course. Of course, he'd likely be blamed for it, but with a murder rap hanging over his head, disturbing the peace with a raucous billiard ball might not make the indictment.

This whole murder accusation thing was less than ideal for a new butler, but he had at least gotten through day two. This evening he had arranged a sizable distraction for himself and Annie. At Stanley's invitation, they would be dining at Cam Logan's place.

Nigel considered the visit more business than pleasure. He had roped Stanley into providing desserts for the wedding and playing the friend card might persuade him to ante up a little extra effort. He needed all the help he could get.

As for Annie? She had no interest in seeing Stanley again, at all. She'd always said he was like a human barnacle attached to her mother's hull, and once he'd scraped himself off, she was more than fine with never again setting eyes on the pudgy gastropod. But the chance to visit the house of Cam Logan—country singer, TV reality star, local legend—was a fish of a different color. Everyone knew she had a place out there, but almost no one had seen it. Nothing was visible from the road. Few locals had ever been invited. There were rumors of castles with dungeons, safari parks, cryogenics labs, and weapons of mass destruction, but in small towns, exaggerations were possible. Nigel and Annie were being afforded a rare opportunity to peek behind the rhinestone curtain.

Through a remotely opened gate, down a two-lane road, through a mile of verdant woods, Nigel drove into a broad, manicured space of attractive outbuildings encircled by a white split-rail fence. The road eventually wound in front of an expansive home built in the Roman villa style.

As Nigel and Annie got out of the car, a man exited the house. Judging by his dress and purposeful manner, Nigel recognized him as a fellow butler assigned to greet the guests.

"Hello," Nigel said to the approaching man. "We're the Blandwater-Cummings."

"You are? Good for you," said the man. He walked on past, climbed into a nearby pickup truck, and drove away.

Nigel and Annie walked through a small courtyard, past a gurgling fountain, to the massive front door.

Stanley answered the bell dressed in expensive, brightly colored leisure clothes chosen for him by someone who didn't seem to know who he was. "Come on in. How are you? Good to see you," he said. "How have you been, Annie?"

"I'm fine," she said, taken aback by the friendliness.

"And how is your mother? Doing well, I hope." He had grown loquacious since leaving Annie's mother. Such verboseness in his previous marriage would have earned him some form of humiliation.

"She's...recovering."

"Oh, dear. I hope you don't mean recovering from my departure. You know, we didn't have much of a marriage."

"No. I meant from the explosion of a hot water heater. She sustained some injuries—"

"Oh, dear. Serious?" asked Stanley, concerned but with a hint of giddiness.

"No. The injuries were mostly to her hair. But that's pretty debilitating for a woman like her."

"Yes, it must be. A hot water heater explosion? I don't understand that. Those things never blow up."

"She had a new one, just installed," said Annie.

"Really? Just installed? There's not much to installing a hot water heater. The installer must have been an imbecile. I couldn't make one explode with dynamite. She should sue."

"I believe it was a factory defect," interjected Nigel. "How have you been, Stanley? You look different, younger."

"Thanks, Nigel. I feel younger. I've lost about ten pounds."

"It'd be eleven if not for that hair," said Nigel, admiring his new crop.

"Let's make our way to the den," said Stanley, motioning them forward. "Honestly, I feel shipshape, sleek, streamlined, like years of clingy barnacles had been scraped off my hull. I've been working out and eating right. Cam's personal trainer and dietitian work wonders. You should try it sometime, Nigel."

"Right. Where would any of us be without our personal trainers and dietitians? Not in Cam Logan's house, that's for sure."

The trio walked down a muralled hall obviously intended to evoke the Mediterranean. Nigel wondered if Cam owned a Mediterranean villa modeled to evoke central Texas.

"Ah, here's Cam now," said Stanley, turning and welcoming her with open arms. Cam walked past the arms and straight to the guests.

Cam Logan looked every inch the star. Annie certainly noticed. Her eyes drizzled the country tart from the top of her luxurious hair to the tips of her manicured toes and then back up again. Size-ups of that intensity were normally reserved for those about to be slammed to the pavement and handcuffed. But in this case, Annie was likely noticing the immaculately polished toenails, the graceful lines of her slippers, the beautiful fabric of her flowing, designer maxi-dress, the vintage art deco necklace and earrings, and her velvet headband sprouting deep blue flowers, possibly sapphires, scattered across a field of silky, golden hair. She admired the art of such presentations even if she didn't indulge herself.

Nigel noticed that Cam Logan looked very well-preserved and maintained for a woman in her fifties. You could see a lot of craftsmanship had gone into her. And money, lots and lots of money. A year's maintenance on that facial skin alone was probably worth a luxury automobile or two.

"I am so glad to meet you," said Annie.

"Me too," said Nigel. "My wife has told me so much about you."

"It's always wonderful to meet my fans," said Cam. No one had mentioned anything about fans but when you're Cam Logan, you just assume. "You're both friends of Stanley, I understand."

"More or less," said Nigel.

"Of course we are," said Annie, driving an elbow into Nigel's appendix. "We've known Stanley for years."

"Wonderful. You can tell me some of his secrets," said Cam.

"Nope. Afraid not," said Nigel. "When you look at Stanley, you're seeing all there is. They say you can't judge a book by its cover, but I say, why not, if the pages are blank."

Stanley smiled and nodded.

The foursome made their way to the dining room, where they occupied the end of a table made for twelve. Wine was provided by a servant in white who appeared to hear but not speak.

"Enjoy the wine," said Cam.

"What kind is it?" asked Nigel.

"It is a Camignon Blanc," said Cam.

"I'm not so knowledgeable about wines. I confess I've not heard of that variety before," said Nigel.

"You wouldn't have. It's a hybrid grape developed by my oenologist. I have my own vineyard."

Nigel swirled the wine in his glass and held it up to the light before gently rolling it under his nose to capture the aroma. It was wine all right. "Here on the property?"

"Goodness, no, not here. In Oregon."

"I see. That sounds convenient. No late-night trips to the liquor store for you," said Nigel. "Under what label do you sell your wine?"

"We don't sell it. We drink it. I used to spend so much on wine, but now that I have my own vineyard, I don't even think about the cost. And it's so much fun. I go up there every fall for the grape harvest. It's become a passion," she said, grasping Nigel's forearm. "I crush the grapes myself, the old-fashioned way."

"The old-fashioned way? What's that?"

"I stomp them to get the juice out."

"You stomp the grapes? Yourself?" said Nigel, holding his glass to the light. "You have special grape-stomping shoes, I suppose?"

"Shoes? Goodness, no! That's not how it's done at all. When I first started the winery, I had a grape press. But when I told my Italian vintner—Dito, a wonderful man—that I wanted to press the grapes myself, he suggested the old-fashioned way of stomping the grapes with the bare feet of a woman. According to him, there's no duplicating the flavor derived from the old stomping methods—something to do with the fungus."

"The fungus?" repeated Annie.

"Don't ask me to explain the science, but I do know it's a lot of hard work."

"Is it?" asked Nigel.

"You can't just walk around on the grapes. That's not

enough. There's a technique involved. It took me three seasons and a lot of personal coaching from Dito to get it right. Now he says I'm the best ever."

"The best grape-stomper?" said Nigel.

"Yes, though stomping is not really the right term. To do it correctly, you must bounce, not stomp, and you rotate your body counterclockwise throughout the process."

"Counterclockwise?"

"In the northern hemisphere. And Oregon," said Cam, "is in the northern hemisphere."

"Sounds very technical," said Nigel.

"And messy," said Annie. "Doesn't the grape juice go everywhere?"

"It's done in a big plexiglass tub to contain all the juice. You don't want to lose a drop after all that work."

"It must get all over your clothes."

"Clothes?" asked Cam.

Annie looked at Nigel.

Nigel looked at Stanley.

Stanley grinned and held up a fresh glass of the foot wine.

"You have some…eh…special outfit for bouncing on grapes?" asked Annie.

"No. Just me," said Cam. "Clothes are forbidden within the grape-stomping tub. It's a law, or a rule or something. Dito explained that clothes harbor contaminates, so to maintain maximum purity, the grape-stomper—me—must be naked. Rest assured, no article of clothing has ever touched the wine you're drinking."

"I find that reassuring. Is it reassuring to you, dear?" Nigel asked Annie.

Annie was busy squinting into her wine glass, which she held over a candle.

"I thought so," said Nigel. "Bottoms up, everyone."

A delicious soup was served, followed by a course of stuffed quail, followed by some unidentified finger food. By the time the main course arrived, the foot wine had taken effect and the conversation had turned more personal.

"So, how did you two meet?" asked Cam.

"She tackled me," said Nigel. "She tackled me in a public park as I was jogging. Threw me down, pushed my face in the dirt, and we've been together ever since."

"How romantic. She saw what she wanted and went after it."

"She thought I'd been molesting young girls in a public restroom."

"And she wanted to reform you—adorable."

"Case of mistaken identity, actually," said Nigel. "A couple minutes later, she tackled a different guy and shoved his face in the dirt. As far as I know, they never dated. You see, Annie was a police officer with the Houston Police Department."

"That explains the lack of makeup," said Cam.

Hoping to avoid a dangerous situation, Nigel spoke up. "The story of how you and Stanley met must be far more interesting."

"Should I tell them, Stanley?" asked Cam.

Stanley smiled and did not nod.

"I was working on my distillery—"

"Excuse me," interrupted Nigel. "Your distillery?"

"Yes, my distillery. It's a pet project, a kind of hobby. I want to produce my own bourbon. Of course, it's a long-term thing. I mean, even when the distillery is operational, it'll be twelve years before my first batch of whiskey. Maybe eleven, if I get impatient. Anyway, I was in need of a veteran pipe fitter to inspect a few of my couplings."

"You do your own pipe fitting?" asked Nigel.

"I love pipe fitting. Some people like knitting, some like fishing—I like pipe fitting. And I'm very particular about my pipe fitting. I wouldn't trust just anyone. Get the wrong person for a job like that and the whole place could blow up. So, I looked on Angie's List, and guess who shows up?"

"Horatio Pipe Fitter?"

"Stanley, the perfect man for the job. He inspected my

couplings, gave me some welding advice, and demonstrated his special soldering techniques. Before you knew it, we were talking stop valves, reducers, and bulkhead fittings over a bowl of caramel popcorn. I'll spare you the gory details, but once the wine came out and the discussion veered into ball valves, orifice flanges, and female threaded Y-fittings, I was a ball of plumber's putty in his hands. He's been here ever since. I believe I can say he's never been happier. Isn't that right, dear?"

Stanley grinned while holding up a glass of Cam's foot wine.

It dawned on Nigel that good fortune hadn't changed Stanley all that much.

"He won't say it, but I will," said Cam. "It was a perfect match. He was a pipe fitter in the middle of a divorce. I was a country star in the middle of a divorce. Amazing, but true. If they put that in a romance novel, no one would buy it. The premise, I mean. They might buy the book. Shit, a romance novel with 'pipe fitter' in the title? I'd buy that."

As dinner skidded toward dessert, conversation devolved into a round robin of personal status reports. After some robust prodding from Cam, Annie discussed her daily activities as a small-town private eye, warning as she went that it wasn't as exciting as one might suppose. She was right. Upon finishing, Annie fell into a rare, sorrowful state, no doubt ruminating on her dull future as a small-town private eye.

Cam, seeing her guest go catatonic, looked to console with harrowing tales of fabulous celebrity-hood. All appearances to the contrary, she was being crushed to a pulp from the inside out by a deepening artistic crisis. The fickle radio-listening public had recently turned away from her brand of pop-country. Country-pop was now the rage, and she doubted her ability to manage the transition. She had heard of suffering for one's art but was dismayed to learn it also applied to music. To make matters worse, she could not find good management advice. Her agent insisted she get a new accountant. Her accountant insisted she get a new agent. Her lawyer agreed with both of them. As if that weren't enough, she also needed a new yoga instructor. The discourse gave her a headache, so she summoned the wait staff to summon the masseuse, a herculean chap who stood behind her rubbing her temples. She appeared to fall into a trance, interrupted occasionally by sips of her foot wine.

Stanley was next. He described his transition from pipe fitter to award-winning artisanal baker. One might assume that such a journey accomplished in the span of a few months by a senior citizen merited more than eighteen words. Stanley didn't think so.

Finally, Nigel discussed his new job at the Sandoval place, describing himself as the estate administrator. "Little did I know," he said, "that I'd be tasked to organize a wedding on my first day. Many thanks to Stanley here for providing the baked goods on short notice. I'm sure they'll be fantastic."

Stanley grinned, nodded, and held up his glass of foot wine. And then, running short of grins, he said, "I hear there was a death on the property out there."

"Yes," said Nigel. "Most unfortunate. Of course, that's an assumption. I didn't know the chap."

"What do they say he died from?" asked Cam.

"A frog in his throat," said Nigel.

"Fatal, is it? A frog in the throat?" said Stanley, his normally pink face having turned a darker shade of pink. He appeared flustered, as if he'd just had frog for dinner before realizing the ramifications.

Nigel had not seen Stanley that color since a deviled egg went down the wrong pipe. He replied, "So it appears. The police have mentioned murder."

"Murder?" said Cam. "A little more toward the front," she said to her temple-rubbing Adonis.

"The frog appears to have been of a poisonous variety. Not only that," said Nigel, "he also had a toad in his mouth. If it was murder, it was by that rarest of fiends, the amphibian killer."

"Do they have any clues—footprints, fingerprints, or such?

Any suspects?" asked Stanley.

"No fingerprints," said Annie. "Amphibian slime is not a good medium. They do have some footprints at the scene. Unfortunately, they belong to Nigel."

"Of course, I've already told the police I didn't do it, so I'm clear," said Nigel. "Want to know my theory?"

"This should be interesting," said Annie.

"A drifter, drifting as drifters do, drifts onto the Sandoval property. He's a herpetologist."

"A drifting herpetologist?" asked Cam.

"Not as rare as you might think," said Nigel. While the others considered the statistics, Nigel continued. "Anyway, the herpetologist carries with him a poison dart frog, perhaps as a pet, perhaps for personal protection, who knows? He sacks out for the night on the Sandoval property. The poison dart frog is, of course, a tropical animal. It would seek out warm, humid conditions. The man, this drifting herpetologist, is also a snorer. You see where I'm going with this?"

"I do, I do," said Cam, opening her eyes. "This drifting, snoring herpetologist was murdered by his own frog. That is a brilliant deduction."

"You're obviously an intelligent woman," said Nigel. "For those who haven't caught up, this poison dart frog seeking optimal tropical conditions in which to pass the night finds the open maw of the snoring herpetologist and makes himself at home. Need I say that having a poison dart frog cuddled against one's tonsils might prove adverse to one's health? In this case, yes."

"What about the toad?" asked Annie.

"The toad crawled into the open mouth after the frog. Perhaps for the same reason, a comfy place to spend the night."

"You seem to have solved the mystery," said Stanley.

"Congratulations. Perhaps you should join your wife in the detective business," said Cam.

Nigel had suggested this very thing some time back. Annie,

after regaining her composure, had said this was why he made a good husband—because he made her laugh. Annie wasn't laughing now, audibly at least, but her head was down and her shoulders were convulsing.

"Let me know when the police confirm your brilliant theory," said Stanley.

"I'll keep you posted," said Nigel.

"Would you like to see the house?" asked Cam with the rejuvenated spirit of one coming off a good temple rub.

"Absolutely," said Annie.

With that, the four walked the premises. The residence was impressive in a way that lavishly constructed and professionally maintained homes often are. It had a music studio, a theater, one of those pools that's half indoors and half outdoors, and a shrine. The Cam Logan shrine room contained awards, photos, framed articles, and a life-sized wax figure of Cam herself, meeting a life-sized wax figure of Oprah. A meeting which, as Cam described it, "Should have been destined to happen."

Clearly, Cam enjoyed playing the tour guide. Stanley followed along with the fish-eyed grin of a lottery winner who'd found his winning ticket while removing gum from his shoe.

"Next, I'll show you my playroom," said Cam, leading the group to an outbuilding through a long, narrow hallway. This was no simple corridor, however, as one wall was constructed of glass, behind which thrived an indoor forest. "To your left," she said, "are enclosures for my tropical animal exhibit. If you look hard enough, you might see the ocelot, or you might not—she's good at hiding. I wanted a leopard but was told I didn't have the space. Some day.

"And here's the bird enclosure, parrots and macaws mostly. Past that you have the South American creepies—beautiful snakes, mostly. A red pipe snake, emerald tree boa, and that neon-looking guy is the eyelash viper. Beautiful, but deadly."

"It must be quite a chore to look after all these animals," said Annie.

"It is, but not for me. I have a zookeeper who stops by, and I have staff do the day-to-day stuff. It's an operation, but it was always my dream to have a zoo. I go to South America at least once a year to find new animals. And," said tour guide Cam, "here is my lagoon. Fully stocked with fish from the upper Amazon."

The corridor opened into a warehouse-sized space containing a lake bordered by lush tropical vegetation and spanned by a foot bridge.

Nigel wondered if she'd considered a crocodile. *Why wouldn't she?*

"And now my playroom, where I keep my toys," said Cam, opening a locked metal door.

Let loose inside the hanger/gymnasium, the visitors spun themselves in silly circles marveling at the vast expanse of adult playthings. Hard to believe that such a vast array of diversions could belong to just one person with just one lifespan.

"You have a large extended family?" asked Nigel.

"Not unless you count ex-husbands," said Cam. "I know it seems a little overwhelming, but what can I say? I like to live."

'Consume' might have been a better description. Nigel's eyes were drawn to a pair of ultra-light aircraft parked behind a five-foot wall of board games.

"How many guns do you have?" asked Annie, staring at an impressively displayed armory in a wall of custom-built cabinets.

"I couldn't say," said Cam. "My first husband was a gun nut, and my third was pretty much a collector—"

"Let me guess," said Annie, squinting at the outstretched muzzle of an enormous gun, which, following its length, led to an ugly, hulking form in drab olive. "He also collected tanks."

"That would be husband number two, the military man. You're looking at Pete, the PT-76, a Soviet construction from the '50s. We had a chance to buy one cheap in Turkmenistan, so we picked it up."

"Does it work?" asked Annie.

"It had better. We spent a hundred grand to make it battle-ready. Of course, I don't have live ammunition, just some practice cartridges that came with it."

"And what"—Nigel pointed to a giant cylindrical cage off to the left—"is that?"

"That is a vertical wind tunnel, you know, for skydiving without a plane. Husband number two—no, make that number three—was hot for me to try skydiving. I wasn't about to get into some creaky-ass plane just to jump out of it, so he bought me this as a persuader. I hated it. Terrible for the hair, so skydiving was a no-go. Six months later, I told *him* to go jump from a plane, 'chute optional. He was gone with the wind, but I got stuck with damn tunnel. Like all this stuff, it was bought with my own money, so I'm stuck with it."

One section of this vast army of misfit toys contained the accoutrements to all the world's leisure sports. There were golf bags, tennis rackets, croquet sets, darts of various types, skis, snowboards, fishing gear, scuba tanks, watercraft, assorted skates, trampolines, bicycles, and, lording over it all, a full-sized skeleton of a *Tyrannosaurus rex*.

"Am I to assume the T rex provides security?" asked Nigel.

"Rex was a gift to the geologist, husband number four. He had a thing for fossils and liked puzzles, so I bought him this set of bones. When they delivered it with a big rig, he was like a boy on Christmas morning. He spent days connecting kneebone to thighbone. If he'd have thrown me a bone once in a while, he might still be around."

In a far-off corner, Nigel noticed a collection of bizarrely shaped furniture hung with shiny chains and soft leather goods. When a grinning Stanley walked into his field of vision, Nigel looked away. After a moment to scrub his mind of disturbing visions, Nigel raised his eyes to see Stanley standing among the articles, smiling like the family cat under the canary cage holding in a mouthful of feathers.

Cam and Annie had gravitated toward the modern weaponry section. Nigel, spotting some Rock'em Sock'em Robots, challenged Stanley to a match.

After what seemed like minutes, Nigel heard Annie's voice, "Ya'll ready to go?"

"I suppose," said Nigel. He was agreeable because a big early lead had dwindled to 46 rounds to 42.

Stanley said nothing, but his sagging lips communicated a reluctance to leave a game in which he'd seized the momentum.

The four returned as they had come, out the metal doors to the lagoon. As Cam bolted the door behind them, the others walked across the bridge. Between squawks of tropical birds, the trio heard a gentle plop from behind.

"Oh, shit," shouted Cam. "My ring fell into the lagoon. This is terrible."

The group backtracked to rally 'round the stricken girl.

"Which ring, dear?" said Stanley.

"The one you picked out. The ruby one. I don't want to lose it. That's *our* ring. You've got to get it back."

"Shouldn't be that difficult. Where'd it fall?"

"There," she said, pointing.

"I see it," said Nigel. "I can get it."

"Let Stanley do it," said Cam. "He's got a trash grabber thingy."

"A thingy?" said Stanley.

"You know, that thing with the claw. I know you've seen it. I used it yesterday to pick up your underwear. It's in the side closet, outside the kitchen."

"Should I get it?" Stanley asked.

"You should get it," Cam replied.

"I'll go get it." Stanley exhaled a large gob of air, and off he went to get the thingy.

"Is it worth a lot?" asked Nigel.

"I don't know. Thirty, forty-thousand, but it's not the money," said a tearful Cam.

"No, of course not," said Nigel, rolling up his sleeve. "I'll see if I can reach it."

"No, don't," said Cam. "You're our guest. Let Stanley do it."

The more Nigel could do for Stanley, the more Stanley might be willing to do for Nigel. Stanley, despite his turtle-like tendencies, seemed the type to avoid moisture on his person. Physical assertion wasn't his thing either, and if Nigel could save him the trouble, old Stanley might reward him with a deluxe treatment on the wedding sweets. Nigel needed all the help he could get.

"I'll just stretch myself out and see if I can reach it," said Nigel, lying down on the edge of the bridge and thrusting his arm into the water.

"Be careful," said Annie half-heartedly.

Nigel understood her attitude. She was being the race car driver's wife, showing appropriate concern while being helpless to stop her man-child husband. She'd been conditioned by dozens of similar scenarios from the past. This time, he was determined to succeed rather than embarrass.

Nigel thrust his arm downward and came up short of the bottom. He edged himself farther out over the bridge and pushed his arm in up to the shoulder. His fingers touched gravel, but no ring. Seeing how he was already soaked to the shoulder, it couldn't hurt to go a bit deeper. He squiggled himself even farther out until half his head was underwater.

"Watch it. You'll fall in if you're not careful," said Annie. She bent down and grabbed his pant leg as if that might help.

"You should stop," said Cam. "Stanley's coming."

At this point, Nigel would sooner plunge in like a pearl diver than give up the search. He stretched his fingers to their max, hoping to feel metal. He didn't. What he felt was his body go stiff and buzzy, like being hit with an electric cattle prod built for elephants. The next sensation was one of hearing his own waffling scream before his mouth filled with green lagoon water.

Annie let go of the pant leg to cover her ears.

Nigel rolled into the water like a quivering log. When he next emerged from the depths, he did so with a mad, flapping, vertical leap. Had Annie been an experienced fisherman, she'd have recognized the move as that of the hooked tarpon realizing it had drawn the attention of a hungry bull shark. As he cleared the water, Annie spotted the source of his torment in the form of a slimy, slender creature lunging for his ankle. This aquatic version of a weenie dog did not bark but crackled as it made contact.

Nigel's upper body landed on the bridge, and Annie helped to pull the rest of him out of the water. Even though his head had been submerged, his hair appeared dry and frizzy. His bulging eyes darted to and fro as if searching for an exit, and his body, stiff as a tree trunk, shuddered as if under attack by a chainsaw.

"Are you all right?" asked Annie.

After a few false starts, Nigel said, "Wh-Wh-What?"

Annie looked at Cam for an explanation.

"I didn't know," she said. "I mean, I told my aquarist I wanted an electric eel. I didn't know he'd gone out and gotten one."

"Wh-wh-why? A-a-a-an eel?" stammered Nigel, struggling both to speak and to not bite his own tongue.

"Who wouldn't want an electric eel?" said Cam. "Maddie's got one. If Maddie's got one, you know they must be something to have."

The logic was indisputable.

Stanley eventually showed up with the thingy, but without electrician's boots or rubber gloves declined to plumb the depths.

The party made their way back to the house, exchanging thank yous, apologies, and *adieus* while studiously avoiding the subject of eels. For Nigel and Annie, it was a night they'd long be unable to forget. Cam, he thought, might not remember it the next day.

11

BASELESS ACCUSATIONS

Some nights don't want you to sleep, and Nigel went through one of those. It may have been the room, thick with the essence of Gastrick, or it may have been the recurring aftershocks from his recent electric eel attack. Whatever the culprit, the old soul refused to lie still with the body. But, sleep or no sleep, Nigel was to report to Mrs. Sandoval for day three of his new career. Days one and two had included disposing of a dead body, catching an old crone flung from a banister, welcoming husbands (past, present, and future), and being implicated in a murder. Not to be overlooked, his leisure time had included two exploding water heaters and electrocution by an eel. He looked forward to day three.

The morning's breakfast failed to compete with an unpleasant aftertaste from the previous night. Unable to ascribe the lingering flavor to any particular menu item, Nigel suspected he was experiencing the aftermath of having one's saliva fried *in situ*. With the taste of eel-generated electricity in his mouth, he made his way to Mrs. Sandoval's office for his morning briefing.

"We didn't see you at dinner last night," said Mrs. Sandoval, picking lint from her commodore's jacket.

"That's reassuring for you. I wasn't there," said Nigel. "I'm sorry if you missed me, but my understanding was that evenings are my own."

"Your understanding is correct. Had a good dinner, I trust?"

"Exquisite. Roast quail, delectable. I could have eaten a dozen. Ever had it? Quail? If you should ever get the chance... And the dessert! Some French thingummy with pancakes and berries and a blowtorch. Absolute heaven—"

"Do you know what we had?" asked Mrs. Sandoval.

"I believe Lysette mentioned pizza."

"Pizza! Yes, we had pizza, Mr. Nigel. That is what we had, from Domino's, I believe."

"Excellent. Tasty?"

"Abuelita had the trots."

"Prefers that to pizza, does she?"

"She had the pizza, Mr. Nigel. First, she had the pizza, and then later, she had the trots. It always happens that way. It is why we do not serve pizza in this house. Do you understand?"

"I think so, but let me read it back just in case. Abuelita doesn't care for pizza. She prefers trots. Got it."

"No, you don't got it," said Mrs. Sandoval. "When I say the trots, I mean the runs. I'm trying to be lady-like. Diarrhea, Mr. Nigel. Abuelita loves pizza, but when she eats pizza, she gets diarrhea. Now, do you understand?"

"I do, I do. I don't wish to pry, but has she ever considered giving pizza a pass, considering how it...eh...passes?"

"She can't help herself. She loves pizza and refuses to believe it's the cause of her discomfort. She'll always blame something else. That's why we must not have pizza in this house, understood?"

"Yes, sorry about that, m'lady. Now I know."

"We employ a cook so that we have home-cooked meals according to our preferences. As the butler, it is your responsibility to see it through accordingly. Is that clear?"

"Exceedingly clear, m'lady."

Nigel was now employing a technique known to veteran

butlers as lady-spreading. Not as diabolical as it sounds, lady-spreading was the practice of strategically sprinkling one's conversation with the word "lady" in its various forms when addressing troublesome female clients. The word possessed a subliminal power to soothe and disarm, especially when applied liberally by British butlers working in North America. Ladling out the "ladies" was the butler's equivalent of twisting a lad's ear and saying, "Act like you been somewhere."

"Good. Let's have no more screwups," said Mrs. Sandoval. "Now, where do we stand regarding the wedding preparations?"

"Uh, dessert catering, check. A tent for the outside ceremony, check."

"You have a minister?"

"I have a suggestion. I still need to call."

"Don't get one of those religious types. They'll spend an hour trying to convert us. The bride and groom have 175 years between 'em. They don't have time for that sort of thing."

"No, m'lady. An irreligious minister. Should not be difficult."

"What about alcohol?"

"For the minister?"

"No. For me—I mean, for everyone. What's your booze plan?"

"Not given it much thought. Have you any suggestions?"

"A margarita fountain. Of course, there should be champagne. Someone might want beer, so a keg, I suppose. And tequila shots. There must be tequila shots. Just make sure we have enough to go around, and someone to serve. And flower arrangements, you'll need to take care of that. And a photographer—nothing too expensive. These are old people. They don't like to look at themselves, nor do we. Oh! And the wedding dress. Have you bought it?"

"The wedding dress? Uh, Stefanie was looking into that. I'll get a status."

"And the groom's suit. You need to make sure the groom's outfit matches up appropriately with the bridal gown."

"I see. Something in crushed velvet, maybe purple," said Nigel. He wouldn't say it, but considering Abuelita's taste in wedding gowns, chaps over bare buttocks might be appropriate groom-wear.

"Don't be silly. Purple at a wedding? Ridiculous."

"If you say so, m'lady."

"And you'll need to check that the rings are sorted out, and a best man, and someone to give away the bride."

"Who would that be?"

"How would I know? I'm not the one arranging this thing. That's your job, Mr. Nigel."

"Of course, m'lady. I will see to all the arrangements."

"And one more thing, Mr. Nigel."

Nigel shuddered.

"The dead man that appeared in our garden the other day, the one you're arranging a funeral for…" Mrs. Sandoval waited for Nigel to acknowledge.

"Yes, I recall the dead man. Go on."

Mrs. Sandoval leaned in and lowered her voice. "Do you, by any chance know who killed him?"

"No, m'lady. Haven't a clue."

"Are you sure?"

"The last time I checked with myself, I had no theory. Why do you ask?"

"That detective here yesterday thinks you did it."

"What? I assure you I did not!"

"Well, he talked to everyone, and he seems pretty certain it was you."

"Did he say that?"

"He didn't stand up and yell 'The butler did it,' but it was pretty clear to everyone that he thinks the butler did it."

Nigel had certainly felt accused during his interrogation, and Abuelita's little tirade hadn't helped his cause, but he figured he was just one of many bushes being beaten by this bungling detective. Rubberface seemed the type to accuse everyone of everything. Learning that he was murder suspect number one, with no number two, was a shock like that of an electric eel, but different.

"Why does he think that?" said Nigel.

"I'm sure the reasons will be described in the indictment."

"Indictment?"

"Wouldn't that be the next step? I'm not so familiar with these things, but the detective talked about an indictment."

"But what evidence does he have, m'lady?"

"You're getting yourself worked up, Mr. Nigel. You need to relax. You said you didn't do it, and I, for one, hope that's true. Just answer one question for me, and then we can forget all about this unfortunate conversation."

"What's that?"

"Suppose you did kill a man on this property—I'm not saying you did, but just for grins, let's suppose, *suppose* you killed a man on this property—would you be clever enough to get away with it? I mean, you wouldn't leave behind clues, would you?"

"What kind of question is that?" said Nigel. "Why would you ask such a thing, m'lady?"

"Mr. Nigel, understand it's my fervent hope that you had nothing to do with this murder. But, if on the outside chance you did, I would hope you would have proceeded with all due discretion. Murder or no murder, I have a household to run. I don't need to tell you about that nutty business with our last butler. To have two butlers in a row hauled away on murder-related charges would severely damage our reputation among prospective future butlers."

"*Your* reputation?"

"Yes, our reputation. You have no idea how hard it is to find a butler in a place like New Antigua, Texas. This is not the big city with butlers on every street corner. No, it's almost impossible to find a proper butler in this town. Between you and me, it's the reason you're working here."

"I'm glad to know I have your confidence."

"You do have my confidence, Mr. Nigel. Believe me, whatever you say stays between the two of us if it might in any way prove damaging to the Sandoval reputation. You have my assurance."

"How very reassuring, m'lady," Nigel said, wiping sweat from his downcast brow.

"You bet. From the first time we met, Mr. Nigel, I felt you were sly. You have that kind of face. And the more I've gotten to know you, the more I feel that way. I believe that no matter what you may have done, you'll not be found guilty. I'm comforted by that."

"I'm happy for you."

"One more thing before you go," said Mrs. Sandoval.

"Yes, m'lady," said Nigel, as his will to live dribbled from his pores.

"You need to move."

"Move?"

"You'll need to move out of Gastrick's old room to make way for Mr. Sandoval. He slept in a tree last night."

"Which tree?"

"I hardly think it matters which tree, since none of our trees have beds. You can move in with Grumps for the time being."

"With Grumps?" said Nigel, trying to recall such a person.

"You know, Gastrick's uncle. The guy you've been delivering food to. There's a sofa in that room. You'll bunk there."

"Yes, m'lady. I'll get on that straight away."

Gastrick had once mentioned something about an aged uncle. As for delivering food to him, that was a new one. Nevertheless, a sweaty Nigel turned to face the perilous day.

"Oh, Mr. Nigel?"

What other torture might be unleashed? "Yes, m'lady?"

"I like what you've done with your hair. Is that a perm?"

12

A MAN WHO'S FIGURED THINGS OUT

Reluctantly, Nigel packed his things and made his way to the quarters of the mysterious ancient one known as Grumps. He knocked on the door.

"Rrrrrghhh?" came a reply.

Taking that as an invite, Nigel eased the door open and poked his head in. An elderly man sat in a cushiony chair hunched over a portable tray table. In the far corner of the room, a television displayed a message indicating no signal available. Nigel couldn't see much of the man's face as it was shielded beneath an olive-green army helmet.

"Hello," said Nigel. "I'm to be rooming with you."

"You bring my dinner?" growled the man.

"Not on this trip, but as soon as I park my bag, I can get you something."

"You better if you want to stay in this room. My nephew stopped bringing my dinner. What's wrong with that kid?"

Of course, the nephew in question was the former butler who'd been in jail the past three months facing multiple charges, including conspiracy to commit murder. News traveled slow in certain parts of the Sandoval residence.

"I think from now on, I'll be looking after your dining needs," said Nigel.

"Where's my nephew?"

"I believe he's away for a while."

"Who are you, and why do you think you can stay in my room? Nobody asked me."

"Sorry about that. There's a bit of a housing shortage, so Mrs. Sandoval assigned me to this room. Temporarily, you understand. As soon as the crises abates, out I go. I promise to be as unobtrusive as possible."

"You ain't planning to sleep in my bed, are you?" asked Grumps, staring at the dead TV. He had not, as yet, bothered to glance in Nigel's direction.

"No, no, I'll be fine on the sofa," said Nigel.

"Good. I don't want you in my bed. You look the type to have bedbugs, or crabs—"

"Rest assured, I don't have—"

"Hair lice, ticks, fleas, tapeworms. I don't need that stuff."

"Goodness, no. Absolutely, I—"

"Stay off my bed."

"For sure," said Nigel. He would not bother to ask how Grumps got his name.

"Where you from?" Grumps asked, directing a squint that communicated where he should go. "You got a funny way of talking."

"I'm from England. Surrey, to be precise."

"England! I might of know'd it. It was an Englander stole my girl back in WW2. Why, if I had my old flamethrower, I'd torch your ass right where you sit."

"That sounds a bit harsh. Let me say that on behalf of English people everywhere, I apologize for the action of the dastard who stole your sweetheart. The depth of your grudge speaks volumes about what a very special girl she must have been," countered Nigel, ever the diplomat.

"Not really. She had bad teeth and pasty skin. They were like that, those British broads, but it gave guys like me hope. Those gals back home wouldn't give a sad sack like me the time of day, but those limey birds suffered from bad vision and poor taste—just the kind of roadkill made to order for a horndog GI like myself. And they loved the chocolate. They'd do anything for it. An-E-thing."

"Really?"

"Yes, really. Just ask your mom," spouted the man. He then lowered his voice and his head. "She was the love of my life, but it all came crashing down. It was on a Tuesday. Tuesdays were never good on the battlefield, but this one was particularly objectionable. Actually, it may have been a Wednesday. Wednesdays weren't good neither. Anyway, on that terrible Wednesday, or maybe Thursday, after a full day of chasing Jerries, I received the letter that would forever change my life."

"A Dear John letter from your English sweetheart?" interjected Nigel.

"You heard this before?" asked Grumps. A tear would have been rolling down his cheek if he hadn't run dry back in the fifties.

"No, but I feel as though I have."

"She wrote me this letter," he said, pulling a folded, brownish slip of paper from a nearby shelf.

"You've kept the letter all this time?" asked Nigel. "That is amazing. How did you manage to save it?"

"Through the rest of the war I kept the letter in the bottom of my boot."

"The safest place," said Nigel.

"I pretended the letter was her face. All across Germany I stepped on it. Even when others collapsed, I had the incentive to take that extra step. When I got home, I took the letter out. It had once smelled of perfume, but no more. I didn't know what to do with it, so I ran it over several times with my uncle's tractor."

"And the letter survived?"

"Of course it survived. That's it right there, moron," he

said, pounding a finger on the fragile brown paper. "But after a few more years of keeping it in the bottom of my shoe, my anger started to weaken. Sometime during the Kennedy administration, I realized my wrath had been misplaced. The letter was not the enemy and never had been. All that butt-clenching anger, that molar-crunching rage—it was fun, but it was getting me nowhere. After splitting a tooth while chewing on some barbed wire, it came to me that I'd been wasting my energy."

"Good for you. Didn't let it get the best of you."

"Absolutely not. It could have, you know. I was in the danger zone. But I discovered my mistake before destroying myself over what? A silly letter."

"Exactly."

"No, it wasn't the letter that deserved my hate, but that rat-faced little Brit, Milton, and all the other rat-faced little Brits like him. That's who deserved my hate. I can't tell you what a revela-tion it was when that light went on. A new lease on hate. A hate so rich and pure, it was like hating for the very first time. My rage bubbled and boiled anew."

"Did you consider seeking help?"

"For what? I never felt so alive. I didn't eat for three years. Not in the conventional sense. I subsisted off the bitter drippings of my own blackened soul. The only way my animus could have been assuaged was to find that Milton and desecrate his body in ways Jeffrey Dahmer only dreamed of."

"Did you look for him?" said Nigel, his knees pumping like pistons.

"No way. The only way to keep the hatred percolating was to stay in my room and brood. If I'd gone out into the world, who knows what would've happened? I might have lost that bitter fire. Then where would I be?"

"I don't know. Not bitter? Did you ever think of finding a new girlfriend?"

"I ask you, what girl would want a guy self-consumed with

barely contained rage that threatened to explode at any minute? Certainly not the sweet, well-adjusted girls I favor."

"I see your point."

"No. Once I got that letter, my fate was sealed. I would never again find that perfect combination of homeliness and desperation combined with an ingratiating laugh and insatiable desire for chocolate. She was made for me and I for her, my one and only."

"May I read the letter?" asked Nigel.

"You can, but only to yourself. I can't bear to hear it again. I don't even want to see your lips move, understand?"

"I'll try," said Nigel.

The brittle, brown, sweat-infused paper carried an aroma slightly akin to Cam's foot wine. Nigel made low humming noises as his eyes progressed down the page.

"No humming noises," growled Grumps. "It's far too painful to hear humming inspired by that letter."

"Sorry," replied Nigel. He finished the letter and turned it over to see if there might be more—a PS, perhaps. "So, your girlfriend was named Wilhelmina?"

"That's right, the most elegant name in the English language. No need to rub it in. Is that your game?"

"No, just checking," said Nigel. "Tell me, Grumps, if I may call you Grumps, when was the last time you read this letter?"

"That'd be February of '45. It was cold as hell."

"So, you read it then, but haven't read it since?"

"That's right. That's what started the downhill slide. What are you getting at?"

"Were you a good reader? I mean like a fifth- or sixth-grade level? Literate, I mean?"

"I was all right."

"So, you received this letter, and you sat down, and you read it?"

"It didn't happen exactly that way. See, we'd been fighting the Jerries since morning, and just before we called it a day, this mortar round lands right smack-dab in front of me. Fortunately, I was on the other side of this little brick wall. That wall probably saved my life, though I've often cursed it. Anyway, the wall protected my body from the blast, but the explosion threw a cloud of masonry dust right into my face. I was blinded. They put a bandage over my eyes and led me back to camp. It was three or four days before I could take that bandage off and see again."

"And you received the letter later that day?"

"That evening."

"So, that evening, while your eyes were bandaged, you received the letter. How did you read the letter?"

"A guy in our platoon, Jester, read it to me."

"Chester read it to you?"

"No, Jester. With a J. He read it to me."

Nigel was beginning to put some pieces together. "This Jester with a J, what kind of a chap was he?"

"Jester was a cutup. You know the type, a wiseass. Always blabbering insults, trying to trick you, playing practical jokes. He'd do anything to put one over on you. Honestly, if we'd a taken a vote for someone to go on a suicide mission, he'd have won. What a Bozo. He knew better than to mess with me, though. I made sure of that."

"Did you?"

"I'd have none of his foolishness. I was too smart for him. What's all this talk about Jester? What's he got to do with anything?"

"Oh, nothing, I suppose," said Nigel slipping the brown piece of paper into his jacket pocket. "Nothing at all. You best forget about Jester."

"I have forgot about him. It's that English bastard I think about. Sometimes I wake up in the middle of the night with my fingernails sunk deep into my pillow," he said, holding up his knotted hands like a pair of talons. "I've got hold of his liver. I can see that sorry English wretch, wherever he is, screaming 'til his lungs pop. Nighttime is the only time I feel any pleasure."

"Gracious," said Nigel. "Maybe you should try knitting. They say it relaxes the soul."

"My soul is a burning cesspool of insatiable hate. Knitting, huh? I like those big needles."

"Perhaps knitting's not your thing. A quiet game of solitaire before bedtime might improve your sleep."

"I do my best work while sleeping. There's nothing I can't disembowel in my sleep. You're bunking here tonight?"

"That was the plan."

"My advice: sleep with your eyes open."

"Not a problem," said Nigel, meaning the part about eyes open. "You said you were hungry. How long has it been since you ate?"

"Seems like forever. I don't keep track. If there's no food, I just chew on my own blackened soul. Vengeance can keep you alive, you know."

"Certainly, but your own blackened soul tends to be high in free radicals. I'll see if I can't pop down and find you something more nutritious."

"And pudding. I want pudding."

"Of course you do. A nice pudding made from the liver of an Englishman. Mmmmm, wouldn't that be nice? I'll be back in a jiffy."

13

BUTLER'S BUSINESS

As it was ten in the morning, the inmates of Asylum Sandoval had rolled themselves out of bed and infested the common areas. In the lounge area to one side of the staircase, the newly returned Mr. Sandoval, in his donated wardrobe, looked less vagrant-like and refreshingly chipper for one who'd passed the night in a tree. His spirits were likely bolstered by the warmth of his daughters, Esmerelda and Stefanie, enclosing him like bookends on the Louis XIV loveseat.

Esmerelda was not Mr. Sandoval's biological offspring but had arrived as part of a package deal when he married Abuelita five decades earlier. By every other account, however, she was his daughter. Essie believed their surprisingly coincidental returns signified some grand cosmic jubilee, her personal Age of Aquarius. She could hardly keep herself corked.

Stefanie, the daughter of the current Mr. and Mrs. Sandoval, had a less romantic view. She put no stock in cosmic coincidences, or in her father's tales. Either he was lying or, as his stoved-in head seemed to indicate, addlebrained. Whichever, he had obviously run out of things to fail at, given up, and boomeranged home. But faults and failures aside, she was overjoyed to have him back. The trio now filled the atrium with choruses from their shared childhood songbook.

Annie had left for the day, but her mother haunted the estate like a gas leak. She floated about the place in her improvised turban and massive sunglasses, watching, listening, and not engaging. Rooms went silent and then empty when she entered —the same effect had she been a meandering skunk.

Mrs. Sandoval, sitting alone in her office, thumbed through a magazine while waiting for the clock to strike twelve. The hour from eleven to noon was her longest—the jittery interval between caffeine buzz and tequila fortifiers when unexpected things often occurred.

Skimming an article on "How to Satisfy Your Man in 27 Easy Steps," she became afflicted with a sudden chill. Looking up with a start, she glimpsed an enormous pair of sunglasses topped by a turban just as they vaporized like a sinister mist. Mrs. Sandoval spasmed in fits and starts as if a handful of her heartbeats had just been stolen. Shaking, she returned to her article, but could not remember what step she was on.

"Completed my move," said Nigel, injecting his head through the threshold.

Mrs. Sandoval popped six inches out of her seat while ripping step fifteen from her magazine.

"My word!" she shouted. "Aren't you butlers supposed to announce yourselves? Scared the living daylights out of me."

Nigel retreated from the doorway for a second approach. "Ahem. I've completed my move," he said. "The gentleman I am to bunk with, do you have a schedule for him?"

"What kind of schedule?"

"I assume he eats. Goes out. Talks to people. I assume."

"Gastrick took care of that. It was his responsibility. Gastrick's gone."

"Indeed he is. The gentleman, Grumps I believe he's called, is still here. He requires looking after."

"See that he is."

"Yes, ma'am. I will see to it, then." Nigel turned to leave.

"Wait, Mr. Nigel."

"Yes, ma'am?"

"You've talked to that Jack Watt, have you not?"

"Yes, ma'am. A good chap. Quite a cheery sort. As an unnamed poet once said, 'He floats with winged sandals above life's catastrophes.'"

"I didn't know he hung around with poets, but his poet friend had him dead on." Mrs. Sandoval rubbed her forehead as if it were cramped.

"You don't approve of him, madam?"

"I approve of him very much. As you say, he's a cheery sort. It's just that ...." She struggled to find the words. It was all very well that Abuelita had found some sap to marry, but having met the sunny Mr. Watt, Mrs. Sandoval seemed conflicted.

Nigel understood. The thought of that buoyant man being shackled to the glum Abuelita was enough to stir up the bats in anyone's belly. She feared the winged vermin might loiter if Mr. Watt wasn't warned, scared off, or tied to the bumper of a truck heading to a faraway state.

Nigel, noting Mrs. Sandoval's anguish, interceded. "I understand your distress, madam. I myself have had similar misgivings."

"What should we do?"

"Nothing," said Nigel.

"Nothing?" asked Mrs. Sandoval.

"Nothing. I believe things will work out in the end."

"How?"

"Has this Mr. Watt eyes to see with?"

"He does."

"Ears to hear with?"

"Those too."

"Legs to run with?"

"Two, I believe."

"There you have it. Everything he needs. I suggest letting nature take its course."

"So, you think when he sees Abuelita for who she is, he'll run for the hills?"

"Wouldn't anyone?"

"Maybe you're right. Let's hope for your sake it works. One more thing before you go, Mr. Nigel. Could you remind me again, who is that ghastly woman creeping around in a turban and sunglasses?"

Nigel was wondering when the howling would begin. One day seemed about right. "That would be Annie's mother."

"Annie, that private investigating lady?"

"Yes, madam."

"And how long is she to stay? That mother, I mean."

"Until her home repairs are complete. I don't have a date."

"Is there anything we can do for her? I mean, to get her out of here sooner?"

"Not that I am aware of, madam."

"I'll tell you, Mr. Nigel. Bringing that lady here is a blot on your record. I mean, I don't mind having guests, but that lady is like some kind of walking *momento mori*. Do you know what I mean?"

"Yes, madam, I understand completely. She makes one contemplate a dreadful death and an afterlife of twisted, never-ending misery."

"Spot on, Mr. Nigel. So you've noticed it too?"

"I dare say, the woman was put on this earth for no other purpose."

"She doesn't even speak. Is she dumb?"

"No, madam. Unfortunately, she is not."

Mrs. Sandoval shivered. "I might not feel so unsettled if she just said something."

"Respectfully, I would disagree. I have heard her speak. Her words, should she choose to communicate, are prone to rankle," said Nigel. "Or worse."

"Worse than rankle?"

"Much worse. I would postulate that engaging her in conversation could have far-reaching repercussions. I would strongly advise against it. Perhaps I should warn the others."

"Do that, Mr. Nigel. For everyone's sake, warn the others."

Nigel made his way to the kitchen where Lysette was preparing the day's lunch. He stood at her side admiring the dishes in various stages of completion.

"Have you made a food tray for Grumps?" he asked.

"If someone orders a tray, I'll make one."

"So no one has ordered a tray?"

"Not since Gastrick been gone."

"Did you wonder if Grumps was being fed?"

"I wondered if he even existed," said Lysette. "I've heard of someone named Grumps, but I ain't never seen no one named Grumps. Is there such a person?"

"In fact, there is. And he must be pretty hungry. How long has Gastrick been gone? Three months? That's a long time to live off the drippings of one's own blackened soul. He must have been eating something."

"I don't know nothing."

Nigel did not wish to discuss it further. The police already had their snoot up his drawers for one murder. If Grumps expired in the night, he didn't want to leave a trail of incriminating conversations. "What do you have that I can take to him now? He could be on the verge of starvation. He's not the kind you could tell by looking."

"We running short as it is, what with all these extra people. You could take him your lunch."

"Fine. I'll put together the tray. From now on, could you put together a tray every day for lunch and dinner? I'll see that you're compensated."

"You know you will."

Nigel prepared a tray from Lysette's offerings and poured a

glass of juice. He was about to wheel the tray out on a cart when a loathsome sound tore through the silence.

"Where's my fiancé?" cackled Abuelita from the atrium. "Where's he gone to? Where's that damned fiancé?"

Wheeling the cart out of the kitchen, Nigel spotted Abuelita, center atrium, spinning around in her wheelchair. The girls, Mr. Sandoval, and Mrs. Sandoval across the way, held up their palms in the universal gesture for "How-the-hell-should-I-know?"

"If you can wait a couple minutes," said Nigel, "I'll help track him down."

"If he's skipped out, I'll track him down myself and skin that sucker alive," said Abuelita. "With my fingernails."

Nigel pushed the cart quickly toward the elevator only to freeze as Annie's mother, conjured up by Abuelita's declarations of violence, materialized at the base of the stairs. The turbaned wraith stood like a statue except for a tongue, strangely unforked, moistening her lips. Nigel averted his eyes. Giving a wide berth, he pushed the cart past the menacing mother-in-law and into the elevator.

As the elevator doors opened, the grandfather clock sounded the first of twelve gongs. He reached Grumps's room as the opening chords of "Tequila!" played, followed by Mrs. Sandoval expressing her relief in the form of a Tarzan yell. Critically needed in two places at once, he served Grumps first based on proximity and starvation. Fortunately, once he deposited the food tray and fixed the TV to receive a signal, Grumps was eager for Nigel to leave the room.

"Tequila!" shouted Mrs. Sandoval as Nigel landed on the first floor.

Nigel hustled to the liquor locker for the desired beverages and glassware.

"Get the lead out, bonehead," shouted Abuelita as Nigel reached the cabinet. "Tequila!" she wailed.

Nigel considered tossing the bottle directly into the restless mob, allowing them to chew off the top and trade open mouth gulps to their hearts' content. Only his butler's training held him back.

As he was prearranging the shot glasses, a lady's shoe came flying into the formation.

"Tequila!" shouted Abuelita, waving her remaining shoe over her head.

"Coming, m'lady," said Nigel.

While reassembling the shot glasses into neat formation, he noticed a movement on the back lawn. Such activity in the light of day was unlikely from any of the current residents. Pulling back the sheer curtains, Nigel saw Abuelita's missing fiancé. The condemned man marched about in the manner of a mechanical toy soldier before stopping to place hands on hips as if lost.

Nigel unlatched the French doors with the intent of asking the doomed man if he'd like a snort. At the first sound of doors unlatching, the man looked up, froze like a statue caught scratching himself, and then hoofed it. To where, who knew? But once he'd decided to go, he went.

A shoe whizzed past Nigel's nose, through the opened door, and out onto the back deck.

"Tequila!" shouted Abuelita. "The next thing I throw will have a blade on it."

14

EVIDENCE PILES UP

Having pacified the thirsty natives and knocked out a lunch of crackers and Vienna sausages, Nigel raced to the front door to answer a ringing bell. Standing before him was Winjack, the rubber-faced police detective.

"You?" asked the detective. "Still here?"

"Why would I not be?" replied Nigel.

"I had an inkling you might have been fired by now."

"It's just my third day on the job."

"Congratulations. You've got staying power, but the week is still young."

"Yes, but growing older by the minute. How can I help you?"

"I would like you to round up all the residents. I have breaking news regarding the dead man."

"Breaking news? Is he not dead?"

"Of course he's dead."

"For a minute, I thought you had a story worth hearing. Nevertheless, I shall rally the inmates." Nigel opened the door wide, allowing the detective to follow him in. Stepping to the center of the atrium, Nigel formed his hands into a megaphone. "Everyone!" he yelled. "Hear ye, hear ye. Inspector Detector is back. He thinks he has news. Rally around, boys and girls. Come one, come all. Step right up. Don't be late. Last one in is a rotten egg."

The residents, who had been centered around the liquor cabinet, reshuffled themselves to encircle the atrium.

"Everyone," announced Nigel. "This here detective has returned claiming he has important information on that unfortunate incident involving a cadaver—"

"What unfortunate incident was that?" asked Mrs. Sandoval.

"The cadaver," said Nigel.

"What about it?"

"It was in the garden."

"Yes, the cadaver in the garden. What was the unfortunate incident?"

"The unfortunate incident was there being a cadaver in the garden."

"We know that already. When you said there was an unfortunate incident involving the cadaver, I thought it must have disappeared, or exploded, or caused a traffic accident. The fact that it was in our garden isn't so unfortunate. If you want unfortunate, imagine how that man felt when he became a cadaver."

The detective nodded his head as if he understood.

"Very well," said Nigel. "Let's show the detective how civilized we can be. Indulge him with all the attention you can muster. No throwing of objects before he's finished. I yield the floor to Detective Winjack."

"Thank you," said the detective. "A surprisingly gracious introduction given your precarious legal situation." He removed a notepad from his trench coat and began reading, "Approximately 9:00 a.m. last Monday morning, an unidentified dead body was reported on this property—blah, blah, blah. In the oral cavity of the deceased was found a toad of a type not known to be injurious to humans. Upon removal of this toad, a frog was found farther down the cavity. This frog was summarily identified as one of the poison dart varieties native to South America. These animals are highly toxic to humans. However, a preliminary toxicology report indicates the man did not die of poisoning from this animal." He closed his notebook.

"So, the frog was *not* a poison dart frog," Nigel proclaimed.

"The frog *was* a poison dart frog," said the detective.

"Are you telling us that poison dart frogs are safe to consume?" said Nigel.

"I would not recommend consuming a poison dart frog," said the detective. "However, preliminary tests indicate that this particular poison dart frog was not poisonous."

"I see," crowed Nigel, pacing in front of the crowd. "Yet you maintain that a murder was committed. Are you suggesting the murder weapon was a non-poisonous poison dart frog administered as an asphyxiant?"

"Are you nuts?" said the detective.

Sensing a moment, Nigel faced the detective with an upturned finger. "Detective, when you found a toad in this man's mouth, you said he died from a poison toad, then you said he didn't. Then you found a poison dart frog in his throat and said he died from a poison dart frog. Now you say he didn't. What next? A salamander in his stomach? Your credibility is ebbing, Detective Winjack, Ebbing. So what actually killed this man, Detective, a blow to the head?"

"Interesting that you, of all people, should mention a blow to the head," said the detective. "According to the coroner, the cause of death was a blow to the head."

Nigel folded back his upturned finger.

The room went silent except for the sound of a dozen ears stretching toward Nigel in anticipation of a juicy confession.

"Why is everyone looking at me?" asked Nigel. "And tuck those ears in. You can't honestly think I had anything to do with this man's death."

"We wouldn't like to think so," said Stefanie, always the voice of reason. "But we would all be more certain if you confessed."

"Confessed? Confessed to what?"

"To whatever you should confess to," said Stefanie. "We're not saying you committed this particular murder, necessarily, but we know there must be things in your past. We can see it in your tormented eyes. Maybe now is the time to bare your soul. You could at least enjoy your jailtime with a clear conscience."

"Jailtime?" protested Nigel. "For what? I haven't done anything, and there's no evidence. Is there evidence?" He hoped there wasn't evidence.

"We know the man was hit sharply in the back of the head, behind the right ear, with a rounded object about an inch in diameter," said the detective. "I'm thinking a ball-peen hammer. Do you own a ball-peen hammer, Mr. Blandwater-Cummings?"

"Own a ball-peen hammer? I don't even know what a ball-peen hammer *is*. What is it?"

"This"—Detective Winjack said, holding up the diabolical implement—"is a ball-peen hammer. Do you know where I got this ball-peen hammer, Mr. Blandwater-Cummings?"

"How would I know? Murderers-R-Us?"

"Your garage."

"*My* garage? How did you get in my garage?"

"Do you deny that it's your hammer?"

"Let me see that." Nigel gave it a once-over. "Aha! This is not my hammer. It's a loaner. It was loaned to me by my father-in-law, Stanley, for working on rain gutters. I've never even used it."

"Excuse me," said the turbaned, sunglassed mother-in-law, speaking for the first time since entering the Sandoval residence. "I have intimate knowledge of this man, Stanley, of whom he speaks. Stanley would never loan out his tools to such a dubious character. Never."

"Thank you for that, miss," said the detective, turning again to Nigel. "Is it not true that there was an explosion and fire at your house the day after the body was discovered?"

"What of it?" said Nigel.

"Fire, that ancient destroyer of evidence. The fire could have been purposefully set to destroy this ball-peen hammer, or any other evidence from any other crimes."

"Other crimes? What *other* crimes?"

"I wouldn't know. But then, I did not start the fire. Of course, arson is a serious crime in and of itself."

"Arson?"

"When you finish the arson investigation at his place," said the turbaned mother-in-law, "you can start one on mine."

"I have one more bit of news before I go," said the detective. "Is Mr. Sandoval here?"

"Yes, sir," said Mr. Sandoval, raising his hand.

"Mr. Sandoval, I have some bad news."

"Oh, dear."

"Oh, dear, indeed," said the detective. "You, Mr. Sandoval, are dead."

"Really? I've felt disoriented lately, but I didn't think it was as bad as that. Actually, I've seldom felt better. What killed me?"

"The cause of death is listed as unknown, but you were declared dead a few weeks ago. No one told you?"

"If they did, I don't remember."

"Did anyone else know that Mr. Sandoval was dead?" asked the detective.

"Everyone thought he was dead," said Stefanie. "You, apparently, were the last to find out. But I have news for you, Mr. Detective. He's alive!"

Stefanie and Esmerelda jumped up in a fit of squeals to caress their dented but reclaimed father.

"You can jump up and down all you want," said the detective, "but it's not as simple as that. He's been declared dead. A person can't just show up after having been declared dead and expect to live as if nothing had happened. Not without going through a lot of hell first. He'll need a new Social Security number for a start. But there's an even bigger issue at stake."

"What are you talking about?" asked Esmerelda.

"He needs to prove his identity. Who are we supposed to

believe? An official document from the Bureau of Vital Statistics
with the state seal of Texas on it, or the word of some old geezer
who turns up with armadillo shell shoes?"

"He's not an old geezer. He's my Papa," protested Esmerelda.

"I'm sure you want to believe that, ma'am, but we need to
establish the truth. For all we know, he could be an illegal alien.
Did he come with any kind of identification?"

"I'm sorry to cause such trouble," said Mr. Sandoval, "but,
no, I have no identification. For a long time—many years, maybe
—I didn't even know who I was. Bit by bit, parts of my memory
came back. Eventually, I remembered my name was Sandoval
and that I came from New Antigua. I hoped that if I could make
it back to New Antigua, I'd find out more about myself. And
now you tell me I'm dead. I had hoped for a better ending."

"Ridiculous!" declared Esmerelda. "You're alive and you're
my Papa. Obviously, any documents declaring him dead need to
be nullified."

"For him to have been declared dead," spoke the detective,
"some member of his family must have filed the paperwork.
There must be affidavits testifying to his death or disappearance.
Who filed the paperwork? Who entered the affidavits?"

Every member of the gathering scanned every other member
of the gathering, expecting to see a raised hand. Instead, every
member of the gathering saw every other member of the gathering scanning all the other members of the gathering while not
raising a hand.

"No?" said the detective. "So, I am to believe that no member
of the family filed for a death certificate or entered an affidavit,
even though we have this brand-spanking new death certificate.
Strange."

"I say this with all due respect," said Nigel, turning to the
detective, "but you seem to be a detective without a clue."

"I believe," said the detective, inspecting the head of the ball-
peen hammer, "that once we've matched this hammer to the
dead man's injuries, I will have far more than a clue."

A shiver traveled down Nigel's back and then up his front. "Do you even know who the dead man is?" he asked.

"As yet, we do not," replied the detective.

"So, you have a dead man you cannot identify, whose cause of death is an ever-changing story, and a live man you seem to think is dead. Please excuse us if we remain skeptical. Am I right, people?"

"Would not surprise me in the least if you did someone in with a ball-peen hammer," replied his mother-in-law.

"Me neither," said Abuelita as her functioning eye punctured Nigel like a flaming icicle.

"Well!" said Nigel. "Thank you all so much for standing by me in my hour of need."

The crowd began to disburse.

"Tomorrow, I'll organize a noose-tying class. Nothing like a good, wholesome, shared activity to warm the blackest of hearts. If the weather's nice, we can build a gallows. I'll contact the local chapter of Habitat for Inhumanity, and, if we all pitch in, we'll have it up by noon. Any volunteers to make the lemonade?"

"Mr. Nigel, please don't be too upset," said Mrs. Sandoval. "It's not that everyone feels you're a murderer. We sincerely hope you aren't. It's just that we feel you're a pretty lousy butler. If you buckle down and become a respectable butler, you might have more people on your side. You can understand that, can't you?"

"I see. A matter of priorities. I get it."

"Good. Now, get me a tequila. This whole thing has made me tense."

When Nigel returned with two shots of tequila—one because she'd asked for it, and the other because she would ask for it—he noticed Annie conversing with the detective. After leaving the tray for Mrs. Sandoval, Nigel hid himself behind some curtains to eavesdrop on their conversation.

"So, you honestly have no idea who the dead man is?" asked Annie in a withering tone.

"As of yet, no. These things take time."

"Maybe I can save you some time," said Annie. "See if your victim doesn't match up to an Emilio Anguilero."

"Emilio Anguilero, eh? This name pop out of a bad dream? An old boyfriend, perhaps? Or something your Ouija board coughed up?"

"Call it a professional hunch. Maybe it's him. Maybe not. If it's him, then you'll have an actual lead toward finding the killer. It'd sure beat pissing in the wind, wouldn't it?"

"I assure you, no one is pissing in the wind."

"Oh, yeah? What's that on your shirt?"

Nigel couldn't see the follow up, but he knew the routine. Annie knew how to talk to these detectives in a language they understood. Nigel turned to sneak away.

"Yoo-hoo, Mr. Nigel," called out Mrs. Sandoval. "I see you! Could you bring me some ice cream? Vanilla custard, two scoops, crush some Tums to sprinkle on top. Thank you."

Nigel felt unnerved, like a chicken finding a snake in its coop. These constant insinuations that he was a murderer made it hard to maintain a butler's reserve. As soon as he could find a moment for himself, he texted Annie to meet him in the study. She wasn't always the comforting type, but he needed the perspective of a professional.

The seldom-used study featured a giant mahogany desk backed by a wall of musty leather-bound volumes Nigel perused while waiting for Annie. He would not have typed any of the Sandoval residents as scholarly readers, but the titles on display contained works of classic literature, philosophy, history, science, and law. Impressive it was, until he reached for Isaac Newton's *Principia* to discover that it was neither leather-bound, nor a volume, but part of a three-dimensional wall façade.

"Okay, what you got?" asked Annie, interrupting Nigel's disappointment.

"Ah, there you are. I thought you might have gotten lost," he said, sliding himself on top of the desk.

Annie leaned against one of the facing chairs. "I was just persuading Mother how harmless you are, even if you happened to be an assassin."

"Were you convincing?"

"Of course. She knows you, and she knows me. I'm packing heat, and I know how to use it. Case closed."

"Good for you, but we both know I'm not the killer. I have an idea who is."

"You think it's Abuelita's fiancé, Jack Watt."

"Correct. We think alike."

"No. Thankfully, we don't. He bears watching, but he's not the killer."

"Why not?"

"Murderers don't stick around for their investigations. If he were the killer, he'd be long gone. I've got plenty of questions about Jack Watt, but he's not the killer."

"Then who?"

"Don't know. But I have an idea who the dead man is, and that's a start."

"How do you know that?"

"The petition filed for Mr. Sandoval's death certificate. Almost certainly, the petitioner was that evil lawyer behind the Abuelita catfishing scheme. To clear the way to inherit her fortune, he manufactured some documents, including that petition for Mr. Sandoval's death certificate. He wanted a clean deed to the estate so once he married and murdered Abuelita, the property would be his, no questions asked.

"The petition included two affidavits from associates of Mr. Sandoval from his South American expedition. They each testified to his disappearance on that trip and their belief that he was dead. Our corpse fits the description of one of those men."

"Great that you figured that out, but what do you propose to do now?"

"I've given the name to Chief Inspector Bozo. If he's even halfway competent, which may be a stretch, he should be able to confirm his identity. If not, I'll have to investigate on my own."

"But what about the killer?"

"I'm researching the other associate. The way I figure it, our dead man was killed by someone who knew him, possibly an accomplice. It may or may not have been the other associate, but I would certainly like to question him."

"But why would they be here at the Sandoval estate?"

"Don't know. That's a good reason to find the accomplice, isn't it?"

"I'll give you a better reason. To keep me off death row. That harebrained detective thinks I did it."

"Get real. Calling that detective a harebrain is an insult to hares. Don't worry about it."

"Don't worry about it? Did you see his performance today? He has a hammer from our garage. If that thing should match the injury, I could be cooked. Fried, I should say."

"Did you kill the guy?"

"Of course not!"

"Then forget about it."

"What if the guy was killed by a ball-peen hammer? What then?"

"Have you ever seen a person's head after a blow by a ball-peen hammer?"

"You mean before Monday? Not that I recall."

"You still haven't. A coroner would not need two days to establish the cause of death for a blow to the head by a ball-peen hammer."

"No?"

"No. You saw the body, right?"

"I did."

"What'd it look like?"

"A dead person."

"Right. A person. A ball-peen hammer would leave something not like a person. More like a bloody mess with bone fragments and scattered brain bits."

"You're making me feel so much better."

"It's my job."

"As a detective?"

"As your wife. My job as a detective is to keep you out of the frying pan."

"I'm feeling pretty hot right now," said Nigel, pulling Annie close and planting a big kiss on her lips.

A shuffling noise forced his eyes open in time to see Mrs. Sandoval beat a hasty retreat.

A private eye might explain away such an indiscretion as an unfortunate requirement of the job. A butler would have a harder time of it.

15

TREASURE OF THE L3 VERTEBRAE

Following dinner, Nigel partook of a solitary walk around the grounds. He did this not to enjoy the evening air, but because the house felt infested with twitches and shudders. The apprehension was palpable even though he strove to keep his hands in open view and had dispensed with articles of clothing capable of concealing a ball-peen hammer. Nevertheless, his presence, without fail, provoked abrupt conversation, ashen complexions, and the voiding of rooms.

Little wonder that in a house containing Nigel, the Ball-Peen Hammer Assassin, and Mother, the Turbaned Death Queen, residents huddled in sheltered enclaves to formulate defensive strategies and escape routes.

Upon returning from his walk, Nigel retreated to his sleeping chambers to find Grumps slumped in his chair, wearing his helmet and watching Fox news.

"Good evening," said Nigel, causing Grumps to belch.

"You must not be very popular down there."

"Why do you say that?"

"Why else would you be up here at this hour? Besides, don't take no genius to see you're not the belle of the ball."

"Maybe I prefer to spend time with you."

"Yeah, right. If it's between me and that Abuelita, I might believe you. She's a piece of work, that one. If I had to choose between spending an hour with her and scrubbing my colon with a Brillo pad, I know which one I'd choose."

"Come now, Grumps. Abuelita must have been something in her day."

"What day would that have been? Halloween, 1900?"

"Laugh if you want, but you know she's getting married on Saturday?"

"I did not know that. The groom is blind, deaf, and stupid, I take it."

"No, no. As far as I can tell, he has all his senses."

"No sense, if you ask me."

"Seeing as how she owns the house we're staying in, we should probably change the subject," said Nigel, even though Grumps was clearly on a roll. "Tell me, why do you wear that helmet?"

"Need the protection. Head injury."

"From the war?"

"After the war. Working on a charter fishing boat. I was the party of the third part in a fight between a man and his wife."

"That's unfortunate. What did he hit you with?"

"She. She hit me. A four-foot hammerhead shark, square on top of the head. I weren't the target, you understand. She was going for her husband. She'd have got him too, if she had caught a six-footer. It was my mistake for gettin' between 'em. Should have let 'em go after each other. Anyway, the lady swung her four-footer, came up short, and crumpled my braincase. Never expected to get waylaid from behind by a fish. You know what started that fight?"

"Who would clean?"

"Drag adjustments on her fishing reel. When he told her to loosen, she'd tighten. When he told her to tighten, she'd loosen. I ain't never been married, but it seems like the kind of stuff you'd work out beforehand."

"Absolutely. Communication is everything. So, you've worn a helmet ever since?"

"Pretty much. I could have got my head fixed. They gave me some money, those two lovebirds. But instead of a metal plate in my skull, I bought a motorcycle."

"Of course you did. You can't drive a metal plate around town. Besides, you already had a helmet."

"Darn tootin'. Maybe if I'd had my Wilhelmina, I'd have cared about a stoved-in head. But seein' what I been through, a dent in my skull seemed fitting, if you know what I mean. It's like those guys who got injured during the war but didn't get their purple hearts until years later. That's kind of what I feel like with my dented skull. Like I really earned it when I got that letter, but the physical manifestation didn't happen 'til I got dinged with a hammerhead. Delayed injustice, you might call it. Funny how things work out."

Funny indeed, thought Nigel, because, as if nailed by a hammerhead, a thought crumpled into his braincase. To his helmeted companion, he said, "You have a lot in common with someone I know. He might make for a better roommate than me. Not English. Would you like to meet him?"

"Be okay, I guess. You know, I don't mind telling you that you're not as bad as you seem. As we've gotten to know each other in these jabber sessions, my desire to disembowel you in the middle of the night has softened somewhat. Of course, you should still sleep with an eye open. I don't have control over my dreams, and I dream big."

"If you'll excuse me, I think I'll go speak to this man about becoming your roommate. You never know...could save a life. Be back soon."

Nigel hurried down the hallway to Gastrick's old quarters. Not wishing to startle the old gentleman, Nigel gently knocked, then whispered, "Mr. Sandoval. Psssst, Mr. Sandoval. Psssst."

"What's happening out there?" asked a scratchy voice from behind the door. "What's going on?"

"Mr. Sandoval, sorry to disturb you. May I come in? I have something to discuss."

"Who are you?"

"It's Nigel, the butler."

"You the one who killed that guy with a hammer?"

"No. Wasn't me."

"Okay. Come on in."

"Thank you," said Nigel, entering the room and shutting the door behind him.

"Sorry about the questions, but you can't be too careful," said Mr. Sandoval. "There's a murderer on the loose, you know."

"So I've heard," said Nigel. Hoping Mr. Sandoval's opening remarks provided a framework for his delicate request, he continued carefully. "I've come to talk to you about tonight's sleeping arrangements. How do you like your room?"

"Pretty tremendous," said Mr. Sandoval. He underscored his answer by dropping open his jaw while pointing his eyeballs upward as if viewing the Sistine Chapel.

"Tremendous?" said Nigel. "You don't find it a little much? Maybe too spacious, a little isolated, lonely, perhaps?"

"It is big. But if you ever spent eight days inside a locked semitrailer with 140 migrants, then spacious, isolated, and lonely ain't the worst."

"No, I suppose not. However, your safety is our chief concern. As you said, there may be a killer lurking on the premises. I don't want you to be unduly worried, but we take the safety of our guests very seriously. That is why we'd like to move you into a room with another resident. It's for your own security."

"You're doubling me up? Putting me in with someone else?"

"For your security, you understand."

Mr. Sandoval pulled at his face.

"It's strictly temporary," said Nigel. "Just until we apprehend this killer."

Mr. Sandoval looked around the room. His shoulders

drooped as if he'd been relegated to the lower branch on a sappy tree.

"The resident you're to share a room with is a combat veteran—"

"Iraq or Vietnam?" asked Mr. Sandoval.

"One of those other wars. It doesn't really matter which war. What matters is that he was on the front lines and saw plenty of action. I assure you, he won't cower in the face of violence...not this chap. He's the sort to be right in the middle of it. Believe me, no killer in his right mind would be knocking on this chap's door."

"A nice guy?"

"Nice? Nice isn't even the word. You two would have so much to talk about."

"Like what?"

"Fish-induced head injuries for a start," said Nigel, feeling he'd set the hook. "He has one; you have one. That alone would be a day's conversation. You two could start a Facebook group together. Wouldn't that be fun?"

"Facebook? Is that like MySpace?"

"Even better. But you've definitely got the right idea."

"Who gets this room?"

"For tonight, it would just be me...as a sort of bait," said Nigel. "We're thinking this room might be where the killer strikes next. Not that we think he will, mind you. But if he did, this room would be the spot."

"What about the clothes?"

"The clothes?"

"The clothes in the room? All the nice things? What happens to the clothes?"

Mr. Sandoval's attire had thus far gone unnoticed. Upon inspection, it was obvious he had embraced the room, wardrobe and all. His head sported a fedora hat with a brim pulled low over a pair of Maui Jim sunglasses. His wiry frame was covered by some form of men's velvet lounge wear topped with a brocaded smoking jacket covered by a loose, satiny robe. His feet, swaddled in red toe socks, were sidled into a pair of open-toed Mexican huaraches. An assortment of rings adorned his fingers.

"The clothes are yours to use," said Nigel, his heart warming at the thought of Gastrick's prized possessions put to good use. He wouldn't need them for at least another five to ten years. "Take what you need, and if you run out, mosey on by and browse to your heart's content."

Heartened by this revelation, Mr. Sandoval retrieved a large suitcase from the closet and began to pack.

Nigel, relieved at the prospect of sleeping with eyes closed, collapsed in a chair. His quiet reverie crumbled when his shuttering eye caught sight of a glistening black-and-yellow object atop the dresser. The object would have gone unnoticed had it not hopped.

"What"—Nigel pointed at the black-and-yellow blob—"is that?"

"That's Glen," said Mr. Sandoval. "He's a nice boy. He goes with me everywhere."

"Correct me if I'm wrong, but isn't that a poison dart frog?"

"Some might call him that. I just call him Glen."

"Why do you have a poison dart frog named Glen?"

"He looks like a Glen. Don't you think he looks like a Glen?"

"I don't care if his name is Glen or Glenda, why do you have a poison dart frog at all? Again, correct me if I'm wrong, but aren't poison dart frogs *poisonous*?"

"I hadn't noticed. This little guy saved my life once."

"You used it to poison an adversary?"

"You seem obsessed with that poison angle. It's the same with the natives down there. You and them must read the same books. Anyway, they're correct about *their* poison dart frogs. They're just not correct about *my* poison dart frog. You see, it's not the frogs' fault that they're poisonous."

"Whose fault is it?"

"The ants."

"The ants?"

"Yes, the ants. The ants are the bad guys. They're the ones that make the poison. When the frogs eat the ants, they accumulate their poison. The frogs are just curators. My little Glen here gets a steady diet of crickets and worms. Not the kind of stuff that a little frog can make poison from." Mr. Sandoval scooped up the little frog, stroked its back with an index finger, and then gently kissed the top of its tiny head. "You're harmless, aren't you, Little Glen?"

Nigel felt like a heel for interrupting, but asked, "You said it saved your life?"

"Once, in the jungle. I was cornered by some hostile types. Happened a lot in those days. With no weapon to protect myself, I popped Glen into my mouth. When the group surrounded me, I opened my mouth and let Glen crawl out. Some of the hostiles looked horrified and some laughed, but they left me alone. Maybe they figured I was crazy, or I was bad medicine, or I was about to die. I don't know, but they let me be, and I got out of there."

"If you want to write a book, I'll be your agent."

"I wasn't the first to do it."

"Did others have poison dart frogs?"

"We all did. They were our pets in the jungle. You couldn't have dogs. They'd get lost or eaten. But not these frogs. Of course, you had to be careful. The wild ones really are poisonous until you get them to stop eating ants."

"And how do you do that?"

"You don't feed them ants."

"Oh."

That was the most coherent discussion Nigel had heard from Mr. Sandoval. Past conversations often left the impression that an unseen third party inside the man's head was conducting its own parallel interview.

Mr. Sandoval began stripping off his assorted garments and

throwing them into the suitcase. He eventually removed a black Harley-Davidson T-shirt to reveal a bare torso that could have been used as a museum exhibit for bones and tendons.

Nigel would have preferred to not see such a display, however, before averting his eyes, a feature on Mr. Sandoval's weathered hide captured his attention.

"Where did you get that?" said Nigel, pointing to a place on Mr. Sandoval's back that Mr. Sandoval could not possibly see.

"Get what?"

"That tattoo?"

"What tattoo?"

"The one on your back."

"There's a tattoo on my back?"

Nigel, having perceived the general direction of the conversation, took decisive action. "On your lower back, left side, there is a tattoo. The tattoo depicts a house. From the right corner of that house is a dashed line in a southeasterly direction to the small of the back, around the spinal column where it terminates against the image of a pot heaped with a yellow substance. Let's presume it's gold. Just off to the side of that dotted line is a notation that says 18p. That is a description of the tattoo on your back."

"Are you sure it's not moles?"

"I'm not a dermatologist, but I suspect it's a tattoo."

"Don't care for tattoos. I should have it removed."

"You don't remember getting it?" said Nigel. "I mean, it's pretty big. It's on your back. You don't recall lying on your stomach for several hours under intense lighting while being painfully punctured thousands of time by a human billboard, and then paying that billboard a good sum of money? None of that stirs up a memory?"

"Afraid not. But there's a period there—like ten or fifteen or twenty years—where I don't recall much. Could've happened then."

"But even if you don't remember getting the tattoo, the thing must mean something. Do you know what it means?"

"Means nothing to me. What do you suppose it means?"

"I don't like to jump to conclusions," said Nigel, "but let's review. There's a house, and a pot of gold, and a line between house and pot of gold annotated with 18p. What do you think it means?"

"What does p mean?"

"What would *you* think p means?"

"In England, isn't p some kind of money?"

"Some people use it for pence. Is that what you think? Eighteen pence?"

"Don't know. How much is eighteen pence?"

"Eighteen pence wouldn't buy the pot, wouldn't even pay the VAT on the pot. Maybe p doesn't mean pence. Maybe it's a unit of distance. Any ideas?"

"P, p, p," whispered Mr. Sandoval, tapping his dented head. "Could mean parsec."

"P for parsec," said Nigel. "Of course. Outstanding. I'm so impressed you remembered. How long is a parsec?"

"Don't know," said Mr. Sandoval.

"That's okay. We can look it up later. Now, about that pot of gold," said Nigel, rubbing together his palms as if praying to some golden idol. "I'm guessing the pot of gold is symbolic rather than literal. What do you think the pot of gold might signify?"

"Gold?" said a hesitant Mr. Sandoval.

"I would guess that actual gold doesn't play into it."

Mr. Sandoval appeared puzzled. After spending two decades wandering the wilderness where every need is immediate and every threat is physical, his skills at metaphor had greatly diminished.

"Pot of silver?" said Mr. Sandoval, stretching himself.

"I doubt there is an actual pot, either," said Nigel.

Mr. Sandoval let his shoulders sag, seeming at a complete loss.

"It's okay," said Nigel. "We shall consider it as unspecified treasure. Now then, the house. What house would that be? Any ideas?"

"A haunted house?"

"Why do you say a haunted house?"

"Does it look haunted?"

"No, not really. It looks like your basic, generic, nondescript house. Again, I suppose it's somewhat symbolic. I doubt the tattoo artist was working from a blueprint. What house do you suppose it might represent, Mr. Sandoval?"

Mr. Sandoval's brain, already pressurized from that dented cranium, must have been buckling under the weight. "Yours?" he said in a low tone.

"Mine, did you say?"

"Yes?" said Mr. Sandoval.

"Why would an image representing *my* house be on *your* back, Mr. Sandoval? Does that make sense?"

"No?" asked Mr. Sandoval after some hesitation.

"No. I would say that it doesn't. What about your house, Mr. Sandoval? Could that be *your* house? I mean, being that it's on *your* back? Do you think it might be *your* house?"

"Yes?" muttered Mr. Sandoval.

"Okay. Let's suppose it's your house. Reviewing what we know, there is an unspecified treasure eighteen parsecs from the southeast corner of your house. Does that make sense to you, Mr. Sandoval?"

"No?"

"No? Why do you say no?"

"Yes?" Mr. Sandoval appeared notably relieved to have only two choices.

"Okay, so you say it makes sense. Good. We're on the same page. Now, I must request—and this is of utmost importance—

that you don't tell any of this to anyone. This is to be our little secret until we figure this thing out, okay?"

The tired Mr. Sandoval mulled possible responses before letting one roll out his mouth. "Okay?"

"Splendid," said Nigel. "We have an understanding."

16

TOO MANY PSSSSSTS

"Grumps," whispered Nigel. "Psssst."

A snore cut to a snort as Grumps launched skyward as if punctured from below.

"Sorry to wake you, but this is Mr. Sandoval. Your fine new roommate."

"You," said Grumps, addressing Mr. Sandoval, "sleep on the sofa."

"Okay," said Mr. Sandoval.

"You English?" said Grumps.

"Nope," said Mr. Sandoval, removing his fedora.

Grumps's steely gray eyes, peeking out from beneath the darkness of his helmet, scanned the new roomie from his huarache-clad feet to the top of his bare, dented head. "Your cranium is concave," he said.

"I know. Hit by a fish," said Mr. Sandoval.

"Hit by a fish? I'll be damned. Looky here," said Grumps, removing his helmet and turning his head to reveal a nasty indentation to the back of his skull.

"Looks like a hammerhead," said Mr. Sandoval.

"Yep. Four-footer. And yours?"

"Arapaima. Five-footer."

"You don't say. I'll bet you got some brain damage."

"Possible, I suppose. I got a ten- or twenty-year memory gap. Maybe there's a connection. And you? Brain damage?"

"Doctor said there'd have to be, but I ain't noticed nothing."

Nigel, feeling like the spouse at a class reunion, fished for an excuse to leave. "As much fun as all this has been, I'll be leaving you two to your little pajama party. Don't stay up too late. Keep the giggling to a minimum for the sake of the neighbors, all right? Bye."

Nigel skipped down the hall to his single occupancy room where a solid night's sleep awaited. He collapsed on the bed face-up to be caressed by a momentary wave of serenity. A serenity born of sleeping alone on a comfy mattress without a brain-damaged, psychopathic killer within stabbing distance. He drifted off to sleep, only to be awoken by a sound reminiscent of an inner tube after being bitten by a snake.

"Pssssst, pssssst. I know you're in there. I can hear you snoring," said a whispering voice from beyond the door.

Nigel put his ear against the door.

"Pssssst, pssssst. Hey, Sugar, your candy store is back in business," said a gruff, sandpapery voice. "In two more days, the shop closes up for good. Indulge your sweet tooth while you can. I've saved all your old favorites and," said the voice, dropping down even quieter, "if you're a bad boy, a really bad boy, I brought my bullwhip."

Nigel wasn't feeling like a bad boy, but before he could disappoint the candy store masochist, he heard the creak of a door followed by the whiz of a receding electric wheelchair. After a moment, he opened his door and stuck his head out. In one direction, he saw Abuelita's wheelchair disappear into the elevator. In the other, walking toward him, was a shuffling, helmeted Grumps. Nigel felt obligated to follow the old guy to assure his safety and prevent any murder he might wish to perpetrate. As Grumps passed, Nigel was reassured by the lack of splattered blood on his person.

The old man, oblivious to Nigel's presence, shuffled down the stairs and into the kitchen. There, he pulled a single slice of bread from the breadbox, obtained a spoon from the silverware drawer, and grabbed a jar of mayonnaise from the refrigerator. A spoonful of mayonnaise was scooped out and plopped into his mouth. After returning the jar of mayonnaise, he devoured the piece of bread. He went about this business in the robotic, emotionless state of one content with a menu of white bread and mayonnaise.

Leaning against the end of the kitchen cabinets by the back door, Nigel recognized that he was in the presence of a sleep-eater, perhaps a habit the man had developed when no one thought to feed him. Asleep or not, it seemed a deficient meal for someone with the run of the pantry. Maybe mayonnaise and white bread constituted the proper antidote for one regularly feasting on their own blackened soul. Or maybe he consumed his sandwiches over successive nights, tomorrow returning for the second slice of bread and the turkey breast. The possibilities were many, but not worth losing sleep over.

Through the window in the back door, Nigel noticed movement on the back lawn. Unable to discern more than shadowy motion, he turned on the floodlights. The figure jumped as if stepping on a live wire before looking back at the house and fleeing the scene. It was Jack Watt, again.

Having seen Grumps back to bed, Nigel returned to his room, removed his clothes, and fell immediately into his deepest slumber...for at least a minute. A dishearteningly familiar sound poked him in the ears.

"Psssssst, psssssst."

The sound came from outside his door.

"Pssssssst, psssssst."

Not again. This particular edition sounded different—moister, more rounded, less sizzly, like an oceangoing raft punctured at the waterline by a marlin.

"Pssssssst, pssssssst."

Nigel was a patient man, but these pssssssts in the night were beginning to wear. He got up and placed his ear to the door.

"Pssssssst, pssssssst."

"Stop pssssssting around," whispered Nigel. "Get to the point."

"Won't you open up and let me in? It's been so long," said a voice that purred like a kitten after lapping up her saucer of tequila.

"Go away," said a pssssssted-off Nigel.

"No. Not goin' away," whispered the voice. "I'm staying right here. It's been twenty years with no wifely attention. Open that door or I'll scream."

If Nigel's tolerance for pssssssts in the night was limited, his tolerance for screams was practically nil. He unbolted the door to admit a wobbly Mrs. Sandoval, shut the door behind her, and flicked on the lights.

The drunk-eyed Mrs. Sandoval stood like a statue—a statue with outstretched hands holding a bottle of cognac in one and two snifter glasses in the other. She wore a flannel robe that provided full cover when closed. It was not closed. The open robe revealed an interior garment that, in another life, would be swaddling melons in a supermarket.

A dumbfounded Nigel, exposed as he was to new aspects of his employer, stood unaware of his own vulnerabilities. As Mrs. Sandoval's eyelids crept northward over her swaying pupils, those vulnerabilities came to light in vivid, if blurred, detail. The flabbergasted Mrs. Sandoval gazed at the dumbfounded Nigel, and vice versa.

Mrs. Sandoval, having expected an open-armed greeting from her long-lost husband was, for the moment, so stricken by the sight of her out-of-place and out-of-dress butler that the sparsity of her own attire had hardly crossed her mind.

Similarly, Nigel, having been roused out of bed and coerced into opening the door by his matronly boss wrapped in cheese-cloth had not, as yet, considered his own lack of attire.

The two parties stood gaping for precisely the amount of time it takes a cognac bottle to fall from a traumatized hand to a carpeted floor. The dull impact jolted the two oglers back to a consciousness they had hoped was a bad dream.

Having suddenly realized she'd left the drapes open, Mrs. Sandoval dropped to a crouch and pulled tight on every swath of flannel she could get a hand on.

Nigel, with nothing to ogle, felt a chill. Not the kind of chill induced by low temperatures, but rather, the kind of chill induced by standing in front of one's employer outfitted in tighty-whities and a pair of dress socks. A hop, skip, and a jump placed the underweared Nigel behind the bed. On the trip over, he managed to snag a comforter.

"Whattaya doin' in this room?" asked Mrs. Sandoval.

Not only did Nigel hear her words, he saw and smelled them billowing forth like tequila vapor smoke signals. "What are *you* doing in this room?" he asked.

"My husband was s'posed to be here. Whattaya done with him?"

"He's rooming with Grumps. I introduced them."

"Why'd ya do that?"

"To foster friendship and goodwill."

"With old Grumps? I don't b'lieve it."

"Really," said Nigel. "That, and avoiding carnage."

"From Grumps? He's ninety-six years old."

"His body may be ninety-six, but his black heart holds the passion of a twenty-year-old Jack the Ripper."

"We need to get Valdy outta there."

"You needn't worry. Grumps craves the blood of an English-man. Mr. Sandoval, on the other hand, is like a fraternity brother —Order of the Cleft Skulls, Fish Chapter. They're probably working on secret handshakes as we speak."

"Well, if Valdy's not gonna be here, then I oughtta leave. Unless... Do you like cognac, Mr. Nigel?"

He did like cognac, but under the circumstances, he preferred sleep. And if not sleep, pants. "That bottle should be saved for your husband, don't you think?"

"You're funny, Mr. Nigel. You know I got lots of bottles."

"I'm talking about that one. The one you brought. That one's for your husband."

"You're too smart. You're not mad at me, are you?"

"Of course not. Why would I be?"

"You can't blame a woman for wanting to be with her husband, can you? Especially after twenty looooong years."

"No, you can't blame a woman for wanting to be with her husband any more than you can blame a husband for wanting to be with a woman," said Nigel. "I'm not sure that came out right."

"I saw you today with that detective woman."

"How unfortunate for you."

"Mr. Nigel, lemme give you some advice. What's your wife's name?"

"Annie."

"Annie? The same as that detective woman? That's a coincidence."

"Isn't it?" said Nigel. He thought of fessing up that she was the wife, but he needed to starve the conversation, not feed it.

"I'm sure your Annie is a won'erful girl. I don't know what she sees in you, but there must be somethin'. Anyway, my advice is to stay away from that detective lady."

"Stay away?"

"Yep. Stay away. She's bad news for someone like you. Bad news. Wanna know why? I'll tell ya. She's young. She's smart. She's good lookin'. She's good. You don't want somebody like that."

"Are you sure?"

"No! A girl like that wants a man that's...eh...smart, and eh...intelligent...and...eh...what's the word I want?"

"Bright?"

"Dashing! She wants a smart, intelligent, dashing man. And that," she said, steadying herself for a big point, "is not you."

Nigel was confused. Not about the words. They were clear enough. But, unless a seven-foot man was standing to his immediate left, the point didn't quit register. Mrs. Sandoval then squinted and dragged her wavering pointer across Nigel's face before also implicating an invisible dwarf to his right.

"You go home to that little Annie," she continued. "That's your best bet, even if she hates you."

"Sound advice," said Nigel, hoping she was wrapping up.

"Absotively. Sure ya don't want some cognac?"

"Pssssst, pssssst," came a sound from the direction of the door.

"Was that you?" asked Nigel.

"Wasn't me," said Mrs. Sandoval.

"You're sure one of your parts isn't leaking?"

"I know when I'm leaking. Ain't me, I tell ya."

"Pssssst, pssssst."

"Well, someone's leaking," said Nigel.

"Pssssst, I know you're in there, Nigel. Open up. Let me in."

"Who's that?" whispered Mrs. Sandoval.

"Don't know," said Nigel, knowing all too well.

Under most circumstances, Nigel would have relished a wee hour visit from the wife. This was not one of those circumstances. He gathered the comforter around himself and made his way to the door, which had a well-defined grease smudge indicating where to place his ear.

"Pssssst. Nigel, open up. What's taking you so long?" said the voice behind the door.

"Sorry. Waking up. Give me a minute. Need to put something away," whispered Nigel. "Hold on. I'll be right there."

Nigel had every intention of showing Mrs. Sandoval the

window, but when he turned around, she was gone. Disappeared. Vanished like a crumpet in the night. Understanding that mediocre minds think alike, he looked toward the window for signs of a quick exit, such as curtains flapping in the breeze. Nope. No breeze. No curtains. Venetian blinds, undisturbed.

"Are you going to open up, or do I have to bust this door down?" said the voice from beyond.

"On my way, dear," said Nigel, scanning the room a final time for telltale signs of the desperate housewife. Seeing none, he opened the door and pulled his wife through. "What a surprise! An unexpected surprise. The most surprising kind."

"What are you wearing?" said Annie. "It's like hugging a sleeping bag. Makes me want to climb inside."

"Is that right?" said Nigel. "Planning to stay awhile?"

Annie held up a bottle of prosecco. "Maybe I will. I couldn't sleep. Mom snores awfully."

"Really? Does fire come out?"

"You know she sleeps with her eyes open? Creepy."

"Reptiles do that, I've heard."

Annie led Nigel to the bed where the two sat down. "I saw you earlier put Mr. Sandoval in with Grumps, so I knew I'd find you here," she said.

"You saw me?" said Nigel. "I didn't see you."

"I'm a detective, remember?"

"I do recall, so what have you detected lately?" Nigel could hardly keep his extremities from bouncing, shaking, or trembling. The intoxicated Mrs. Sandoval, in a scarcely clothed state, lurked nearby, and he needed to get one of these women out of his room. For now, he'd keep the conversation going until something came to mind.

"That fiancé of Abuelita's is up to no good," said Annie. "I don't know what yet, but he's got something in mind that doesn't involve a wedding."

"Abuelita has the worst luck with fiancés. Damages my faith in the internet. It's a shame, a sweet girl like that living alone.

She needs a nice husband. The kind that can take a whuppin'. Maybe it'll work out for the best."

"Another thing," said Annie. "Different topic, but that Cam Logan/electric eel thing bothers me."

"Bothers you? I should say it bothered me. I spent forty bucks on hair relaxers."

"Cam's story about her aquarium keeper putting it in the lagoon without her knowledge—not credible."

"Do Cam Logan and credible belong in the same sentence? Take Stanley. What's she doing with him? Unless the answer is footstool—not credible. And that hair of hers, it sparkles. What is that? My Dad had a bowling ball that looked like that, but hair? Not credible."

"You're right—nothing credible. It's impossible to know what to believe about her."

Nigel offered no comment, hoping Annie would detect a conversation run dry and say something like, "Just a thought. Must be running along."

She said nothing like that. Rather, she unleashed the kind of smile Nigel saw far too rarely.

He returned a smile of his own, the kind that said, "Cards?"

Annie looked down at her bottle of prosecco, and then, with a slow, deliberate motion, brought her head up to unleash a side-eye so smoldering it needed an ashtray underneath it.

Nigel hated to extinguish the flame, but the situation had grown far too combustible. "You know what I discovered today?"

"What?" she said, turning the side-eye into a snide-eye.

"Mr. Sandoval has a poison dart frog."

"What? A *living* poison dart frog?"

"A living, pet poison dart frog, just like the one in the dead guy's throat."

"How is that possible? Isn't that extremely dangerous?"

"Not according to him. Dart frogs are only poisonous if they eat ants. No ants, no poison. He said all his South American buddies had these dart frogs on no-ant diets."

"Interesting."

"Yes, isn't it?" A pause ensued that Nigel rushed to fill. "Indeed, but what about the killer? That detective thinks I did it. If we don't solve the case, he's going to roast me on a spit."

"Let him. That two-bit Colum-boob is a dumpster fire. As long as he's chasing your ass, he's out of the way. You just keep your nose clean so he doesn't have anything to pick at," she said, tweaking Nigel's nose with a forefinger. Annie's expression changed from playful to perplexed. "What is this?"

"What is what?"

"There's something under my foot," she said, reaching downward. "It's a fancy glass."

"Indeed," said Nigel, wondering what had become of its owner.

"Have you been drinking on the sly?"

"Not me. This is Gastrick's old room. You can find all kinds of surprising things in here."

"But it smells of alcohol," said Annie.

"Does it? That's from yesterday. Yesterday there was alcohol. I recall now. Yesterday there was drinking, of course."

"Smells fresh. Doesn't smell like from yesterday."

"Did I say yesterday? It's been a long day. No, I meant earlier today. When I helped Mr. Sandoval move, he had a bottle of cognac. He had a snort in a snorter, or I should say a snift in a snifter. I remember now. He neglected to take his glass. I guess he'll have to snift straight from the bottle. Him and Grumps are probably all snifted out by now."

"Is that the bottle?" said Annie, pointing to a bottle of Remy Martin on the floor by the nightstand.

This was getting out of control. *What next? A melon bag?* "Did I tell you that Mr. Sandoval has a map?" he said, desperate to deflect. He hadn't wanted to mention the map, but circumstances had forced it out of him.

"A map of what?"

"Well, kind of map-like, possibly."

"A map of what?"

"It might be moles."

"Moles? He has a map of moles?"

"I mean, the map might not be a map, but rather, a collection of, you know, map-like moles, or spots, or blemishes, or freckles. Maybe ticks. I didn't look that close. It looked kind of like a map, but I need to check it again later...in case something moves."

"So, this map is on his body?"

"I guess it would be, wouldn't it? That's usually where the moles are."

"What makes you think it's a map?"

"Let's not jump to conclusions just yet. I'm just sort of halfway thinking it might be a map. Not sure yet. It's an imagination thing, like looking at clouds. You know, where one person just sees clouds, another sees a unicorn slurping a smoothie while another sees garden nymphs sponging down Albert Einstein. Anyways, just thought I'd mention it for future reference."

"Pssssst."

17

SLEEPLESS NIGHT, FITFUL MORNING

"Did you hear something?" said Annie.

"Probably a mosquito," said Nigel, hoping it might buzz away.

"Sounded like a leak."

"They do that, mosquitos, so I've been told."

"Pssssst."

"There it is again," said Annie. "Was it you?"

Nigel peaked inside his quilted wrapper. "Thankfully not. Probably a passing snake."

"Snakes do that when they pass?"

"Depends on what they had for dinner," said Nigel. He hoped it wasn't Mrs. Sandoval from somewhere inside the room. In her state, one would think she'd have been pssssst out already.

"Pssssst."

"It's coming from the hallway," said Annie.

"Good. Let them pssssst in the hallway to their heart's content."

"Psssssst."

"It's at your door," said Annie. "You better see who it is."

"All right. For no one but you, dear," said Nigel, arranging his comforter like a bloated toga. He made his way to the door, placing his ear in the usual spot. "Who is it?" he whispered.

"Sorry to disturb you, Mr. Nigel," said the hallway prowler, "but we've run out of toilet paper."

"Is that you, Mr. Sandoval?"

"Yes, it's me, Mr. Nigel."

"How are things, Mr. Sandoval?"

"We've run out of toilet paper."

"Aside from that, all good?"

"We need toilet paper."

"You've been out rolling houses, haven't you? I told you two to behave."

"No, Mr. Nigel, we haven't. We just need a roll of toilet paper."

"I'll see what I can do. You'll not waste it foolishly, will you?"

"No, Mr. Nigel. We wouldn't," pleaded Mr. Sandoval. "Could you hurry, please? Grumps is waiting."

Surprising, thought Nigel. Grumps didn't seem like the waiting type.

"Okay, Mr. Sandoval. You wait there, and I'll fetch you some."

Nigel had a decision to make. Behind door number one lay a closet he suspected of harboring extra toilet rolls. Behind door number two was a bathroom containing toilet paper, if not extra rolls. Behind either door lurked a possible fiasco in the form of a sloshed and netted Mrs. Sandoval. Relying on simple logic for his toilet paper search, Nigel went with number two. He took a deep breath and waved to his wife on the way in. Annie, perched center-bed like the final tart on the dessert tray, raised an eyebrow as if to suggest the night was still young.

Nigel felt the night growing old and more crotchety than any night had a right to. He knocked on the bathroom door before barging in, then closed the door behind him. To his great relief, no one was waiting to greet him. To his chagrin, neither were spare rolls of toilet paper. While unspooling a kindly number of sheets from the one available roll, discordant male and female voices arose from without. Distinct words could not be pulled from the general squawkery, but he expected the worst because that was the kind of night it was.

The commotion ceased when Nigel entered the room. Annie, still sitting center-bed, was now wrapped in a sheet. She looked like Mount Fuji sprouting a head. In an opposite corner stood Mr. Sandoval, stoop-shouldered in satiny pajamas, addressing a wall.

"I'm so sorry, Mr. Nigel. I didn't know you had company. I waited outside, but that lady was coming. I didn't want to be seen."

"What lady?" asked Nigel.

"That turbaned lady with the dark glasses. The one that looks like Mother Satan. I'm sorry, but she scares me."

This, from a man who had once fought off a jaguar with a fish. Nigel understood. "It's quite all right. She scares me too."

"Thank you for understanding," said Mr. Sandoval.

"Here are your provisions," said Nigel, handing him the folded pile of tissues.

"You don't have a roll?" asked Mr. Sandoval.

"Sadly, not tonight," said Nigel.

"Mr. Sandoval," said Annie.

Nigel's ears stood on edge. Unless Annie had a spare roll of toilet paper up her nightshirt, addressing Mr. Sandoval meant nothing but trouble.

"Nigel was telling me," Annie continued, "that you possess a map of some kind."

"A map, ma'am?" said Mr. Sandoval.

Nigel, facing Mr. Sandoval with his back to Annie, began a series of hand gestures intended to advise Mr. Sandoval to withhold certain information.

Mr. Sandoval, having some familiarity with the sign language of Amazonia, gave Nigel the thumbs-up, likely thinking the butler was wishing him well with his bathroom adventure.

"A map," repeated Annie. "He said you may have a map on your body."

"Ah!" said Mr. Sandoval. "You must mean that treasure map tattooed on my back. Now I remember. Mr. Nigel saw it earlier today."

"Can you show it to me?" asked Annie.

"Do you have any tattoos, ma'am?" said Mr. Sandoval, implying interest in a game of you-show-me-yours, I'll-show-you-mine.

"No, afraid not," said Annie.

"Now, now, now," interjected Nigel. "It's entirely premature to mention maps, or treasure."

As if the word "treasure" had been some secret code, the closet door burst open like a failed dam, spilling the liquified Mrs. Sandoval into the room. Mrs. Sandoval's robe—unencumbered as it was by belt, clasps, or buttons—fluttered behind her as she bounded out of the closet with outspread arms. Below the flapping robe, for all to see, was the undernetting that served little purpose but to keep Mrs. Sandoval herself from flapping. In her exuberant escape, she hopped on Nigel's protective covering, pulling the comforter to the floor.

While Mrs. Sandoval engulfed the awestruck Mr. Sandoval, Annie launched herself into Nigel's personal space with quite a different attitude.

And there they stood, the four of them: Mr. Sandoval in his silken PJs, Mrs. Sandoval in her melon net, Nigel in his socks and tighty-whities, and Annie in her tank top.

"Pssssst."

Annie looked at Nigel.

Nigel looked at Mrs. Sandoval.

Mrs. Sandoval looked at Mr. Sandoval.

Mr. Sandoval looked at Annie.

When all that looking yielded nothing, they tried again, shifting one person to the right. After several iterations, the group shrugged.

"Psssssst." It came from behind the door.

As the four stood looking, the door creaked opened.

"Where the hell is my toilet paper?" said a craggy voice from a helmeted head. Upon seeing the miscreants, Grumps's eyes widened. "What the hell? Ya'll having a party, and no one invited me? Damn! How often does this happen?"

Grumps left Nigel's room properly equipped for his important business. The Sandovals, man and wife, had comported themselves more like distant cousins. Not anymore. They left the room like a pair of naughty teenage lovers determined to make up for lost time after being grounded for twenty years. Annie was the last to go, but she did not go easily.

To Nigel's great consternation, Annie had fallen ass over tits for one of those ridiculous conspiracy theories. Somehow during the night's activities, she'd gotten it in her head that Mrs. Sandoval was more than just an employer. Of course, he challenged this assumption, vigorously.

"Absurd," said Nigel. "Unfounded, illogical, unsubstantiated, ludicrous, balderdash."

"Balderdash?" said Annie in a tone that would make a balder dash if balders were capable of such.

"And poppycock, and anything else you can think of that means rubbish. What possible evidence do you have for these outlandish suppositions?"

Of course, Annie, the former police detective, was expert at providing evidence, and she did so with painstaking thoroughness. Her case rested on these basic facts: (a) Mrs. Sandoval was in Nigel's room at 2:00 a.m. concurrently with (b) a bottle of cognac and two cognac glasses; (c) Nigel was in a state of near undress, (d) Mrs. Sandoval was in a state of near undress, (e) Mrs. Sandoval was hiding in a closet, and (f) as she was leaving, Mrs. Sandoval said to Nigel, "Remember what I told you," as she did that "skin the carrot" thing with her fingers while glaring at Annie.

Nigel sat quietly for the testimony. After Annie rested her case, he noticed that his eyes blinked more than usual.

"Well?" said Annie. "Don't just sit there blinking your eyes. Say something."

"Is that all you got?" asked Nigel.

"Is that all I've got?"

While awaiting his wife's reply, Nigel recognized that he'd tweaked one of those nerves with direct ties to the powder keg.

"I see your point, but you've got it all wrong. It was all a matter of circumstance. As a matter of fact, everyone involved had the noblest intentions. Mrs. Sandoval wanted only to reconnect, so to speak, with her long-lost husband. She came to the wrong room because I moved her husband to Grumps's quarters so that the two might establish a brotherhood based on their shared experience of fish-based head trauma. Mr. Sandoval arrived on a mission to help a friend avoid a hygienic catastrophe. And you? You apparently came to make life miserable for your do-gooder husband. If you persist with this evil fantasy that me and Mrs. Sandoval were, eh, playing a game of hide the bishop, you go right ahead, but let me say this. I will never, ever have a passionate interest in a woman whose name begins with Mrs. Not going to happen. If that lady came to my room looking for sex, she was going to leave disappointed, because when it comes to that sort of thing, the only one I'll be disappointing is my wife. Now, Mrs. Blandwater-Cummings, the ball is in your court. You may stay here if you fancy a quick disappointment, or you may leave."

Annie opted to leave, but not out of anger. Rather, she wished to be back in her room when Mother woke up—one of those mysterious rules of etiquette between a daughter and her dragon mama. Nigel's speech had effectively pinched the fuse just short of ignition.

Relieved he was, but still haunted throughout the night by

psssssts, as if his brain had sprung leaks. Despite the sleep-deprived torment, sleeping in was not an option. Today everything had to come together for tomorrow's wedding. The tent and furniture were to arrive, the flowers would be delivered, the minister and the photographer would be briefed, and the dress would be fitted. Was there a chance all these things would go as planned? Any of them?

18

A HEART-TO-HEART

Breakfast was not a catered affair at the Sandoval estate, but Nigel spent a good half-hour moving various items from the kitchen to the adjoining buffet court. As might be expected, few guests were astir at the seven o'clock hour. Decanting the milk, he received a call from a person representing the minister he'd booked as the wedding's officiant. One might have expected a secretary. If the voice belonged to a secretary, it was one who'd weathered a long career boxing on the undercards.

"Dis da man what booked Rev'rend Bilcher for da wedding tomorrow?"

"Yes, I had him booked for a three o'clock ceremony," said Nigel.

"He won't make it."

"He won't? Why not?"

"A accident."

"Oh, dear. I hope no one was injured."

"Not dat kind of a accident. An incident might be a better description. He's gonna be away awhile."

"I had paid a deposit in advance."

"Really? How much?"

"A hundred dollars."

"You don't say. Dat explains where he got da money. We thought he was flat broke, but now we know."

"You'll send my deposit back?"

"Naw. The rev' would have to do that, but he ain't gonna be available."

"But if services are not rendered, you have to return the money."

"Naw, buddy. *I* ain't gotta do nothin'. It's Rev'rend Bilcher who oughtta return your money, but he ain't gonna be available. If I was you, I'd write off that hunnerd as a charitable contribution."

"A contribution to what?"

"The Rev'rend Bilcher Housing Fund."

"Is that an accredited charity?"

"Not likely, but I can tell you, your hunnerd dollars has contributed mightily to the good reverend having a roof over his head and food in his tummy for da next six months. Dat ain't no lie."

"I would rather have my money back."

"Yeah? Here's what you do. In six months, maybe nine, you call this number. If he answers, ask for da money back."

"He'll give me a refund?"

"He probably won't answer. Probably have a different number, maybe a different name, maybe a different state. But you can try."

"I will be reporting this to the Better Business Bureau."

"If that's your thing, go right ahead. You be you. It'll keep you outta trouble, keep you from doing anything rash. Take care, you." He hung up.

Nigel had been up less than an hour and already his day was heading in reverse. Then Mother rolled in like a Mongol horde looking for plunder.

"Where's the kiwi and the avocado?" said the turbaned fright.

"I don't believe we have kiwi. There's some guacamole dip in the refrigerator," replied Nigel.

"I didn't ask for guacamole. I asked for avocado. I'm not about to put guac on my face. How about papaya? Have any papaya, Nile?"

"No, no papaya. And the name's Nigel."

"Nigel, shmigel, no papaya, no avocado. What kind of place are you running here?"

"Not a smoothie shop, but we have apples, bananas, oranges, peaches, strawberries, pineapple, lemons, limes, and mango."

"I need something for my face, not my stomach."

Now he got the picture. Nigel sensed an opportunity to start healing old wounds. "If you're looking for a fruit mask, I can whip one up in a snap. Butler's training, you know." Butler's training had nothing to do with it, but Nigel had seen his wife make one. It was not rocket science. More like an opportunity to clear away overripe fruit.

"I'm skeptical, but you can give it a try, Nyland."

"Coming right up. The name's Nigel."

After the disastrous water heater episode, any success would bolster his reputation. He pureed a mango, added a tub of blueberry fruit-on-the-bottom yogurt, dropped in half a banana too bruised to eat, and squeezed in some lemon juice. It came out thin, so he added some corn starch, and voila, a facial mask more than adequate for a dragon.

"Here you go, Mother dear," said Nigel, handing her a dish of the stuff. "If this doesn't work, nothing will."

Even through the sunglasses, Nigel sensed Mother's eyes revving themselves into burning lasers. He moved away before the killer rays got a lock. She grabbed a few edibles and left with her dish of fruity face de-ager.

Members of the household filtered in and out of the kitchen over the next hour, keeping Nigel busy with assorted cleanups and errands. The tent company arrived at nine to set up the tent and chairs. He walked the crew around to the garden area and instructed them as to the orientation and placement.

Near one corner of the tent was the hole that had been discovered last Monday along with the body. Not only was the hole and its dirt pile still present, but a twin hole with a twin dirt pile had materialized fifty feet away. Nigel scanned the surroundings for signs of a new body. The lack of one put a hole in the theory that the hole was an aborted attempt to dispose of the corpse. Regardless of their origins, both holes needed to be repaired before the wedding. It wouldn't do to have holes lying in wait to break the legs of unsuspecting wedding goers. At least, not if he wasn't allowed to pick and choose which legs.

By the time Nigel returned to the house, every inmate was up and about and wanting some service or another. Abuelita's voice rose above all others as she had, once again, misplaced her fiancé.

"Where's Jack? What's happened to Jack?" she'd say. "Have you seen Jack? Has anyone seen my jackass fiancé?"

For two people on the verge of marriage and living in the same house, Jack Watt and Abuelita spent a surprising amount of time apart. Most couples, under such circumstances, attach themselves to each other's hips and exhibit the kind of earnest affection that drives closest friends and dearest relatives to hide in closets. Not these two. Abuelita could not keep track of Jack Watt's whereabouts. Jack Watt likely found this to be her most endearing quality. Stefanie, her of the AWOL husband, looked upon the separations as training. Nigel held out hope that Jack Watt had wised up and permanently decamped.

"I will see if I can find your precious Jack," said Nigel. Wrangling wayward fiancés might not have been in his job description, but this was one task Nigel would be happy to fail at. What a relief that would be.

Nigel's search for Abuelita's missing fiancé left him feeling like a beekeeper searching for the queen of the hive. Everywhere he went, occupants scattered and buzzed, but with no sign of the royal prize. Having searched the house proper, he ascended to the attic where small round windows provided sweeping views in every direction. To the east, in the far distance, he spotted a lone figure of a man where one ought not to be.

A ten-minute hike put Nigel within shouting distance of the flighty fiancé. Jack Watt, surprisingly, had turned out to be a thoroughly likeable guy, one of those easygoing types supremely relaxed within his own skin. A skin that Abuelita was soon to bore herself permanently under like some aged blood-sucking tick. Why a guy with Jack's charms would invite such a tragedy was beyond comprehension. What Jack needed was a nudge—a nudge away from a future of crushing anguish, hellish torment, and harrowing agony. Then again, maybe that's what was missing in Jack's life.

"Hey, there," Nigel yelled to Jack, who was seated on a stump.

"Who goes there?"

"It's me, Nigel, the butler. Sorry to disturb you, Mr. Watt, but your lady has become agitated. I think she's a bit paranoid that you'll slip into the woods never to return."

"Nothing of the sort," said Jack Watt, spinning around on his stump. "Just need me some personal time. I'm a loner at heart, a lone wolf."

"Understood. I've got a touch of the independent streak myself. Of course, I'm married, so the wife sets some limits."

"Keeps you penned in, does she?"

"Oh, I wouldn't say that," said Nigel, gazing toward the horizon, beyond which, somewhere, free men were gallivanting. He wasn't a smoker, but a drag would have been nice. He pulled up a blade of grass and placed it in his mouth. It tasted awful. Like grass. And dirt. "Actually, you're pretty spot on. That's me all right, a wolf in a cage. A lone, wild wolf yearning to be free. In a cage." He stole a glance at Jack to see if he might have turned pale. Nothing. "But for me it's worth it. I love my wife."

"You're a lucky wolf in a cage then," said Jack.

"I hope you're as lucky." Nigel looked for signs of downcast. Nope. "I don't know if Abuelita mentioned it, but she's already lost one fiancé. That man went to jail before she could reel him in. It was just as well. He was planning to murder her. My point is that Abuelita suffers from paranoia when it comes to losing another. She gets a little antsy. She'll want you around…all the time, if you know what I mean."

"Not likely. I need my space." Jack Watt had a way of making even stark statements sound reasonable and fun.

"I'm totally with you on that, you bet," said Nigel, rubbing the back of his own neck. "I hope I'm not being intrusive here, but it might be something you and Abuelita should discuss, this need to be alone. Just to make sure you're on the same page, maybe you could have that discussion before the wedding…like this afternoon. A little discussion could save a lot of time and trouble on things like, oh, I don't know…wedding arrangements. Why, just the other day, I heard about a husband and a wife on a fishing trip—"

"Did you and your wife have one of those discussions? About the cage and the wolf, I mean."

"Oh, yes, a whole series of them. Best talks ever. You been married before, Jack?"

"Yep."

"Good, so you know what I'm talking about. How did your previous marriage, eh, turn out, if you don't mind my asking?"

"Died."

"Died? You mean your marriage died?"

"Wives. Wives died."

Nigel's instincts told him to steer away from what could be a sensitive subject. "Sorry to hear that. Maybe this time will turn out better."

"How's that?"

"Well, maybe this time your wife won't die."

"So, a divorce would be better? Or, better yet, I die?"

"No, of course not," said Nigel, pulling up another blade of grass.

"Those are the only other options," said Jack matter-of-factly.

"I just meant that you wouldn't have to go through another grieving process."

"To avoid that, I'd have to die first. Is that better?" Jack's logic was unassailable.

But Nigel wasn't finished. "You could die together," he said.

"Together? Like what? A murder-suicide?"

"No, nothing like that. I mean, in your old age, after a life well spent, you die together, the two of you, in each other's arms, while you're both asleep. That's what I had in mind."

Jack Watt looked at Nigel as if a pig with wings had just squeezed itself out of his butt. "You're a romantic, you know that?"

"Maybe this is not the best discussion for us."

"You brought it up."

"Not my intention, I assure you. I was just inquiring as to your previous marriages."

"Is that what you came for?" Strange as it may have seemed, Jack Watt still had a twinkle in his eye and a chuckle in his voice.

"Not particularly, but that's where the conversation went. What would you like to talk about?"

"I was out here alone, which might indicate talking wasn't on my agenda. I'm here to commune with nature and meditate."

"Meditation! Now that's something we could talk about. How did you get into meditation?"

"It was recommended to me."

"I see. Who recommended it to you?"

"The warden was the first one. Then there was the psychiatrist. Then there was my fourth wife."

That was a lot of information for one statement. Nigel wasn't sure where to begin. "Your fourth wife?" he said, working in reverse order.

"That's when I finally took it up. After my fourth wife."

"After your fourth wife recommended it, you started meditating?"

"Not immediately. Later. By then, I would have tried anything."

"So, meditation has helped?"

"Has it ever. The jitters stopped. The impulses died down. The voices went away. What a difference. I wholeheartedly recommend it. You seem like the type could use it."

"Doesn't work for me. I get queasy."

"That's what I said until I hit rock bottom and got serious about it. You just haven't hit rock bottom yet. I sense you're not far away, though."

"Nice to know. That reminds me, I know you aren't involved, but that detective wants to question you about the dead body."

"No can do, pardner. Talking to a cop would be a trigger. Could undo years of anti-anxiety therapy. If they want to talk to me, they'll have to arrest me. Besides, from what I understand, they already know who did it."

"And who would that be?"

"You're asking me? I thought the butler knew all. Don't expect me to spread any rumors. Not my thing. I'll just say this, watch out for that bottom, pal. It's rocky down there."

Being warned about rocky bottoms by someone facing a future with Abuelita did not comfort Nigel in the least. "I'll keep that in mind. Maybe we should go to the house now. I hear Abuelita is ready to try on her wedding dress. She might want your opinion."

"That's bad luck, isn't it, to see your gal in her dress before the wedding? I don't put much stock in superstitions, but maybe this time I'll adhere."

This guy's strategy seemed to be to avoid the bride as much as possible before the wedding. When considering his marriage partner, Nigel had to admit the plan had appeal. Taking a different angle, he said, "If it's not too much of an imposition, may I ask what brings you two together for these solemn vows? I don't mean to pry, but you two don't seem to be diving head-long into each other's moistened eyes, if you get my drift. Or have I missed something?"

"You're asking if we're in love?"

"Or at least finishing each other's sentences."

"There's all kinds of reasons to get married. True love might be the worst of them."

"A fascinating opinion."

"My dad never married for love, but he was the envy of every man in the state. He married my mother, his first wife, sometime before I was born. I barely knew my mother. She died when I was very young, on Valentine's Day, from food poisoning traced to chocolates. Very rare."

"It must have been a shock."

"Those who saw the look on her face said it was. She was not a pretty woman, but she came from a rich family. Her daddy owned trains. Rumor had it that he protected his daughter from cruel taunts by keeping her hidden. This was untrue. He just kept her away from the tracks so she wouldn't stop the trains.

"My dad, to hear him tell it, was the handsomest boy in Oklahoma. Of course, he was from Texas, but he sometimes crossed the border where the competition was weaker. He had his choice of any young maiden in the territory. Based on unspoken practical considerations, he chose for his wife the homely, spinster daughter of the state's wealthiest railroad magnate. By most accounts—Dad's in particular—my father was a kind and faithful husband for three years. And then, when I was four, Mom passed away from the toxic bonbons.

"Dad was so grief-stricken that he used hundred-dollar bills to wipe his tears, and when the tears had dried, he used the same bills to light cigars. He never let good money go to waste. For six weeks, Father grieved, and on the seventh, he inherited.

On the eighth, he remarried. His first marriage had been subject to unseemly insinuations that he was a gold digger, that he had married an aged, homely woman solely for money. He proved these conjectures baseless with the unveiling of his second wife, a penniless, but awesomely attractive young girl.

"My dad and his new wife traveled in different social circles, occupying different homes on the same block. They maintained an active married life, however, with regular get-togethers at his place on Tuesday and Saturday nights. Then came the year 1968, arriving like a thunderbolt just as 1967 petered out.

"First, there was the Great Collapse—a devastating financial event not widely known outside the family circle. My father had staked the family fortune on the Raiders to upset the Green Bay Packers in Super Bowl II. Sounds like folly today, but Father had it on good authority that Bart Starr, Green Bay's quarterback, had lost three of his best fingers and his second-best thumb due to frostbite. The account may have been overstated given that Starr completed 54 percent of his passes. The family wealth disappeared overnight.

"As if that weren't enough, several months later, the wife died in a tragic accident involving a mechanical failure during a scenic drive on a mountain road. My dad, driving at the time, escaped death in a most miraculous fashion. His car door spontaneously popped open as he was, according to his own eyewitness account, pushed gently outward by a mysterious force as the steering wheel came off in his hands. My father, an otherwise irreligious man, declared his salvation a purposeful act by the Holy Hand of God. This went down well with the community police chief, a deacon in the local chapter of the Church of the Holy Rollers. My father, so appreciative of the officer's kind assistance, sold the wife's house and donated the proceeds to the police chief's church fund."

"Money well spent, I'm sure," said Nigel.

"A lesser man would have been crushed by such events, but not dear old Dad. Defying all expectations, he married an attractive, age-appropriate, self-made rich woman. To the best of anyone's knowledge, they lived harmoniously for the next four years until Father's head tragically collided with a frying pan as it was being held in his wife's hand. It was the final tragedy in father's life until six years later when, at a fish market, he slipped on a jellied eel and slid into a vat of boiling kelp."

"That was a life," said Nigel, summing it up.

"I owe so much to the man."

"Really? How so?"

"Well, you know what they say, 'Like father, like son.'"

"I've heard that, but what does it mean, really? I mean, to you?"

"The father sets the path. The son, willingly or unwillingly, has no choice but to follow. Isn't that what it means to you?"

It could not have been more chillingly explained. Nigel appreciated this little heart-to-heart but was experiencing more than his usual share of unease—an unease shared with Catholic priests of the New Jersey dioceses when taking confession from their most generous benefactors. While feeling no personal peril, he was not so sanguine about Abuelita's prospects. A strange case, Abuelita. The most generous appraisal from the most desperate matchmaker would not have certified her better than third-rate goods on the marriage market, yet homicidal fiancés formed a line outside her door. *Karma*, Nigel supposed.

Despite the past abuse, Nigel understood a butler's duty to protect his client no matter how scaly a creature she was. But what could he do without appearing insubordinate? Giving a frying pan as a wedding gift might be misinterpreted. Restoring her access to firearms could result in immense collateral damage. *What to do?* His heart fluttered, and then, an idea.

"I've been meaning to bring up a rather delicate issue," said Nigel. "Perhaps now is a good time."

"Shoot," said Jack Watt.

"Abuelita, though she may appear as tough as boot leather—"

"Doesn't she? The other day, I swear I heard her thigh bone snap. I don't think she even noticed."

"Yeah. That happens. As I was saying, she may seem like a tough old broad, but she is actually quite weak."

"Really? Like how?"

"Her heart. It has a condition. It must not be exposed to excitement of any kind."

"But snapping bones are okay?"

"Bones are bones, she has a bunch of them, but only one heart, and it's weak. Any exciting, stimulating, or physically assertive experiences could be dangerous, resulting in instant heart failure. You must be very careful not to excite her."

"You talking honeymoon stuff?"

"Precisely. Honeymoon stuff—the worst thing imaginable. She should not be encouraged to even think about the honeymoon stuff. I recommend staying completely away from her after the wedding."

"Completely away? Maybe you haven't noticed, but she seems to be—how to put it delicately—hot to trot on all the honeymoon stuff. Why is she so eager if it might kill her?"

"Oh, she doesn't know. And this is crucial—she must *not* know. A shock like that could…could stop her heart. And you know what they say."

"What do they say?"

"Stop the heart, and…and the rest stops too…and quick."

"They say that?"

"Some do."

Jack Watt pursed his lips and furrowed his brow. "So, you mean, even after the wedding, I'm not to—"

"No! Absolutely not," said Nigel, feeling he'd formulated a deal-breaker.

"How about—"

"No, no, no, not that either. Far too risky. And you must keep the secret. In fact, it's better if you don't even talk to her after the wedding."

"Let me get this straight. After the wedding, I should stay away from her, not talk to her, and no honeymoon hoopla. Is that what you're telling me?"

"You got it."

"Okay."

"You mean you're good with that?"

"Sure. Why not?" Jack Watt registered a disappointment equivalent to a schoolboy's upon learning the cafeteria had run out of creamed spinach.

"It's a rather extreme request," said Nigel. "I dare say, most bridegrooms presented with such a revelation the day before the wedding might have a rethink. Do you need some time—maybe an hour to mill it over?"

"No, don't think so."

"Are you sure? You might be in shock. Sit down and take a deep breath."

"I am sitting."

"Most men in your situation would be lying down, or more likely, running away. You could do that, you know, run away."

"But most men are not marrying a special girl like my little hen."

"No, they most assuredly are not."

Nigel's creamed spinach analogy had been a good one, but there was always that one kid who went for the goop. The pathologically obliging Jack Watt seemed intent on having his creamed spinach, though for what purpose? The wedding was going ahead as planned.

"Well, then, is there anything I can do to make your separation more tolerable?" asked Nigel. "Reading materials, perhaps?"

"Nope. I'll be fine," said Jack Watt, before reconsidering. "There is one thing."

"What is that?"

"She's going to be all over me once the ceremony is done. If you can do something to keep her away, it'd be a big help."

19

EXPLOSIVE PREPARATIONS

Nigel would have preferred to catch a comfy spot on the undercarriage of a train bound for Saskatchewan, but out of a sense of duty, he legged it back to the Sandoval house of horrors. As much as Abuelita wanted her Jack, Nigel left him perched on his stump to exorcise those voices from within. He approached the house feeling sadly demolished. He had held high hopes for Jack Watt, a fellow sane person within the crazy Sandoval constellation. Nigel had envisioned a future with the two of them standing shoulder to shoulder, nudging each other's ribcages and suppressing chuckles while observing the antics of the inmates. Such merriment seemed unlikely if Jack proved to be, as Nigel suspected, one in a long line of serial spouse-killers.

Still, Nigel hoped they could remain friends. After all, besides having an uncommon (for the Sandoval environs) level of lucidity, they were also both under suspicion for murder. These ugly conjectures, for the time being, were more of the embarrassing gas leak variety. But, should they condense into something more offensive, could one have a more valuable friend than Jack Watt, who'd been around this kind of thing all his life? Probably not, as long as you weren't his wife.

Nigel had not yet traversed the atrium before being accosted

by the half-sisters, Stefanie and Esmerelda. A trailing whir
alerted him to search for open manholes, haystacks, or portals to
a new dimension.

"What do you think?" asked Stefanie, stepping aside to
expose Nigel full-on to the most gruesome spectacle he'd ever
had the displeasure to witness.

Abuelita's pruny face contorted into a jack-o'-lantern smile,
derived, it seemed, from some twisted satisfaction at being
repackaged in red satin and black lace.

Confronted with such an abomination, Nigel rocked back on
his heels.

Abuelita looked all the world like a crypt-keeping saloon girl
from a Wild West horror show. Her gown's plunging neckline
left large tracts of long-neglected wastelands exposed to vulnerable retinas.

He averted his eyes, but what he had seen could not be
unseen. "You look like you're ready for...eh...a dance," said the
horrified Nigel.

"I am," said Abuelita. "After the marrying. This here's my
wedding dress. It goes on hard, but it comes off easy. If you think
this swings, you ought to see what I got for the honeymoon. It's
magic—it disappears." She exploded with a cackle that also
contained magic—it made the stomach try to digest itself.

"How are the arrangements going? Do you need any help?"
asked Stefanie of the shaky Nigel.

"The minister canceled this morning. It'll be difficult to find a
replacement on such short notice."

"I'll do it," said Esmerelda.

"You'll find a minister?"

"I'll *be* the minister. I'm ordained. I got papers and everything. I can do it."

"I didn't know you were a minister. What church?" asked a
skeptical Nigel.

"The Church of Humming Moon and Singing Stars."

"Ah, yes...and where would they be headquartered, this church?"

"Luna," said Esmerelda. "Luna-by-the-Sea."

"California, I take it."

"Oklahoma. But it's a church of the natural order. Their dominion knows no bounds. They operate in all quarters of the known and unknown universe. Even space! So much better than some county justice of the peace."

"Well, if you're legally qualified, then I'm all for it. One more thing off my list."

"I need to prepare—remarks to write and herbs to burn. This will be so much fun."

Sometimes it seemed as if Esmerelda had left as an angry, sullen eighteen-year-old and returned forty years later as an excitable sixteen-year-old.

"Take me outside," said Abuelita. "I want to see the tent."

The group had scarcely moved a yard before freezing at the sight of a deathly vision in turban and sunglasses advancing from the back deck. Nigel peeled off to the right. The others, lacking a coherent escape plan, cowered in place.

As he bounded from the room, Nigel overheard Esmerelda say, "My god, what happened to your face?" Exploding out the back door, he heard a spine-withering, "What!"

The rapidly moving Nigel noted, out of the corner of his eye, the fully erected wedding tent. As he jogged past, he was joined by Tom, the amiable team foreman for Weddings-in-Tents. Tom, a burly veteran of two tours in Afghanistan, needed a sign-off to send the team home. It was a stroke of good fortune, then, for him to catch Nigel galloping through the area. Nigel scribbled on his clipboard while Tom ran alongside. Handing back the clipboard, Nigel veered toward the northwest, while the foreman, hearing a siren-like wail, dived belly first to the ground and covered his head.

Nigel recognized the unearthly wail as that of a demon in a

sour mood. He sprinted north-by-northwest in search of a faraway stump to sit upon.

Nigel drove into town for his dinner rather than risk a chance meeting with the fire-breathing dragon-in-law. During his escape, he had caught only a glimpse of the wailing ghoul. That glimpse had been sufficient for him to see that visible portions of her fair complexion had shade-shifted toward something approximating raw hamburger meat. While one might speculate as to the catalyst for such a transformation, he chose not to. It wouldn't matter because he was already certain that a fruit-based facial preparation had been assigned the blame. Looking on the bright side, no one had died. Actually, someone had. Scratch the bright side.

Returning to the estate, Nigel made his own inspection of the wedding tent. Inside, an assortment of cleanly arranged chairs and tables awaited tomorrow's ceremony. He tried to envision tomorrow's solemn proceedings, complete with flower arrangements, guests, minister (Esmerelda), and the saloon-succubus bride and her serial-killing groom wheeling/walking down the aisle.

Nigel felt a sense of accomplishment. A week earlier, he could not have imagined himself planning a wedding, but now, mere hours from the event, a sense of pride washed over him. But the pride in his head was counterbalanced by a less sanguine sense at his core that was harder to define. He had not been pregnant, but the distress in his gut suggested he might soon give birth to a colicky hedgehog baby. He hoped that wasn't the case. Clearly, the impending marriage, which Nigel foresaw as a colossal catastrophe for all concerned, weighed on his mind. These thoughts he expelled from his head, choosing instead to revel in the satisfaction of knowing he'd done his part to make it all happen.

He stepped out of the tent and inhaled the gentle, fragrant air of a quiet evening. The shadows had grown long, but enough sunlight remained to operate machinery.

A few minutes later, a wide-eyed and white-knuckled Nigel motored around the tent atop a jerking, sputtering, insect-like mechanical contraption. The small, yellow machine bucked and bounced like a geriatric mustang set upon by bees. He wrestled the vehicle toward hole number one located a few feet from one corner of the tent.

The back deck of the residence filled with the full cast of inmates drawn outdoors by the racket from Nigel's newfound toy.

"What's he riding?" asked the mother-in-law.

"It's that backhoe," said Mrs. Sandoval. "It's been in the garage for ages. I'm surprised it still works. But what's he doing with it?"

Mrs. Sandoval was generous in her description of the machine. A backhoe would more fairly describe its larger sibling. Nigel's little gizmo was a micro-backhoe, also known as an excavator. This motorized riding implement, built for light digging and heavy cursing, was best suited for sandcastle construction.

"Do you know what you're doing?" yelled Annie.

"Has he ever?" said her mother, looking more mummified than ever in turban, sunglasses, and veil.

"Maybe you should wear a helmet," yelled Annie.

"We all should be wearing helmets," said her mother.

Nigel did not acknowledge. His preference would have been to perform this operation quickly and covertly, but there was no turning back. He attempted to placate the crowd with a wave, almost losing his seat in the process. He two-handed the controls and set about the task at hand.

To dig out a pre-dug hole using the JCB 8000 CTS Micro-Excavator would be the work of a minute in the hands of a skilled operator. A skilled operator, Nigel was not. His biggest stumbling block was operating what were euphemistically termed "the controls." The controls hardly seemed controlling. Obstinate, ornery, and temperamental, the machine had been designed as a robot version of the pack mule.

While struggling to govern the mechanical beast, Nigel received all manner of unwanted advice from the onlookers crowded at the porch railing. They seemed to regard the activity as a kind of spectator event—man against machine. He suspected a good portion of the crowd was pulling for the machine and not above using sabotage to ensure its success.

"Back up about two feet," yelled Stefanie.

"No, he needs to move forward a half foot if he wants the rock bucket to extend beyond the hole," shouted Stefanie's husband.

"I beg to differ. Judging by the length of the dipper arm, a full extension should provide ample reach. Of course, if he's going to do that, he'll need to drop the stabilizer arms. No telling what might happen if he doesn't drop those stabilizer arms," shouted Esmerelda.

"Either way, he'll need to move one foot to the right," said Stefanie's husband.

"Only if the swing arm doesn't have a rotational joint," yelled Jack Watt.

"You are correct, of course. If the swing arm has a rotational joint, he'll need to rotate the arm ten degrees to the right," yelled Abuelita.

"Your right or his right?" shouted Mrs. Sandoval.

"Amateurs," Nigel grumbled.

The advice, well-meaning though it was, served only to frustrate the contraption, which became ornerier and more uncontrollable with each directive. No matter how hard Nigel jammed the levers or how many times he punched various buttons, the machine refused to do his bidding. Even so, he managed to align the machine for a dig. After several false starts, he forced the excavator to scoop. By the fifth scoop, the process had become systematic. On the sixth, the scoop encountered a solid object. Just what Nigel had hoped for.

These mysterious holes had appeared for a reason. The occupants of Castle Sandoval weren't the types to dig holes for recreation. No, these holes existed to put something in or take something out. Once Nigel had spotted Old Man Sandoval's torso map, he was determined to investigate, and what better place to start than with starter holes? The current holes, too shallow for decent treasure, may have been dug by hand and abandoned before hitting paydirt. If that was the case, Nigel was there to finish the job.

The five-gallon scoop, rising from the depths, cradled a cylinder. Nigel climbed off the excavator and knelt to inspect the object.

It was rusted and ancient with a plastic lid. Inspection revealed it to be a coffee can—Maxwell House, Good to the Last Drop. The can was light, too light to contain precious metals. Dollar bills, perhaps. Nigel pulled off the lid to find paper, rigid, warped, water-damaged paper. He extracted a piece of the contents and held it high in front of his face to catch the evening light. From the bound collection of pages, he unfolded an uncommonly long sheet—Janice Raymond, Miss December 1974. Nigel had discovered a stash of *Playboy* magazines.

Vintage *Playboys* in mint condition might sell for folding money, but not these. The bounty did not justify a tattoo. He dropped the can in the hole and reburied it.

Nigel wasted no time digging into hole number two as the chief source of illumination was now the backyard's floodlights, making it difficult to see. The spectators continued to mill around the deck, though taking less interest in the excavations. The more anonymity, the better, as far as Nigel was concerned.

With a better command of the machine, he had mined seven scoops of dirt within minutes. One more would be his last. He sent down the bucket and hit something hard. Not only was it hard, it sounded hard and hollow, like a safe. He raised the bucket and tried again, hoping to get underneath the object to lift it out.

Nigel didn't remember what happened next, but those on the deck would describe it for years to come. A great flash of light coincided with a hollow boom. A cannon shot was how it was described by describers who had never heard a cannon being shot. Against the great blinding flash could be seen the dark shape of the excavator flying upwards and spinning in a pirouette. Coming off the excavator, also in silhouette, was a man "flying" end-over-end in a northwesterly direction.

Once the spectators had overcome flash blindness, they watched with hanging jaws as a great geyser of blue flame twisted its way toward the heavens. This cyclonic inferno would have been the sight of a lifetime if not for what came next.

The fire, having sampled the corner of the white tent, and the tent, having experienced the fire's hot licks, began a torrid, all-consuming affair. Within minutes, the tent was a massive, roiling fireball.

"Oh, the humanity!" yelled Jack Watt.

He could yell that because no humanity was at risk.

Within seconds of the blowout, Annie had located Nigel crawling around in the glow while muttering something about Miss December. With him slung over her shoulder, she trudged back to the house and deposited him on the steps of the back deck.

"Spectacular, old man," said Jack Watt. "Can't wait to see how the wedding turns out."

20

LAST-MINUTE SUPERHEROES

Nigel awoke and saw the envelope on the floor by the door. Someone had shoved it under the crack without bothering to pssssst. The envelope, he supposed, contained a note someone wanted him to read. To read it would require picking it up, which would require getting out of bed. Therein lay the problem.

Nigel didn't see how he could do it. A night's sleep after being tossed thirty feet by an explosion lacked its usual restorative powers. He felt as if someone had entered his room during the night and starched his body. Stiff it was, like a case of *rigor mortis* without the comfort of dying.

Ten minutes later, he had reclaimed enough of his joints to slide out of bed. A few minutes after that, he retrieved the note— a missive from Mrs. Sandoval requesting his presence first thing in the morning.

Nigel was neither surprised, nor particularly unhappy. A little disappointed maybe, but also relieved. He just hoped the dismissal would be effective immediately, relieving him of the wedding and funeral duties.

By the time he entered the foyer, the house was abuzz. A biggish guy in a blueish jumpsuit walked swiftly toward the back of the house while a smallish chap in a greenish jumpsuit lounged near the door. Nigel sidestepped a nondescript sort in a brownish jumpsuit to get to Mrs. Sandoval's office.

"Good day, m'lady. At your service," said Nigel.

"I hope you're okay after yesterday's misadventures. I regret that we couldn't talk last night, but your condition and my condition put us in no condition to have a frank and meaningful discussion. Now that we have our wits about us, I want you to understand that explosions on this property without prior consent are unacceptable. Such activities are not what I hired you for. Do we have an understanding, Mr. Nigel?"

"What?"

Mrs. Sandoval winced while leaning back in her chair. "I said, 'Do we have an understanding?'"

"Could you repeat…a little louder, perhaps? My ears," he said, pointing to the organs in question before opening his fists to suggest an ear-shattering explosion.

"Don't blow things up," shouted Mrs. Sandoval.

"Sorry. Won't happen again," Nigel shouted back.

Another jumpsuited person, medium-smallish in a grayish tone, stepped in to procure Mrs. Sandoval's signature.

"Who"—Nigel twirled a pointed finger—"are they?" He brushed his hands across his chest as the universal sign for jumpsuit.

"Mr. Nigel, I'm not hard of hearing. You don't need to use sign language."

"What?"

"They're from the gas company," she yelled. "Here to repair the gas line."

"Repair the gas line?" said Nigel. "The one that blew up?"

"Yes," yelled Mrs. Sandoval.

"So, the explosion wasn't something I did?"

"What?" said Mrs. Sandoval, dropping her jaw far enough for her tongue to ooze out.

"So, the explosion wasn't because of something I did?" yelled Nigel.

"Of course it was something you did! You struck a gas line," yelled Mrs. Sandoval. "Those holes were dug by the gas company. Didn't you see the flags?"

"The what?"

"Flags."

"Flags?" said Nigel. "Small, yellow flags?"

"Yes," shouted Mrs. Sandoval.

"Oh," said Nigel. Not the time to go into detail, but he thought the gardener had been mapping out his garden.

"What about the wedding?" yelled Mrs. Sandoval.

"Should we cancel?"

"No, we're not canceling. Do you have everything arranged?"

Arranged? thought Nigel. *The wedding venue is now an ash-filled crater. At least the bride isn't wearing white.* Making use of his disability to buy time, he said, "What?!"

"The wedding?" yelled Mrs. Sandoval. "Is everything arranged?"

What is the opposite of arranged? Deranged? Thinking quickly, he replied, "What?"

"The wedding is today at three o'clock," yelled Mrs. Sandoval. "Be ready. Minister, flowers, drinks, music, food. Got it? Three o'clock."

Food? thought Nigel. *No one mentioned food before.* "What?" he said, hoping she might give the whole thing up.

"Get it done!" shouted Mrs. Sandoval. "Get. It. Done."

Nigel walked out of Mrs. Sandoval's office marveling that he still had a job. Marveling wasn't the word, actually. Regretting was the word. But there was no time for wistful thinking. He needed to get to work. What he really needed was to have his eardrums pierced to let the ringing out and the sound back in.

Nigel looked at his wrist, which served as a reminder that he'd given up wearing a watch three years ago. Had he been wearing one it almost certainly would have reminded him that zero hour was far too near.

What had Mrs. Sandoval rattled about?

The minister — that would be Esmerelda. Thank God, or whatever her preferred deity, for Essie.

What else?

Flowers — arriving soon.

Drinks — never a problem in this house.

Music? Where did that come from? What kind of music? Music had to be a bottom-of-the-list priority.

She mentioned food. What a sucker punch. Did she mean cake? Was that enough or did she want more? A regular meal? Finger foods? What? The cook doesn't even work on Saturdays.

Too late for legitimate catering, Nigel would have to run to town and rustle something up.

Just then, he caught sight of Stefanie waving her arms like one of those yellow-jacketed chaps at the airport who distract pilots as they park their planes. He had learned to ignore stuff of this nature, but she was making it difficult with her imploring gaze and flapping mouth.

Nigel turned to attend to her crisis when he heard a faint ring. For all he could hear, it might have been the doorbell or a fly colliding with a dinner fork. Just in case, he opened the door where he was greeted by Stanley's backside. Stanley's front was engaged in holding one end of a large rectangular box, the other end being held by a young man dressed, as was Stanley, in baker's whites.

"The cake. Excellent," said Nigel, holding the door open wider. "Come this way, Stanley. Follow me."

Once the box had been walked back to the kitchen and deposited on a serving cart, Nigel peeked inside. "Let's have a look, shall we." He knew this wouldn't be Stanley's best, but even Stanley's nominal efforts were...

"Mmmmmmmmm," said Nigel. "Not conventional, I'll say that. What would you call that style? *Avant garde?*"

Unlike the multi-tiered structure so popular among wedding cakes for the last hundred years or so, this one incorporated a modified slab concept. A large rectangular slab abutted against an upright half-disk that was flanked by two small towers. The entire construction was covered in solid white icing with the sole exceptions of a violet inset in the front of the disk and a light blue square in front of the cake structure.

"Very solid looking," said Nigel, as he circled the cake in search of a flattering view. "Monolithic, you might say."

Nigel was grateful for anything at this point. Even a cake that looked like a future monorail station for New Faberville, West Oakdale, and Luddingtontown. He imagined himself cutting and plating the thing before anyone got a proper look. This daydream was interrupted by the sight of Stanley rummaging frantically around the corners of the cake box.

"Damn! Where's that bride and groom?" said Stanley. Turning to his assistant, he continued, "Did you check what was in the other box?"

His assistant's head remained motionless.

"Ehhhhhhh," said Stanley, stamping his feet as he pulled two objects bagged in clear plastic from the corner of the box.

Nigel had never known Stanley to get upset. He was typically impassive unless a dessert had crossed the event horizon of his mouth. Now Stanley began to sag, first the brow, then the mouth, and finally, the shoulders—left, then right. All this sagging must have meant something.

Nigel braced himself for terrible news.

"I have to apologize," said Stanley. "I've been in such a rush, I had no time to design and decorate a proper wedding cake. I had to make do. I was already booked to produce a birthday cake for an eight-year-old based on the Hall of Justice from the Super Friends. With so little time, I doubled the recipe and made two identical cakes. I delivered the first one this morning and came here to deliver the second. I hate to tell you this. I am so very sorry, but there's been a mix-up. You've got the wrong figurines. Somehow, instead of Spring Bride and Dashing Groom, you've ended up with Wonder Woman and Aquaman."

Showing no emotion, Nigel stared as if unable to comprehend the magnitude of the offense.

Under the crushing weight of silence, Stanley shuffled and stammered and searched for a suitable explanation. "I can't tell you how sorry I am. It's been so rough of late. I don't like to bring up my personal life, but Cam has been like a bear with a burr up her behind. I don't know what's gotten into her. She just won't be happy. It keeps me up at night. A baker wakes up early. Yeast, you know. When the alarm is set for five, and you're walking the floor until three…it doesn't make for happy baking. The business is collapsing, and I'm at my wits' end. Of course, you don't need to hear my problems. You've got a wedding to produce. I'll see what I can do to get your figurines here before the wedding starts. Please, say you'll forgive me."

Nigel issued no response.

Stanley sagged again, starting at the knees and working upward.

Recognizing that Stanley's mouth had stopped moving, Nigel said, "What?"

Stanley backed out in defeat.

Nigel waved goodbye. Today was a day for making do and moving on. Besides, that Wonder Woman was pretty hot.

Replica of a fictional government building or not, the cake would have to suffice. The saving grace for this wedding was that no matter how badly things balled up, the principals wouldn't have decades to brood over it. That uplifting thought returned a bounce to Nigel's step.

Food was next on the agenda. There were plenty of microwave popcorn to go around, but he feared more might be expected. He galloped through the kitchen toward the back door as Mrs. Sandoval stepped in front of it.

"Where's the ceremony to take place?" she asked.

"Eh, the Great Hall," said Nigel, preparing a stiff arm.

"The Great Hall?"

"I mean the salon," said Nigel, feinting left while planting his foot for a plunge to the right.

"Salon? You mean the entrance hall?"

"Check."

"But there are no chairs."

Trivial details, thought Nigel, drawing close to the blocking Mrs. Sandoval.

"A stand-up wedding. Latest thing. Good for the health. Cam Logan had one," yelled Nigel while drawing in his stomach and sliding to her right.

Mrs. Sandoval spun around as he clipped her shoulder on the way out.

By the time Nigel made the final turn toward the Sandoval estate, the kung pao chicken and beef broccoli vapor was thick enough to slice with a chopstick. Halfway down the drive, he noticed a pedestrian in the road ahead. Could Jack Watt have come to his senses at the eleventh hour? If so, Nigel would give him a lift to the bus station and provide him with all the Chinese takeout he could bear.

As Nigel closed, he saw it was not Jack, but Mr. Sandoval fleeing the nuptials. The man walked in a slow shuffle but, sartorially speaking, he had spanned continents since first arriving. His current outfit, displaying not a single piece of roadkill, consisted of the most extravagant threads from the vintage section of Gastrick's closet. A smart fitting Nehru jacket topped a pair of purple paisley bell-bottoms. Esmerelda's work, perhaps.

"What ho," yelled Nigel sticking his head out the car window. "There's a wedding up at the house in an hour. If you keep walking this way, you'll miss the festivities."

"It's my ex-wife, isn't it?"

"She's just the half of it. There's a chap too."

"I don't want to see it."

"Honestly, I don't want to see it either, but I'll show up for the party. Skip the vows. They're for cows. Here to browse, then carouse. That's my motto."

"You don't have a dent in your head."

"No, admittedly not, but I wouldn't let that stop me. I think we can find you a nice hat."

"I don't want to see my ex-wife get married. I don't have a problem with her doing it, I just don't want to see it."

"I'm with you. I don't want to see it either, but if you drink enough, it'll be blurry."

"Right," said Mr. Sandoval, slipping his hand into his knap-sack and pulling out a bottle of the brown stuff.

"I see. Having your own party. If you're going to do that, the least I can do is provide dinner." Nigel reached to the backseat and grabbed one of the twenty-four bags from Panda Empress. "I hope you like Chinese."

"If I don't, the birds will."

"I'd like nothing better than to stop and share a stump, but duty calls. *Au revoir.*"

21

THINKING OUT OF THE BOX

After shuttling twenty-three bags of Panda Empress and two large pizzas into the kitchen through the back entrance, Nigel inspected the entrance hall. He was comforted by the sight of several lovely flower arrangements, delivered as promised. He was less comforted by the sight of a casket.

There, at the geographic center of the entrance hall, atop a waist-high platform, sat a gleaming, copper-colored, highly unanticipated casket. One might have thought that such a thing appearing midday, mid-residence, out of the bloody freakin' blue, would have attracted a crowd. Not, apparently, at the Sandoval estate.

Nigel circled the burnished receptacle in a clockwise direction. Having completed the circle, he repeated the process in the anticlockwise direction. He squatted and looked underneath for hidden panels, thinking someone might have booked a magician for the wedding, then backed away and scratched his head. He didn't recall ordering a casket. The flowers had been absurdly expensive, but not casket-level money. Stepping up to the handsome object, he rapped softly three times on the lid.

No reply.

He lowered his ear to the copper-clad box.

Quiet as a tomb in there.

Nigel stepped back to contemplate. Opening it did not appeal. He had seen enough movies to know that uncorking random coffins seldom ended well. He decided he had not contemplated enough.

He gazed at the fancy corpse container for some time before noticing that the lid was not tightly shut, as if an object impeded its full closure. He peered into the meager separation. Darkness. Pulling away, he spotted the source of the obstruction—the tips of three fingers.

Nigel leaped three feet up and two back. *Not right*, he thought. *Not right at all.*

He'd been under the impression that caskets were like Disneyland rides—hands should remain inside at all times. Occupants of caskets should be, on the whole, pretty darn well behaved. He could not envision a scheme where fingers should be given outside access. Coming as it did minutes before a wedding, the whole scenario was too troubling by half.

Nigel had no choice but to open the deathly box. *How? From behind? Should I lift and duck? Should I have a mallet and wooden stake handy?* He opted for the quick peek.

Placing two hands flat on the casket lid, he pushed just enough for a glance inside. As soon as eyes met interior, Nigel dropped the lid and stiffened as if run through lengthwise with a skewer.

"Owwwww," came a voice from the interior.

"Eeeeee," came a voice from Nigel's interior.

"What happened? What are you doing?" said a muffled voice from within.

"Esmerelda?"

The casket lid pushed upward from the inside. Within lay an almost unrecognizable version of Esmerelda. This woman's philosophy as far as facial upkeep had previously tended toward the painfully natural. On this occasion, however, she had gone full-on cosmetological. Colors from the rainbows of every planet smudged her face.

"That hurt my fingers," she said through turquoise-colored lips.

"Sorry. Didn't expect to see you there. You're okay? I mean, not dead or anything?"

"Do I look dead? I just wanted to engage the experience. Never been in a coffin before. It's a trip. I was a bit nervous about the wedding, so I crawled in here and pretended to be dead. What a gas! It made me feel so...so...*alive*."

"Yes, I've heard death does that for a person."

"Then you opened the lid and the spell was broken."

"Sorry to have resurrected you. Believe me, not my intention, but when I saw this casket where a wedding is about to take place, something came over me. Curiosity, I suppose."

"How long to the ceremony?"

"Twenty minutes, but I've not seen a soul. Perhaps everyone has found a casket to curl up in. Now that you're up, help me push this one to the side."

"Push it to the side? Why? It's beautiful."

"Beautiful maybe, but hardly appropriate."

"It's completely appropriate," said Esmerelda. "Like a wedding, the casket is a symbol of passage, of transformation, a part of the great continuum—"

"More like the great discontinuum."

"I say we keep the casket here for the ceremony. It works. A casket at a wedding ceremony—a token of mystical crossings, of life's great bridges. Magical. If we had a birth symbol, we'd have the whole set."

"Maybe I can run to the hospital and find a woman in labor. While I do that, you can arrange a human sacrifice. Let's not do this thing halfway."

"You're being sarcastic, aren't you?"

"You think? Maybe coming across an inhabited coffin has given me a different perspective. But you're the officiant of this wingding, so if you want a casket, we'll have a casket. It just seems to me that the bride and groom, given their…eh…stage in life, might feel they're being rushed. I mean, having a casket at their wedding seems a little suggestive in all the wrong ways. And, knowing what I know about this couple, they don't need suggestions."

"Don't be silly. A casket awaits us all. But not me, no. No casket, no graveyard. I'm to have a sustainable death. Just my nude body in a field under a newly planted tree to be called Esmerelda."

"A fruit tree, no doubt."

"Mmmmmm. Organic apples."

"While you're picturing yourself transforming into apples, I'm going up to see how the groom is getting on. You might want to check on the bride. If either one is making trouble, we've got a place to stuff them." Nigel turned to walk away but, unfortunately, his hearing had returned sufficiently to sense the doorbell.

Opening the door to an overly familiar droopy-faced detective, Nigel said, "Oh, it's you."

"It is I. I'm glad you're here, Mr. Blandwater-Cummings."

"That makes one of us." Nigel assumed the detective's visit was for a bad reason. He had not been known to visit for anything else. But when the detective led off his visit with a prolonged demonstration of neck elasticity, Nigel grew impatient. "Is there something I can get you? An Uber, perhaps?"

"What is that?" said the detective, extending an arm to point around Nigel.

"You're a detective, and you have to ask that?"

"Is that a casket?"

"A tisket, a tasket, a copper-colored casket. I'll bet they never make fun of you down at the station."

"What is a woman doing in that casket?"

"What do women usually do in caskets?"

"She's sitting up," said the detective.

"Let's take that as a positive, shall we? Maybe the funeral home will give us a refund."

"That's Esmerelda. I talked to her the other day."

"So, it *was* you. We knew something got ahold of her. Boredom drove her to an early grave. I'll say one thing, you're cleaner than a ball peen hammer."

"She's walking away."

"Is she? She must have heard your voice. I'd be walking too if I wasn't paid to stand here."

"Are you finished with this nonsense?" said the detective.

"If you don't like my nonsense, then tell me who you wish to see so you can get on with your own."

"I'll see you, for a start."

"You've already seen me. I'm tired of being seen. We should stop seeing each other."

"Come Monday, I am confident—"

"Come Monday you'll be confident? I bet you say that every Saturday."

"On Monday, I am confident that I'll be returning with a warrant for your arrest."

"A warrant for my arrest?" Nigel carried a long fuse, but recent events had burned it down considerably. With a fast-approaching wedding ceremony, he had no time for this detective. What he did have was a head of steam in need of a vent. "You can't fool me, see," he said in his best American gangster. "I know your game, see. You got nothin', copper. Nothin'. Threaten me with this phony warrant story so I'll leave town, eh? Claim the killer skipped just as you were closing in, eh? Take credit for solving a crime with no evidence, eh? It's a frame-up, I tell ya, and it ain't gonna work, copper. You know why it ain't gonna work?"

Not expecting such an onslaught, the detective stepped back while flashing a greenish tint in the vicinity of the gills. "Why?" he asked with a fragile bravado.

"Because I'm stayin', see. I'm callin' your bluff, flatfoot. You ain't pinnin' no rap on me. You dirty rat—"

"Detective Winjack," interjected a dragonly female voice. "I'm glad you're here. I have observations that might be of interest. Certainly of more interest than anything from this imbecile."

Mother-in-law led the detective away by the forearm, her head covered in a one-piece turban/veil ensemble.

Nigel had never seen her in such a getup, but the beige, sparkly material looked familiar. As she walked away, the headgear's twin tails entwined at the back of the neck and trailing down her back gave up its secret. They were the sleeves of one of Annie's favorite blouses.

With zero hour fast approaching, Nigel bounded up the stairs to the groom's quarters. "Doing okay in there? Need anything?" he asked after knocking.

The door opened. Jack Watt displayed himself in a standard black tuxedo. "What do you think? Adequate?"

"Adequate, yes," said a wincing Nigel. "If adequate were adequate."

"What do you mean?"

"I'll alert you here and now, Abuelita, your little chickadee, will not be dressed in traditional garb. Not by a long shot. You've seen a peacock?"

"Sure."

"A toucan?"

"Yeah."

"A bird of paradise?"

"In pictures."

"Take one of each, toss them into a blender, whirl them around a bit, and look inside. That's Abuelita's idea of a wedding dress."

"You think she'd prefer something a little louder?"

"Louder? Something that screams bloody murder, I should think."

"I chose this because nobody told me different. Truth is, I'd rather wear almost anything else."

"That's the spirit," said Nigel.

"If you have a better idea, I'm game."

Nigel led him to Gastrick's closet, the contents of which had barely begun to be plundered. The former butler/convict was a man not of style, but of 800 styles, if one cared to stretch the word to its limit. The possibilities for an adventurous groom were endless.

Jack Watt, as it turned out, had a fine eye for the ridiculous. He held a jacket up to his neck. "Eh? What dya t'ink hyere?" he said in his best Bronx.

"What's up, doc?" said Nigel, the suit appearing to be a knockoff of an original worn by Bugs Bunny in *Racketeer Rabbit*— wide-lapels, double-breasted, gray with triple thick chartreuse pinstripes.

Jack found a blood-red dress shirt, which he matched with a black tie dotted with images of garish socks. The ensemble was bottomed out with the matching black socks spotted with images of brightly colored neckties.

Jack Watt put on the suit, though it may be more fitting to say the suit swallowed Jack Watt. Once unshackled from the closet, these were threads on a rampage. Jack, playing the part of the colorless mannequin, would be its hostage for the evening.

Nigel and Jack took a moment to admire their creation. It was the kind of suit that preceded the wearer into any room, screaming, "Pull my finger."

"You've somehow captured the spirit of this solemn occasion perfectly," said Nigel.

22

WITH THIS RING

At the appointed time, guests congregated—not as planned in the great white tent that now floated as fine ash across Louisiana —but in the home's central entry hall. Let us set the scene.

Esmerelda, seated in a lotus position atop the casket, welcomed the guests with closed eyes and crossed arms. An unearthly hum was sometimes emitted during her meditations. Or were they incantations? Stefanie the Sane stood wrapped in her own arms while semilistening to her semimonthly husband prattle on about the craftsmanship of casket makers. Nigel's private eye wife occupied her own bubble a few feet from her invisible ghoul mother, who was busy filling the head of that rubber-faced Columboob with her own convenient conspiracies. Grumps, suspended between a folding chair and his army helmet, watched for any signs of Englishmen. Even before the principals arrived, the scene had the look of a Halloween party waiting for the arrival of the punch bowl. Mr. Sandoval, not present but presumably sharing the shade of a large tree with a sizable bottle, was probably by now warm and fuzzy.

Nigel and Jack Watt sauntered down the stairs and assumed positions in front of the casket.

"Well, here we are," said Nigel.

"Here are we," said Jack.

Jack Watt, being the groom and wearing as rude a conversation piece as had ever been exhibited inside the gates of Asylum Sandoval, had expected a few high-fives and "look at yous." The lack of any such reaction—of any reaction at all—left him feeling severely self-conscious. It was like showing up at the office in clown makeup and having no one notice. Perhaps the clothing choice was too subtle for the audience.

Nigel, catching Annie's eye from across the room, nodded and winked. Her blank gaze turned into a pucker at the sight of Jack's suit. Jack Watt, perhaps sensing the reaction, straightened the knot on his sock-tie and pulled up his tie-socks. Nigel assured him he looked splendid and that it would all make sense once the bride appeared. The bride and Mrs. Sandoval, however, were nowhere to be seen.

"Pssssst."

"Is that you?" a haunted Nigel said to Jack Watt.

"I hope not," said Jack Watt to the haunted Nigel.

"Pssssst."

"Sure it isn't you?" asked Nigel. "Check your suit. Your left shoulder looks low."

"Pssssst. Mr. Nigel, pssssst," whispered a voice.

Nigel shuffled toward a drapery that had apparently learned to speak. "What's up?" he whispered to the talkative curtains.

"Abuelita is ready. Position the groom and start the music."

"The music?"

"The 'Wedding March.' When the music begins, Abuelita will enter from the east."

"From the east?"

"Yes, but we're waiting for the music."

"Very well," said Nigel, not feeling very well at all. He shuffled to Jack Watt. "Your bride will come from the east," whispered Nigel.

"Which way is east?"

"Don't know. Keep your head on a swivel. When you see

your bride, you'll know where east is because she'll be coming from there when she comes."

"And she'll be drivin' six white horses when she comes? When she comes?"

"Don't know for sure about that," said Nigel. "Be ready for anything." He hoofed it for the kitchen, stopping long enough to announce, "Wedding. Warning. Wedding to begin in five minutes. Warning. Wedding. Take your places, people."

In the kitchen, Nigel rummaged through drawers to locate a roll of parchment paper. Pulling a comb from his pocket, he quickly constructed his musical instrument.

The residents milled about like cows awaiting a hay drop while Esmerelda remained motionless atop the casket, positioned between two small containers emitting acrid clouds smelling of marijuana, rubber, leaves, gunpowder, and toast. In other words, every variety of smoke native to Texas. The irritating atmosphere was soon made more so by a tuneless series of blips, warbles, hums, and drones emanating from the kitchen. The raspy sounds eventually congealed into a recognizable tune. Recognizable, perhaps, but not pleasant. New Antigua had heard nothing like it since that Fourth of July celebration in 1997 when the high school orchestra played "Flight of the Bumblebee," triggering a mad orgy among the city's cicada population.

"Is that 'She'll Be Coming Around the Mountain'?" someone asked.

Indeed it was, but Nigel was just tuning up. After flexing his embouchure with the familiar foot-stomper, he burst from the kitchen blowing a full-chested comb-kazoo version of Mendelssohn's "Wedding March." While the interpretation was hardly on par with say, the New Antigua Saxy Ladies Quartet, most felt it surpassed Clem Spetz's dog whistle rendition since it could be heard.

As previously foretold, Abuelita emerged from a direction, possibly east. The whizz from her wheelchair added a nice harmony to Nigel's buzz-comb recital. That is, until he modu-

lated up half an octave upon seeing her glide forth in a traditional, cream-colored, brocaded wedding dress covering every
limb and boob.

Where was the crimson and black lace? Where were the
nauseating displays of corrugated flesh? What had happened to
Abuelita? Had she, at the last minute, been exposed to a mirror?

As Nigel finished the "Wedding March," Abuelita positioned
herself beside the awaiting Jack Watt. Polite applause flittered
through the atrium as she brought the chair to a standstill
without the aid of a shinbone, a rare feat.

Jack did not appear inspired. He fidgeted as if infected with
wedding lice. He pulled and scratched and wiggled like a snake
needing to shed its chartreuse pinstriped skin.

Nigel, looking at the two lovebirds, felt justified in forgetting
to hire a photographer.

Abuelita should have been enjoying one of life's great sugar
highs but wore a scowl as if holding in a mouthful of vinegar.
Stationed directly behind her, Mrs. Sandoval had the look of one
fresh off a skirmish with an ostrich. Nigel figured Abuelita's
wedding dress switcheroo had not gone down without a struggle. The changeup would rankle all the more once she'd bagged
an eyeful of her husband-to-be dressed to the nines and three-
quarters and then some.

With all assembled, eyes turned toward Esmerelda. The eyes
of Esmerelda, however, were nowhere to be seen. She was
looking within. After a contagion of side-eyes and shuffled feet
among the spectators, Nigel took matters into his own hands.

"Ahem," he said.

Esmerelda moved not.

People blinked, and the grandfather clock ticked, tocked,
then ticked again.

More decisive action was needed. "Ahem," said Nigel, posi-
tioning a finger to tap the lotus-seated Esmerelda's knee.

"Don't touch," said Esmerelda, raising her open hands. The
left palm displayed an image of the sun nicely rendered in felt-

tip, and on the right palm, a companion felt-tip of the moon, probably Earth's, and a generic star. Her eyes remained closed. "I'm summoning. We shall not have a wedding without the aid of the spirits."

"What the hell?" said Abuelita. "We got tequila, vodka, and bourbon. What more do we need? Gin? Let's move this thing along."

Eyes still closed, Esmerelda moved her opened hands in broad slow-motion arcs while incanting, "Moon eclipses sun. Sun eclipses moon." She brought her busy hands together in a praying motion. "Bless this celestial union. Sun and moon, Venus and Mars, fire and water. May the heavens forever smile upon these two blessed virgins—"

"What?" said Abuelita.

"...so they may, with your bountiful grace, please the good earth, please one another, and please the future with the fruit of their love." Esmerelda raised her head and opened her eyes. "Does anyone here today, relying on the great truth that dwells within the earth and the infinite wisdom that falls from the stars, have reason why these two should not be joined in spirit as husband and wife? If so, sayeth now."

Esmerelda could have been reading a terms-of-agreement document, given the crowd's reaction. Had she worded it differently, like, "If anyone thinks this is a bad idea," there might have been a bull-rush. But Essie wenteth not there.

"Who will be giving away the bride?" asked Esmerelda.

This question elicited a good deal of eye talk among the hostages, but no volunteers.

"Who among ye shall hand over this beautiful bride?"

After several minutes of no takers, Nigel stepped up, and offered, "If you put it that way, I'll do it."

"Excellent," said Esmerelda. "Who are you?"

"You know who I am," said Nigel.

"What is your relationship to the bride? Are you her father?"

"You know I'm not," said Nigel.

"A good friend?"

"Nope."

"A caretaker?"

"Certainly not."

"Could you please state your relationship to the bride?"

"I'm her butler."

"So, you, as her butler, will be giving her away to this man."

"Yes, ma'am. That man there, in the green pinstripes."

"Do you wish to make a statement to the bride's future husband?"

"Sure," said Nigel, turning to Jack. "Good luck, buddy. Better you than me."

"Very well," said Esmerelda. "Before this lovely bride and this chosen groom exchange vows among this gathering of friends and family and the divine entities kind enough to accept our invitation, I will say a few words regarding the venerable state of matrimony—marriage, as it is commonly known.

"Marriage began thousands of years ago as a property deal. A man would take a wife in exchange for property—pigs, cows, coins, or other wives. Compared to today, the wife lived in bliss —cooking, cleaning, sewing, washing, caring for kids, and in her spare time, being grateful to have found an owner. The wife of old held a position comparable to that of the modern pet dog, if the dog had to work eighteen-hour days.

"But times changed. Women of today have discovered their true value. Modern men, by contrast, are seldom worth more than a kick in the head. These modern cavemen no longer purchase wives because they can't afford it. And yet, your typical 'man' enters into marriage as if he's receiving a free, life-time pass to hop aboard the Boom-Boom Express whenever he likes." Esmerelda thrust an index finger toward the sky. "No, sir," she barked. That index finger dropped down to point at Jack Watt's forehead.

Jack, as cool as they come when talking about strangely

dying wives, turned white and emitted a squeak like a mouse seeing his reflection in a cat's eye.

"A wife," Esmerelda continued, "is not a piece of real estate to be purchased and used at the husband's discretion. No, a wife is like a high-rent, luxury apartment requiring a continual, never-ending stream of compensations to ensure access. The husband, when he says, 'I do,' may as well be signing an eternal, unbreakable lease."

Jack stood strong, but his Adam's apple was searching for a way out.

"A marriage is not all about the husband," said Esmerelda. "The wife also has obligations. She is the landlord and must not be lazy. A proper wife must hold the husband accountable. Like the song says, 'a woman is a woman, but a man ain't nothin' but a man.' The wife must be understanding. She must understand that the male of our species is weak, he is slothful, he is a deceiver, and he will take what he has not earned. A good wife is all that elevates her man beyond the trash under his sofa cushions. How does she do this? By making him pay. And pay. And pay. Keep it up, girls. It's a never-ending job. But it's his only hope." Esmerelda smiled at the congregation.

The ladies smiled back.

"So, here we are," continued Esmerelda. "A deal is to be struck this afternoon. We have this...*interestingly* dressed man and this lovely bride." She turned to Jack. "Do you, Jack Watt, take Amalia Gallina de la Cruz Huerta Sandoval to be your lawfully wedded wife, to love, to honor, to cherish, to spare no personal indignity in pursuit of her comfort and well-being, to disregard all personal pain in providing her an endless array of pleasures, to spare no expense in the pursuit of all that she wants, as long as you both shall live?"

"I do," he said between clenched teeth. The clenched teeth may have been a necessity because he looked like he was about to belch up a bullfrog.

Turning to Abuelita, Essie said, "And do you take this man,

Jack Watt, to be your lawfully wedded husband as long as you shall choose?"

Jack's hand began to rise until it was pushed down by the force of Esmerelda's eyebrows.

Too late.

Abuelita did not answer, but instead, began the lengthy, arduous process of standing up. She performed an inventory of all the necessary systems both for her and the chair, followed by an unbuckling, and then a second inventory. She began the standing procedure by squiggling her left side forward by a centimeter followed by a centimeter squiggle for the right side. After fifty moves per side, she was ready for the tricky bit.

Jack had to be wondering if his vows were in effect should this operation end tragically.

Abuelita rolled onto one butt cheek for the final ascension. Mrs. Sandoval buttressed the chair as Abuelita began the push to a standing position. The congregation held their breaths, turning slight shades of blue as they listened apprehensively for the soft crack of powdery bones. Abuelita planted both feet on the floor and pushed herself up to a standing position, receiving a heartfelt ovation for her success.

As always, Abuelita faced the opposite direction after a chair exit. "Where's the preacher?" she snapped. Reorientation remained an elusive skill.

"Over here," said Esmerelda.

"What the hell?" Abuelita followed her neck around for a 180-degree spin. "Ah, there you are. I do."

"Jack Watt—"

"What?"

"You may place the ring on your bride's—"

"Hold on," said Jack.

Nigel, lost in a rumination on the optimum ratio of kung pao chicken to broccoli beef orders, resurfaced after a sharp bump to his elbow.

"Pssssst."

That sound again. Nigel tried to ignore it.

"Pssssst. Old man, the ring, please," whispered Jack Watt.

Nigel looked around and then felt another bump to the elbow.

"Ring, please," whispered Jack through the left side of his mouth.

"What ring?" whispered Nigel through the right side of his mouth.

"You're the best man—"

"Surely not."

"You're it, Hoss. Hand me the ring."

"What ring?"

"No time for jokes. Ring, please."

Nigel searched each of his pockets in the off chance there might be a ring in one of them. Coming up dry, he reached a hand into his jacket's inner pocket and came out with extended thumb and forefinger a half-inch apart. With his other hand, he grasped Jack Watt's nearest dangling limb, bent it up from the elbow, and turned its attached hand palm up. Nigel, in a motion reminiscent of a mother bird feeding her nestling, delicately placed thumb and forefinger, half-inch apart, onto Jack's outstretched palm before flipping his hand away like a mother bird gone to find another worm.

Jack Watt looked into his palm, and then turned to Nigel, who busied himself by studying a far corner of the ceiling. A mother bird must allow her flailing chicks the opportunity to fly, and what better time for Jack Watt to fly than now? He looked at his palm again, then reached toward it and came away with extended thumb and forefinger, half-inch apart. He grasped Abuelita's left hand and slid extended thumb and forefinger, half-inch apart, down the length of her bony ring finger before patting her hand and retreating.

Abuelita held her hand out, then drew it close to her good eye, then extended it out again. She flipped her hand over, then felt her ring finger with her other hand. She looked up at Jack.

Jack Watt was busying himself by studying a far corner of the ceiling.

"I now pronounce you husband and wife. You may kiss the bride, if she's willing," said Esmerelda.

Nigel, in an inspired bit of improvisation, ran to reset the grandfather clock to 11:59.

23

WEDDING SPLASHER

Before the first refrain of "Tequila!" echoed through the hall, the natives demanded their liquor. Nigel was all for it. Thrown together after all the explosions and whatnot, the festivities might have seemed threadbare to the unencumbered intellect.

Let no intellect be unencumbered, thought Nigel. Lacking the legal authority to pump the place with laughing gas, he leaned hard on the alcoholic retardants. Unfortunately, he could lead his inmates to booze, but he couldn't make them drink themselves silly. Scarcely a round had been poured before inquiries began to pile up. Who was in the casket, they wanted to know, and where was the food?

One by one, Nigel sectioned off individuals for dinner service, personally shepherding them through the kitchen for entree selection and microwaving, before plopping them down at the dining room table. A considerate host, as Nigel had learned, encourages social mingling and interplay by placing guests into thoughtful juxtapositions, thus ensuring a convivial discourse. He wanted none of that. Letting these yahoos mix it up at his Chinese buffet could easily lead to mob action. His plan was to isolate the inmates to a maximal degree. Snide remarks could be tolerated, but he wasn't about to have this rabble forming into a cabal. The dining room table seated twenty-four, perfect for maintaining a healthy disconnect among his twelve diners.

Six had chosen the plastic trays of kung pao chicken, while three chose plastic trays of broccoli beef. Abuelita wolfed down the special bride's pizza. Not surprisingly, the evening's two most irksome guests, Rubberface and Stefanie's husband, abstained after examining the fare. The last guest had hardly been served before a chorus of "Cake!" erupted in the dining hall.

Nigel arrived with more alcohol, but the respite was only temporary.

"Cake, cake, cake!" came the call soon after everyone's drinks had been stiffly freshened.

A second appearance of the alcohol cart failed to quell the ugly scene, so Nigel wheeled the cake out to a crowd that was seriously under-lubricated for the journey ahead. The room quieted as he unveiled the cake.

The initial reaction was mixed. That is to say, not everyone hated it in the same way.

"What the hell?" said Abuelita. "Who ordered that thing?"

"That's a wedding cake?" asked Stefanie.

"Looks like the old city hall in Dusseldorf before we bombed the shit out of it," said Grumps.

"It's the Hall of Justice," said Stefanie's husband, a man whose mission, it seemed, was to reappear at two-week intervals to reinforce everyone's negative opinions of him.

"No," corrected Nigel. "It is a representation of the ideal wedding chapel where perfect unions are formed."

"Looks like the Hall of Justice to me," said Stefanie's husband.

Mrs. Sandoval leaned closer and said, "What is this Hall of Justice?"

"The international headquarters for the Justice League," said Stefanie's husband like an expert on architectural baked goods.

"The Justice League? A political organization?" said Mrs. Sandoval. "Do they make good cakes?"

"They don't make cakes at all," said Stefanie's husband. "The Hall of Justice houses the Justice League of America, the umbrella organization for many great American superheroes, like Superman, Batman, Wonder Woman, and Aquaman."

Stefanie, hearing her chosen lifelong partner expound so expertly on the topic, turned as red as Superman's cape.

"Why have such a cake at a wedding?" said Mrs. Sandoval.

"Good question," said Stefanie's husband, bouncing on the balls of his feet.

Nigel replied, "The cake is not a Hall of Justice cake. Nothing to do with that building, or superheroes, or the Justice League. How anyone could think such a thing is beyond me."

Stefanie's husband harrumphed, but otherwise, silence prevailed. The rebellion had been quashed.

Jack Watt reentered the room after, perhaps, some time spent in a closet enjoying a good cry. He made a beeline for the controversial dessert. "My, my, that is a superb representation of the Hall of Justice. One of the finest I've seen in cake form. Wherever did you get it?"

"I was just explaining," said Nigel, "that this cake has nothing to do with any Hall of Justice. Any resemblance to that structure is purely coincidental."

"Hey, look what I found," said Stefanie's husband, holding up two figurines. "It's Aquaman and Wonder Woman. They must be getting married in this ideal wedding chapel. Or, just maybe, they arrived by mistake, having confused it with the Hall of Justice to which it bears such an uncanny resemblance."

The doorbell rang.

Nigel ran to the front door like a starving man to a dinner gong.

"Well, Stanley, I didn't expect to see you here," said Nigel to a harried-looking version of the man.

"I said I'd come with the correct figurines," said Stanley, holding up some objects wrapped in plastic.

"Fine. You are just the man I want to see."

"I am?"

"Absolutely. The wedding party has just been admiring your cake."

"Oh, dear," said Stanley, backing away.

Nigel grabbed him by the shoulder. "Everyone wants to meet the creator of that fascinating dessert. But before I introduce you, there's one thing you should know about that cake."

"What's that?"

"A number of guests have gotten into their thick skulls that your cake represents the Hall of Justice, that kind of superheroes' clubhouse."

"They're right."

"No!" said Nigel, seeing Stanley had failed to grasp the situation's nub. "They are not."

"No?"

"Can't be, old man. This is a wedding. Superheroes aren't a motif. Not here, anyway. You need to snatch that rumor by the neck and strangle it," said Nigel, demonstrating how one might go about it if rumors came in the form of small animals.

"Strangle it?" said a horrified Stanley.

"Like you've never strangled before," said Nigel. "Put it down, man. It's got to be done."

"I'm not sure I can do it."

"Of course you can do it. Let 'em know that when you slapped that thing together, superheroes never crossed your mind."

"Is that right?"

"It's got to be right. Superheroes aren't your vibe. You wouldn't know a superhero if it flew out your arse. Just remember that."

Stanley nodded, horizontally at first, then at Nigel's prompting, vertically.

"Great. Superheroes? Not your thing. Play dumb. If anyone can do it, Stanley, you can." Nigel led the baker into the dining room at a brisk trot. "Everyone," he announced to the table of cake-starved diners, "it is my pleasure to announce the arrival of Mr. Stanley Dillard, the baker-artiste of this exquisite cake. Questions have been raised regarding this fabulous cake's *moderne* design. I'm sure Stanley would be happy to answer any and all inquiries regarding this unique dessert. Without further ado, I give you the great Stanley."

Stanley took a half step sideways and froze in place. Somehow, he had detected the presence of his shrouded ex-wife. The effect was that of a deer on a railroad track caught in the headlights of two trains, one from each direction.

"What inspired you to make such a cake?" asked Stefanie's husband.

"Inspired?" squeaked Stanley, sounding like a mouse having an awkward puberty.

"Surely you must have been influenced by something," said Stefanie's husband. "What was it?"

Stanley felt something cold pierce his heart. His ex-wife had just skewered a kung pao chicken bit with her fork.

"The Hall of Justice," blurted Stanley between stabbing pains in his chest.

Nigel made a coughing sound, which he coupled with a rooster kick to Stanley's ankle.

Stanley hopped to one side and shivered a bit. "But no superheroes," he exclaimed. "Superheroes were the farthest thing from my mind when I slapped that thing together."

"The Hall of Justice, but no superheroes?" said Stefanie's husband. "Does that make sense?"

"Superheroes are not my vibe," said Stanley, looking to Nigel. "I wouldn't know a superhero if it flew out my arse."

"Flew out your what?" said Mrs. Sandoval.

"Arse," murmured Stanley.

"What does that mean?"

Stanley didn't know. He knew nothing about what super-heroes typically flew out of. His confidence was ebbing fast.

The doorbell rang.

"Excellent," said Nigel, making a line for the door any bee would be proud of.

Opening the door, a surprised Nigel said, "Good evening, Cam!"

As usual, she looked amazing for a woman of her years—skin stretched and puffed, makeup finely stenciled, hair sparkling like glitter-flaked fiberglass.

Nigel wanted to swab a finger on her skin to see if it returned with a buttercream frosting flavor.

"Where's that man?" said Cam, pushing herself into the entry hall.

"We have several on the premises. Is there a particular one you wish to see?"

Cam spun around. Her casual dress would have been a favorite in the closet of most women, and certain men. Her outsized gestures hinted that she'd come to the party well-primed. The open bottle of wine in her right hand reinforced the notion.

"That baker, baker, caker, maker. You know who."

"You certainly would have received an invite had we known of your interest," said Nigel. "Would you like to congratulate the lucky couple?"

"Lucky couple of what?"

"The newlyweds. We've just had a wedding."

"That's why Stanley is here, is it? I came to get him. This is no place for him."

"I see. I believe he's in the dining room with the wedding party. Wouldn't you like to join us? We're about to have cake. I'm sure the guests would be thrilled to meet you."

"Would they? They must live boring lives." Cam took a swig from the bottle of her foot wine. She widened her eyes while wiping her lips with the back of her hand. "Is that for the wedding?" she said, nodding at the casket.

"Of course," said Nigel. "Why not?"

"Cool. Anyone in there?"

"No, ma'am, but we're expecting a body any time now."

"Dead?"

"Quite."

"That's good, but I'm not waitin' for him. Where's Stanley? Got to get him outta here. Weddings, dead people. There's a cop car out there." Cam took a swig of her wine and then yelled, "Stanley!"

"Walk this way, please," said Nigel, ushering the wobbly singer toward the dining hall. "Everyone, may I have your attention, please?" he announced. "I would like to introduce Ms. Cam Logan."

Reactions varied throughout the room.

Cam, the consummate professional, raised a hand to her forehead in the manner of a salute. Finding that she held a bottle in her saluting hand came as an unpleasant surprise. She swayed a bit before recovering sufficiently to take a swig. "Pleased to meet you all, but I'm just here to haul away the baker," she said.

"You can stay for cake, if you like," said Stefanie. "I'm a fan of your music."

"If you insist," said Cam, waiting for people to insist.

"Please do," said Mrs. Sandoval. "It's too bad our former butler isn't here to meet you. He had a poster of you in his room."

"Did he? Wonderful. Where is he?"

"He's in jail, awaiting trial for attempted murder," said Mrs. Sandoval.

"Wonderful. If you give me his name, I'll send him a shaving kit. Or maybe I should send him a shivving kit. Hah!" The reaction was muted given the relative lack of ex-cons on the guest list. "Don't y'all know a joke when I make one?"

By now, Stanley had placed the bride and groom figurines

artfully between the Hall of Justice structure and the buttercream reflecting pool.

"That's your wedding cake? Whose idea was that?" said Cam. "That there's the Hall of Justice."

"No, no," said Nigel. "Not the Hall of Justice. This is the Heavenly Temple of Marital Bliss, isn't it, Stanley?" He looked around, but Stanley had vanished.

"Who's the lucky couple?" asked Cam.

Abuelita raised a bony finger while draining a flute of champagne.

Jack Watt, having just returned from a stint in the pantry to pull out some hair, halted in the doorway when he saw Cam Logan. He had the look of someone noticing his afternoon picnic had been joined by a rampaging elephant.

"Speaking of the lucky couple, here's our groom," said Mrs. Sandoval, nodding toward a thunderstruck Jack Watt.

Upon seeing him, Cam Logan tilted her head like a cocker spaniel hearing a cricket. She righted her melon and began squinting. "Mack? Is it Mack?" she said.

"You've mistaken me for someone else, I'm afraid. The name's Watt, Jack Watt."

"Don't I know you?" said Cam.

"Have you been to Cincinnati?" said Jack.

"Yes."

"Is it nice? I've heard a lot about their botanical gardens."

"South America. Was it South America? Years ago?"

"Sorry, does not ring a bell. I don't get out much, but I believe I'd remember meeting you. You are?"

"Cam Logan. The singer, Cam Logan."

"The singer, Cam Logan? Is there a dancer as well?"

"I am *the* Cam Logan."

"*The* Cam Logan. Now I'm impressed. I'm Jack Watt, but I'm not *the* Jack Watt. One of scads, I presume."

"I'm not sure I like your attitude," said Cam, taking a swig of foot wine.

"Would you get a load of that! She doesn't like his attitude," spouted the mummy dragon, uncoiling for the first time this evening.

Stanley's ex, the veiled menace, had sat dormant while Stanley's current girlfriend was paraded in with metaphorical trumpets. But dormant doesn't mean idle. She was an expert at brewing a pestilential atmosphere, and she appeared ready for a cloudburst.

Stanley must have seen it coming and had already taken cover. He had prayed that Cam Logan and his ex would never cross paths, but here they were, two of the world's most formidable vipers within striking distance. He'd felt his end was near, and it was. In his current fetal position, he could practically kiss his end goodbye.

"And you are?" said Cam Logan. "Let me guess, Mata Hairy?"

"Listen to this woozy warbler," said the veiled dragon. "Keep it up, slut, and we'll find out what you're made of from the inside out. I'll tell you what I think. Under that bag of pickled skin, you got some botox, some silicone, a gallon of alcohol, and there must be formaldehyde. What you *ain't* got is talent."

"I know who you are. You're Stanley's old bitch. Let me put it to you straight. Stanley is a sorry pimple of a man, a lump of slime, a zit on my ass. And," she paused for a chug of foot wine, "he's ten times the man you deserve. Of course, that makes him one-tenth the man I deserve. But, hey, sometimes a girl needs a man to twist a heel into. If anyone should know that, it's you."

"I know about that too," interjected Abuelita without choosing sides. "There's just a couple of things men are good for, and that's one of them."

Hearing this exchange, Stanley felt the door to his love life slamming shut...ten years later than it should have.

"You listen to me, you polyester pimp muffin," said the dragon. "I gave that sorry-ass piece of whale blubber the wife he deserved. If he wants to be with you, then you clearly don't know how to properly torture the lumptard. My suggestion: Tie him up and sing to him. No auto-tune, just the hits. That ought to shrivel whatever manhood he's got left."

"What are you laughing at?" said Cam to the detective.

"I love a good cat fight," said the detective, his face flapping from side to side as he wiped away tears of mirth.

"Yeah? I make cat food out of types like you."

"You should not threaten an officer of the law."

"You? An officer of the law? Where's that no-good boyfriend of mine? Stanley, get out here."

"Maybe he's run away," said Jack Watt. "I would."

Quite an admission, considering what Jack had not run away from.

Cam lifted up the tablecloth and shouted, "Stanley, come out from under that table. I know you're there. I can hear you sniveling. Time to go home. There's an acid bath and a salt rub waiting for you. If you don't snap to it, I'll leave you to that invisible woman."

Cam Logan left the premises holding Stanley by the ear.

"That woman knows how to treat a man," said Esmerelda.

"Wedding chapel cake? Anyone?" offered Nigel.

24

FIT FOR A FUNERAL

Nigel awoke feeling a certain measure of accomplishment at having done so. Yesterday's wedding with vows properly exchanged and no fatalities, he decided, was cause for self-congratulation. After three days of butlering the Sandovals, Nigel had become an expert at finding bright sides.

He sauntered into Mrs. Sandoval's office the next morning to be received by the top of her head. "Ahem," he announced.

Mrs. Sandoval elevated the coconut. The rims of her eyes matched her scarlet Mountie jacket. "Mr. Nigel, you were told not to serve pizza in this house, were you not?"

"Yes, I was. But the circumstances merited special consideration."

"By circumstances, I assume you mean Abuelita's wedding. A special circumstance, yes, but a circumstance that should have absolutely precluded the serving of pizza. Abuelita spent last night—her honeymoon night—alone, welded to a toilet, blowing out her colon. Her new husband was not allowed within two rooms of her."

"I bet he didn't complain."

"What kind of remark is that?" said Mrs. Sandoval, knowing full well what kind of remark it was. "Your time here, Mr. Nigel, has been eventful in the worst possible ways. I don't see how you can continue to work here. If I don't see a marked improvement by the end of the month, you will be dismissed. I'm letting you know now so you can adjust...or prepare. Do you understand?"

"There is something I should tell you, m'lady."

"Make it good news. Is it good news? I need good news. Does it involve a resignation?"

"No, not at this time. It involves Abuelita's husband. I suspect he may be an assassin."

Mrs. Sandoval fell back in her chair with enough force to cause her Mountie hat to slide off the back of her head. "What? Another one? Are you kidding? What's the story this time?"

"His father had a somewhat checkered history, wives dying in odd ways at opportune times. I'm afraid the son has not fallen far from the family tree. He bears watching."

"And how do you know this?"

"He told me."

"He *told* you? Don't people keep this sort of thing to themselves? How does that even come up in a conversation? 'Nice weather we're having. Dear old dad would have loved it. He was a wife-killer, by the way.' Was that pretty much how it went?"

"Not entirely, m'lady. The important thing is to keep Jack and Abuelita apart until we can ascertain his true intentions. I managed to do it last night, but we have to stay vigilant."

"Wouldn't it have been better to bring this up *before* the wedding? I mean, how long can you keep a newly married couple apart?"

"It may not be so difficult. I've already talked to Jack about it. He's amenable."

"You talked to Jack about it? You talked to Jack, the supposed murderer? You suggested he stay away from the victim for a while, and he agreed? Does that not strike you as being surprisingly cooperative for a murderer? I may have the wrong impression, but I think of murderers as strong-willed, unaccommodating types. You're telling me we've been blessed to have an obliging one?"

"He thinks Abuelita has a heart condition. I've warned him against placing her in an excitative state."

"Oh, now I understand. The murderer has been kind enough to refrain from any activities that might lead to the victim's death. Immensely thoughtful. How lucky we are to have such a well-behaved killer join the family. Aren't we lucky?"

"I'll keep a close eye on him."

"If you think I'll sleep better knowing that you—"

"Excuse me," interrupted Esmerelda, poking her head into the office. "Does anyone know where Papa is?"

"I haven't seen him today," said Mrs. Sandoval. "How about you, Mr. Nigel? Have you seen Mr. Sandoval?"

"No. I ran into him—"

"*Ran* into him?" said an alarmed Mrs. Sandoval.

"Figuratively speaking. I encountered Mr. Sandoval yesterday walking down the drive about an hour before the wedding. He was seeking a quiet outdoor venue suitable for draining a flask. I have not seen him since."

"I'm worried," said Esmerelda. "His brain isn't completely right, you know. He has lapses. The other day he asked me if I'd seen his llama."

"Did you check with Grumps?" asked Nigel. "They were rooming together."

"He was no help. Kept talking about some Englishman by the name of Disgusting Stink-Breath Weasel-Face. Said if he got his hands on the guy, he would rip out his small intestines, fashion them into a noose, and hang the little snot-nosed Limey until his lying British eyes popped out of their sunken British sockets. I have a feeling he was talking about you, Mr. Nigel."

"Sunken sockets? What does he mean by that?"

Esmerelda shrugged. "We've got to find Papa. He's not alto-gether well. He may have roamed jungles for twenty years, but he's not equipped for a place like modern-day New Antigua. He doesn't even Google!"

"Very well," huffed Mrs. Sandoval. "Who's available for a search party? There's me, there's you—"

"There's me," volunteered Nigel.

"There's that detective lady. She might be useful. Not her mother, though. Too creepy. Abuelita and Grumps are of no value."

"There's me," said Nigel.

"There's Jack Watt," continued Mrs. Sandoval. "But he doesn't know his way around town. Besides, Mr. Nigel seems to think he's a murderer."

"Should we notify the police?" said Esmerelda.

"Let's leave that to Mr. Nigel." Mrs. Sandoval turned to Nigel. "Please call that detective that's been hanging around. You two have so much to talk about anyway. Let him know that Valdy has disappeared and we'd like him back. You can also present your latest murderous husband theory, if it makes you happy. The fact that you'll be explaining it while not stuck in a doggie door at 2:00 a.m. might lend your story a certain *gravitas*. Some form of evidence might help as well."

"I will notify the detective of Mr. Sandoval's disappearance."

"One other thing, Mr. Nigel."

"Yes?"

"The body should arrive this afternoon."

"The body, m'lady?"

"The body, the dead body, the one to be buried. It arrives this afternoon. Take care of it."

"Take care of it, ma'am?"

"Of course, take care of it. You're the butler. You should know what to do with a cadaver. You went to a school, didn't you?"

"Yes, m'lady, a butler's academy. Mortuary services were, somehow, absent from the curriculum. Nevertheless, while you're scouring the countryside for Mr. Sandoval, I shall bone up on the subject. Who will be making the delivery?"

"I don't remember who. They shouldn't be hard to identify. They'll be carrying a dead body. Let them in."

"Do you have a preferred location for storing a dead body, m'lady?"

"Gracious, Mr. Nigel. There's an empty casket sitting in the middle of the entrance hall. I suggest you use that."

"Very well."

"One more thing, Mr. Nigel. I want the funeral completed sooner rather than later. Make it on Monday."

"On Monday? Today is Sunday, m'lady."

"Yes, so I've given you an extra day. Use it wisely."

———

With half its population combing the countryside for the stray Mr. Sandoval, the old country club settled into an uncharacteristic serenity. Nigel took advantage of the break by settling into the study's overstuffed executive chair for a few winks. One, maybe two, was all he got before being awoken by the sound of a doorbell. He ran to the peephole and was disappointed to see not a dead body, but a living detective.

"Oh, it's you," said Nigel.

"You needn't sound so disappointed. You have at least one more day of freedom. Tomorrow may be a different story, but today I'm only here to acquire some technical details."

"Let's get on with it then. I'm expecting a body."

"You're expecting somebody?"

"Not *some*body. *A* body. The dead guy."

"The body of Emilio Anguilero?"

"If that's the dead guy, then yeah."

"That's what the casket is for?"

"Look at you! And no one thought you could be a detective. You've earned your trench coat today."

"Never mind the wisecracks," said the detective as he stepped forward to enter. "I've got a few questions for you."

If Nigel was to be the party of the second part in this conversation, he saw no need for the party of the first to enter the house. They were conversing just fine where they stood with the detective outside and Nigel filling the space between the doors. "Ask away. A lot of good it'll do you. I'm innocent, I tell you."

"I'm guessing you take a large shirt and about a thirty-four inseam pants. That about right?"

"Right enough."

"You prefer orange or stripes?"

"I don't believe that's something you need to know."

"Your hat size would be what? About seven and a quarter?"

"I don't know my hat size. What is this anyway? You buying me an outfit for Christmas?"

"Not me, but the penal system likes to know things in advance."

"The penal system? You need to clean those ears, Bub. I told you before, I'm innocent."

"Well, just in case, they like to have things in order," said the slimy detective, clearly enjoying the moment.

"When do prisoners get to wear hats, anyway?"

"Not a hat, precisely. More like a cap. It's only for a certain class of prisoner. What's your favorite food?"

"What? Now you're planning my Christmas banquet?"

"Mr. Blandwater-Cummings, you can't be so naive. These cases take a long time. They drag out. I'm as optimistic as the next guy, but this Christmas is out of the question. I mean, even for the world's fastest murder conviction, capital cases are granted automatic appeal. We're talking two years, minimum."

"Oh, now I get it," said Nigel. He had grown tired of playing the part of annoyed butler. With his employer off the premises, he could drop the veil and act like what he really was—an irate wrongly accused murder suspect. "This is harassment. This is trespassing. Are you going to leave peaceably, or do I need to call the cops?"

"Call the cops? That's rich, Mr. Blandwater-Cummings.

That's rich. Call the National Guard as well, why don't you? How about the French Foreign Legion? How about—"

Had Nigel carried about his person a flatulent toad, he'd have used it to cork that blabbering mouth. Being a toad short, he kicked the detective in the shin.

The blabbering stopped.

For one glorious moment, Nigel reveled in the sweet silence of stunned stupefaction. Then he slammed the door.

If the detective was shocked, Nigel was hardly less so. Applying a fast-moving toe to the shin of the law was not just un-butler-like, it was un-Nigel-like. An unholy array of invectives began filtering through the door. They produced in Nigel a warm self-satisfaction, like that experienced after performing a good deed or eating fine chocolate.

With the screaming detective safely partitioned, Nigel turned to more urgent matters. He needed an officiant for the funeral and decided to contact Reverend Bilcher, his no-show for the wedding. Though unlikely to be available, Nigel had already paid a deposit. Perhaps he could get something for his money.

"Could I please speak to the Reverend Bilcher?"

"He gone. Ain't comin' back."

"Is there someone working in his place? Perhaps someone from his organization?"

"Dis is Breadbox, the good pastor's partner in crime, youse might say, but let's keep dat to ourselves. What you need?"

Nigel recognized the voice, though he'd not previously heard the name. The man's speech patterns—think Bugs Bunny after a pistol-whipping from Elmer Fudd—suggested he'd had a career as a prizefighter in Brooklyn, or possibly the Bronx. The nickname, Breadbox, implied a propensity for attacking the midsection. His opponents, Nigel inferred, had gone for the head and enjoyed considerable success.

"Well, Breadbox, we talked earlier about a wedding the reverend was unable to officiate."

"I remembers you. You from New England."

"Not *New* England. Just England."

"One of dem places, yow, sure. If ya want your money back, ya gotta call the reverend, but he ain't answerin'."

"Yes. Cheers. What I'm calling about now is that I have a funeral to produce and need an officiant. I wondered if he had an affiliate who could fill in."

"I could do dat."

"You, Breadbox?"

"I done funerals before. There was Jimmy Three-Nostrils. I did his just before they never found him again. And then there was Knuckles Houlihan. He had two services, the one I did for the boys and the other one in dat church for his wetsack wife. That church had the service without no body. How you figure a funeral with no body? A miracle, I guess. Dat's the church for ya. This gonna be in a church?"

"No."

"Good. I don't do no church services. Too restrictin'. And then I did a funeral for Crossfire Callo. That was some service."

"Why? What did you do for Crossfire?"

"Well, I was readin' dat t'ing, you know, what they call it where you say da nice t'ings?"

"A eulogy?"

"Dat's right. I was readin' dat oology, and all hell broke loose. People there didn't like me sayin' nice t'ings about Crossfire. My philosophy is once a guy got whacked, you say nice t'ings. Don't matter no more 'cause they ain't around to get the swellhead. But these people—musta been friends and relatives of people what got whacked by Crossfire—and there was a lot of 'em, I mean, Crossfire was a great guy, but he was messy, ya know. That's why they called him Crossfire. Anyways, I was just sayin' a few good words and these people take a 'ception—"

"Excuse me, you said 'the people take a cepshun?'"

"Yea, you know, they took a 'ception. They didn't like the nice t'ings. Anyway, there was practically a brawl right there in the cemetery. I had to knock out a few guys before order was restored. Fortunately, there was about a hunnerd cops there. They always took an interest in whatever Crossfire was doin'. I'm pretty good at keepin' order, myself. I ain't afraid to knock a few heads, if the situation calls for it. Ya think there'll be any roughhousin' at this funeral? I get extra for bodyguard work."

"No, I expect this funeral to be quick and nonconfrontational."

"Closed box?"

"Excuse me?"

"Da box, will it be closed so's you can't see the stiff?"

"We may have it open."

"Really? I never done one like dat. In my experience, da body's pretty chewed up. How'd da mug die?"

"Blunt force trauma to the head. A ball-peen hammer, I've been told."

"Chief," said Breadbox, adopting the tone of a drill instructor after being shot in the foot by one of his recruits. "You serious? Whacked with a ball-peen hammer to the nugget, and you're goin' wit' an open box? Dat is twisted. You seen this stiff yo'self?"

"Yes, I saw him just after death."

"And he looked okay? I mean his head wasn't crack-a-noodle-do'd?"

"No, I didn't even see blood."

"Dat's peculiar. Don't sound like no ball-peen hammer I ever knew."

"Interesting you should say that. My wife suggested the injuries were not consistent with a ball-peen hammer."

"Far be it from me to crawl into your private life but sounds like dat wife knows what she's talkin' about when it comes to busted up heads. I never seen no ball-peen hammered noggin, but I seen a hand...and a knee...and a elbow. In my humble opinion, a ball-peen hammer injury to the head is not consistent with da proper application of an open-box funeral. No, it ain't."

"I'll take that as expert advice. So, Breadbox, can I count on you to say a few words on the dead man's behalf?"

"If dat means dollars in my pocket, sure. What do you know about da man?"

"Nothing. Nothing at all. Nobody does."

"Poifect. Dat's the way I like it. An open field to ex-cise my poetic instindts. You can count on me, Chief."

Just as Nigel concluded terms and conditions with the eloquent Breadbox, the doorbell did what doorbells do. The opened door revealed a significantly overdressed man flicking a smoking cigarette butt at a passing butterfly.

"Oh, Mr. Sandoval?" he said, unbending himself while wafting away the smoke. "May I express our sincere condolences? We have come to deliver your dear, departed loved one." The man handed Nigel a card. "Chip's the name."

"I am not Mr. Sandoval. I'm the butler, Nigel. I'll accept delivery. You can cut the condolences. The body is neither dear nor a loved one to anyone in this house. He just happened to wander by and expire on the lawn."

"Very well. Is Mr. Sandoval or Mrs. Sandoval home? We'll need someone to identify the body."

"No, Mr. Sandoval is not home. He's been lost in the woods since yesterday, and Mrs. Sandoval is out looking for him."

"I see. Would you be able to sign off on delivery?"

"Yes. I thought I made that clear. You've been in this business too long, Chip. You're taking on the characteristics of your freight."

"I'm sorry, sir, but it's customary to get a signature from someone listed on the invoice. Where are we to place the deceased?"

"Right there," said Nigel, pointing. "In the casket, if you don't mind."

"I'm sorry, sir, but we cannot place the body inside the casket. We can place the body beside the casket, if that's okay?"

"Why would that be okay? If you can place the body *beside*

the casket, surely you can place the body *in* the casket. Saves you from bending over."

"Our invoice lists a 5-1-3, delivery of embalmed remains," said undertaker Chip, raising the document. "That is, placing the body in supplied containment, at a place specified by the accepting party within restrictions hereby specified, yadda, yadda, yadda," he said, lowering said document. "Placing a body in a casket would require a 5-2-5, that's mortuarial staging. That's an extra service."

"Could you put the body on top of the casket?"

"Yes sir, we can do that."

"So, if I ask you to put it on *top* of the casket and then I *opened* the casket, the body ends up *in* the casket, doesn't it?"

"Well, technically, no. Under a 5-1-3, the body is to be delivered in the supplied containment carton. Respectfully, sir, I don't think you want the supplied containment carton placed in your lovely casket. Ruins the effect."

"Picture this, Chip. You and your partner there are lifting the supplied containment carton to be placed on top of the casket, which, circumstantially, has just been opened. Suddenly, you stumble—maybe because I've kicked you in the googlies if that helps—and oops, the body rolls out of the supplied containment carton and into the casket. Do you see how something like that might happen, Chip?" Nigel patted the back of Chip's shoulder because Chip seemed the type to appreciate a pat on the back of the shoulder.

"I'll tell you what," said Chip. "It's no skin off my nose. I mean, it's as easy one way as another. But if we do what you want off the record, so to speak, it would just be a body dump. No staging of any kind. You would be responsible for that."

"Of course, absolutely. But at least the body would be in the casket where it belongs."

"You'll need to sign this delivery form stating that we performed our work as specified. You can't complain about the delivery once you've signed this form. It's a release that states we delivered as per *our* orders and *your* guidance. Is that understood?"

"Sure, no problem. Just put the body in the casket," said Nigel, signing Chip's document on the dotted line.

"Very good," said Chip, patting Nigel on the back of the shoulder even though Nigel wasn't one to appreciate a pat on the back of the shoulder. "Open up the casket, and we'll bring in the departed."

Chip yelled to his colleague in the van, "Orloff, we're ready for the body. It's a casket dump."

The two men soon wheeled in a heavy-duty cardboard container that they parked alongside the casket.

"Nice casket," said young Orloff. "Thirty-two-ounce brushed copper, Regency hardware, by Elysium-Hope, I believe."

"Enough of the showroom talk," said the more businesslike Chip. "Ready? One-two-three, dump."

The two lifted and twisted the carton until the body rolled into the casket with a thump-de-thump.

"That's one down, one to go," said Chip. "To the chariot, Orloff."

"Wait a minute," said Nigel.

"No wait-a-minutes," said undertaker Chip. "You signed and that's final."

"I signed for delivery of *a* body, but not *this* body."

"What?"

"I was not expecting an old lady in a blue dress. My corpse was a male, last time I checked."

"You checked?" said Orloff.

"Not anatomically, no, but he wasn't wearing lipstick or a wig."

"Crap!" said Chip. "Lesson learned. Always match the box to the address. This could have been bad."

"I consider it bad already," said Nigel.

"No problem. Nobody's been buried yet. We just put this

body back in its box and get yours out here. We'll get 'er done lickety-split."

Despite the undertaker's glowing optimism, poor Mrs. Steif —her name in life if they'd tagged her right—proved not so willing to reinhabit her carton. One suspected she might have been a crusty old soul, for even as a lifeless shell she put up a fight. But back in her box she went, though in a condition— disheveled wig, bent glasses, and smeared lipstick—she wouldn't have been caught dead in, had she been alive.

Chip and Orloff returned with a body reassuringly tagged as "No name—male." This was more like it. The two body couriers plopped corpse number two into the casket, this time landing with a da-thump-a-dump.

Though reassured by a familiar face, a different issue soon diverted Nigel's attention. "Wait a minute. Where're his clothes?" he asked.

"Did someone pay for clothes?" asked Chip.

"Don't know."

"Did someone bring clothes to the funeral home?"

"Not to my knowledge."

"In that case, he doesn't have any."

"He did have clothes. I saw them. He didn't die naked."

"He can't be buried in those clothes. Wouldn't be legal. Those clothes had to be destroyed."

"But he can't be buried like this. Look at him. For God's sake, he's in a sheet."

"Shroud," said Orloff.

"Fine, a shroud. Is this how you operate? Just dump the body in a shroud and leave?"

"No, it isn't how we operate. It's what you asked for. If you would like a mortician to help with body prep, you can call the number on my card. That's the best I can do."

"But the funeral is tomorrow at noon. Would they have time?"

"Not likely. Maybe someone else."

While Chip and Nigel squabbled over the cadaver's scant wardrobe, Orloff entertained himself by giving No-Name Male the once-over.

"How'd this man die?" said Orloff.

"Blunt force trauma," said Nigel. "A ball-peen hammer to the head."

"A ball-peen hammer?" asked Orloff. "Naw, I wouldn't think. I had an uncle done in with a ball peen. His skull was like a jigsaw puzzle."

Two days ago, Nigel hadn't known what a ball-peen hammer was. Now it seemed that ball-peen hammers ranked even higher than fish for blunt instrument assaults. "You had an uncle killed with a ball-peen hammer? How often does that sort of thing happen?" he asked.

"The mob," said Orloff. "The ball-peen hammer is an old classic. But this guy, no. He took a hit, but not by a ball peen."

"You're the third person to say that," said Nigel. "What do you think he was hit by?"

"Couldn't say, but the mark here indicates something with some texture to it."

"Orloff here is studying forensics," said Chip. "This job gives him a chance to practice his art. He should tell you about that murder case he helped solve. Guy had a gash in his head that turned out to be from a ninety-pound sturgeon. Can you believe the guy was whacked by a fish?"

Nigel, having little time to engage in fish stories, ushered the two toward Mrs. Steif's destination.

Nigel found dressing a dead body to be more pleasant than a conversation with the mother-in-law, but less pleasant than being shocked by an eel. The cadaver seemed as averse to being dressed as Nigel was to dressing it. The two made a bad team, but eventually came to an arrangement.

Having finished the task, Nigel took a moment to reflect on his tumultuous first year as a butler. Of course, with 359 days yet to go, the year might yet smooth itself out, but it had, in his mind, irrevocably earned its tumultuous stripes. The lingering question was whether it might yet plummet to the ranks of horrific or grisly.

From his first moments as a butler dispensing with a stray cadaver, to the latest task of threading that late gentleman's legs into a pair of borrowed trousers, any sense of a soothing routine had, thus far, escaped Nigel's grasp. Old Winpole had preached how the unforeseen, the unexpected, and the unfavorable were to be taken in stride by the competent head servant. The consummate butler, in trying times, must be unflappable. Nigel, admittedly, was flapped. How could he not be? In addition to the hijinks involving Mr. No-Name Corpse, he'd franticly coordinated a wobbly wedding, planned a last-minute funeral, installed a pair of exploding water heaters, survived an electric eel attack, detonated a gas pipeline with accompanying inferno, found and lost a misplaced husband, welcomed a murderous fiancé, and, last but not least, become a murder suspect. In outline form, maybe it didn't sound so bad, but it kept him up at night. That, and all the psssssssting at his bedroom door.

Week two will be better, he told himself.

But he could not rest on his laurels. A corpse, no matter how nattily dressed, needs a hole to be planted in. The tiny backhoe, even after being blown several feet into the air, still functioned. Functioned, as in could still dig a hole while rattling like souvenir kidney stones in an empty beer can.

A great ditch required commemoration of some sort, especially if there's a body in it. Time did not allow for the purchase of a proper gravestone, so Nigel turned to the maintenance shed that was chock full of artifacts from the estate's old golf course days. He waded through the dusty clutter of signs, flags, poles, and fencing—items disappointingly but not surprisingly lacking the best qualities for commemorating the dead. Venturing deeper into the darkest recesses, he spotted something more to his liking—a brass sundial mounted in a cement pedestal. Though nonstandard, this grave marker would serve as poignant reminder, especially when viewed at night, that for the dead, time was not a thing. How better to add a touch of class to a garden being repurposed as a depository for wayward corpses?

Nigel wiped away a layer of dust and grime from the weathered face to uncover a motto encircling the dial. It read, "Always Time for Golf!" A wonderful sentiment had the deceased been a golfer. Nigel decided that he must have been.

"What's up?" said a female voice, coinciding with a poke in the ribs.

Nigel experienced one of those jarring moments when, instead of finding oneself tied to a concrete slab amid leaping flames being gigged with a pitchfork, one finds oneself sprawled on a loveseat in a mansion accompanied by the wife.

"Oh, it's you," said an alarmed Nigel, seeing Annie prepped for another poke. "I was having a lie-down after dressing a dead man and digging his grave. How's your day been?"

"Not good," answered Annie. "Looked all over for Mr. Sandoval. No luck. Mrs. Sandoval is frantic. Stefanie and Esmerelda aren't much better."

"Any clues?"

"Just his backpack and a tray of half-eaten Chinese dinner down by the creek."

"He was kidnapped while eating?"

"I imagine he ate as much as he could stomach. It was the broccoli beef. He probably just moved on, but to where, I don't know."

"You don't think someone picked him up?"

"My theory is that he went out wandering. Think about it.

The man lives like a hobo for twenty years. He comes home to a family he hardly remembers. Everything is different. He's a stranger in a strange house. Having seen what's here for him, he might need some self-time to think things over."

"Like he's a lone wolf."

"You know, when my family used to get together for Thanksgiving—I mean, the whole family with aunts and uncles and cousins and grandparents, the whole shebang—after about six hours, people would start to disappear. They'd take walks, drift off to quiet rooms, hide in closets, whatever. You get my drift?"

"You mean your mother."

"What?"

That "What?" had an edgy, switchblade quality to it. Nigel felt his spine constricting. "She would take walks, your mother, would she?"

"No. I meant that people get overstimulated in busy social settings. This may be why Mr. Sandoval has gone away. For him, leaving the house for a night, or a week, or a month is no big deal. Maybe he'll come back, or maybe he's decided he doesn't want to spend the rest of his life here."

"So, you don't think he's been abducted?"

"Who would do that? And why? I suspect he's wandering around out there. You saw him before the wedding? What was his state of mind?"

"Whatever his state of mind was, it was likely to change because he carried with him a bottle of state-of-mind changer. He was going to wait out the wedding. He said he didn't mind his ex-wife getting married, but he didn't want to see it."

"I suppose that's reasonable," said Annie. "Tell me, what do you suppose went on between Mr. Sandoval and Mrs. Sandoval the other night after they left your room?"

"Oh, I don't know. Man-and-wife stuff?"

"You think? Mr. Sandoval is advanced in years and seems pretty frail."

"He may be a wreck of a man, but a wreck of a man is still a man. And Mrs. Sandoval is still a woman."

"What do you mean by that?" said Annie, sharpening her tongue.

"She is, isn't she? At least, she still acts like one."

"What do you mean by *that*?" said Annie.

Nigel realized he'd struck some kind of nerve. Silly place for a nerve, but he'd pull back the drill nevertheless. "I just mean the old gal hasn't given it up yet. Still polishes the hooves and coifs the mane. You know, the feminine habits that any thoroughly disinterested person might notice. Why this interest in their love life?"

"The state of their relationship might give insight into why Mr. Sandoval would leave or stay. Put yourself in his place. Would settling down with the old wife be a sunny day at the beach, or a slow roast in hell?"

"I see what you mean."

"And what does Mrs. Sandoval know about that map on his back? She must have heard us talk about it in your room. Did she know about it before?"

"No, she didn't."

"How can you know that?"

"I believe the tattoo was obtained in Brazil," said Nigel, enjoying the rare opportunity to know something his wife didn't.

"Why Brazil?"

"The tattoo has a kind of treasure emblem on it with the inscription, *tesouro*. I looked it up. It means 'treasure' in Portuguese. I suppose Mr. Sandoval could have gotten it in Portugal, but since we know he just wandered back from Brazil, let's assume he got it there. Therefore, Mrs. Sandoval wouldn't have known about it."

"This inscription, are you sure it's not moles?"

"Ah, now that you mention it, could be. Portuguese moles."

"Right," said Annie. "Supposing Mrs. Sandoval had never

seen it, could she still know its secret? Does she know what Mr. Sandoval might be hiding?"

"If she does," said Nigel, "she knows more than Mr. Sandoval does. He has no idea what the map means."

Nigel rested his weary gray matter while Annie's tireless cogs continued to gyrate.

"Changing topics," she said, "did you see that detective today?"

"Yes, he came by, as gristly as ever, I'd say. If I'm to believe him, he'll have a warrant for my arrest tomorrow."

"I told you to forget about that. Did you tell him about Mr. Sandoval?"

"Mr. Sandoval?"

"Yes, about Mr. Sandoval being a missing person. Mrs. Sandoval said you were to call the detective."

"Ah, I don't recall that I happened to mention anything about Mr. Sandoval."

"Wait," said Annie.

Why did Nigel, upon hearing the word 'wait,' suddenly want to run away? He had known that word for a long time and was pretty clear on the definition, yet when Annie said it the way she did, waiting was not what came to mind

"Let me get this straight," continued Annie. "You, the last known contact for Mr. Sandoval, talked to a detective but neglected to mention that he was missing? You, who are also the prime suspect for a murder. Tell me you didn't do that."

"I didn't do that."

"Oh, thank God."

"The murder, I mean. The other thing I did."

"How could you do that?"

"Sorry," said Nigel. "One can hardly be expected to think of mislaid people while being fitted for the electric chair. I mean, I'd have gabbed about the vanishing Sandoval until I was blue in the face if that detective hadn't insisted on taking orders for my last meal. I got distracted."

"Nigel, Nigel, Nigel, you are now not only the prime suspect in a murder case, but also the primary person of interest in a missing person case. Until one of these cases is resolved, you are, as the police say, in deep shit."

"You told me not to worry about the murder case. You're changing your mind?"

"No, but when they've filed you as a murder suspect, you don't want to hand them addendums. You should be on your best behavior."

"Really? I probably shouldn't have kicked him then."

"You kicked the detective?"

"Just a little bit, in the shin. He'll survive."

"Nigel, Nigel, Nigel."

This saying of Nigel three times followed by a disgusted look was some kind of evil spell, probably conferred from her mother. Wherever it came from, it worked. Nigel's bottom heated up just as if he'd taken smacks from his mum.

"You said you dressed the body. Where is it?"

"In the casket, last I saw. Why?"

"I want to take a look." Annie didn't wait for permission. In an instant she was up and striding for the casket with Nigel in her wake.

"Before you look, I need to warn you. I don't want you to be shocked by what you see—"

"Nigel, I've seen dead bodies in all kinds of conditions. Nothing here is going to shock me."

"I know, but I just want to let you know beforehand. The body—"

Annie popped the hood.

"Nigel, you didn't," she said upon seeing the body. "First the wedding and now the funeral?"

"I kind of wanted to bury the memory."

"You should have put the cake in there as well."

"It's not so bad, really," said Nigel. "The green pinstripes give him a little color. Goes with his complexion."

Annie let out a snort. "You even used the tie with the socks on it."

"Goes with the suit."

"A red rubber nose would go with that suit."

"Gastrick didn't have any for some reason."

"Okay," said Annie, stepping away from the casket. "Now I have to compose myself."

"That's funny," said Nigel. "You're composing while he's decomposing."

"Maybe *you* should wear the red nose." She stepped back up to the casket, reached her hand around the corpse's neck, and wrenched his head to the side.

"What are you looking for?" asked Nigel.

"This. The point of impact."

"Ah, I see," said Nigel. "In my opinion, the impact was made by a non-smooth article, something with texture."

"That is a very astute observation," said Annie, poking the area at the back of the head.

"I also believe he was not killed with a ball-peen hammer. A blow by a ball-peen hammer would have rendered his skull into a jigsaw puzzle."

"A jigsaw puzzle?"

"You know, pieces."

"Those are intelligent observations," said Annie. "Who gave them to you?"

"Orloff. Orloff and Breadbox."

"Orloff and Breadbox? Is that a comedy team?"

"Orloff, the mortician's assistant, and Breadbox, the eulogist."

"You've been talking to the experts?"

"Do you concur with their expert opinion, doctor?"

"I find myself in general agreement with Orloff and Breadbox. A ball-peen hammer makes no sense at all. Whatever hit him struck with speed, not weight. A heavy object, like a ball-peen hammer, carries a crushing power behind it. That's not evident here. This was done by a lighter object at high velocity. This man did not die from a crushing blow, but from a hematoma—a secondary effect from a blow to the head, probably from a projectile."

"Brilliant, Dr. Annie. You should form a company—Annie, Orloff, and Breadbox: Forensic Analysts."

"Unfortunately, none of this tells us who did it."

"No, but eliminating a ball-peen hammer as the weapon of choice means they can hold off fitting me for an electric skullcap."

"They don't use electricity anymore," said Annie. "Too cruel."

"Someone needs to tell that to the eels."

25

BUTLER OR NOT, HERE WE BURY

The flowers arrived at ten. Breadbox, the officiant, arrived at eleven-thirty. The tequila hour arrived at noon. Nigel had not arrived at all.

These events, arriving as they had without a butler to deal with them, left Mrs. Sandoval less than jolly. The wedding had been a rather rocky affair, which was no surprise considering the collection of livewires at the heart of it. This funeral, by contrast, where nothing much depended on the outcome, should have been a relaxed, pleasant occasion. But an increasing gall built within Mrs. Sandoval at being put in such a somber, dour mood.

Where is that damn butler? Mrs. Sandoval asked herself as she sat tequila-less in her office.

"I haven't seen the damn butler," said a husky voice that seemed to materialize from within her ears.

The startled Mrs. Sandoval reared back on her chair expecting to see a ghost. She saw one. The veiled dragon lady had materialized at her office door.

"Looks like it's going to be a nice day for a funeral," said the shrouded, sunglassed head. "Perhaps your damned butler has met with a dreadful accident. Wouldn't that be just awful?"

"It certainly would," said the shaken Mrs. Sandoval. "He's in charge of the funeral."

"Whoever put that man in charge should be buried along with the body."

"I beg your pardon?" said Mrs. Sandoval.

"Hmmmm," said the dragon spirit before disappearing.

Nigel had been right. The lady rankled when she spoke. Mrs. Sandoval scarcely had time to blow the tension out her nostrils before Breadbox knocked on her office door.

"Yo, sorry to interrupt lady, but it's near to one o'clock. I gotta be out by two, so we need to get this t'ing started if it's all right wid you."

"Very well. The butler is supposed to be in charge, but he's disappeared. I suppose I can round up the mourners, and we can get this over with."

"May I have a word wi't you about the deceased? Let me be da foist to say, I am truly sorry for your loss, ma'am."

"That's nice of you, but don't waste your breath. I'm just throwing the funeral."

"Very generous of you, ma'am. Did you know da dead guy well?"

"Nope. Not at all."

"Can you tell me anyt'ing about him?"

"Nope. Don't know anything about him."

"I understand he died by a ball-peen hammer to the head. Is that correct?"

"Could be."

"A most unfoitunate accident."

"Accident? If it was an accident, I'd say not only unfortunate, but unprecedented. If you'll excuse me, I'll corral the mourners. Give me ten minutes."

"Yes, ma'am. If you's to be so kind, where will the funeral take place?"

"We'll just gather around the casket. It'll be a stand-up funeral."

Breadbox looked concerned. "A stand-up funeral? You mean, I need jokes?"

"I mean the mourners will be standing."

"Dat's a relief. I'm short of material as it is."

"We'll have a brief ceremony beside the casket, and then we'll move it outside to the gravesite. Can you double as a pallbearer?"

"For ten extra, sure. One more t'ing, Miss."

"Yes?

"I saw some broad, looked like a mummy with sunglasses. Is she gonna be at da funeral?"

"I suppose. Why?"

"She scary, that's all. I'll have to keep my eye off her when giving da oology, or I be gettin' da shakes."

Breadbox drifted off, presumably to prepare an information-free eulogy, while Mrs. Sandoval headed upstairs to roust the inmates. Having corralled the herd and driven it downstairs, she disappeared. In a fit of propriety, she had taken the time to lock the liquor cabinet, but not before a couple of lightening rounds with Jose Cuervo. A refreshed Mrs. Sandoval reappeared to the awaiting mob of the usual suspects—Stefanie and husband, Abuelita, Grumps, Esmerelda, Mr. Sandoval, and Annie with mummy. Only Nigel and Jack Watt, presumably on one of his walks, were missing.

Mrs. Sandoval waddled up to the casket and opened the lid. "Begin," she declared to Breadbox, who was standing alongside.

"Don't he look peaceful? That is one sharp suit. It does my heart good to see a man meet his maker in some fine threads and an unbroken face."

Mrs. Sandoval turned to the crowd. "I'm happy to announce that officiating today's funeral, we have Breadbox."

Before Breadbox had spoken a word, the doorbell rang.

Mrs. Sandoval opened the door hoping to see Nigel ready to assume his role as funeral manager, a role she'd happily hand over as soon as she'd lopped off one of his appendages. She was disappointed.

"Oh, it's you, Detective. What's the news?" asked Mrs. Sandoval.

"The news?" asked the detective, standing in front of two uniformed officers.

"About Mr. Sandoval?"

"What about Mr. Sandoval?"

"Haven't you been out looking for him? Didn't you talk to the butler yesterday?"

"I did, but not about Mr. Sandoval. What's this about Mr. Sandoval? Is the butler trying to pin the murder on him?"

"Mr. Sandoval has been missing for over a day," said an increasingly distraught Mrs. Sandoval. "The butler was supposed to tell you. I thought you were searching for him."

"I know nothing of this. We are here for that butler, Mr. Nigel Blandwater-Cummings."

"You can come in and wait. He's out just now."

"What? He's out? Out where?"

"I don't know. He didn't say."

"So, Mr. Sandoval disappeared and now the butler is missing. This is very suspect. I will have my man call this in immediately." The detective stretched his neck to view the motley gathering around the casket. "So, what's going on here? A party?"

"A funeral for that dead man. Come in and join us. The more, the merrier, but we need to get on with it."

"Very well," said the detective. "This is Officer Blake and Officer Boykin. I promise we'll be unobtrusive."

The officers took up positions behind the crowd as they faced the casket and Breadbox at the center of the entrance hall.

Mrs. Sandoval rejoined the crowd and commanded, "Step on it, Breadbox."

"We are gathered here today on this solemn occasion," he enunciated in a loud clear voice, "to mark the passing of this man...this man..." Breadbox gestured toward the man, who offered no response. "Excuse me," said Breadbox, bending toward Mrs. Sandoval, "what's this man's name?"

"I don't know," said Mrs. Sandoval. She turned to the crowd. "Anybody know this man's name?"

"What man?" said Grumps.

"Just a moment," shouted back the detective, retrieving a paper from inside his trench coat. "Emilio Anguilero."

"Thank you, Detective," shouted Mrs. Sandoval. "And just think, that butler said you were good for nothing." She twirled a pointed finger.

Breadbox looked confused but proceeded. "This man... Emily-o Angle-io, eh, what he said, was, as far as we know, a fine man. We gather here today to commiserate his life. Does anyone have some kind words to say about this man? Anyone?"

Had this been a nighttime event, there would have been crickets. As it was, the grandfather clock stood tall. Tick-tock.

"Anyone at all?" said Breadbox. "Anything? Doesn't have to be much, a Bible story, perhaps?"

Esmerelda raised her hand.

"You there," said Breadbox. "Spill it."

"He was killed on the night of a new moon."

"Now we're talking," said Breadbox. "Killed on the night of a new moon. That tells us something about the man. What does that tell us?"

The listless mourners blinked their eyes and shifted their weight from one leg to the other. Some twice.

"Tells us he weren't no werewolf," said Breadbox. Clearly, he was an experienced professional. "We also know he ain't no vampire 'cause he stayed right there in that coffin. Anything else? Anyone?"

"He had a frog in his mouth," shouted Mrs. Sandoval.

"And a toad," added Abuelita.

"This I didn't even know," said Breadbox. "Now, that's some interesting facts. I never know'd anyone died with a frog and a toad in his mouth. I once know'd a dead man had a canary in his mouth, but a frog and a toad? Never. That's a new one. Wonder what it means?" He stroked his lantern jaw before continuing. "How a man dies can say a lot about how he lived. We find dis man here died the night of a new moon with a pair of reptiles in his mouth. What does this say about the man? I'm going to say it indicates he was a dedicated family man, loved his mother, and was a pillar of da community. How's dat? And he loved dogs." He let loose a broad smile, which might have been blinding if not for all the gaps. He then turned to the cadaver and shot him with his finger as if to say, "Gotcha, buddy."

Turning toward the crowd for the big finish, he continued. "One more t'ing I can say about our dear departed is dat he wasn't done in with no ball-peen hammer to the head. A pea brain can see that. This is a fine-lookin' corpse. No ball-peen hammer here. We ain't morons, is we?"

The question froze the listless crowd. Eyeballs rotated about in their sockets searching for Nigel as they tended to do in this house when imbeciles or morons were mentioned.

"Anyone have anything to add?" asked Breadbox. "Fine. I now, by the power vested in me, declare this man dead and gone to the maker of his choice. Let bygones be bygones. May he rest in peace. Amen."

Nigel had grossly underestimated the time to get there and back. He got up early thinking he needed about three hours. The poor little excavator, which he'd reckoned could go about five miles per hour, must have been clanking along at about three. The entire expedition had taken almost seven hours. Still, it had been worth it.

He turned the tiny excavator off the highway toward the Sandoval estate. A couple minutes later, he steered off the road and into a small clearing where he killed the clattering engine. A gentle breeze rustled through long grass and shuffled fallen leaves as birds sang in the sunshine. Nigel heard none of it. After seven hours of the excavator's clamorous cacophony, his offended ears had exchanged hearing sounds for generating them. His head vibrated from the inside with an angry buzz.

After dismounting from the bouncy metal insect, Nigel found the solid earth shakier than he had remembered. He reached a palsied hand into his mouth and extracted a bothersome nugget from under his tongue. He placed the foreign body, a crown that had shaken loose a mile back, into his pants pocket.

His bones ached, the world quivered, and his martyred cell-phone lay crushed along the shoulder of a country road, and yet, he was elated. He placed a hand on the dirt-encrusted, cast iron pot that was his prize. It had been where old Mr. Sandoval's back had told him it would be...kind of. That is, once Nigel determined the map pertained not to the current estate but to the old Sandoval house that had been destroyed in a fire many years ago.

Even with that revelation, the search had not been simple. The property was now abandoned, fenced off, and overgrown, with only slabs of cement indicating the former habitation. Nigel had ruled out that 18p dealt with parsecs. That would have required interstellar, warp-speed travel—unlikely for old Mr. Sandoval. He speculated that p meant paces, an imprecise but traditional unit for buried treasure maps.

On site, he matched the bare foundation to the structure on the tattoo. But, after several unsuccessful excavations, he surmised the tattoo might have been directionally flipped. Perhaps the tattooist had been looking in a mirror or had used a reversed stencil. Either way, the treasure lay toward the outer reaches of the pelvis rather than the coccyx.

With this hypothesis, Nigel went to work excavating a broad semicircular swath. At a depth of less than two feet, pay dirt announced itself with a clank. He maneuvered the excavator's scoop underneath the foreign object and lifted out a dirt-encrusted cauldron—round, black, and mysterious. As it turned out, the pot depicted on the map was not metaphorical, but a close representation of the genuine article. The ancient kettle was capped with a lid, which could not be pried open with finger-nails or keys, meaning the contents remained a mystery. The pot was so heavy, he carried it home using the excavator's scoop as a satchel.

Nigel stood back and admired the pot, not for its physical attributes or its promise of riches, but for the solid detective work it represented. He imagined the excitement to come when he presented the lost treasure to its rightful owners, the Sandovals.

As he remounted his rickety metal insect, a large SUV zoomed past. Behind glass the color of basalt, Nigel could see neither driver nor passenger. However, based on a rhinestone-bejeweled script that stretched from rear wheel to front headlight spelling out the name Cam Logan, he believed the driver to be Cam Logan. If not Cam Logan, it was Cam Logan's biggest fan not named Cam Logan.

Cam Logan barreling down this road made no sense. But nothing about her ever did.

26

OLD FRIENDS, DEAD FRIENDS

Annie had heard of certain unprincipled comics who, hoping to bolster their *cachet*, salted their audience with paid laughers. Listening to Breadbox's eulogy, she felt like one of those except she was not getting paid and she was not there to laugh but to mourn. Not a great gig. Since the departed was an unknown quantity, the presented material lacked a certain immediacy, in her opinion. She used the time to consider the unanswered questions surrounding the deceased's demise. Unfortunately, Breadbox's eulogy, as entertaining as it was, failed to provide the grist for any new theories. Then, as pallbearers were being sorted, the doorbell rang.

Everyone knew of the butler's absence because Mrs. Sandoval had made it a theme. The crowd crackled with excitement at the prospect that Nigel, oblivious to his master's rage, stood behind the door.

With each dingdong, Mrs. Sandoval stiffened but held herself in check, allowing the free flow of rings to underscore the lack of a door-answering butler. Eyes opened wide, tongues licked lips, and hands pressed against hands as the door swung open to expose the victim.

"My goodness, where have you two been?" asked Mrs. Sandoval.

The battle royale would have to wait because standing at the door was, no matter how hard one squinted, not Nigel. Instead, a ragged Mr. Sandoval huffed while a tattered Stanley puffed. The pair looked as though they'd run through a briar patch before being caught by a badger.

"Have you two been out on a bender?" asked Mrs. Sandoval, as if she disapproved.

"Kidnapped," panted Stanley.

The detective pushed his way through the crowd to secure a more advantaged position. "Kidnapped?"

"Kidnapped by who?" asked Mrs. Sandoval.

"Whom," corrected Mr. Sandoval.

"Kidnapped by *whom*?"

"Cam," said Stanley. "After we left here Saturday evening, she chained me up—"

"Chained you up?" said the detective. "With what?"

Stanley often hesitated to speak up because he feared being the dumbest one in the room. He now paused to commemorate the passing of a baton, then replied, "Chains."

"Hmmmm," murmured the detective.

"She chained me up in her car, and later, when she saw Mr. Sandoval, she chained him up." Stanley paused in case the detective had another question. He did not. "She had us trapped. We escaped this morning."

"Let me get this straight," said the detective. "Cam Logan, the female country star, has been holding the two of you against your will? Cam Logan, the one with the golden hair and that mansion up near No Way? The Cam Logan that sings that song, 'Hydrating for You'? That Cam Logan?"

"No," said Mrs. Sandoval. "'Hydrating for You' was by Lauren Lamb. Cam Logan sang 'Greasy Backhand'."

"I thought that was Tammy Gobel," said Stefanie. "Cam

Logan sang, 'Cocoa Butter Cowboy,' or was it 'My Lanolin Lover'?"

"I don't care who sang what song," said the detective. "What I want to know is how one small woman could hold two able-bodied men against their will. How old is she? Like fifty-five?"

"Maybe, but she doesn't look a day over forty-five," said Mrs. Sandoval. "She probably uses that moisturizer made from platinum dust and goat poop."

"I don't care about song titles or moisturizers. I want these two gentlemen to explain how they were held against their will by a middle-aged, female country singer."

"She's the spawn of the devil, she is," said Stanley, sounding like an ancient mariner.

"She'd give that first wife of mine a run for her money, I'll tell you that," said Mr. Sandoval.

"What's that supposed to mean?" cackled Abuelita as her head spun around on its stalk. "Spawn of the devil, my ass. You ain't seen nothin' yet."

"Just a minute," hissed the veiled dragon lady, appearing amongst the crowd like a she-demon sprouting from hell. "I don't like to hear this term, 'spawn of the devil' tossed around in such cavalier fashion. This gutter-slime country singer, Cam Logan, only wishes she were a spawn of the devil. She's not worth a hellhound's poop, I assure you of that."

"I believe that lady knows what she's talkin' about," said Breadbox.

"An Englishman," said Grumps. "If you want a real spawn of the devil, look for an Englishman. To rid the world of such a menace, you must drive a stake through its heart and that's just for a start. Any Englishmen here?"

No hands went up.

Grumps huffed.

"We can't just stand around discussing the devil's spawn," said Stanley. "Cam could be coming as we speak. We need to marshal our forces and prepare our defenses. We may not have much time."

"Calm down," said the detective. "We have three officers of the law here. A middle-aged, female country singer is hardly a threat. If you wish to file a complaint against her—"

"File a complaint?" said Stanley. "After everything she did to us?"

"What did she do?"

"She chained us to a distilling pot and demanded we hand over a map of some sort. We didn't know what she was talking about."

"Right, and what else?"

"She drank wine in front of us and wouldn't give us any, most of the time."

"But some of the time she would?"

"Yes, but only a little."

Annie watched this scene from the shadows while trying to piece things together. The mysteries were certainly stacking up faster than the clues. The big revelation was that Cam Logan knew something about a map and was desperate to get her manicured talons on it. One could only suppose that the map in question was the one on Mr. Sandoval's torso. But, while Cam knew *of* a map, she apparently had no idea that it came in tattoo form. How did she know about the map, and did she know what the treasure was? This wasn't Annie's case, but she was already envisioning a friendly interrogation of Cam.

"I hates to interrupt this brilliant police work, but we need to get this man buried," said Breadbox. "I need some pallbearers. Raise your hand to volunteer."

While Breadbox counted hands and worked out positions, the haggard Mr. Sandoval stumbled up to casket's edge to view the body. The pallbearers encircled the casket, and Breadbox was poised to close the lid, when Mr. Sandoval said the most interesting thing.

"I know this man."

One could have heard a pin drop if not for the sound of heads spinning.

Mrs. Sandoval was the first to speak. "How do you know this man? From where?"

"Not sure," said Mr. Sandoval. "In my past. Not my youth, but sometime later." He knocked a fist against his dented cranium. "There're memories in here that don't want to come out. What's this man's name?"

"What was his name again?" called out Mrs. Sandoval.

"It was...give me a moment," said the detective. "Emilio Anguilero."

"Doesn't sound right to me," said Mr. Sandoval. He bent over to look closely at the corpse's face. "Does he have a tattoo? On his arm, maybe?"

All eyes looked at all the other eyes. All the other eyes were blank.

"We could look," said Esmerelda in a spasm of practical thought.

"Good, Essie. Take a look," said Mrs. Sandoval.

Esmerelda stepped up to the waxy figure in the green pinstripes. She hesitated before backing away. "This seems like police work. Doesn't the detective know if there's a tattoo?"

"I don't catalog tattoos unless they have relevance to a case," said the detective.

"I believe we've established relevance," said Stefanie. "Go to it, Detective."

Stepping up to the body, the detective asked, "Which arm?"

"Try the left," said Mr. Sandoval. "Then try the right."

"His left or my left?"

"Take your pick."

The left arm revealed nothing. He pulled back the sleeve for the right arm and *voila!* "A snake," said the detective.

"No, not a snake," said Mr. Sandoval. "I remember now. It's an eel. His name is Anguilero—in Spanish that means something like eel person. He was called Eel. I still can't place him, but he gives me a bad vibe. Maybe it's because his name is Eel. Or maybe it's because he's dead. Or maybe it's that suit. I don't know." He sat down at the base of the casket stand, rubbed his dented head, and set about to remember a man named Eel.

Mr. Sandoval wasn't the only one rubbing a body part. The room was alive with stroked chins, scratched scalps, wrung hands, and fingered temples, all for the purpose of unlocking the inner Sherlocks. This revelation, the connection between the long-lost family member and the unknown corpse, had everyone reviewing the facts.

Annie, as one might expect, was a few lengths ahead of the pack. That said, she didn't have this figured out by a long shot. One now had to wonder about the timing of Mr. Sandoval's re-entry into society, coinciding as it did with the mysterious murder of an old colleague at the estate. Even more puzzling was the issue of geography. How did two men, acquaintances separated by decades and thousands of miles, turn up unexpectedly at the same location? Coincidence? Sure. Annie would happily drink a toast to such a miracle except for the fact that one had been murdered.

But Annie was not completely clueless. She knew something about this Emilio Anguilero. He had been on the Brazil expedition when Mr. Sandoval disappeared. He was one of two people to submit affidavits declaring their belief that Mr. Sandoval was dead. His help had undoubtedly been solicited by Abuelita's previous fiancé, the evil lawyer. The same lawyer who'd planned to marry Abuelita, kill her, and claim her inheritance.

Annie had a lot to think about. These new revelations combined with what she already knew placed the crosshairs directly on Mr. Sandoval as suspect number one. On the one hand, she could easily concoct scenarios in which Mr. Sandoval might have had a motive to kill. On the other, she had known many murderers, and Mr. Sandoval wasn't one. Or, if he was, he was the most brazen and cunning she'd ever come across.

Of course, the other great revelation of the day was Cam

Logan's knowledge of a map. This kind of loopy factoid was what Annie referred to as a screwball, and this one came with hair grease on it. Nutty as it was, she knew not to ignore a pitch just because it came from left field. But still, Cam freakin' Logan, the country singer with the electric eel. And, just five paces eastward lay the mortal remains of a man, name of Eel, with a tattoo of an eel. It made one think, and that's what Annie was doing.

The rest of the congregation, being composed of types who required stimulation for thinking, continued to rub, scratch, wring, and finger the pertinent parts until the door was flung open.

Jack Watt, upon surveying the crowd of self-massaging thinkers, called out in his cheerful way, "Who died?"

Several heads and fingers motioned toward the casket.

"Oh," he said.

Mr. Sandoval, who had been in deep thought, stroking both dented and undented portions of the braincase, arose from the floor and carved a path toward Jack. He stopped just inside his personal space and looked him dead in the eye.

Jack's eyes, by contrast, shifted to the left, then the right, as if looking for a referee to step in.

"Mack?" said Mr. Sandoval.

Jack's brow furrowed.

Annie moved closer to see if there might be perspiration.

"Mack? Is that you?" said Mr. Sandoval.

"Don't you mean Jack?"

"Mack," said Mr. Sandoval. "Mack Wynn, isn't it?"

"If by Mack Wynn you mean Jack Watt, then you've got me right down to the socks."

Mr. Sandoval stepped back and pulled at his face, disappointed that he could no longer trust his own memory.

Annie suspected his memory was better than he gave it credit for. The name Mack Wynn had struck a bell. He was the submitter of the second affidavit. To recap, Mr. Sandoval and the two men who had recently declared him dead had, after twenty years apart, arrived at the Sandoval estate seemingly independently. Of course, the declared dead man was alive and one of the declarers was dead but, dead or alive, somehow they had reunited twenty years after their failed Amazon expedition.

Of course, the bull's-eye that had been on Mr. Sandoval's back now had a companion piece to go on Jack Watt's (or Mack Wynn's) back. The fact that Jack was the only one of the triplets to escape a murder attempt suggested he might need to explain a few things.

"You remember Eel?" asked Mr. Sandoval, hoping to find a shard of his memory that could be trusted.

"Eel?" repeated Jack Watt. "Ah, yes. Slender creature, swims in the sea, not good eating, too fishy."

"No, I mean our guide, Eel, the one who took us down the Amazon."

"Eel, the guide?" asked Jack Watt, rolling his eyes upward while tapping his chin. "I went on so many trips."

Annie could see the dillydallying, the stall, hoping for a way out. She had seen it a million times—a man struggling not to lie while avoiding the truth.

"There was this trip," Jack mumbled. "Over twenty years ago, I think."

"Yes! Yes! You were there. You were a financial partner. There was Eel, the guide; and me; and Dig, the archaeologist. We looked for the lost city of Kubao."

"Kubao? Yes, I recall." Jack pushed his head forward for a closer look at the man. "Valdy? Is it you, Valdy? How could it—"

Mr. Sandoval puffed up as if he had an air pump connected to his heel. "Yes, it's me. You remember. We remember. I thought I'd forgotten everything about those days, but I remember you, and I remember Eel."

"That's incredible, Valdy. Fantastic. How long have you been alive? Am I the last to know?" asked Jack Watt.

Fantastic it may have been, but Jack had the look of someone hit between the eyes with a sock full of marbles. He was genuinely surprised, make no mistake about that. But surprise comes in many varieties. There's joyful surprise, angry surprise, disappointed surprise, and many others. Jack seemed, more than anything, to be in the shock-surprised category.

Annie noticed Jack glancing toward Abuelita, perhaps feeling self-conscious about having just married his old friend's ex-wife. Or maybe he wondered what her reaction would be, learning of this connection to her ex. If she cared, she didn't show it.

The joyful reunion of old colleagues quieted quickly, as if a 500-pound gorilla had just taken a seat in the corner.

"Seriously," said Jack Watt, trying not to look serious. "How long have you been back in circulation?"

"I was away quite a while," said Mr. Sandoval. "I got back here on Wednesday."

"On Wednesday, you say? The same day I arrived. My, my, isn't that a coincidence?" Jack Watt had that knock-me-over-with-a-feather look. In fact, it was worse than that. He stumbled over to the sofa and fell into it without the aid of a feather. "I didn't think you were alive," he said.

"That's too bad. A little marital advice from me could have saved you a lot of misery."

"I certainly didn't connect you with this place."

Ah, but Jack knew more than he was letting on. The death certification papers would have contained Abuelita's name and this address. He should have had no trouble connecting his old friend to the asylum. In Annie's experience, men that have two names can't be trusted, and Jack Watt/Mack Wynn was proving the rule.

It would have been fun to materialize out the woodwork, expose the con, and demand an explanation. But that's not how cases are solved, not if you want convictions. Confrontations work in books and movies, but in real life, keeping eyes open and beak to the ground was how to pull up the worms. Besides, the afternoon had fairly swarmed with revelations. Who knew what the evening might bring?

"It's wonderful we had this little reunion," said Breadbox. "But if youse wants my help putting this man in the ground, we better hurry it up."

Twenty more minutes in the tiny excavator and Nigel had kerchuggathumped his way to the estate entrance. Rattling up the drive, he noticed Cam Logan's SUV parked off to the side a good 200 yards from the house. Why it should be parked there and not, say, in front of the house was yet another Cam Logan oddity he would let slide. He clattered past with his precious cargo on down to the garage.

Once inside, Nigel turned the scoop downward until the pot rolled out. The four-foot fall to the pavement produced a seismic thud that jolted him through his seat. He slid down to examine the pot lying at the center of a network of radial cracks in the cement.

The impact had shaken off the dirt crust encasing the surface of the object. Nigel reexamined the lid, which was so tightly fitted that hardly a seam existed to facilitate its removal. Either by design or by some decades-long chemical process, the lid had become one with the pot. The thing could have been smashed into a building, and the lid would have stayed put. No less than an acetylene torch was needed. Fortunately, he knew where to get one and the man who could use it. Stanley, it appeared, was good for more than just Hall of Justice cakes.

Nigel rubbed the black cauldron. No genie appeared. He put his ear to the filthy thing and tapped it with the blade of a screwdriver. He heard no hollowness. The pot must be filled to the brim. He was determined not to think about gold, but gold was what he thought about. After all, what were buried pots discovered from secret maps supposed to contain?

Of course, Nigel had no claim to the gold, but he wasn't after riches, though he'd take them in a heartbeat if offered. No, he was more into redemption. While he might be a simpleton, he was not a simple man. Wealth was not his thing, nor did he harvest great pleasure from a job well done, which explained a lot. Nor did he gain much lift from compliments or positive feedback, though he'd heard good things about them. Nigel's secret superpower, his unique inborn ability, had always been to create huge expectations for himself that then boomeranged toward continuous and sometimes spectacular failure. This sort of thing he had elevated to an art form, a kind of gruesome spectators' sport for friends, colleagues, and lucky bystanders. However, as accomplished as he was in that field, he had not reaped many benefits. Worse, certain people used his exploits for their own personal enrichment, be it through increased comparative social standing, cover for their own bad behavior, or that thing the Germans have a word for about joy from another's misfortune.

It's not that people are cruel—most, some, a few found something to like in Nigel—but there were those certain individuals who reveled in his downfall more heartily than seemed appropriate. When he slipped on the banana peel, so to speak, some chuckled behind their hands while others threw down bars of soap hoping for an encore. Nigel's joy would be presenting those disbelievers with one blinding, incontrovertible success, rather than just another calamity. He'd waited a lifetime for the opportunity. And now, as he hugged the dirty pot full of *tesuoro*, he could almost hear the joyful noise of his detractors' molars being ground into tooth dust.

But first he had to get the treasure out of the garage.

Nigel squatted down, placed both palms against the pot, and pushed with all his might. The heavy pot rolled a half-inch before encountering an impassable obstruction, possibly an ant.

While resting, he heard noises from the house.

27

FUNERAL, INTERRUPTED

The pallbearers—two officers, the detective, Breadbox, Jack Watt, and Stefanie's husband—shuffled the casket through the back French doors, onto the back deck, and down the trail to the garden burial site. The operation proceeded seamlessly except when Stefanie's husband let slip his corner while exiting the house (due, he claimed, to a minor earthquake) and again when descending the patio steps. Goes to show that greasy bounders are ill-suited to pallbearing. In neither case did the occupant make a fuss.

Those glitches aside, the funeral party shuffled to the gravesite like a collection of self-absorbed zombies mesmerized by the afternoon's revelations. Thoughts of "who's really who," "what's really what," and "how does this affect me?" had pushed the whole planting-a-dead-stranger thing into the mind's back shelf. The funeral might well have been postponed if not for the hustling Breadbox, who had an upcoming appointment to meet a man who owed another man.

Arriving at the gravesite, the pallbearers found no provision for relieving themselves of the casket. Had they anticipated the brevity of Breadbox's remarks, they would have deposited the box directly, but instead, they slid the coffin onto the large mound of dirt piled graveside.

Breadbox wasted no time. "We pay our respects to Emlio Ang-ly-er-o—"

"Emilio Anguilero," corrected the detective.

"What he said," continued Breadbox. "He passes out of this life and into the next. Ashes to ashes, doit to doit, the woims crawl in and the woims crawl out. Though with a fine box like dis, not for a while." Breadbox closed the book—*Harry Potter and the Goblet of Fire*—and concluded, "Let's get him in the hole, boys. Slide 'er down."

The officers and the detective grabbed hold of the casket and eased it down the sloping dirt flank toward the grave. As the box edged toward the loamy depths, a bang and a clang convulsed the crew.

While cowered heads turned this way and that, Grumps provided clarity. "Incoming!" he yelled while flattening himself like a halibut on ice.

Other members of the group, having less experience at bombardment, jerked their heads about on their stalks like turkeys hearing a chop.

Annie dropped to the ground and saw a golf ball sail fifty feet past the funeral party. Turning her head to the opposite direction, she saw a figure with a long gun. "Everyone down," she shouted.

A second report from the rifle was accompanied by the overhead whistle of a second golf ball. The ball shot past the gathering and skipped far down the grounds.

"Two o'clock," shouted one of the officers. "Gunman has an AR-15 with suppressor. And someone is playing golf."

Annie rolled her eyes, figuratively if not literally. The two o'clock designation meant nothing since people were scattered in every orientation. And, of course, there was no suppressor and no golfer. Someone was firing golf balls with a specially outfitted rifle. While not as deadly as a bullet, a high-velocity golf ball strike would do serious damage. As a matter of fact, Annie felt certain she was looking at a murder weapon.

"She's here," shouted Stanley. "She's here. She's here to kill us all."

"Everyone," shouted Annie, "the gunman is in the woods just past the garage. Crawl over to the grave and get in. Officers, stay low, keep under cover, and fan out."

"Is it an Englishman?" shouted Grumps. "If it's an Englishman, I'll take him."

Annie looked around for the officers. She saw one of them scrambling up the patio deck and making a leap for the French doors. The other must have been in the hole. She had visions of a frontal assault with guns ablazin'—something she'd always dreamed of—but with no gun, the dream lacked credibility. Looking around, she saw that everyone had made it to the hole except for Abuelita, who sat high in her wheelchair, holding up a middle finger.

Another shot rang out. The golf ball clanged off the wheelchair. One could only imagine the damage done by a high-velocity golf ball connecting with Abuelita's leathery hide. Neither were built to withstand such an impact. Clearly, Abuelita needed to be extracted from the chair and moved to a safer place. Annie readied herself for the rescue.

Abuelita would have none of it. The chair bucked into gear and advanced toward the gunman at battle speed, which, on good pavement with a favorable tail breeze, was three miles per hour. Across the grassy, uneven terrain, staying upright, much less moving forward, might prove a challenge.

Abuelita's defiant move earned Annie's grudging admiration. Watching the wrinkled wheelchair-bound battle-axe advance into the teeth of withering enemy fire reminded her of herself fifty years in the future. As much as she would have liked to watch, Annie could not stand idle while the brave old bat got pummeled by golf balls. She raised herself for a charge, when out the corner of her eye, she spied a gangly, cloaked figure galloping on a path to intercept the creeping chair. Puffing like a locomotive and scarcely breaking stride, Annie's mother latched onto the screaming invalid, swinging her out of her seat belt and away from the chair in a single motion. Judging by the scream, the crone appreciated being jerked from her wheelchair even less than being shot at with golf balls. She put up a fight, but within a few steps, the stampeding Mother held one leg securely to her chest while the remaining Abuelita parts bounced upside-down off her back like a bony rag doll. The veiled Samaritan, screaming hag attached, hoofed it to the house, snorting like a Clydesdale delivering Budweiser up San Juan Hill.

With Abuelita out of the picture, Annie was now the target of opportunity. She crawled toward the gravesite, lucky to avoid a ball striking the ground two feet from her head. Scrambling around the pile of dirt, she found conditions in the grave to be… well, grave.

At the sound of the first shot, the casket had been allowed to drop uncontrolled into the hole. Landing on its side, the box had opened like a book, exposing the dead Emilio who, for good reason, looked cramped and uncomfortable. The ditch, *his* ditch, created for his sole personal use, was now being shared with a detective, a police officer, Stefanie and her husband, Mrs. Sandoval, Jack Watt, Breadbox, Grumps, and Stanley. That's ten in a grave—not customary. The defunct Emilio, disheveled as he was, could not complain. He held the horizontal position. The remaining occupants compacted themselves into the available space like puzzle pieces. Annie had no space to enter but was, for the moment, safe behind the mound of dirt. Nothing, however, prevented the shooter from repositioning for a better angle.

"Hey there, Mr. Policeman," said Annie. "If you're not going to use your gun, I'd like to borrow it."

"Sure. Borrow the gun," said the officer. "But you can't borrow the bullets."

"Why not?"

"Ain't got any. If I had bullets, *I'd* be using the gun."

"You carry a gun but not ammo?"

"Normally I'm loaded, sure, but I'm off duty. Me and Boykin just showed up 'cause Detective Winjack wanted a show of force. It was either show up or buy the next keg for bowling night."

"So, a show of force means empty weapons?" asked an incredulous Annie.

"Emphasis on *show*. Safer that way."

Another blast sent a golf ball glancing off the gravesite mound, scattering dirt on the crowd below.

"Right," said an annoyed Annie. "Hopefully your bulletless partner will be back soon with a weapon, some ammo, and a SWAT team."

"Perhaps the reverend could say a prayer for our rescuers," said Mrs. Sandoval.

Eyes swiveled toward Breadbox who was pulling loose dirt from behind a cauliflower ear.

"Would you like to conduct a prayer, Reverend?" asked Stefanie.

Having completed the detail work, Breadbox looked up. "Who? Me?"

"Who better?" asked Mrs. Sandoval.

"Anyone, probably," said Breadbox. "I just do funerals. I don't do estemp'raneous prayin', especially not for no cops. No offense. What I need to do is get out of here. I got a business appointment in forty-five minutes, and if I don't get there, he'll get away. I mean, the deal will get away. The deal won't be executed, I should say."

"We can't just stay in this hole all day and let this maniac take potshots at us," said Stefanie's husband.

The regulars had been waiting for Stefanie's husband to voice his opinion. Unfortunately, there wasn't much they could do about it. And, while no one could argue with his reasoning, no one was going to feed the beast by agreeing either.

As if to punctuate his point, a shot rang out and a golf ball buried itself in the dirt a few inches from Annie's head. The shooter had repositioned, forcing Annie to do likewise on the opposite side of the pile. Everyone else scrunched a little lower.

"Protect us, Lord," said Breadbox, "'cause I don't wanna die by no golf ball in no grave hole. Is that irony? Are you being ironic, Lord? If so, please stop. Amen."

Through the garage's clouded window, Nigel had watched the procession to the gravesite. The funeral had done well enough without his services, so he dampened the urge to sally forth. Easy to do since his urges were nicely saturated to begin with. Besides, the march to the gravesite looked to be a sullen affair that did not comport with his current ebullient state of mind. Better to keep the sunshine contained within its vessel for now. Post-burial, after the lamenters had absorbed their full allotment of gloom, he would stroll in with the radiant glow and proclaim treasure for one and all. Perhaps he should have hidden in the fireplace.

Nigel sat himself down on his immovable treasure pot to wait for the funeral to expire. Before long he drifted into a familiar dream—familiar but with variations. Nigel returning as the conquering hero by way of lion-drawn chariot was the usual stuff, but this time, a black pot rested near his sandaled feet. Assorted laurels, rose petals, and celestial virgins were tossed in his direction by the adoring crowd. In return, he flung droplets of olive oil and sweat he'd collected along the way. Nothing was too good for his fans. When his lions stopped to replenish themselves with roadkill they'd killed on the road, the multitudes parted as if combed on either side. From the furrow emerged the empress, Annie, a vision in white mini-toga, rose petals in her hair, rose petals in her teeth, and scabs on her knees. She slunk toward the chariot to a chorus of whistles—"Sweet Georgia

Brown." She placed a delicate, porcelain hand on Nigel's scabbard—

The proceedings went poof with a bang.

Nigel jolted awake. *Strange sound for a funeral*, he thought. Perhaps they'd dropped the casket from a great height. Doubtful. Maybe they'd saluted the man's passing with the discharge of a firearm—well within Breadbox's wheelhouse. A second bang got him to the window.

He watched his swath-headed mother-in-law hoofing it to the house with what appeared to be a huge, hideous insect on her back. One could only hope. He thought he heard a horse but didn't see one. In the other direction, Abuelita's wheelchair lay on its side, and some distance beyond was the gravesite, now abandoned. The only sign of life was a shoe peeking out from behind the mound of dirt. Another shot rang out. Nigel saw a streak over the grave accompanied by a puff of dust from the pile. The shoe disappeared for a second to be replaced by Annie scrambling around the corner of the dirt pile. She was under attack.

The octogenarian Abuelita weighed a scant ninety-eight pounds, mostly hide, bones, and rancor. Carrying the old viper around on one's back must have been like lugging around a leather sack full of petrified elbows.

If anyone was suited to this task, it was Annie's mother. She, of unknowable age, had the back hide of a triceratops thanks to a skin regimen of topically applied stiffeners and a nightly bed of nails. She was also strapping and fit, as vinegar drinkers tend to be. If she consumed extra calories, they didn't stick around. Sizzled away, most likely, by the continual need to produce fresh supplies of venom.

These two spirited ladies were much alike and, as one might imagine, had hated each other from the outset. Mother plopped

Abuelita onto the sofa and huffed like a hippo after a pearl dive. Underneath the swaddling, her straining nostrils flapped on the exhale and ballooned on the inhale.

"You sound like a damn horse," said Abuelita.

"This horse just saved your life," huffed Mother.

"I didn't need savin'," said Abuelita.

Though many would have agreed with Abuelita, Mother had indeed saved her life—the kind of compassionate act Abuelita could never forgive. To make matters worse, Abuelita had been focused on taking down an enemy, which she lived for. The interruption was inexcusable.

"You stay here and rest up. I'll be down soon," said Mother.

Abuelita sat and listened to the occasional golf shot. Frustrated and angry she was—in that respect, a day like any other—but she was also sleep-deprived, owing to last night's pizza revolt. Her eye, the functional one, soon closed as she drifted into dreamtime.

Abuelita found herself in a vast stadium filled to capacity with cheering fans. Her box seat, next to the handsome, shirtless young emperor, provided prime, unobstructed views of the stadium floor. A gate opened, and a lion-drawn chariot entered. The driver, an imbecile, smiled with rose petals in his hair and a laurel around the neck. He waved to the crowd. Spectators burst into hysterical applause, anticipating the show to follow. He was a fool, this chariot driver. He had no idea. He flicked his whip to move his lions. They moved all right. They bound out of their harnesses and began searching for someone with a whip. Abuelita jumped out of her seat and dumped her entire basket of rose petals on the hungry lions. The crowd erupted in a chorus of whistles—"Sweet Georgia Brown."

A sound jolted Abuelita from her reverie. The shrouded sphinx was on her way out the door with a golf club over her shoulder and a bucket of balls in her hand. "Where do you think you're going?" she said to Mother.

"To play a little golf."

"Break a leg," said Abuelita. She meant it.

At the gravesite turned foxhole, Stefanie's husband prattled on. "We've got to do something even if it means someone has to sacrifice for the good of the whole. Someone needs to confront the killer face-to-face while the rest of us escape."

"You volunteering?" asked Breadbox.

Any of Breadbox's fellow foxholers would have known he was wasting valuable breath.

"I think it's pretty obvious who should act as the decoy. This brave man here," said Stefanie's husband, rubbing Grump's bony shoulder. "A member of the dwindling Greatest Generation, an heroic war veteran who's already demonstrated the intestinal fortitude required to stand in the face of enemy fire, a man who has already led a full and happy—"

"*Not* happy," corrected Grumps.

"…a full and complete life, and he has his own helmet. He's the perfect volunteer. We are so lucky to have counted him as our brave and loyal friend, courageous to the very end."

"Who are you?" said Grumps.

Another shot rang out as a ball whistled over the hole at supersonic speed.

"Time for great men to stand up and be counted," said Stefanie's husband, scrunching down while giving a thumbs-up sign under Grump's helmet.

"He can't go out there," said Stefanie.

"Why not?" said her husband.

"Grumps can barely walk. He'd be taken down in a minute. What kind of decoy would that be?"

"Not as spry as I used to be," said Grumps. "Now, if that were an Englishman…"

"I'll go," said Stanley.

"You?" asked Stefanie, beating everyone else to the punch.

"Excellent," said Stefanie's husband.

"It's me she wants," said Stanley. "I'm the cause of all this. I see no choice but to confess. I'm the killer."

"You? You're the murderer?" said the detective. "That can't be. I don't have a warrant for *you*."

"It was more an accident than a murder," said Stanley. "You must believe me. I never intended to kill him, not in a million years."

Another shot sent a ball bouncing off the dirt pile a foot from Annie's head. The shooter had once more repositioned, forcing her to scramble around the dirt pile again.

"What was your motive?" asked the detective.

"The two of them, this Eel person and Cam, were having some kind of relationship. I saw the text messages. I confronted Cam with the evidence. She didn't deny it, but insisted she wanted it to end. But she was afraid of Eel, afraid of what he might do to her. A person named Eel cannot be trusted, too slippery. Cam cried on my shoulder, right here," he said, pointing to his chest. "She begged *me* to do it, to end *her* affair. She convinced me that Eel was the type who would never hit a man, only a woman. He'd listen to me, she said. It was the only way, she said. So, she arranged to meet Eel here at the estate. Only I would show up in her place. She said he was in for one eel of a surprise. Cam's clever like that."

"But why here?" asked Mrs. Sandoval.

"I supposed he was staying here."

"He was not," said Mrs. Sandoval.

"Be that as it may, Cam arranged for the meeting to take place here. Eel was waiting on this very spot. I engaged him in small talk to assess his character. He struck me as taciturn and abrupt, seemed to have no interest in the weather. Not the type you can trust. He then implied I should leave because he was there to meet someone and three would be a crowd."

"He implied it? How did he *imply* it?" asked the detective.

"He said, 'I'm about to meet someone, and three would be a crowd. You need to scram.'"

The detective looked satisfied with that answer.

"I then informed him," continued Stanley, "that Cam would not be coming. I told him she considered him nothing but a terrible, awful, horrible mistake. I told him that between seeing his face again and having ptomaine poisoning, she'd choose ptomaine, but he didn't know what that was. So I told him she thought he was on par with a foot fungus."

"And this infuriated him?" asked the detective.

"Not all that much, but when I told him that she chose me over him, he became agitated."

The burial party looked at Stanley, then looked at the dead man spilling out of his casket, and then looked at Stanley again. Even in the silly suit and having been dead for a week, Eel held a decisive advantage in the looks department. Personality-wise, it would have been a close call if they had both been dead, but with Stanley doing all the talking, the edge would have gone to Eel.

"He seemed at first disbelieving," said Stanley. "Then he laughed, hysterically so. It was super annoying. He stomped his feet and took a frog out of his pocket, a pretty yellow frog. He said to me, 'This frog is deadly poisonous, and you, my friend, will eat it.' I said, 'Will not.' He said, 'Will.' I said, 'Will not,' and I pushed him. Surprised by my assertiveness, he stumbled backward and fell. His mouth was open. It was always open. I think he was a mouth breather. The frog went right in."

"Into his mouth?" asked the detective.

"As if it owned the place. But after a moment, he got up—"

"The frog?"

"The man. The man got up, brushed himself off, stood up like he was about to burp out a frog, and then collapsed. Dead, it appeared. Poisoned, I assumed."

"Stanley," asked Annie, "by any chance, when this guy

dropped was there also a sound?" Another shot rang out as a projectile buried itself at the base of the dirt pile. "Like that?"

"Now that you mention it," said Stanley, "there could have been. But after having just killed a man, I didn't think much of it. I was flustered."

Annie looked up to relocate the shooter. The attacker was at the edge of the woods, but not in the commanding offensive position she expected. She saw the gunman, rifle in hand, dive and crouch as a white object zoomed past and ricocheted off a tree. The assailant was being assailed. The gunman, using a tree as cover, raised the rifle from a sitting position and fired toward her rival sharpshooter. Annie saw an opportunity.

"Guys," said Annie, addressing the ladies and gentlemen of the ditch, "I have an idea. Everyone needs to sit tight and not do anything stupid. Are we clear on that?"

"That's a good idea," said Mrs. Sandoval. "I'm glad you thought of it."

Annie took off running in the direction of the shooter.

28

NIGEL MAKES HIS MOVE

The shrouded dragoness anchored herself at the northeast corner of the house and teed up a ball. She adjusted her sunglasses and scanned the distant woods for signs of a golf-ball sharpshooter. A creeping figure of decidedly assassin-like nature provided her a target. At 150 yards, she'd have been better off with a five wood, but she'd make do with her three.

Golfing had been her thing in high school, and she'd played it through most of her adult life. It was only after marrying Stanley, the lout, that she had put away her clubs. Stanley and golf had never got on. He wanted a game that looked hard but played easy, not the other way around. All the romantic blithering in the world couldn't save a game that mocked its own players at each and every hole with that contemptable contrivance known as par. Stanley's problem was that he'd made the game too complex. His wife understood that true enjoyment came, not from holing the ball in X number of shots, but rather from knocking the crap out of something with a club.

Mother addressed the ball. "Goodbye, Stanley."

Whoosh. She let loose with a furious swing and watched the distant figure cower as the ball sailed overhead and bounced off a tree.

Too much Stanley, she thought.

She teed up another ball as a gun sounded and a ball screamed past her, ricocheting off the brick house. The shooter may have had a marked advantage in power, but at 150 yards, her incoming could almost certainly be avoided. Such was not the case for those at the gravesite, a mere 50-yard range.

Bring it on. Mother was plenty game for a bout of golf dodgeball. She stood straight to address her second ball before noticing movement at the gravesite.

Annie was making a run toward the shooter.

Brave, but not smart, thought her mother. Hoping to draw attention away from her girl, she laid into the ball but spun off a worm-burner. That's what happens when you slack off the practice sessions for a few years. She refocused on the battlefield to find her girl.

Annie, hiding behind the abandoned wheelchair in a prone position, righted the chair and spun it around so the back faced the shooter.

Mother teed up another ball while Annie, hunkering in the chair, moved in reverse toward the shooter. Mother swung true, launching the projectile on a perfect arc toward the edge of the woods.

The ball had eyes, as they say, curving directly onto the target's head. The crouching figure flopped.

Mother whooped like a hooded banshee. She still had it.

Nigel jumped back as the deflected golf ball banged against the door's small window. He grimaced, not at the ball's impact on the window but at its impact before it struck the window.

From the safety of the garage, he had watched a policeman meticulously prowling his way through the woods, tree by tree, toward the gunman. The officer's mission, Nigel reckoned, was to put a definitive stop to the golf ball gunman's havoc-wreaking. To this end, he had secured a position behind a nicely placed tree almost within leaping distance of the shooter. The officer had made the sign of the cross before rising to make his final charge. He took no more than two strides before dropping like a uniformed sack of potatoes, the unfortunate result of a golf ball strike to the cranium. The golf ball shooter, it seemed, had an accomplice.

Nigel looked across the way and saw Annie had moved from the pile of dirt to the abandoned wheelchair. He watched as she positioned the wheelchair's back toward the shooter before placing herself in it. The gunman fired at her, but the ball bounced off the back of the chair.

Smart, he thought. *As long as she keeps her back to the shooter and her head ducked down, she can zoom right out of range.*

The wheelchair kicked into motion but not away, as Nigel had supposed. Instead, she rocketed three miles per hour in reverse toward the gunman. *What is she doing?* After considering, he concluded she must be playing the part of a diversion in a coordinated dual-pronged assault. Annie was to provide a distracting frontal offensive, allowing the officer to attack unde-tected from the rear. A brilliant plan, if not for a second golf ball shooter. Brilliant or not, Annie was now seriously exposed from two sides and totally unaware that her partner had gone tits up, so to speak.

When plan A fails, it's obviously time to pull plan B from wherever one keeps a plan B. He guessed Annie didn't have one because she wasn't a plan B type of gal. He recognized, as he had so many times in his life, that he was Plan B. His mission could not have been simpler: Save Annie from a pair of golf ball assas-sins. Nigel's brain went to work, as it did in times of crisis, like an under-lubricated steam-era machine.

Annie bounced and jiggled in the wheelchair as it plowed forward in reverse. The back of the chair had taken some hits, but the padded seat dulled the impact to a sharp thud. She'd counted ten golf balls launched so far. She would have traded her left arm to know how many were left.

Annie knew something about these active shooters. If they intended to survive their assaults, an alarm clock in their head triggered a switch from attack mode to survival mode. Annie wanted to speed that clock. By challenging the shooter, she would feed a growing paranoia that opposition forces were closing in. At some point, the shooter would opt for survival and make a run for it.

If the assailant was Cam Logan as she suspected, Annie felt confident she could run her down. While Cam was physically fit, owing to her cadre of personal trainers, there was little chance she'd have worn appropriate footwear. Tackling her would be an honor and a pleasure. If she put up a fight, a black dirt facial could be in her future.

Of course, all this presupposed a sane and rational gunman who preferred living to dying. With criminal profiles of AR-15 golf ball assailants in short supply, sane and rational might be giving credit where credit wasn't due. This, however, was something Annie scarcely considered as a golf ball whizzed past her head at 130 mph.

As long as she could maintain a safe distance and a back-facing orientation, Annie felt protected. That is, until a ball sailed past from the opposite direction. The shot missed her by a mile, but she was alarmed. A second attacker from the opposite direction put her in grave danger. She looked toward the house, eventually finding the unmistakable visage of her swaddle-headed mother. A reflecting glint exposed the swinging of a golf club as a turf scorcher skipped past toward the shooter.

Annie had an ally, though not necessarily a helpful one. While Mother might draw the shooter's fire, she might also endanger Annie with errant shots. Furthermore, she might be resupplying the shooter with fresh ammo.

Having closed the range to an uncomfortable degree, Annie shifted the wheelchair into forward mode to increase the distance. After giving the shooter a chance to run for it, she'd make another charge if needed. That was the plan, but a beep from somewhere on the wheelchair implied the plan might need an adjustment. A red light flashing on the tiny control panel indicated the battery had fallen to recharge level.

Annie's worst nightmare was to become an unarmed, stationary target in the open field. She piloted the chair forward with the hope of making it out of potshot range. As the chair whirred forward at a glacial pace, golf balls sailed past in both directions, two striking her chair without inflicting damage. The battery became her least critical problem when the chair bottomed on a small rise. One powered wheel rotated uselessly in the air while the other threatened to spin her into a dangerous position.

If this were not bad enough, Annie glanced houseward to see Mother hopping awkwardly in a failed attempt to avoid a ball strike to her hip. Annie put her head on a swivel, alternating views of the shooter in one direction and her mother in the other. Her mother was down, but seemingly from nowhere, a small padded figure shuffled out to administer aid. Perhaps the first responders had finally arrived.

Annie's attention returned to her own predicament when a ball clanked hard off the right wheel of the chair. The arrival direction indicated the shooter was on the move. She tried to realign the chair for a proper blocking angle but could not. The worst-case scenario had arrived. Left unarmed and immobile in an open field, her situation hovered between serious and grave.

She abandoned the chair as a sitting device and prepared to use it as a shield for the expected barrage. Behind it she cowered. Annie hated cowering. Cowering felt like helplessness, and helplessness made Annie want to destroy things.

Annie, the former marine, couldn't live with the idea of her last check being cashed by a golf ball while cowering behind a wheelchair. If she had to go down, she would go down standing and swinging. Maybe when the others saw her at full gonzo, they'd be inspired to join the fun. Otherwise, she'd likely go down in a hailstorm of golf balls.

However, before she stood to make her final stand, a warbly voice arose from the gravesite. "Cam. Cam. Over here, Cam."

While Annie was not the one being paged, she nevertheless turned to see who was doing the paging. Rising from the grave was a droopy-headed figure in a chartreuse pinstriped suit. Across the way, the shooter lowered her weapon and trotted toward the limply resurrected figure.

"Eel?" yelled out Cam. "Is that you?"

The dead man rose to a full "standing" position, albeit with an extra set of arms coming out from below the armpits. One of the extra arms wrapped around the dead man's waist while the other held the head upright via the chin.

"Don't shoot, Cam. It's me."

Annie recognized Stanley's voice. A standing dead man needs its support system, and this one had Stanley.

Cam also recognized the voice, judging by her transition from a jog to a plod. "What do you think you're doing, Stanley?" she asked, as if he'd been caught pilfering the foot-wine.

"Let's go home, Cam. Take me back to Cam-A-Lot. I know you came to save me, but violence is not the way. It would be best for everyone if we just gave ourselves up and let justice run its course. I might get some jail time, you might get probation, but all this mayhem will just make it worse. Eventually, I'll get out, and then we'll have the life we've always dreamed of."

"Waiting for Prince Charmless to get out of prison is not the life I dreamed of, Stanley. If you hadn't noticed, I'm not the waiting type. Now, where's the map? I want that map."

Before Stanley could reply, a clatter commenced from the direction of the garage. The clatter was soon joined by an unholy choir of rattles, sputters, and clangs. The source of the racket soon revealed itself. But revealing oneself is not the same as explaining oneself.

All the various players in what had been a pitched battle halted their desperate activities to gawk at what they saw. Even the cadaver in the chartreuse pinstripes appeared to be stroking his chin, albeit with someone else's arm.

The little excavator had no on-board sound system, leaving Nigel to improvise. "Da-ta-da-da-dum, Da-ta-da-da-DUM," and so on and so forth, he sang in a strong voice. That's Wagner's "Ride of the Valkyries" for those who don't read music. He could barely hear himself over the noise of the clanky contraption, but he imagined his adversaries cowering in shock and awe.

Not that he'd be able see their reactions or much of anything else. The excavator, in its native state, had sadly lacked protection from would-be assassins not named the sun. The original cockpit infrastructure, composed of four metal poles supporting a tiny roof, needed stout reinforcement to stand against a team of determined golf-ball riflemen. In a brief few minutes, he had transformed the skeletal vehicle into an armored fighting machine by enclosing the cockpit with a motley collection of signs, boards, and scrap metal. The trade-off for this increased pilot protection was a near-total reduction in his field of vision. The supposed advantage of sight as a battlefield attribute was about to be tested.

With his view of the world reduced to a single knothole in a piece of scrap fencing, Nigel went into battle with a distinct lack of situational awareness. Vital information, like where the hell the enemy was, eluded him in the opening moments and improved only sporadically thereafter. Nevertheless, he pushed the machine forward at maximum speed, pursuing a zigzag pattern in hopes of catching a glimpse of the enemy through his knothole.

To an outside observer, the mobile scrapheap appeared to be driven by a blind drunkard, a notion reinforced when the excavator plowed into the only object in the whole field, Abuelita's wheelchair. In a race of straight-line speed, the excavator and wheelchair would have been well matched. In a contest of brawn, the excavator held a slight advantage. Nigel brought the scoop down on the chair several times, crumpling it to a degree, before discovering wide-open territory to the obstacle's left. Or right if he'd chosen to go that way. After overcoming this inconvenience, the search for something to confront continued.

Had one observed the movements of Nigel's excavator from the air, it would have resembled that of a cockroach after being sprayed with dollar store bug killer. Energetic but aimless about describes it. Nevertheless, he eventually located the shooter through his knothole. He had hoped the shooters, once confronted with the futility of war against a mechanized opponent, would cast aside their weapons and reach for the stars. Should they refuse, he would have no choice but to run them down. How to make them stand still while he did so was an issue he'd not yet addressed.

This very point became more than a hypothetical when the sniper demonstrated an unfortunate tendency to move. Every move by the assassin required Nigel to resume a scattershot ramble across the field until he'd once again realigned his knothole with the peppy killer. Exasperating hardly described the situation. Of course, in his makeshift cocoon, Nigel could play this game all day as long as his fuel held out. Suddenly, fuel level was something he wished he'd checked before leaving the garage.

It was during one of these recalibrating rambles that Nigel heard a loud pop, sending him two feet into the vertical.

The first appearance of Nigel's improvised tank had been met with, for lack of a better word, befuddlement. Of course, impressions were more nuanced than that. Annie was also concerned, the Killer was also dismissive, Stanley was also annoyed, and on and on. But all were befuddled.

Annie had abandoned her wheelchair shield to avoid being crushed by Nigel's tankette. She'd had little choice but to adopt the moving excavator as cover though his erratic driving meant she'd also had to walk around like a drunk person following a lost snake.

The negotiations between Cam and Stanley had immediately ceased so Cam could assess the threat level of a creeping junkpile. After a few watchful moments, Cam regarded the junkyard curiosity not as a threat, but as a nuisance. Mostly because of the noise. With occasional sidesteps to confuse the mechanical monstrosity, she resumed the discussion with Stanley.

"I want the map."

"What?" replied Stanley, struggling to hear above the clattering din.

Annoyed and impatient, Cam lifted the rifle to her shoulder and fired at the excavator's makeshift shack. The golf ball struck center-panel of what had once been a wooden sign proclaiming, "Golf Shop."

Nigel's work in the construction field prior to his latest creation had primarily involved building structures out of playing cards. It was this experience that he had applied to his most recent tank project. The weakness of such a background became nakedly obvious when that "Golf Shop" sign split down its long axis. As it turned out, the sign had served as a kind of supporting structure. Once split, the sign folded, relaxing its obligation to support its neighbors. The neighbors, in turn, relaxed their obligations to support their neighbors, and so forth and so on, until no board, plank, or panel supported any other. Gravity took care of the rest.

Nigel had seen the concept play out many times, but never from the inside. The work of ten minutes had disintegrated in seconds. A discomforting breeze wafted across his neck.

Before the slats had even hit the ground, Cam had reloaded and retargeted her weapon at what appeared to be a spot right between Nigel's eyes. "Turn that damn thing off," she said, while looking down the barrel of her weapon. "We're having a discussion here."

With the uprising quelled, Cam turned back toward the grave and yelled, "The map, Stanley. Where is it?"

"What map? I don't know what you're talking about," said Stanley from behind Eel. "Whatever is mine is yours, but please stop going on about this map. I've already confessed. They know I killed this guy," he said, thumbing the chest of his human shield. "They know it was an accident and that I acted in a jealous rage."

"You confessed? To who?"

"The police."

"When did you go to the police?"

"The police are here."

"Here?! Where?"

"In the ditch."

"The police have been in the ditch this whole time? While I've been shooting up the place? What kind of police are they? This town deserves better than that."

"I'll take that up with the city council when I get out of prison," said Stanley. "But for now, you need to lay down that gun. As things stand, given your celebrity status, I'm sure you'd get off with community service and a stint in rehab. Also, your music sales would spike, and you'd get a lucrative book deal."

Stanley looked exhausted. He wasn't used to holding up a dead man by the armpits, nor speaking in paragraphs. After a breath he continued, "But none of that can happen if you keep going on about this silly map. No one knows what the devil you're talking about."

"If you don't know," said Cam, "then you better send out that Mr. Sandoval. He knows. Send him out, or I'm going to start plugging people."

"If I knew about a map, I'd tell you," said a muffled voice from deep within the grave. "I don't know about any map."

"In that case, the only question is who gets it first," said Cam.

Nigel found the conversation frightfully confusing. He'd left the house this morning as the prime murder suspect and the possessor of the map. Now Stanley was confessing to the murder, and Cam wanted the map. It was all double Dutch to him. Double Dutch, yes, but double Dutch that worked in his favor. Not having a monopoly on murder charges had to be a good thing. And he had already recovered the treasure.

The most immediate problem at hand was the gun aimed at his forehead. Nigel's frontal lobes, averse to high-velocity golf balls entering their space, made a persuasive argument that if Cam wanted a used-up treasure map, then she should have it.

"I have the map," yelled Nigel. "I'm the one you want."

All eyes turned to Nigel sitting in the tiny excavator surrounded by golf course-related debris.

"And just where did *you* get the map?" asked a skeptical Cam.

"Off a body," said Nigel.

"So, you got it off of Eel, did you? How long have you had it?"

"Since yesterday," said Nigel, which was not a stretch since he'd drawn the Sandoval map yesterday from memory. If Cam wanted to believe it came from Eel, so be it.

"Put the map here," she said, indicating a spot a few yards in front of her. "Lay it right there on the ground and then get back into your little Tonka toy. And don't nobody else move," she said, swinging her gun around.

Slithering off the excavator with hands in air, Nigel duck-walked toward Cam and kneeled, as one does in the presence of a golden-haired goddess. He slowly pulled the map out of his trouser pocket and laid down the offering a safe distance from her manicured toes before crab-walking his way back to the security of his excavator.

She picked up the map. "Okay, everybody, I'm going to ease on out of here. Try to follow, and it'll be the last thing you do. I suggest saving your stupidity for something important."

"Cam," yelled out Stanley, "don't you want me to come along?"

"No, Stanley. Forget about Cam Logan. She's a figment of your imagination. If you're lonely, get yourself a dog."

Cam Logan backed away into the woods.

29

GRUMPS GETS HIS CHANCE

Now that the danger was over and the shooter had left the scene, law enforcement arrived in great numbers, spreading themselves about the place like a horde of beetles. Nigel found their effectiveness questionable, but they did a fair job of not bumping into each other while telling the residents they could rest easy.

"We'll have the perpetrator apprehended in no time," said each and every cop to each and every non-cop.

If nothing else, the non-cops had to be heartened by the sheer multitude. How many it took to apprehend a woman in the woods, who knew? More than three, obviously.

The home's exhausted occupants and guests, nursing their physical aches and emotional wounds, arranged themselves haphazardly in the atrium. The detective paced the room like a cat whose mouse has disappeared into a wall. Mr. Sandoval stared into space; perhaps, after the morning's revelations, reworking the puzzle of his lost years. His rediscovered colleague, Jack Watt, appeared surprisingly placid, even pleased. Had he been a pipe smoker, he'd have been smoking one now. Grumps sat compacted into his seat like a man trying to boil his own blood. Stefanie rubbed her forehead while her husband, across the room, glowered as if a chunk of smelly cheese had lodged in his nostril. Mrs. Sandoval needed a drink because she didn't have one.

Annie held an ice bag on her mother's bruised thigh, marveling at how fast the ice melted. Had she lifted the veil from her mother's face, she'd have seen a woman feverishly plotting to get uneven. Her rescue of the wretched Abuelita had placed her in a splendidly exploitable position over her rival hellmate. But then, Abuelita, evil sorceress that she was, had turned the tables with her act of craven selflessness. Taking advantage of a moment of weakness, the old crone had perpetrated a blatant act of vindictive goodwill. The veiled one could not let this cruel act of kindness go unchallenged.

Abuelita, wrapped in a suit of comforters and memory foam, must have been feeling a sense of relief. Her "deliverance" by that loathsome veiled creature would have led to repugnant expectations of gratitude, which, fortunately, she had neutralized by her own "rescue" of the hooded hellhound. How the invalid Abuelita had found the energy to cushion herself up and pull that lizard queen to safety was anybody's guess.

The person that might venture more than a guess was Esmerelda, who had experience in the black arts. Essie, however, was strangely subdued. Probably because she was reading people's auras and disturbed by what she read.

Lumbering into this muted assemblage were two tired cops to see the pacing detective.

"You got her?" asked the detective.

"Afraid not. We've combed the entire area. Not a sign of her."

"She must be around. Female country singers don't just vanish into thin air. If you've secured the perimeter, then she must be hiding on the premises. Look high and low. I want her found, understand?" said the detective, pointing to a spot on the ground where he wanted her placed.

The two sweaty cops did not offer the detective a salute or a "Yes, sir." Rather, they exchanged knowing looks. The same knowing looks Nigel had seen aunts exchange on various occasions, usually accompanied by a pat on the head.

"Well, listen to you," said cop one, while scouring the detective with an abrasive eye. "Haven't we gone and gotten ourselves all high and mighty now that you're Mr. Detective? Funny how I don't recall *you* scaring up that many lost country singers in your patrolling days."

"Okay, okay, enough of that," said the detective.

"Perhaps Your Lordship would like me to perform a jig in his honor," said the cop, adopting the role of silly manservant to his Royal Highness, the Detective. "And when I have completed my jig, may I have the honor of delivering Your Lordship a fresh crumpet?"

"That's enough."

"Let me assure His Majesty, the royal crumpet shall be delivered with the utmost care, in a manner befitting food destined for thine royal mouth with nary a single instance of contamination from yon scallywag's nasty bits."

"That'll be enough, Dodds. Don't make me report this to the captain."

Dodds and his snickering partner accepted the rebuke and left to conduct their business.

Meanwhile, Grumps's helmeted head twitched on its stalk like a nesting emu sensing a dingo. Once he'd located the *faux* British cop, he glared at the officer as if he'd just made off with one of his eggs.

"He's a Brit," said Grumps under his breath. "I heard British. British, British, British." So agitated was he that poetry spouted from his lips, "Fee-fi-fo-fum, I smell the blood of an Englishman." One could see his veins popping to the surface as they plumped with rage hormones. Within minutes, his muscle capacity doubled to half that of an average healthy man.

The crowd knew something was up when Grumps repeatedly pounded a shot glass on his helmet, producing a sound like one of those boxing bells being struck by a shot glass.

"Errrrrgh," said Grumps.

Anyone looking into his face would have known that "Errrrrgh" meant "My name is Inigo Montoya," or words to that effect.

Grumps rose to his feet, tottering for a moment until the blood caught up to his brain. His upper lip curled skyward, exposing where a sharp, fearsome canine tooth once was. His chest heaved outward as rejuvenating air rushed in to compete for space with the indigenous mucus. His blood raced through rock-rimmed arteries. "Errrrrgh," he repeated for clarification.

The rustle of clothing, the creak and pop of aged joints, and then, a sharp, metallic thunk followed by a clankity-clank-clank, were the sounds of a ninety-some-year-old man on the attack. The target of this orgiastic rampage remained unscathed, untouched, and unaware, having been twenty-five feet away at rampage start and twenty feet away at rampage end. The assault had been foiled when Grumps's left heel held its ground against Grumps's right foot. While his feet fought to a stalemate, the remainder of Grumps fell forward like a slow-motion tree. His helmet (head inside) collided with the sofa's polished oak armrest before spilling onto the marble floor (head not inside). The crowd, their heads having snapped to the sound of metal on wood, were treated to the sight of a nonagenarian collapsing very gently onto an octogenarian.

The most calamitous impact of Grumps's fall was borne by the helmet, which may have saved his life. The rest of the action took place in relative slow motion as Grumps creaked downward one rusty part at a time, onto the soft, cushiony Abuelita. The words soft and cushiony had not been applied to Abuelita for decades, but on this occasion, they fit. Her improvised padded suit came in handy a second time by protecting the colliding bodies from the many bony protuberances on both sides. An embarrassed Grumps was helped off Abuelita and carried to a distant chair for his own protection.

Seeing this painful episode, Nigel wondered if it wasn't time for an intervention. The news would be harsh, the impact possibly severe. Could his fluttering heart take it? Not the kind of thing to face without a bracer.

Nigel gulped down a couple of stiff ones and dove right in. Kneeling beside the gore-starved old man while studiously avoiding eye contact, he said, "Grumps, I think there is something you should know."

"He's British, isn't he? You gonna to tell me he's special forces or something? Doesn't matter. I'm ready."

"Nothing like that. I'm sorry to disillusion you, but that man is not British."

"I heard him talk. I know the accent when I hear it. He's pure limey."

"Sorry, he's not. He was putting on an accent, and not a very convincing one at that. All over the map, he was. Cockney, Queen's English, the South, the North, a total mess. Putting that aside for the moment, let's talk about your old girlfriend."

"Raquel?"

"There was a Raquel?"

"Who you talking about?"

"Wilhelmina, your old English girlfriend. The stuff of dreams."

"I wouldn't go that far."

"Go as far as you like. She's your girlfriend."

"Aahh," said Grumps with a faraway look in his eyes.

Nigel found it disconcerting to see a fifteen-year-old's inquisitive passions staring back through a ninety-five-year-old's eyes.

"As far as I like?"

"Sure, why not?"

"Because she's not mine," said Grumps. He held up two clenched, bloodless fists. "She left me for an Englishman." His hands trembled and his teeth chattered. "Errrrrgh."

"That's what I wanted to talk to you about. I'll try to let this cat out easy, but I'm not sure I can without a few scratches. I want you to keep in mind that I am merely a messenger. I'm not Wilhelmina, or Milton, or Chester—"

"Jester?"

"Right, Jester. I'm not any of those people. Keep that in mind, okay?"

"Got it. You're you. Check."

Nigel felt he should ease into the conversation. "So, how are you feeling, Grumps?"

"What kind of a question is that?" asked Grumps. "You gonna talk about the weather next?"

"Fine. I'll get straight to the point. Remember the letter?"

"What letter?"

"The one from Wilhelmina."

"Wilhelmina sent lots of letters."

"Yes. Specifically, the one you carried around in your shoe for years. The one you had up in your room. The one I read."

"Oh, that letter."

"Yes, that letter. You told me that you had never actually read that letter."

"Jester read it to me."

"Right, Jester, the practical joker. By any chance, do you know where Jester lives these days?"

"No. Do we need Jester?"

"It'd be great to have him in the dungeon for game night, but no, we don't need Jester. You see, when Jester read that letter to you…" Nigel paused for a moment, and continued, "…well, he didn't."

"He didn't?"

"No, he didn't."

"Didn't what?"

"Read the letter to you."

"Yes, he did. I heard him."

"No. What he said was not what was in the letter."

"What did he say?"

"You know, about Wilhelmina finding another man. The letter didn't say that."

"It didn't?"

"No."

"What about the part about not wanting to see me anymore?"

"Nope. Not in the letter."

"What about the part about her moving to Scotland to be a salmon rancher?"

"Was that in there?" asked a puzzled Nigel.

"That's what I'm asking."

"No. That wasn't in there either."

"Did the letter say she wanted to see me again?"

"Yes."

"Dang," said Grumps, indicating a certain disappointment at wasting seventy of his best years. "Did the letter say she would be waiting for me?"

"Yes."

"Dang. Do you think there's a chance she might still be waiting for me?"

"No."

"Dang. In the letter, did she call me Biscuit?"

"Yes."

"I never liked being called Biscuit. Why the hell would she call me Biscuit?"

"In Britain, a biscuit is a cookie."

"What? Are you sure?"

"Yes."

"Well, that's not so bad, then, is it?"

"No."

"Did she sign her name with a little heart over the *i*?"

"I can read the letter to you, if you like?"

Grumps knew that even if Nigel read the letter to him, it wouldn't answer his question. The old man had a blank stare, as if watching his last seventy years unfold blank frame by blank frame. He sighed, stuck a finger in his left ear, and twisted. He didn't know what else to do. "No. I don't think so. I think I'm over it," he said, peering into the middle distance. "That whole hating thing was, quite honestly, starting to bring me down. Gave me heartburn at night. Such an outlook might not be the healthiest thing in the world."

Nigel could see the man churning through deep, existential thoughts. "Is there anything I can do for you?"

"I need to get me one of those iPhones," said Grumps. "You know about Tinder?"

Nigel sensed a man on the road to recovery. Released from the singular, all-consuming hate that had hardened him for so many years, a transformation was taking place right before Nigel's eyes. The creased and folded skin of Grumps's face, reminiscent of low-quality papier-mâché spread thinly over the cracked hide of a rhinoceros, appeared to soften as if some merciful fairy had sprinkled it with fairy dust. Before Nigel could ask, "What's Tinder?" an infectious cough swept across the room.

"Stop that," yelled Abuelita. "What the hell do you think you're doing?" She coughed while waving her arms through a white, smoky cloud.

"Sorry," said Stanley. "I was just shaking out my baker's hat. I didn't realize it was covered in powder."

"What is that?" said Stephanie.

"Powdered sugar, I think," said Stanley, licking his finger. "Mixed with a bit of grave dust."

30

A PENNY DROPS ON STANLEY

Mrs. Sandoval propped up the foam-wrapped Abuelita, coughed for a spell, and ordered Nigel to fetch the tequila.

Nigel wondered what had taken so long. He had big news to spill, and it was building inside him like water behind a dam. But big news wasn't a thing to be released in drips and drops. No, he wanted big and splashy, a veritable tsunami of glad tidings. To get those floodgates opened good and proper, strong lubricant was needed

"Yes, ma'am," said Nigel. "Coming right up. I'll bring the bottle and glasses, and some champagne."

"Champagne? Have you lost your marbles?" said Mrs. Sandoval.

"I've had a premonition that we shall need it."

Nigel sauntered to the liquor cabinet, narrowly avoiding a collision with the detective on the way. Rubberface had taken to pacing again and didn't seem to care whose foot he tripped over in the process. He had much to think about, the detective, but an afternoon spent in a hole with no room to pace seemed to have mucked up the works. The works were double-stepping now.

Before Nigel had poured the first drink, Mrs. Sandoval,

appearing underserved and overwrought, blurted out, "I don't understand."

"What don't you understand, Mrs. Sandoval?" asked the detective.

"What just happened? Why was Cam Logan shooting at us with golf balls? What's this about a map? I feel like I'm in some third-rate mystery novel. Fourth-rate, maybe. This is my home. I should understand what happens in my own home, shouldn't I?"

"I will fill you in on the details after conducting some important police business." The detective turned to Stanley. "You are under arrest for the murder of Emilio Anguilero. You have—"

"Wait a minute," interrupted Annie. "You're arresting *him*?"

"We all heard his confession. It is my duty to arrest him."

"Not if he didn't commit the murder. How can you possibly arrest him after what we just witnessed?"

"We witnessed a crime, Miss. That does not discharge me from my duties as a detective in a murder case. If you would be kind enough to refrain from these outbursts, I will conduct my arrest."

"If you do, you'll be making a fool of yourself."

"Indeed," announced Nigel, popping open a bottle from the cart he'd loaded up with a dozen shot glasses and two ice buckets cradling champagne bottles. "Tequila, anyone? Everyone?" He'd hoped the previous discussion had been settled but, judging by the looks from the detective and Annie, it appeared not.

"The only thing Stanley confessed to," said Annie, "was shoving a man."

"He confessed to the killing," said the detective.

"A couple days ago you said that man, Anguilero, died of a blow from a ball-peen hammer. How does shoving someone comport with death by a ball-peen hammer?"

"Good point!" said Nigel, handing Annie a shot glass of tequila.

The detective pumped himself up, gathering hot air to expel in Annie's general direction, one might assume. "As the suspect himself explained, he pushed and the man fell backward. It would seem evident that the man's injury occurred when he fell onto an object."

"A ball-peen hammer, was it?" asked a smiling Nigel.

"The hammer was a working assumption. It could have been a rock."

"It was not a rock," said Annie.

"Oh, no?"

"No. He did not fall on an object. As the suspect explained, the man rose again after falling, before falling a second time. This second fall, the suspect says, may have been accompanied by a blast. I assure you, it was. Anguilero was killed by a strike from behind. By a golf ball, Detective Winjack. He was struck with a golf ball."

"Ha!" said the detective. "Your theory does not hold water. The death occurred at night, in the dark. Who plays golf in the dark? Not me."

"You play golf, Detective Winjack?" asked Nigel.

"No, but if I did, I wouldn't play in the dark. How could I find my balls?"

"Detective, I don't believe you could find your balls on a sunny day at noon if they were in your pants pocket...or thereabouts." Nigel handed the detective a shot of tequila.

"In this case, there would be no need to find a ball," said Annie, downing her shot, "because no one was playing golf. Someone—I shouldn't need to say who—was hiding in the shadows with a golf-ball-shooting rifle. A single shot from that rifle killed Anguilero."

"But why?" interrupted Mrs. Sandoval, coming up from shot number two. "Why were they on my property? I don't know any of these people."

"I expect Stanley can explain," said Annie, turning to Stanley, who was sitting on the second step of the staircase, peering through the railing like a convict.

Stanley turned even whiter than usual. Now the center of attention, he clearly would have preferred to be back in a ditch. "I'm not sure I can. Cam set up the meeting. Why here? Because that's where he was. My job was to show up and tell him he needed to find another girl."

"So, you told him that?" asked the detective.

"I did. He laughed and threatened me with the poison frog. As I said before, I pushed him. He went down, and the frog jumped in his mouth. He got up and then went down again."

"From a golf ball to the back of the head," said Annie.

"I suppose," said a forlorn Stanley. "My dear Cam. Poor, weak Cam felt she needed to protect me. She couldn't help it. She chose me over him."

"Ha!" shouted Mother, ejecting the tiny nonword like a venom-soaked spitball.

Eyes widened and jaws tightened all around. Those who had not yet availed themselves of a fortifier charged the liquor cart.

Stretched out on the loveseat like a relaxing cobra, Mother continued. "Stanley, you blind little toad. Go out and have a look at the body in the casket. That man, dead as he's been for the better part of a week, would still give a girl a better time than you. I'm sorry to break this distressing news—perhaps someone can fetch you a box of Kleenex—but that country-fried tart of yours was a bad shot when it counted. You know what I mean, Stanley?"

Stanley's face crumpled as if it had taken spit from a cobra. "I do *not* know what you mean."

"No, of course you don't. Have a seat, Stanley. Brace yourself."

Stanley was already sitting, but he curled his hands around the stair rails.

"This is going to hurt you a lot more than it hurts me," said Stanley's ex. Under the veil and sunglasses it was difficult to detect, but her voice suggested a twinkle in her eye. "What I mean, Stanley, is Cam missed. There, I said it. Now you know what the rest of us know. *You* were the target, Stanley. She was aiming at *you*. She wanted that man and his map—not you. You're barely a man, and you have no map. The sooner you understand this the better. Your precious Cam was just a two-bit, third-rate country singer with bad aim. It pains me to say this, Stanley, but if she were any good with a golf ball gun, you would be in that box."

"The madwoman rants," said Stanley, standing up. "Have you ever heard such a preposterous thing in your life? It makes no sense...does it?"

"Care for a tequila shot?" asked Nigel. "Take two, on the house."

Stanley clamped his mouth shut as if he'd been offered brussels sprouts. He stepped off the stairs and lumbered toward the group to plead his case. "But we had a life together, me and Cam. That's what she wanted. Not some carefree fling and a map. I must be right...right?"

"Stanley, remember that little episode with the electric eel?" asked Annie.

"The one her aquarist left behind?"

"It wasn't her aquarist left behind the eel, Stanley. Strange as it may seem, I think the eel was left behind by that guy called Eel, and it was intended for you. Remember, you were supposed to reach into the lagoon. When Nigel went in, murder plot number one was foiled."

"But Nigel survived."

"But that's Nigel. Had you gone in, I suspect you'd have received a little something extra to make sure you didn't."

"Shocking," said Nigel.

"Most likely," said Annie.

"But what about our life together?" said Stanley. "We had everything going, the bakery, the distillery, I made his and hers back scratchers. How could she just throw that away?"

"Because of you, Stanley. There was you," said Mother.

"Stanley, you remember that giant warehouse with all the entertainment equipment?" asked Annie.

"Of course. Cam's toy box."

"Right. Cam's toy box. How many husbands did Cam have?"

"Six, I think."

"How many boyfriends?"

"I have no idea."

"My point is that Cam is a woman with a short attention span. You were together how long? Four months?"

"And twelve days."

"Twelve days too long, probably. Past your expiration date. You should feel good to be alive."

"Tequila?" Nigel offered to Stanley. "How about three?"

"That's all well and good," said Mrs. Sandoval, "but that doesn't answer the question of 'why here?'" She flipped a third, or was it a fourth, tequila shot. She wanted answers and wanted them while she was still conscious.

"The map," said Annie. "The map, it would seem, has something to do with this place."

Ah! The map. Nigel detected an opening. "Ahem," he said. "I may have some pertinent—"

"But a map of what?" asked the detective. "Cam believed that Mr. Sandoval knew something about this map. What about it, Mr. Sandoval? What do you know about this mysterious map?"

31

PENNIES FROM HEAVEN

A few seconds ago, Mr. Sandoval had been relaxing on one of the comfortable salon chairs, falling in and out of sleep. Suddenly he was set upon by a trench-coated detective asking questions for which he had no answer. "I don't know about any map," he said, shaking his dented head. "There's so much I don't remember."

"You obviously remember this gentleman," said the detective, indicating Jack Watt sitting opposite. "And the two of you knew the deceased. If I'm to believe the story as presented thus far, the three of you once tramped around South America together, searching for relics. And now, these many years later, by sheer coincidence, the three of you end up on this estate. And, lo and behold, one of you is dead and the other two know nothing about it. More than odd, if you ask me."

"Odd?" asked Mr. Sandoval.

"More than," said the detective, "if you ask me."

When asked about his past life, Mr. Sandoval adopted the expression of a third grader asked to recite his multiplication tables through the twelves when he'd only ever got to the tens. "We were all on that Amazon expedition, but my memory is fuzzy about those days. Got hit by a fish, you know. How long has it been? Twenty years? Very fuzzy."

Fuzzy recollections about some long-ago jungle junket were all well and fine, but surely, they could wait an hour. Nigel, on the other hand, had up-to-the-minute blockbuster stuff, no fuzz attached.

"Mr. Sandoval has had a hard day. We've all had a hard day. I suggest—"

To Annie a hard day meant more questions needed to be asked. "So it falls on you, Mr. Jack Watt, to tell us what took place in that jungle twenty-odd years ago. This should be interesting."

Jack Watt had spent the last ten minutes staring glumly at the floor before hearing his name. Now he reacted like a man with cookie crumbs on his mustache. Before speaking, he slid a hand down the lower part of his face. Had he a mustache harboring cookie crumbs, that mustache would have been cleared of morsels.

Jack, a clean-shaven man, let slip a wry smile. "I guess I have no choice but to tell my story, do I? It's not that I wished to conceal the truth, you understand, but some truths are better left unsaid. At least, that's what I thought. But, under the circumstances, I'll lay my cards on the table.

"I first met Mr. Sandoval when he was seeking financial backing for his Amazon expedition. Being an amateur archaeologist with a surplus of cash, the thing was right up my alley. I agreed to underwrite the whole expedition with the sole condition that I was along for the ride."

"Excuse me," said the detective. "May I ask where this surplus of money came from?"

"Kapok."

"Kapok?"

"Well, at first. My dad was big into kapok. I took over the company and expanded into jute."

"Jute?"

"Maybe I should just tell the story. Your skimpy grasp of the plant-derived commodities market might prove burdensome.

Anyhow, the expedition started with high hopes and dry feet. A leaky boat took care of the dry feet, and our guide, the late Mr. Eel, made short work of the high hopes. Usually, rivers have two directions—upstream and downstream. Eel had a talent for going side-stream. Our anthropologist—Dig was his name—became doubtful about the mission's prospects and abandoned the expedition at one of those river villages. Getting back to civilization cost him an arm and a leg."

"River bandits?" said the detective.

"Cannibals," said Jack. "Anyway, the rest of us continued on. Not only did the mission's prospects dim with each passing day, so did our expectations of ever returning to civilization. Mr. Sandoval and I pledged to one another that if one of us didn't make it back, the other would take care of the widowed wife. Two days later, Mr. Sandoval disappeared. He and Eel had gone ashore to pee, and only Eel returned. Eel organized a search effort, which turned up nothing."

"He went ashore to pee, you say?" asked the detective.

"Well, that was the number one thing, I suppose."

"And the number two thing?"

"Number two," said Jack Watt. "May I proceed with the story?"

"Please do, but let's stick to the meaningful facts."

"It didn't dawn on me at the time, but if Eel had perpetrated a foul deed, he needed only assign himself the relevant search sector to ensure the body would not be found. Just the sort of shenanigans you might expect from a guy named Eel. After a couple of days, we ended the search and left the area to notify the authorities."

"You didn't follow up on the pact to take care of his widow?" asked Mrs. Sandoval.

"As it turned out, I couldn't. For unknown reasons, all the contact information for Mr. Sandoval was bogus. All the expedition's contracts and documents had false addresses and phone numbers. Likewise, his personal effects, outside of a couple photographs, had no personal data. The man wanted to be a mystery and had done a good job of it. I was at a loss as to how to get in touch. It wasn't until I received an affidavit a few months ago that I had any information as to his widow's whereabouts. That's when I got in touch."

"What about Eel? You had recent contact with him?" asked the detective.

"None. I didn't know if he was alive or dead. Didn't care."

"But he likely also received an affidavit request," said Annie.

"I suppose."

"Did you know anything about a map?"

"Never heard about a map."

"Right," said Annie, crossing her arms the way skeptical inquisitors often do. "So, a few months ago, you had no idea this place existed, and now you're here and married to Abuelita. What's more, you just happened not to mention that you were part of Mr. Sandoval's expedition. That's quite a turn of events. Care to explain?"

"Not especially, but I suppose it looks bad if I don't. You see, before receiving that affidavit, the only item I had relating to Valdy was this picture."

He pulled from his pocket the picture he had so enthusiastically ogled upon first arriving at the asylum and held it up for all to see.

Upon viewing the photo, the men folk did funny things with their breath—some inhaled, some exhaled—all while suppressing a whistle. The female contingent, except for Abuelita, looked skeptical, as if suspecting trick photography.

"Pretty hot, eh?" said Abuelita.

"Epic," whispered the detective.

"Hot indeed," said Jack Watt. "My sentiments exactly. Of course, what I didn't know when I saw the picture twenty years ago was that it had been taken thirty years before. I thought Jack must have had a young wife stashed away. Fast forward to my receiving the affidavit sent from this address. I remembered our pact, and I remembered that picture. Remembering the picture was easy because it was taped to my mirror."

"Before, you mentioned a wife," said the detective. "Didn't she object to you having that picture?"

"If she'd been alive, she'd have given me hell about it. I haven't been struck by lightning, so I suppose she's moved on. Anyway, I contacted Galena—that's her name. I call her Little Hen, ya'll call her Abuelita. I contacted her, but I didn't tell her exactly who I was. My identity, I figured, could be a touchy subject given the circumstances of Valdy's disappearance. I sort of introduced myself as a friend of a friend with some interest in establishing ongoing contact, if you get my drift."

"So, from that beginning, we're to believe a romance blossomed?" said the detective.

"If that makes it easy for you, sure."

"But Mr. Watt, the picture you've shown us today—May I see it again?" Jack held up the photo and then pulled it down quickly as the detective moved in for a closer look. "Yes, wow. This picture does not, how to say this gently, accurately depict the woman you married, if you understand my meaning."

"What is he saying?" crowed Abuelita.

"I get your drift," said Jack.

Expecting Jack to elaborate, the crowd cleared a flight path between him and Abuelita. Jack just winked.

"Okay, let me wade a little deeper," said the detective. "It's all well and good to want to marry a photograph. May I see the photo again?" Jack held it at arm's length toward the detective before pulling it back, causing him to stumble forward. "Oh, yeah. We can all appreciate that, but at some point, you must have become aware that a photo is not real life. Certainly, not in this case. Let me see that photo again for a comparison." Jack moved the photo in a large circle causing the detective's jowls to flutter as his head followed the movement. "Yabba-Dabba. When did you become aware of this great discrepancy?"

"What's he talkin' about?" said Abuelita. "Is he sayin' I don't look like myself? I need me one of them golf ball guns. I know just where to aim it."

"Calm down, dear. Let me handle this," said Jack, moving to Abuelita's side. "When Jack Watt makes a commitment, Jack Watt sticks to it. If I promised an expedition buddy to take care of his widow, then you can be damned sure Jack Watt will take care of his widow. And if I tell a woman I'm going to marry her, then you can be damned sure I'm going to marry her. And if that woman/widow happens to be"—Jack placed his hands over Abuelita's ears—"a gargoyle, then so be it."

Abuelita looked up adoringly at her husband. No objects were thrown. She was either too enraptured by her husband's rare physical contact, or she didn't know what a gargoyle was.

"But, of course, that's all academic now," continued Jack. "We'll get this fixed up and sorted out, and I'll be on my way." He held up a shot glass and smiled as if conducting a toast.

Mrs. Sandoval turned to Jack Watt. "I must say, no matter how much tequila I drink, I still can't get my head around this thing. You said you pledged to take care of Mr. Sandoval's widow?"

"That's right. I'm sorry it took so long, but I think everyone here can agree I made a good faith effort," said Jack. "But, of course, as it turns out, with Mr. Sandoval's return, my dear Little Hen already has a perfectly good husband. As much as I hate to face facts, our marriage cannot be. Annulment, I believe, is the process for this sort of thing. Just one of those things that didn't work out. I am crushed, rest assured, but I shall always have my memories," he said, looking one more time at the photo before shoving it back in his pocket.

"But," said Mrs. Sandoval, "she's not the widow. I'm the widow."

"What?" spat Jack Watt.

"What?" said Mr. Sandoval, taken by surprise at having produced a widow.

"I mean, I was," said Mrs. Sandoval. "I mean, I *would* be the widow if he were dead. Abuelita, you'll be pleased to know, is not Mr. Sandoval's widow but his ex-wife. I'm the second wife. I'm the widow…if he were dead, I mean."

"Now I'm confused," said Jack. "You're not Mr. Sandoval's sister?"

"Absolutely not! That would be against the law. Besides, I'm too young to be his sister."

"But I didn't know you were his wife. I mean, I didn't know he'd married twice. So, this means…?" Jack Watt staggered as if he'd gulped from the vessel with a pestle to discover the brew was not true.

Abuelita puckered her mouth and airmailed a lamprey's kiss.

Jack tried to return a smile, but the smile never got past the larval stage.

"Time for celebration," said Nigel, clasping Jack's shoulder. "The annulment has been annulled. I never sufficiently congratulated you on your recent betrothal. I'm sure you two lovebirds will be ecstatic together. 'Til death do you part, in sickness and in health' and all that rot. One other thing," said Nigel, pulling Jack closer. "That little directive about throttling down the passions? Forget about it. The old gray mare has come through with a clean bill of health. Consider the sanctions lifted, the embargo repealed, and the harbor open for business. Harvest those oats, young man. Show those spring bunnies a thing or two. All the best to you and the missus. Care for a tequila? Here, take a bottle. Don't drink it all in one gulp." Nigel placed the bottle in the stunned man's lap.

Jack's mouth, hanging open as it was, suggested a funnel might be of use.

"Mr. Watt, or is it Mr. Wynn?" asked Annie, provoking barely a blink from the ossified newlywed. "You seem to have accumulated two names. What is it? Watt or Wynn?"

Jack Watt resurfaced to an extent, though his jokey self had been supplanted by a soul-shattered version. "Mama named me Jack Earl Watt. Mack Wynn was a pen name I used for my amateur archaeological work. You see, I didn't want those in the jute business to know I was moonlighting. They frown on that sort of thing…the jute traders do. So, for anything archaeological, I was known as Mack Wynn. Otherwise, I'm Jack Watt."

Interesting as all this was, it didn't soothe Nigel's lip, which he'd been biting since kapok was the buzz. "Now that that's all sorted out," he said, "I have some news—"

"But," interrupted the detective, "none of this explains the murder or what happened today. We have a crazed country singer with demonstrated proficiency of the possible murder weapon, screaming about a map. But nothing definitively ties her to the murder. How did Ms. Logan get involved with Mr. Anguilero?"

"We're back to the murder? Come on," said Nigel, thinking they'd all had enough of murder for one day.

"What can you tell us?" asked Annie, turning to Stanley, who'd returned to his perch on the stairs.

"Cam collected South American animals for her zoo," said Stanley. "She knew this man as a guide and an animal wrangler and, I suppose, for other things. How they came together here recently, I haven't a clue."

"I'll tell you my theory," said Annie. "Sometime during the ill-fated Amazon expedition, Eel learned about Mr. Sandoval's supposed treasure map. Supposing it a quicker path to riches than an aimless river safari, he whomped Mr. Sandoval on the head with a fish and left the two of them to rot in the jungle. With the map now in his possession, and the fish-whacked Mr. Sandoval out of the way, the treasure was within his reach. Or so he thought. The scheme developed a major hole when it was discovered that Mr. Sandoval had left no valid contact information."

"Are you saying that this Eel person would have contacted us?" asked Mrs. Sandoval.

"Not at all. Eel needed the contact information to make sense of his map. Treasure maps don't come with coordinates, and Mr.

Sandoval's was no exception. Maps of this kind rely on local familiarity of a particular area. A map that marks a treasure based on its location relative to a rock or a tree is worthless if you don't know which rock or which tree. This is the situation that Eel found himself in. He had a map, but without the necessary context, had no way to use it."

"But he found out where we live," said Mrs. Sandoval.

"Precisely. Fast forward to a few weeks ago. Eel receives a document from this very house claiming to be from Mr. Sandoval's wife. Suddenly, he has a possible reference point for his map. Not only that, he has Cam, an old friend living in the area who might serve as a guide, among other services. Suddenly, Eel had a pathway to the treasure."

"Indeed he did," said Nigel. "If you will allow me—"

"But why was Cam Logan so desperate to get the map?" asked Stefanie. "She doesn't need the money. She should be burying treasure, not digging it up."

"Not the case," said Annie. "Certainly, she made a lot of money, but money goes through that woman like poop through a seagull. I looked up the ownership of her estate in New Antigua. She recently sold it."

"Cam-a-Lot? She sold Cam-a-Lot?" asked Stanley.

"Sorry, Stanley, but yes. I suspect she's sold other properties as well. If she's in dire financial straits, a tax-free pot of untraceable money would be just the thing to keep her in the lifestyle to which she's accustomed."

"Won't happen," said the detective. "We have the place surrounded and the roads barricaded. It's just a matter of time before she's apprehended."

As eager as Nigel was to spill his big news, something about Jack's story tugged at him. That something was pretty much everything. "Excuse me," he said, turning to Jack. "The other day you related a rather interesting autobiography of yourself. I'm not certain what I've heard today squares very well with that account."

"Fool!" yelled out Abuelita. "Stupid fool."

"You're addressing me, ma'am?" said Nigel. She was prone to such outbursts, but the context baffled.

"You see anyone else who fits that description?" she replied.

Several were within eyeshot, but Nigel withheld.

Abuelita cracked a grin like the kind carved into pumpkins. "You hear that, Jack? He swallowed it hook, line, and sinker. What'd I tell you?" She spit out a cackle straight from the depths of her well-used gallbladder.

"That's really something," howled Grumps, slapping his knee. "I've got a bridge for sale. It goes straight to Brooklyn."

Even Stefanie's leper husband seemed in on the joke. "When Jack told me that story, I said, 'Nah, even dimwitted Nigel couldn't believe such a thing. He may look like an ass, but he must be smarter than one.' But once again, I overestimated you." Laughter had not been part of this man's repertoire, but now he was whooping like a hyena. Most unpleasant.

"Now, now," said Stefanie. "Go easy on Nigel. This whole episode is as much a testament to Jack's storytelling ability as it is to Mr. Nigel's gullibility."

"It's a monument to both," said the detective. "A shame we don't have the video. Remember that snake fight? Remember the video, him and that anaconda?" The detective bent forward and put his hands on his knees. His rubbery face turned crimson as his body convulsed. Had he been in a restaurant, alarmed diners would have lined up to apply the Heimlich.

"Everyone, everyone," said Mrs. Sandoval, trying to instill order within the rollicking mob. She'd jumped the gun, though, and had to pause for a snort, followed by a titter, and then a guffaw. Over time, she regained control of her diaphragm, wiped a tear from her eye, and announced, "Let's get back to business. It serves no one's interest to antagonize the butler. We knew when we hired him, he was no Sherlock Holmes."

"No, but I bet you didn't think you were hiring Elmer Fudd?" said the veiled sphinx.

Once the latest round of hysterics died down, Jack Watt turned to Nigel. "I'm sorry, old man. Me and the missus played what you might call a practical joke. That little memoir about all those unfortunate wives was right out of a dark comedy. She thought you wouldn't catch on for at least another week. To your credit, you forced it out of us. Congratulations."

Have your jollies, thought Nigel. *The shoe will soon be down the other throat.*

A sweaty policeman entered the house and walked directly to the detective who struggled to straighten up from his laughter-induced abdominal cramps.

"Excellent," said the detective. "You've come to tell me she's been captured."

"Not exactly," said the breathless cop.

32

A CAT OUT OF THE BAG

"You're not going to tell me she's still on the loose, are you?" asked the detective. "Of course, you're not. You'd make us all look like fools if that's what you came here for. A lone middle-aged woman in the woods stands no chance against the concentrated will of the entire Tonkawa County Sheriff's Department. None at all. Now, what did you want to tell me?"

The officer spent a moment examining the ceiling before resetting his gaze on his own fingernails.

"Well, I'm waiting," said the detective. "What's the good news?"

"The suspect is…not…completely captured at this time."

"Not *completely* captured? What? You've got hold of her leg? What does this mean, 'not completely captured'?"

"We found a bracelet, sir."

"Uggggh," said the detective with a good bit of vibrato applied by his quivering clenched fists. "So, this aged female country singer, minus a bracelet, has vanished. Slipped away. And, I might add, with a treasure map."

"I wouldn't worry about that treasure map," said Nigel.

"Why not? Are you saying the map you gave her is not genuine?"

"Oh, it's genuine all right, but—"

"I need to know about that map," said the detective. "What was on it, where you got it, and what's significant about it? I need to know."

"I'm glad you asked," said Nigel. "However, this information needs a public airing. If you'll hold on to those horses of yours, all will be revealed soon enough. First, I need to administer a few doses of the old elixir." He stepped to the front of the room and thunked two shot glasses together to draw attention.

Thunk. Thunk.

"Everyone, please. Please listen up, everyone. The bar will shortly close. If you'd like another shot, or two, or three, place your orders. I'll see that you're all nicely placated before we reconvene this little get-together in the garage for an important announcement."

"The garage? Did you buy a car?" asked Stefanie.

"Is this some kind of joke?" asked Stefanie's husband.

"You better not be trying to pull a fast one," said the detective.

"No, no, and don't be ridiculous," replied Nigel. "If any of you don't wish to go and hear this fabulous news, then by all means remain behind. No doubt you will hear about it *ad nauseum* from your more adventuresome colleagues. Your absence will be your own regret—"

"Blah, blah, blah. We hear you. Shut up and get to pouring so we can get this thing over with," said Abuelita.

For a few serene moments, all the incessant blather was displaced by the melodious clamor of drinks being ordered, the gentle chug of bottles being drained, and the convulsive gulp of throats chokin' em down before last call.

The entire troupe—healthy, walking wounded, wheelchair-bound, and stumbling inebriates—toddled out to the garage. Nigel led the way, gobbling up the pavement with large, jaunty steps while cradling two pails filled with ice, stemware, and bottles of champagne.

The trailing parade of hostages included the estate's three original ladies and the men they were legally bound to; Annie and her mother; the detective and his two accompanying deputies; and Stanley, Essie, and Grumps. Not attending was Breadbox, who had slipped away earlier to fulfill his commitment to meet a man who owed another man. He would miss that appointment, however, owing to his detainment by the sheriff's deputies. This had nothing to do with the day's exertions, but was, rather, a matter of routine for both the department and for Breadbox.

Once in the garage, the fourteen captives formed themselves into a disorderly semicircle in the space previously occupied by the excavator. Nigel assumed a position as the ringmaster just in front of his precious artifact.

The pot, that dark, inscrutable enigma, seemed to speak to him like ye olde Excaliber spoke to Arthur. "I'm yours," it whispered. "Take me!"

"Okay!" replied Nigel, though silently and not in so many words.

"Did you say something?" said Stefanie.

"No, absolutely not," said Nigel.

"I saw your lips move."

"Just warming up," said Nigel, raising his hands to signal an announcement. "I want to thank you all for making the trip over. I believe you will find it more than worth your effort."

"What effort?" howled Abuelita.

"Easy for you to say," said the hobbled dragon lady. "You were pushed here in a wheelchair."

"Damn right!" said Mrs. Sandoval. "I had to stagger here all by myself."

"We are gathered this evening," continued Nigel, "for an auspicious announcement."

"What's he say?" said Abuelita.

"Something to do with ostriches," said Esmerelda.

"No," said Stefanie. "I think he means something crazy."

"Let me rephrase," said Nigel. "I am here to make a propitious announcement."

"Phfffft," phffffted Abuelita. "He's making up words."

"He means good news," said Annie, turning to Nigel. "Plain English, *por favor*."

"*Por fav*-what?" said Nigel.

"Talk," said Annie.

"Right-ho. Thanks for the translation," said Nigel. "I've gathered you here tonight for what may turn out to be an exciting, possibly even life-shaking presentation. Not to overplay the moment, but not since the opening of Al Capone's vault—"

"Al Capone had a vault?" asked Stefanie.

"Yes, he did. They opened it."

"What was in it?"

"Not important right now. Let's skip past—"

"This Al Capone character," said the detective. "Is he the same Al Capone that used to sell life insurance?"

"Let's forget I mentioned Al Capone, shall we?" said Nigel.

"Now I remember who Al Capone was," said Grumps. "Why are we talking about Al Capone?"

"We aren't," said Nigel. "Before relating this momentous proclamation, I feel it necessary to share some of the recent history that brought us to this point."

"Oh, God. Did he say history?" asked Esmerelda.

"Crap on the history. Just tell us what the hell is going on," crowed Abuelita.

"My leg was aching, but after listening to him, it's my head," said the mummy Mother.

"I'll make this short," said Nigel. "As you are all aware, this afternoon's assailant held a particular predilection for a certain map."

"I wasn't aware," said Abuelita.

"Most of you were aware—"

"What's a predilection?" asked Abuelita.

"The assailant desired a certain map," continued Nigel. "I

appeased that assailant by providing her with the map in question. You might well ask yourselves, how did I come to have this map."

"I asked you that twenty minutes ago," said the detective. "You're stealing my questions."

"I will now answer your question. I got the map through serendipity."

"Sarah who?" asked Esmerelda.

"Sarah Niponny," said Stefanie. "Is she still around? I thought she must be dead."

"Not dead," said Mrs. Sandoval.

"You've seen her?" said Stefanie.

"No," said Mrs. Sandoval.

"Then, how do you know she's not dead?"

"She couldn't be. Not if she's handing out maps."

"I mean to say," clarified Nigel, "that I obtained the map through a purely inadvertent process—a happy accident, if you will. If I may proceed, the original map was in the form of a tattoo on Mr. Sandoval's back—"

"Were you giving him a massage?" asked Stefanie.

"A massage? No, I wasn't giving him a massage. Why would you think I was giving him a massage?"

"How else would you find his tattoo?"

"No," said Esmerelda. "Mr. Nigel already said he got the map through Sarah Nipponny. It was Sarah who gave the massage that caused the happy accident. Sarah Nipponny then gave the map to Mr. Nigel. Is that what happened, Papa?"

"What?" said Mr. Sandoval.

"Everyone," said Nigel, "let's table this discussion for now. The history is not important."

"I see," croaked Abuelita. "He wants to give us a history lesson until inconvenient facts emerge. Suddenly, the history isn't important. Where have we seen that before?"

"We've gotten sidetracked," said Nigel.

"Cover-up!" shouted Abuelita.

"As I stated earlier," said Nigel, "Mr. Sandoval had a tattoo on his back depicting a map. This map, one might assume based upon the strident efforts of various dark forces to obtain it, held valuable information. Our current understanding suggests that this Eel character, whom we buried today—"

"Not buried," said Stefanie. "I'm not sure he's even in the casket. He's definitely not buried."

"This *soon* to be buried Eel character died trying to pry loose the secrets from this map. His accomplice, the country singing star, Cam Logan—famous, beautiful—"

"What?" said Annie.

"...once attractive, rich—"

"Not rich," said Annie.

"A fading beauty, declining wealth—"

"Broke," said Annie. "More debt than most industrialized nations."

"Let me rephrase," said Nigel. "Cam Logan, this once mildly attractive, somewhat famous, soon-to-be destitute, has-been singer, threw everything away, including her sad-sack lover, Stanley, to get her manicured claws onto Mr. Sandoval's back map. Why? What would the foot-wine-swilling Cam Logan want from Mr. Sandoval's back map? Mr. Sandoval had wandered through the wilderness for two decades, oblivious to the ink on his back and the secrets that it held. What secrets? What could be of such import that it found itself inked onto an old man's crusty back skin?"

"I wasn't always old, you know," said Mr. Sandoval, remembering a time when his back skin was quite supple.

"Through the many years, these secrets kept to themselves," said Nigel. "Available only to those who had witnessed Mr. Sandoval take a shower or swim at the beach. This Eel character would have been just such a person."

"You think he was watching me take showers?" asked Mr. Sandoval.

"He would have had the opportunity. Anyway, he knew of

the map and believed it described the location of an object of great value. Perhaps he knew what was there, or perhaps he merely divined that it was valuable because its location was inked on a man's body. Whichever, Eel would not live to find the treasure."

"Cam Logan now has the map," said the detective. "She could be digging it up at this very moment."

"No, she could not," said Nigel, "because, ladies and gentlemen, the treasure is right before your very eyes." He moved to the side, revealing the black cauldron to all.

There followed what might be described as a stunned silence without the stunned part. Aside from the occasional pop of a craning neck, the audience remained respectfully silent for several seconds until a hushed murmur arose. The audience members, growing restless, conversed among themselves in whispers. Quiet they were, but not so quiet that anyone in the room had difficulty hearing them. Topics ranged from unfettered screws to the wringing, cracking, and busting of body parts. After another few seconds, an unpleasant voice sliced through the babble.

"I don't see anything. Where is this treasure?" asked Stefanie's husband.

"You don't see it?" asked Nigel. "It's right before your eyes. How could you not see it?"

"Where?" demanded Stefanie's husband. "Is it behind that wrecking ball?"

"Wrecking ball?" said Nigel, his voice quavering just a tad. "Is that what you think this is?"

"Well, I haven't examined it, but from here I'd say it was a Phipps and Belson 800-lb. Micro-Destroyer Model 3C. They haven't made those since the '80s. It'd be a collector's item, if people collected such things."

"They don't?" asked Nigel.

"Not worth the shipping costs," said Stefanie's husband.

"Otherwise, I'd have kept ours. Got rid of it years ago. Buried it in some vacant lot. Now, where's this great treasure?"

The question, it seemed to Nigel, had become fraught. He closed his eyes, hoping for the appearance of a magic portal he could disappear into. Had he been welcomed by a dapper gentleman in red offering a forever office job in a windowless cubicle between the breakroom and the bathroom, Nigel would have enlisted without hesitation. Of course, the minute he signed, the fountain pen—a gift from the tail of the man in red—would have burst into flames.

It all became academic, however, when Nigel opened his eyes to find no magic portal. Instead, he stared into a roomful of budding vigilantes. The impatient mob shuffled their feet, rubbed a few facial features, and practiced glaring. Skepticism, knee deep from the beginning, rose to the eyeballs. Nigel felt like the old Eskimo who, after walling himself into his igloo for the night, detects the stinky breath of a polar bear.

"W-when I said tr-treasure," stuttered Nigel, "I didn't mean to imply treasure in the conventional sense, necessarily."

"Just what *did* you mean to imply?" asked Stephanie's husband, loudly tapping his foot as if Nigel's fingers were underneath.

Nigel detected a shift in the crowd's demeanor. Impatience had given way to disappointment, frustration, and fury. He didn't want to admit it, but he could see their point. They had been ushered out to the garage and wanted something for their effort. They deserved an explanation.

Why not be a man about this, he thought. *Come clean and own up. What's the worst that could happen? Dismemberment, disembowelment, disfigurement?*

He decided not to dwell on the negative and thought back to the teachings of his butler mentor, Old Winpole, for pertinent pearls of wisdom. Unfortunately, the 'Pole had dropped plenty of pearls on serving up soups, but not so many on self-defense or evasive running.

"Well," said Stefanie's husband, "what *did* you mean to imply by an unconventional treasure?"

A vision glared in Nigel's head of himself being torn apart, which he found unpleasant. He looked at the crowd looking at him. Every eye, thirteen and a half pairs, brandished a carnivore's glint. He recalled Old Winpole's story about his difficult first week. How Nigel would have liked to make a trade. But then, a particularly feline recollection from old Winpole's memoir exploded like a flash grenade inside his brain. As anyone who's been within spitting distance of a flash grenade will tell you, they blind, stun, and disorient to beat the band. And that's when they explode *outside* the skull. In Nigel's case, blind, stun, and disorient were all to the good, allowing him to act without the distraction of thought.

"A leopard," said Nigel. As soon as the words bounced back to his ears, he realized he'd taken a swing for the cheap seats.

"A what?" asked Stephanie's husband, while the rest of the crowd mouthed the words.

"Leopard," murmured Nigel, softening the initial pronouncement, which had seemed a bit stark.

Watching the crowd for their reaction, he noticed their mouths move. They looked like a choir hitting the first note of "The Star-Spangled Banner." The eyebrows too moved in unison, the interior portions sailing skyward while the eyes below widened. Abuelita's brows moved to such an extent that a space appeared between the left and the right.

Nigel's little gambit seemed to have paid off. The hypnotic spell of vengeance was broken. Invoking the image of a lovable, spotted cat had done the trick. The audience became less focused on removing his appendages and more focused on preserving their own.

"Unholster your weapon," shouted the detective to his accompanying officers. "Be ready. He could pounce from any direction."

"Everyone, form a tight circle with the women toward the

center," shouted Jack Watt. "Look toward the ceiling. Leopards are climbers. They attack from above."

"I need a gun. Where's my gun?" shouted Abuelita.

A number of shrieks ensued, which Nigel could only attribute to the untimely appearance of leopard-shaped shadows. Observing this bedlam, he had to reassess his strategy. Had he known these people shared an inordinate fear of leopards, he'd have chosen a bear, but would that have been too much?

"Everyone, please," said Nigel. "There is no need for panic. The leopard will not harm you."

"Not if I get a shot at him," said the officer.

"Do not fire your weapon. That would only make him angry," said Nigel. "He's quite a nice leopard. Housebroken, even. Perhaps we should all go back to the house and leave him be."

"Leave him be?" said the detective. "A dangerous animal can't be left to be. He could ravage the countryside. I won't rest until this animal is found and dispatched."

"Detective, let's be rational. Cam Logan is the wildcat you need to find. Wouldn't that be a better use of your time? She's far more dangerous than any leopard, if you ask me. She taunts people, shoots golf balls, and her carbon footprint must be atrocious. You need to get your priorities straight. Ten leopards wouldn't equal the mayhem in Cam Logan's pinky finger."

"Cam Logan was an emergency," said the detective, "but Cam Logan *and* a leopard is a crisis."

"I'll make a deal with you, Detective. You see that these people reach the house safely and take care of that marauding Cam Logan, and I'll deal with the leopard problem. Do it my way, and we needn't mention this leopard business to anyone."

"But I need to call it in."

"Call it in? I won't hear of it. I'm not going to see your reputation destroyed."

"What do you mean?"

"Why, you've already lost one major criminal today. I don't

wish to rub this in, Detective, but where were you when Cam Logan was terrorizing the place? Cowering in a ditch, that's where. Of course, me and you understand why. But they won't."

"Who won't?"

"Them," said Nigel, directing his gaze upward and toward the southeast. "The naysayers, the press, the bloggers, the mayor, the vigilantes, the animal rights activists. They're always out there, waiting to attack over the smallest things. It'll be ten times worse if they found their new detective had misplaced a major criminal *and* a leopard on the same day. Careers don't progress after a thing like that."

"No?"

"Not for someone like you, no, sir. Letting your proud reputation get entangled with a runaway leopard is a sure way to see it shredded. I'm guessing you don't want that."

"Preferably not."

"So, if you'll escort these people to safety, I'll do you a solid and subdue these leopards."

"Leopards? There's more than one?"

"You never can tell."

"But what do you know about leopards?"

"What do I know about leopards?" asked Nigel. "Look at me, Detective. Do I look like the kind of chap who doesn't know about leopards? You may as well ask what *don't* I know about leopards, Detective. What *don't* I know?"

"Okay, what *don't* you know about leopards?"

"Everything, detective. Everything. Did you know a leopard can't change his spots? I did. Known it since I was a tot. You leave the leopard to me. If you value your career, you'll get these people rounded up and into the house. I'll take care of that kitty."

The detective sheepishly accepted this partitioning of responsibilities, and Nigel breathed a sigh of relief. Even so, he shivered as if sensing the stalking gaze of some deadly animal. He was right. When his eyes met Annie's, he felt his retinas sizzle. He flashed her a furtive thumbs-up, which she may have missed, coinciding as it did with her pupils rolling up in their sockets.

The detective herded the quivering masses out of the garage and up to the house, though not without some protest. The short-legged members of the group wanted to stay, feeling leopards were best confronted as a tight group with the larger members protecting the perimeter. Those with longer shanks felt that leopard encounters were best experienced on the open prairie with plenty of space to run. The short-leggers made the argument that a human, no matter their leg length, could not outrun a leopard. The leggier types did not disagree. Outrunning the leopard had not crossed their minds.

33

LEOPARDS HAVE LIMITATIONS

With the garage cleared of people and large cats, Nigel merely had to wait. Wait for how long? The time required to subdue a leopard in a garage was not something he'd ever calculated. Probably not long, since Mrs. Sandoval would be nursing a powerful thirst.

There was one problem, however: the total absence of a leopard. If Nigel had any talent for reading a crowd, this one came across as pretty darned snoopy. Especially relating to topics like unfettered leopards on the premises. Might they ask to see a body? They might. So, how does one demonstrate the nullification of an animal that doesn't quite exist?

A viable plan proved so elusive that Nigel resorted to deep breathing to center himself. The centered Nigel then relieved his frustration by kicking the wrecking ball. The wrecking ball was, for some reason, harder than he'd expected a wrecking ball to be. His toe made clear that from this point forward, items with "wrecking" in their title were not to be kicked. He soothed the affected member by hopping wildly to and fro for as long as it took to smash a portion of his face against a sign that read "Bag Drop." His toe wasn't so much a focus after that.

The silver lining to all this mirth was a bright idea. With a severe limp and a ravaged face already in the repertoire, Nigel was halfway to passing for a man who'd gone hand-to-claw with a leopard. After a bit of de-rusting to reduce the tetanus threat, he applied a wire brush to leopard-vulnerable areas of his skin and clothes to complete the illusion. Then he gathered an assortment of debris calculated to equal the volume of a good-sized leopard and shoved it into a sack. This he dragged out to the gravesite, flinging it in such a manner as to suggest to the casual observer the interment of a large, dead cat.

Nigel climbed aboard the excavator and began shoveling in the dirt. As he dropped in his fifth scoop, he noticed an arm clothed in chartreuse pinstripes. Apparently, no one had exercised the initiative to place poor Emilio Anguilero back into his casket. He lay just where he had fallen, half exposed to the open air. Nigel took action to remedy that situation. A half-dozen scoops, and the arm was invisible to the naked eye. A hundred more scoops and it was four feet underground.

Having provided the substitute leopard with the burial it deserved, Nigel returned to the house, developing as he went the gimpy lope of a man after nine rounds with a panther. The main entry hall, he found, resembled the far end of a bowling lane after a strike. Exhausted bodies lay strewn about the place in all manner of unnatural orientations.

"I trust all are present and accounted for," said Nigel as he walked into the encampment.

"Tequila!" shouted Mrs. Sandoval.

"Tequila!" screeched Abuelita.

"What happened to you?" asked Annie as he sauntered toward the liquor cabinet.

"A bit of a tussle," said Nigel. "Those leopards, agile creatures, all claws, put up a fight."

"Did it?" asked the detective in a tone that suggested the twirling of a mustache.

"More than you'd think," said Nigel.

Nigel then noticed Annie passing behind the detective with a peculiar look on her face. It was a desperate sort of look, like that of person screaming with their lips stapled shut. What she was going on about, he couldn't say. Probably not the weather.

"Since arriving here at the house," said the detective, "we've been discussing a few issues, and we're confused on a number of points. Perhaps you could clarify?"

Clarify? Nigel realized he was swimming with crocodiles and preferred the waters as murky as he could get them. Besides, he was in no mood to answer questions from the detective who, one day earlier, had been sizing him up for striped pajamas and a skullcap.

"Happy to help if I can," said Nigel, meaning not a word of it. "I hope you'll excuse me while I attend to my chores. Mustn't keep the ladies waiting."

"Of course," said the detective, eyeing Nigel as if through a monocle. "Excuse me, but you've gotten quite a shiner. I don't recall seeing that before. Is that recent?"

"Those things happen when you fight a leopard."

"A leopard did that?"

"I don't know if it was the leopard, exactly. I may have knocked into something during the heat of battle. We were going at it tooth and nail there for a while, that leopard and me. You know how it is when you fight a leopard. Things get frantic. See the scratches?" Nigel held up his arms for all to see.

"Those are from the leopard, are they?" asked the detective in a tone guaranteed to offend any self-respecting leopard. "I would have imagined that a leopard's claws would have ripped the skin right off. Those look more like paper cuts."

"I assure you, no paper was involved." Nigel was growing tired of this inquisition. A man who'd just put down a leopard ought to have earned the right to butler in peace.

But the detective persisted. "This brings us around to an interesting point. In the garage, you talked about the map and its implication for some kind of treasure. Then, you introduced the concept of a leopard—"

"The concept of?" asked Nigel. "Did you say, 'the concept of?' What are you implying? That my arms were shredded by a concept? If that's a concept, it's a pretty well-developed one. I'll say that."

"I mean, it came out rather sudden. When one is talking about found treasure, a leopard is not the first thing that comes to mind."

"Maybe not *your* mind."

"Tequila!" shouted Mrs. Sandoval.

"Coming," said Nigel, wheeling around the liquor cart.

The peevishly persistent detective followed. "So, you're saying you followed this map, this twenty-year-old map, and it directed you to a leopard? That seems odd, to say the least."

"I'm not saying it *wasn't* odd. Did I say it wasn't odd? Odd pretty well describes it. Finding a leopard was a new experience for me, and I've lived some. But there it was. I followed the map. X marks the spot. X has a leopard on it. You can't argue with facts."

"Was the leopard tied up? Was it roaming free? Was it sitting in that spot for twenty years just waiting for a map reader to come along? How can you explain such a thing?"

"In my experience, you follow a map and strange things happen. You're the detective. You explain it. Tequila?"

The shock of the leopard, so effective early on, seemed to have dissipated. Industrial amounts of tequila and a change of topic were in order.

"That's a nice trench coat, Detective. Members Only?"

"This map you talked about," continued the detective. "Is it the one on Mr. Sandoval's back?"

"If you're referring to his back map, sure. Speaking of Mr. Sandoval's back, I've always wanted a trench coat like that, wrinkly and ferociously lived in."

"Did you ask Mr. Sandoval what the map was for?"

"He doesn't know. Doesn't remember that far back."

"I believe he does, Mr. Blandwater-Cummings. With a little help from his friends, that is. We've been able to deduce what the map points to."

"A leopard?" said Nigel, starting to sing in order to drown out the detective. "It's another tequila meltdown—"

"Not a leopard," said the detective. "A swimming hole."

Nigel stopped preparing drinks in mid-concoction. "A what?"

"A swimming hole. A favorite hideaway of Mr. Sandoval's that he called the Honey Pot."

"Why would he have a swimming hole called the Honey Pot tattooed to his backside? Are you nuts, man?"

"You can ask Mrs. Sandoval about it. She can tell you about the Honey Pot. She and the Honey Pot go way back, but not as far back as Abuelita and the Honey Pot. And before Abuelita and the Honey Pot, there was Sovia, a stewardess from Finland, and the Honey Pot. Are you getting the picture, Mr. Blandwater-Cummings? The map doesn't point to any treasure unless your idea of treasure is a bimbo's nest."

"I wouldn't call Sovia a bimbo," said Mr. Sandoval.

Abuelita's arm was cocked and loaded with a shot glass, but she did not hurl. Her eye glazed over like a tuna's encountering a school of herring. Too many targets.

"But the treasure pot on Mr. Sandoval's back," argued Nigel, "is labeled *tesouro*, which means treasure in Portuguese."

"Did you happen to examine the inscription?"

"I didn't examine it. I read it."

"Had you taken the time to inspect it more closely, you would have seen that the word *tesouro* had been crudely superimposed over the original inscription of Sovia. Mrs. Sandoval didn't much like her husband having another woman's name tattooed on his back, so while he was in Brazil, he had it altered to something a bit less troublesome. And there you have it. No treasure."

Nigel felt trapped, but not finished. "Well, that explains it all nicely," he said.

"Explains what?" said the detective.

"The leopard. It was there to guard the Honey Pot."

"No one is going to believe that," said the detective.

"You're telling me this whole hubbub—the death, the assault, the golf balls—was over a swimming hole?" said Nigel. "There's a pool out back, if you haven't noticed. I'm sticking with the leopard."

"That's not what the map pointed to," said the detective. "I'm sure this Eel saw the tattoo and, like yourself, figured it represented an object of great value."

"How much does a leopard pull on the open market?"

"Would you forget about that confounded leopard?"

"Easy for you to say. You didn't have to fight the beast."

"Should we call someone to look at your wounds?" asked Stefanie.

"Look at his wounds?" asked the detective, laughing.

It was a mocking laugh. The kind of laugh a man who puts down leopards with his bare hands wouldn't stand for. Nigel wished he would stop.

"He didn't fight any leopard," said the detective. "Don't you see? There was never a leopard. He made the whole thing up. Ho-ho-ho. He made up a leopard."

"Is that true?" asked Stefanie. "Why would you make up a leopard?"

Nigel said nothing. Had he the anatomy to do so, he'd have kicked himself where it hurt. Why had he so rashly blurted out "leopard"? "Bear!" would have been so much easier to explain.

"Get me a tequila, Mr. Nigel. While you're at it, get us all a tequila," said Mrs. Sandoval. "Once you've done that, you may retire to your room and pack your things. Tonight will be your last night under this roof, and tomorrow will be your last day as our butler. I told you that any more shenanigans would lead to your dismissal. Making up a leopard qualifies in my book. We can't tolerate the kind of mayhem caused by made-up leopards. That's not what I expect from a butler."

"Yes, ma'am. You are quite within your rights to give me the boot," said Nigel, handing her a tequila.

"Mother," said Stefanie, "are you sure you want to fire Nigel? Perhaps he's a compulsive liar."

"I would not say compulsive liar," said Stefanie's husband. "I'd say pathological liar. Tomorrow he may claim there are elephants or monkeys on the property."

"And he's a pervert. Add that to the list," said Abuelita.

"And an all-purpose imbecile," added the veiled mother-in-law. "Some might say buffoon or moron. I prefer imbecile. It covers the spectrum."

The clunk of a shot glass hitting an army helmet called everyone to attention.

Grumps turned to the crowd. "Listen to all of you," he said, pushing himself out of his chair while using Abuelita's head as a support. "You're being awfully hard on Nigel. While I get that he's not solid butler material, you all act as if he's good for nothing. I'd wager he's good for something. He just hasn't found out what yet. You can't just throw a man away because he hasn't found his purpose." Grumps turned to Nigel. "Don't you listen to them. I've never encountered such bitterness in all my life. A pack of vipers, they are. Ain't they never heard of letting bygones be bygones? Don't they know the power of forgiveness? Time to move on, folks."

Nigel patted the old man's shoulder, possibly the first direct human contact the grumpy old man had felt in fifty years.

"Are you sure you won't stay, Nigel?" asked Stefanie. "Maybe in another capacity? Sometimes leaves need to be raked."

"No. My work here is done. I've made my mark. I have learned so much here in my, what, seven days? All good things come to an end, eventually."

Annie watched this drama unfold from a darkened corner. Being at her husband's side during an avalanche of humiliation wasn't, in her opinion, a good place for a wife to be. The whole mess had to be embarrassing enough for poor Nigel without sharing eye contact with his supremely competent wife. She would wait for a more private time to let him know that her faith had not wavered. In her eyes, he was no more of a doofus now than on the day they'd met.

She had never been a proponent of Nigel's butlering career anyway. As far as she could tell, his skills and those of a competent butler scarcely intersected at all. Even the best butlers may have struggled to juggle the collection of cracked coconuts interned at the Sandoval place. Throw in a murder, a funeral, a wedding, and a golf ball attack, and it was hardly any wonder that Nigel, needing to smooth things over, had concocted an imaginary leopard. Leave it to him to overdo it. A black bear would have been quite sufficient.

Sad did not adequately describe Nigel's emotions at losing his butler's job. Relieved was more like it. His head had been crammed with doubts from day one. The dead body probably had something to do with it. Dead body or no, the doubts were well founded, because it had all been downhill from there. Like a rampaging snowball with Nigel trapped at its core, the job had carried him straight into a brick wall. His one week as a butler seemed more than adequate. When your most notable accomplishment is avoiding the electric chair, it's time to move on.

Still, as he entered his room, Nigel found the sense of failure hard to shake. Most of his expensive butler's training had yet to be utilized. The section on mixing drinks had come in handy, but not much else.

However, just because he had lost the war didn't mean he hadn't won a few battles. He had gained experience in administering to the needs of the random dead, learned how to operate a mini-excavator, and was now an expert on how not to install a gas water heater. The week had not been a complete disaster.

One skill Nigel had learned in butler's school was how to pack a suitcase. Walking into his closet to retrieve his bag, he noticed something peculiar. The fridge-like case that had housed the ancient pair of boots was empty and the front glass had been shattered. This was strange for several reasons. The boots were among the least practical pieces of footwear in the closet. Their leather appeared hard and brittle, and the stitching looked as if it might pop at the slightest pressure. Besides that, they weren't even fashionable.

Earlier that morning, Nigel had noticed nothing amiss. The glass shards scattered on the floor would have been hard to miss walking around in his stockinged feet. Who in the house besides Gastrick, former butler and eccentric collector of antique footwear, would have wanted the dilapidated boots? The estate had plenty of loose screws rolling about, but none that Nigel would match to this particular nut. Be that as it may, someone now had a new pair of very old boots.

Nigel's instinct was to report the missing boots. But upon reflection, he saw no upside to involving himself in another brouhaha for which he'd likely be blamed. He cleaned up the glass and resolved to remain silent. Discovering missing boots would be someone else's affair. As he bent to dump the shards into a rubbish bin, something in the darkest corner of the closet caught his eye. A shiver shimmied down his spine. He saw a gun. Not just any gun, but an assault rifle with a cylinder attached to the barrel. A cylinder of golf ball-sized dimensions like the one he'd seen aimed at his forehead earlier that day.

How many assault rifles are fitted for shooting golf balls? Had Nigel been asked that question twenty-four hours earlier, he would have said none and considered the questioner a silly drip.

But, after encountering his second of the day, Nigel concluded it must be a thing. What a sheltered life he'd led.

He retreated from the closet, sat down on the foot of the bed, and thought about what it all meant. Not a thing came to mind before he noticed himself, across the room, looking at himself. This should not have been news given there was a large mirror in his direct line of sight. However, he appeared to be looking at himself through an orderly collection of letters, words, and paragraphs. Nigel stopped thinking for a moment and took to reading. The message, written in bold letters—the only kind possible when written in lipstick—read:

Don't try to find me. You won't. I'm gone. The good life awaits.

Sorry for any damage done. If I wanted to kill, would have used bullets. Then I would hit what I aimed for. Ha ha!

Tell Stanley he wasn't the absolute worst. The bakery is all his, the lucky SOB. Not the parting gift I'd planned.

Take care of my sweet Zuela.

Cam Logan,
P.S. Thanks for the gifts.

So, there it is, thought Nigel. *The suicide note without the suicide.*

It had to have been written very recently. Cam could still be nearby—in the house, even. Dashed odd behavior, breaking into a house to trade a golf ball-shooting assault rifle for a pair of old boots. Then again, it was just the kind of thing Cam Logan might do.

Nigel reread the message, provoking a new set of questions. *Who is Zuela? A daughter? A pet name for her gun?*

Nigel's thoughts on the matter were interrupted by an odd

yowl. He didn't think it was his stomach, though it sounded about that close. He sat perfectly still.

A faint sound of breathing tweaked his nerve fibers in a discomforting way. Then a low growl turned his bones to butter.

Hold on! thought Nigel.

34

NIGEL CHANGES HIS SPOTS

The residents and visitors milled about the entrance hall, reasoning out the day's events and, more joyfully, assigning blame. As one might expect, the leopard's share was dumped upon Nigel, the banished butler. His collection of misdeeds had been so gleefully recounted that most in the room never expected to see his face again. Surely such a man, even one of constrained intelligence, would see the benefit of shimmying down a drainpipe in the dark of night and disappearing under a manhole cover.

So, imagine the surprise when, through this nest of venom-spitting vipers, Nigel zoomed past on his way out. He did not say "hello," "good night," or "*au revoir*." Opening his mouth to speak would have created extra drag.

"What the blazes was that?" asked Mrs. Sandoval.

"It looked like that butler, but I wouldn't have thought he could move like that," said Stefanie's husband.

"Maybe he set himself aflame," said Jack Watt. "Did anyone notice if his hair was on fire?"

"Hair on fire doesn't make you run like that," said the fire-tested mother-in-law.

"I'm sure that was Mr. Nigel," said Mrs. Sandoval. "But what was that thing running after him?"

"You mean that leopard?" asked Stefanie.

"A leopard?" asked Mrs. Sandoval. "Wouldn't that be a coincidence!"

The detective, who'd just belly-laughed his way through fifteen minutes of Nigel/leopard-inspired ridicule, felt the need to weigh in. "I'm no expert in these matters, but I do not believe that was a leopard. Too small."

"A *young* leopard?" asked Esmerelda.

"Don't think so," said the detective.

"A cheetah?" asked Stefanie.

"Had the beast been a cheetah, the butler would have been brought down before he reached the door, and the animal would have been feasting on his liver by now. No, the animal in question was not as fast as a cheetah. This animal would require several hundred more feet before bringing down its butler prey. My guess is a serval."

The spirited chatter had the usual effect on Stanley. Like one of those insects that mimic desiccated leaves or tree bark, he faded into his surroundings. However, had anyone taken the time to examine the mouth parts of this wallpaper stain, they'd have seen movement—a sure indicator that Stanley had something to say, if only to himself.

"Not likely a serval," he mind-muttered. The number of large, spotted cats with leashes and rhinestone-studded collars in greater New Antigua had to be somewhat limited. But Stanley knew of one such animal, and that animal was an ocelot. Not being absolutely certain that *this* ocelot was *that* ocelot, he remained silent. He had already used more than his allotment of words for the day.

"Excuse me," said Stefanie, "before we discuss the animal's taxonomy, I would point out that it was last seen chasing Nigel out of the house. According to the detective, Nigel might be fighting for his liver by now. Shouldn't we intervene in some way?"

"I would not think a full-grown human would be regarded by an animal of that size as food," said the detective.

"How about as sport?" suggested mother-in-law.

"Blake," shouted the detective to his uniformed partner. "Go out there and see if you can find that cat before it kills someone."

"Out there?" asked Blake, nodding toward the front door open to the dark cat-infested night. He put a hand on his sidearm and looked back at the detective before looking down at his own feet.

"Yes, of course, out there. Don't dawdle. Find that animal!"

"How?" asked Blake.

"It's a cat, Blake. Make some cat noises or mouse noises, and see if she comes. If not, listen for a growl."

"Or a man screaming," said Abuelita.

Mr. Sandoval walked up and put a hand on the officer's shoulder. "Watch your back, son. Them jungle cats like to sneak up on you. They're masters of the concealed ambush. Mind your neck. They can smell blood coursing through the jugular."

"You've seen this type of cat?" asked the officer, buttoning his shirt collar.

"Seen? No. You don't *see* a jungle cat. At least, not until he's got his claws in you and he's biting your nose off. If you still have your eyes, that's when you'll see him."

The officer, feeling his prominent nose, did not appear terribly appreciative of the advice.

Jack Watt stepped in to calm the officer. "You just do your job, son. My old friend is just trying to throw a scare into you."

"Ha ha," said the policeman. "I get it. Making stuff up to scare the policeman."

"I didn't say anything about making stuff up," said Jack. "I said he's trying to throw a scare into you. He's doing you a favor. You're about to enter the cat's world. You need all the adrenalin you can get."

"Right." The cop took two steps for the door before turning around. "Anyone want to come along?"

The night air, heavy and still, became heavier and stiller. The chirping crickets became sitting-on-their-hands crickets.

After the officer trudged out the door to shouts of "Good luck," and "Show no fear," the conversation turned to Nigel's fate. The inmates, with Annie abstaining, had split into three philosophic camps.

Camp one discussed, sometimes in heated debate, the feeding habits of predatory cats. Despite a healthy give and take on the subject, the group united in their belief that Nigel would eventually turn up, in pieces, across disparate locations, over an extended period of time. These were the realists.

Camp number two advanced variations on a theory that Nigel would have escaped being eaten but was never to be heard from again. They speculated that he would rendezvous at some predetermined location with the murderous Cam Logan, whereupon the two would run away together to live the remainder of their lives in the perpetual torment of each other's company. These were the romantics.

Camp number three believed that Nigel, having failed his every endeavor in spectacularly public fashion, would take the hint and withdraw from polite society, spending the rest of his days as a hobo, an illegal migrant to Mexico, or a telemarketer. These were the existentialists.

In the end, the three camps agreed to disagree about Nigel's fate and turned instead to guzzling champagne. Imagine, then, their collective dismay when Nigel strolled through the front door accompanied by a large, spotted cat. Those who were seated stood up. Those who were standing, leaned back. Annie, seated on the second step of the stairs, stayed put. All of them gaped, fishlike, at the unmauled butler and his fish-eating cat.

Nigel, noting the champagne flutes, said, "I see you haven't missed me too much."

Mrs. Sandoval, a devout existentialist, wobbled forth. "We didn't expect you back...so soon, I mean."

"Out for a walk," said Nigel. He felt a strange power over the gathered cabal. A power not unlike what a large cat must feel when walking into a dinner party uninvited. He stepped forward, noticing as he did that the crowd stepped back.

"You...you found the leopard," said Esmerelda. "What a lovely little leopard."

Mrs. Sandoval turned to Stefanie's husband. "You said the leopard was made up. That looks pretty real to me."

"That's no leopard," said Stefanie's husband, resorting to technicalities.

"Shhhhhhh!" said Nigel. "I wouldn't say that in front of her. She has aspirations."

"As I said before," interjected the detective, "I believe what we have here is a serval."

"Not a serval," said Stanley. "This is an ocelot. I recognize this animal. It belongs to Cam."

"You're just telling us now?" asked the detective.

"I wasn't sure before. I didn't get a good look. This is the cat all right."

"Stanley is correct," said Nigel. "Her name is Zuela, Zuela the ocelot. Cam Logan left her here hoping she would find a good home. She also left her weapon. In exchange for it, I believe she may have taken a few items."

"How do you know this?" asked the detective, stroking his mustache as if he had one.

"I saw the gun myself. Cam left a note upstairs on a mirror."

"She might still be in the house then," said the detective. "We need to search the house and vicinity."

"I suppose you should," said Nigel. "I don't expect you'll find her."

"Did she say where she was going?" asked Stanley.

"You're not thinking of going after her, are you, Stanley?"

"She needs help. She may be ill, mentally ill."

"She doesn't need your help, Stanley. As a matter of fact, she left a message for you."

"She did?"

"Of sorts. She said you weren't the worst."

"Really?"

"Yes, sir. 'Not the absolute worst' were her exact words."

"Ha!" said Stanley's ex, the swaddled dragon. "If that's the case, she must have been with some real losers!"

"Well," said Nigel, "Cam may have been a murderer, a thief, a deceiver, a profligate, and a con, but I'm pretty sure she wasn't Stanley's worst, either."

Stanley and Nigel exchanged fist bumps while the veiled dragon hissed like a goose laying a pineapple.

"One more thing, Stanley. She also said that the bakery was all yours, debt-free."

"Cam always had a kind heart." While Stanley rolled his eyes upward as if an angel sat on his forehead, the rest of the party exchanged sideward glances as if to say "What the devil is to be done with him?"

"Well, Stanley," said Nigel, "I don't wish to tarnish that image. I mean, she has good qualities, I'm sure, but for the sake of balance, I'll throw this out there. She tried to kill you. Twice."

"I never expected her to be perfect."

"Well, if you look at it that way, you weren't disappointed," said Nigel.

The front room filled once more with policemen tasked with combing the far corners of the estate for any sign of Cam Logan. An inhuman scream sent them scurrying as a group toward the east wing. Not surprisingly, it was Abuelita.

"She took it," said Abuelita, transforming pain into anger.

"Don't upset yourself, dear," said Jack Watt. "Whatever it is, we'll replace it. What did she take?"

"The photograph. It can't be replaced. It can't be."

"Maybe it can. A photograph of what?"

"Me."

"A photo of you? I'm sure you have others. Why so upset?"

"Not just me," said Abuelita. "Me and the 1967 Dallas Cowboys, signed by every player and coach."

"Oh," said Jack Watt. "That might be difficult to reproduce."

"No shit," said Abuelita. "You don't know what I had to do to get that picture."

"Really? What did you have to do?"

Abuelita looked at him sternly. "There are things a husband should never ask his wife."

EPILOGUE

Several days passed before the Sandoval Estate was thoroughly cleansed of its police infestation. A more normal routine settled on the place, though the stress from a busy week of death, wedding, funeral, and assault had left its mark.

Nigel's mummy-in-law, the shrink-wrapped zombie, left even before her house had been rebuilt. The early departure was forced upon her by a pattern of physical threats—made by her toward Abuelita, and Abuelita toward her. This was sadly predictable, for in the face of grave danger, each of the ladies had performed a selfless act of courage to save the other. These complementary acts of virtuous heroism had created a sort of post-heroic stress disorder, diluting the black vitriol so integral to their self-identities. Not that they would admit it, but the two felt starkly alien stirrings of gratitude and humility. This created a discomforting internal dissonance, as if their dark acidic blood had been infused with a dose of vanilla ice cream. In such a state, they could hardly stand themselves, much less each other. The other occupants of the house, it may be noted, never detected a difference.

Mother-in-law left to stay with Annie at the newly repaired Annie-and-Nigel homestead, while he remained behind at the

Sandoval Estate. He found it easier to face a revolving cast of lunatics than one barking mad mother-in-law. He'd wait until she cleared the premises to return home.

Nigel's firing had been temporary. Once Mrs. Sandoval surmised that his leopard story was more exaggeration than outright lie, she found a path to forgiveness. She cared far less about the species of cat than about having a butler for the Christmas eggnog season. Nigel's rehiring did not come without a fight, however. He protested valiantly, assuring Mrs. Sandoval that, make-believe leopard aside, his past execution was a strong indicator of future performance. To illustrate, he reenacted his greatest hits and misses complete with sound effects and a small explosion. It was all for naught. Once Mrs. Sandoval learned that Nigel's eggnog contained both bourbon and brandy, the rehire was assured.

Of course, Abuelita vehemently disapproved. Jack Watt, on the other hand, looked forward to the sideshow. This was as close as they would ever come to agreeing on anything. Though no one had expected it, no one understood it and, like mayonnaise on scrambled eggs, no one wanted to think about it, the newlyweds got along fine. For reasons best left unprobed, the marriage worked for them. A contributing factor may have been Jack Watt's acceptance of Nigel's plea to dispense with any semblance of physical contact. In fact, Jack embraced the concept of celibacy with fervor. The entire household knew this because Abuelita would remind them several times per day, using her most colorful language.

Stanley went back to his bakery, not only to bake but to live. He could not go back to Cam's estate. It had been sold and swept clean of anything soft for him to lay on. Stanley's growing notoriety as an artisanal dessert chef dipped for a while as his imaginative baked goods took on darker tones. Blackened heart cookies and red velvet mausoleum cakes proved not as popular as his earlier, more playful creations. In addition, he swore off women for good.

Women did not complain.

Stefanie and her husband, Stefanie's Husband, went about their business as usual. No one knew what that was, but it was greatly appreciated because it kept the pestilential windbag away for long stretches at a time. Everyone relaxed, especially Stefanie.

A reward was offered for information on Cam Logan's whereabouts, and Esmerelda tried to win it by means of mental telepathy. After many failed attempts owing to "contaminating crosstalk," she constructed an isolating lead box to be worn as a helmet. The heavy contraption proved unwieldy and claustrophobic but did cure a case of hiccups. Essie eventually gave up her telepathy endeavors to craft a line of spiritually infused, lead-lined planter boxes.

The stresses of that eventful week had unnerved Mrs. Sandoval to the extent that she resumed asking for tequila before noon. Nigel was diligent not to facilitate such a habit, but was instructed to serve a midmorning alcoholic eggnog from Thanksgiving until New Year's. This tradition, he learned, was unbreakable. As a matter of fact, his eggnog was such a hit that Mrs. Sandoval suggested augmenting the tradition to include the days from New Year's to Thanksgiving. Nigel managed to head off the proposal with a visit from New Antigua's premier cardiologist. A great relief to him since daily eggnog production was fairly energy zapping.

Of all the residents at the estate, the grandest transformation by far was seen in Grumps. Having been so enamored with gore-spattered vengeance, he had over time lost touch with life's simple pleasures. Once his all-abiding thirst for bloody retribution had been exposed as an inconvenient indulgence, he emerged from his self-imposed hate-filled cocoon into a fresh, expansive rainbow-colored world of new possibilities. Of course, being ninety-five-years old was somewhat limiting, but perhaps less than in the revenge game. This reformed hermit began taking walks—many walks, several per day, outside, in the sun, in the rain, and sometimes, in the dark. Upon his return, he would comment, whether or not anyone was listening, on how bright was the sun, or how wet was the rain, or how grassy-smelling smelled the grass. He was quick with a compliment and only rarely mentioned murdering someone. The other members of the Sandoval estate, who previously had regarded Grumps as something along the lines of an ugly piece of furniture no one would buy, came to regard the kindly old gentleman as more like a friendly stray cat they had no qualms about feeding.

Grumps was sometimes accompanied on his walks by Mr. Sandoval, who would relate episodes from his twenty years of aimless strolls across the Americas. Grumps, in turn, would relate episodes from his fifty years of sitting in a room day after day. The two had lived scarily parallel lives. Both had experienced a rebirth. In Mr. Sandoval's case, a spiritual evolution had formed through his two-decade sojourn. In Grump's case, a momentary insight had revealed that a practical joke had caused him to throw his life away. And, of course, there was that unbreakable bond known only to the small fraternity of brothers with skulls caved in by fish.

So, what became of the off-target murderess, Cam Logan? Who knows?

After nabbing the boots, the signed team portrait, and a few kabobs, she vanished. How she got away or to where, no one knows. She had already sold off most of her properties to pay her debts and needed the treasure, one would speculate, for a smooth landing into the fugitive life. Unless she's hanging out at the Honey Pot, she's still on the run.

On the run, but likely not alone. Undoubtedly, there are people who know things. There must be. A rich person, if they're to maintain a certain lifestyle, can't vanish without help. And anyone who knew Cam Logan knew she would not be giving up her lifestyle. Even if she was no longer Cam Logan, the star, she was still *somebody*, and that somebody required a small army of financial managers, fitness trainers, mental health gurus, plastic surgeons, domestic workers, dietitians, and a handful of world-class enablers. Such an entourage would be tough to conceal even for an experienced drug lord, much less a newly notorious country singer. Cam Logan would turn up somewhere, someday. Probably sooner rather than later.

So, mystery 1A, the identification of the killer, has been solved, but what of mysteries 1B and 1C?

1B. How did a frog end up in a dead man's gullet, and

1C. How did a toad end up in his mouth?

To know that, you'd need to know about the man, Emilio Anguilero.

So, what do we know about this man called Eel?

Not nearly enough.

The rubber-faced detective knows something. Annie knows more than he does. Cam Logan knows more than she does. The FBI knows more than Cam does. The CIA knows more than any of them.

And Nigel?

Well, Nigel knows how to make a devastating eggnog and that's enough for now.

THE END

The end? Not really. The mystery pile just gets deeper from here. Can a certain butler keep from putting his foot in it? Do you have to ask? Get *The Demented Defective* to see Nigel in it up to his neck.

GET A FREEBIE!

Hey reader, D. R. here. If you'd like a little more D. R, then sign up for my newsletter and download this free novelette.

If *The Dating Defective*, a joyful one-hour read, were to appear on the retail market, it would command a price of $1999.99. That's why I'm giving it away for free. Who needs that kind of money? In addition to this epic, you'll receive infrequent emails keeping you abreast of my novelistic mishaps. To sign up, just go to www.drlowreyauthor.com.

By the way, congratulations on finding me. Not many have. Why not poke those D. R. Lowrey-illiterates by entering an Amazon rating or review for *The Butler Defective*. (On the Amazon book page, look to the left in the review section) D. R. would sure appreciate it.

ABOUT THE AUTHOR

D. R. Lowrey, the non-award-winning, critically-untainted author of comedic fiction, writes from the hothouse of Houston, Texas, often while not wearing a shirt.

It wasn't always like this. For years, D. R. clung tenaciously to a shirt-wearing job that paid real money in exchange for his soul. When that job went kaput, he investigated the possibilities of a career in the hardware retail business, or, alternatively, writing fine literature. Fine literature, as it turns out, is hard to write. Harder even than selling door hinges. Having acquired such wisdom, D. R. took to writing stuff more aligned with his true personality—uncultured, absurd, insubstantial. He now foists these works upon the reading public.

Some refer to his books as a "beach read." D. R. disagrees. He feels that if you require a beach to read a book, your time is better spent wading amongst the sharks and stingrays. He suggests reading in the comfort of your own living room, preferably on furniture suitable for napping, while siphoning a favorite beverage. Experience shows that after extensive siphonings, his books do indeed start to resemble fine literature...what with the words, punctuation, and all.

D. R. enjoys thoughtful, non-violent interaction with his readers. He views such discourse as an ongoing referendum on whether to write or sell latex paint.

Check out www.drlowreyauthor.com if you're desperate for something to do.

The Bumbling Brit Abroad Mysteries 1 - 4
Read the entire Nigel saga!

Book 1: Defective for Hire

Nigel escapes the rat race by settling in smalltown Texas. Tranquility he wants, but the town has other ideas. Animal attacks, interminable to-do lists, and an unwanted murder soon have him yearning for simpler days among the rats.

Book 2: The Butler Defective

For most butlers, cleaning up after a murder would be the absolute worst. Not for Nigel. When his arrival as the new English butler coincides with the discovery of a dead body, conclusions are easily drawn, but not easily dismissed. There'll be a lot more cleaning up to do if he's to avoid hard time in the Big House.

Book 3: The Demented Defective

Every person in New Antigua, Texas seems to have just stepped off the crazy train. So why is Nigel the only one hiding from the whitecoats with the butterfly nets? Could it be they're out to silence the one person who knows the town is the epicenter of a global telepathic struggle?

Book 4: The Dancing Defective

Have things finally settled down at the Sandoval estate? Yes, but only because the Sandovals have all vanished. If Nigel is to find them, he'll first have to solve the big mystery behind all the extreme nuttiness. And even that is not enough. He'll also have to dance!

Made in the USA
Monee, IL
07 December 2023

48179605R00204